Brandon ~~has~~ ... family's fortunes, his heroic actions elevating his father to the governor's seat in Kayolin. Gretchan Pax, priestess of Reorx, has negotiated a treaty to end the long enmity between the hill dwarves and the mountain dwarves who have been exiled from their home in Thorbardin.

Yet that ancient kingdom, proudest Dwarf Home of them all, has been savaged and torn by civil war, and now suffers under the merciless thumb of a powerful dark wizard. Sealed against the surface world by a virtually impregnable gate, the dwarves of Thorbardin struggle to survive and to avoid their insane monarch's wrath. Outside of that gated mountain, Gretchan, Brandon, and exiled king Tarn Bellowgranite strive to create an artifact blessed by Reorx, Father God of all the dwarves—an artifact that will smash the gate and allow Tarn to reclaim his throne.

But there are more dangers than even the mad wizard awaiting in the underground realm: a powerful Chaos Dragon surges through Thorbardin, wreaking massive death and destruction, and a beautiful dwarf enchantress strives to keep her master pleased, even as she schemes toward his betrayal.

Ultimately the threat of complete destruction vies with the hopeful blessing of Reorx himself.

One or the other will determine the Fate of Thorbardin.

DOUGLAS NILES

Dwarf Home
A veil of secrecy shrouded the dwarven kingdoms of Krynn when the War of Souls finally came to its bloody end. Now the veil is torn away to reveal the bitter enmities festering under the mountains.

The Secret of Pax Tharkas
The Heir of Kayolin
The Fate of Thorbardin

The Rise of Solamnia
After the Second Cataclysm, Solamnia is in turmoil. But there is one man, an outlaw, who might be able to face down Solamnia's enemies and make an empire out of a shattered land.

Lord of the Rose
The Crown and the Sword
The Measure and the Truth

Elven Nations
Only the oldest child can inherit and the twins born to the Speaker of the Stars accept that—until the depth of the siblings' rivalry is revealed and the resulting war shatters a nation irreparably.
Three books now in one complete omnibus edition.

Elven Nations

PAUL B. THOMPSON, TONYA C. COOK, AND DOUGLAS NILES

The Age of Mortals
Wizards' Conclave

Douglas Niles

Dwarf Home • Volume Three

The Fate of Thorbardin

Dwarf Home, Volume Three
FATE OF THORBARDIN
©2010 Wizards of the Coast LLC

All characters in this book are fictitious. Any resemblance to actual persons, living or dead, is purely coincidental.

This book is protected under the copyright laws of the United States of America. Any reproduction or unauthorized use of the material or artwork contained herein is prohibited without the express written permission of Wizards of the Coast LLC.

Published by Wizards of the Coast LLC

DRAGONLANCE, DUNGEONS & DRAGONS,, WIZARDS OF THE COAST, and their respective logos are trademarks of Wizards of the Coast LLC in the U.S.A. and other countries.

Printed in the U.S.A.

Cover art by Matt Stawicki

First Printing: January 2010

9 8 7 6 5 4 3 2 1

ISBN: 978-0-7869-5150-5
620-24069740-001-EN

The sale of this book without its cover has not been authorized by the publisher. If you purchased this book without a cover, you should be aware that neither the author nor the publisher has received payment for this "stripped book."

U.S., CANADA,	EUROPEAN HEADQUARTERS
ASIA, PACIFIC, & LATIN AMERICA	Hasbro UK Ltd
Wizards of the Coast LLC	Caswell Way
P.O. Box 707	Newport, Gwent NP9 0YH
Renton, WA 98057-0707	GREAT BRITAIN
+1-800-324-6496	Save this address for your records.

Visit our web site at www.wizards.com

To Kayli and Angela

2009—Onward and Upward!
You go, girls!

Prologue

A Treaty for the Ages Yet to Be Lived

This document, yet to be negotiated, shall be agreed upon between the Dwarves of the Mountains and the Dwarves of the Hills at the conclusion of the Tharkadan War. I, Gretchan Pax, Priestess of Reorx—He who is the Master of the Forge and the benign patron of *all* clans of dwarfkind—hereby vow upon my honor and my life to remain at the bargaining table and to hold here the principal negotiators until such time as the completed treaty shall be officially and irrevocably signed.

We representatives of the two mighty clans of the Dwarf Peoples meet in the great hall of Pax Tharkas. This vast chamber has only recently been scoured of the blood spilled in yet another futile and destructive war between our peoples. All acknowledge the tragedy of this long-held hostility among us, of which the Tharkadan War is only the most recent example.

Herewith and present, as the pact is documented and copied and secured, are the following notable representatives of the Neidar and Mountain Dwarves. Each will affix a signature as a personal pledge to honor this treaty. All are seated at the large, circular table in the center of the great hall, and each has pledged to represent his or her respective faction with truth, honor, and dignity:

For the Mountain Dwarves in Exile—

Tarn Bellowgranite, former king of Thorbardin and now the ruler of Pax Tharkas. At his right hand:

Otaxx Shortbeard, chief general among Tarn Bellowgranite's garrison forces, and a lifelong follower, adviser, and compatriot of the former king.

Mason Axeblade, the field captain in direct command of the Tharkadan troops.

Tor Bellowgranite, the young son and chief heir of the Bellowgranite family, who will observe the proceedings as a proper introduction to the responsibilities of sovereignty and command.

For the Hill Dwarves of the Kharolis environs—

Slate Fireforge, descendant of that legendary clan and the righteous voice of reason who sought to prevent the war that his clansman were ensorcelled into commencing.

Axel Carbondale, Chief Captain of the Foothill Clan and now commander of the hill dwarf army.

To moderate this treaty, hearing the words of both parties and seeking to glean the wisdom and to cull the animosity from the participants, the following are agreed:

Crystal Heathstone, royal heir of the hill clans and wife of Tarn Bellowgranite, as such being the former queen of Thorbardin.

Gretchan Pax, humble cleric and most unworthy scribe. Also, the primary author of this document, though it is agreed that other voices shall make themselves known in these pages, with proper annotation.

For purposes of this treaty, the disputes addressed shall extend back to the time of the Cataclysm (sometimes called the First Cataclysm), during which the foundation for eternal war was so unfortunately laid.

It is our resolve, underlined by the authority of Reorx himself, that this agreement shall be regarded as a permanent renunciation of such misguided violence. That is, that war between mountain and hill dwarf shall not only cease for all time, but that the two nations shall agree to cooperate and assist each other by whatever means possible in striving toward the goal of a world that is secure for all dwarfkind.

(NOTE: Tarn Bellowgranite wishes to state, on behalf of the mountain clans, that it has long been his objective to attain such a goal. He has ever striven to avoid military conflict with the Neidar, he declares, and in fact has taken a Neidar woman for his wife these past many years. He has never authorized a military venture against the Neidar, he adds, and was plainly shocked when such a venture was directed against his own people in this hallowed place.)

(NOTE: Axel Carbondale wishes to respond, on behalf of the hill dwarves, that the Klar raiding parties that so frequently sallied forth from Pax Tharkas were under the authority, if not the direct command, of Tarn Bellowgranite. Axel queries how it is that these raiders were known, by proof and by witness, to return to Pax Tharkas with spoils gained from their attacks against the Neidar, and that no visible effort was made to punish them or to return said spoils to their rightful hill dwarf owners.)

(NOTE: Mason Axeblade wishes to note, on behalf of the military garrison of Pax Tharkas, that the Klar are notoriously difficult to control. Furthermore, their captain, Garn Bloodfist, is currently chained in the Tharkadan dungeon, charged with disobedience of his thane's direct order.)

(NOTE: Crystal Heathstone, Neidar maid married into a mountain dwarf clan, wishes to suggest that such bickering is pointless and that perhaps it would be useful to allow Gretchan Pax to continue to moderate the negotiations.)

And thus the discussion and treaty-making resumes . . .

The story behind this proclamation commences with the Cataclysm and the wounds that were torn into the fabric of dwarf history even as that reign of destructive violence tore away at the flesh and the blood of the world itself. The world of Krynn was torn and ravaged by the vengeful might of the gods. Seas flooded formerly prosperous farmlands. Mountains rose where placid lakes and glens had once held pastoral sway. And the peoples of Krynn, human and elf and dwarf and all the rest, could only cower and seek shelter from the immortal onslaught.

What were the exact events of that dark storm? Today none may know for sure, but all have their beliefs. The hill dwarves claim that their mountain cousins sealed the gates of Thorbardin before them and ignored their frantic pleas for succor and protection. In the aftermath, more hill dwarves perished than can be counted among the stars in the sky.

The mountain dwarves claim that they offered that shelter willingly, that the gates were held open for as long as survival allowed. When none of their outside-dwelling kin presented themselves, the mighty portal was sealed. By the time such hill dwarves as had survived the initial catastrophe reached the gates of Thorbardin, there was no simple means of communication between the outside and underground worlds, and thus the plight of the exposed Neidar was for the most part unknown.

(NOTE: Slate Fireforge, on behalf of the hill dwarves, thinks that the latter explanation is disingenuous, er, "hogwash.")

(NOTE: Tarn Bellowgranite, speaking for the mountain dwarves, wonders what magical enchantment exists in the ancestry of Slate Fireforge that he may know such a fact with any degree of accuracy.)

(NOTES, ad nauseam: The ancestry of a great many dwarf families is questioned, sometimes in distasteful specifics, by others present. The negotiations are suspended for a day of feasting and celebration.)

Upon resumption of the talks:

Whichever version of the story is true (and it should be noted that they are not mutually exclusive—G.P.), the result was a cultural scar that has not only lasted for many hundred years, but continued to fester and rot and inflict further damage as the years passed by. Within the century after the Cataclysm, the disputed history was distorted and expanded beyond all recognition by the cruel devastation of the Dwarfgate War, in which whole mountains were destroyed and the power of the villainous wizard Fistandantilus corrupted dwarves and men alike into a fever of murderous combat.

At the conclusion of that war, Thorbardin was bruised and battered and sealed against the world. The hill dwarves were shunned by their undermountain kin and left exposed to the vagaries of existence in an outside world controlled by humans and elves. The wounds of the Dwarfgate War, it is safe to say, created an infection that has never healed.

All gathered here can agree (in principle! No notes are required at this point.—G.P.) that it was this infection that left the hill dwarves vulnerable to the persuasions of the apparently stalwart Harn Poleaxe as he made the case for a war against Pax Tharkas. All now see that Poleaxe was possessed of a dark, evil force, and it was this force that compelled him to march toward war. Because of the bitterness abiding in dwarf hearts, that compulsion was all too easily made real.

It was the protective eye of Reorx himself that prevented the war from rising to the level of catastrophe. For bitterness, hatred, and cruelty existed on both sides. All present admit observing the corruption of Harn Poleaxe when it was revealed by the light of the Forge. His control by a dark power was made manifest that day.

At the same time, all now know that it was the scheme of Tarn's captain Garn Bloodfist, he of the Klar clan, to lure the entire attacking force of hill dwarves into Pax Tharkas—and hence, to crush them beneath a mountain's weight of stones by releasing the massive trap within the ancient fortress. Contrary to the will of his king, Bloodfist nearly succeeded—until the presence of Reorx was made brilliant and true in this very hall, revealing the dark enchantment of the attacking hill dwarves and thwarting the Klar's lethal plan through his most humble agent, the gully dwarf known as Gus Fishbiter.

(NOTE: Tarn Bellowgranite wishes it made known and recorded that Garn Bloodfist, in his efforts to release the trap, was acting in direct opposition to the orders of his thane.)

(NOTE: Axel Carbondale suggests the above note is irrelevant, as it was not the actions of the mountain dwarves that thwarted the mad Klar's plan.)

(NOTE: Otaxx Shortbeard wishes all to know that he and his thane really, really tried to stop Garn Bloodfist.)

(NOTE: Crystal Heathstone suggests, yet again, that the negotiations resume under the auspices of Gretchan Pax.)

And so it shall be done:

Now, in the wake of the battle, on this floor scoured of blood, we strive for a pledge of peace. It is fitting that we make this effort in Pax Tharkas, for though it is a fortress in war, this mighty edifice was originally constructed as a symbol of lasting peace between diverse peoples.

Our goals are three and range from simple to complex.

FIRST, we declare that a state of peace exists between the exiled mountain dwarves who dwell in Pax Tharkas and the hill dwarves of the Kharolis Mountains. Any further raids, coercion, kidnapping, extortion, or other acts of violence between these two peoples are expressly forbidden and shall be punished by the combined might of two nations.

SECOND, the dwarves of Pax Tharkas shall grant free passage through their mountain pass to their kinfolk, the Neidar. The gates shall remain open, the road unblocked, and none shall require any toll or other charge be affixed to this passage. Hill dwarves who journey this way shall be accorded the comforts of any standard wayfarer's house, including food, drink, and shelter at reasonable rates.

In addendum, there shall be no restrictions, tariffs, or undue taxes placed upon mountain dwarf merchants who wish to do business in the communities of the Neidar. Neither shall they be subjected to discriminatory rates when applied to such necessities as food, drink, and shelter.

THIRD concerns a goal for the future. For reference, it should be noted that the mountain dwarves in exile have been driven from Thorbardin by cruel repression. The fanatical thane Jungor Stonespringer used the person—and the life—of young Tor Bellowgranite, at the time a mere infant, as leverage to compel his father's departure. Following that exile, the lone remaining gate of the kingdom, once known as the North Gate, was sealed, and it has nevermore been opened since that time.

Yet all agree that Thorbardin is the key to the future of all dwarfkind. The fate of Thorbardin is the fate of the dwarves themselves. It is hereby resolved that the current government of Thorbardin is false and illegitimate and that it shall be the goal of hill dwarf and mountain dwarf alike to restore the true high

THE FATE OF THORBARDIN

king—Tarn Bellowgranite or his heir—to the throne under the mountain.

Adding urgency to this objective, it has been reported that, within the sealed kingdom of Thorbardin, a bitter civil war currently rages between the forces of King Stonespringer and the rebel army of a powerful and wicked dark wizard.

(NOTE: Tarn Bellowgranite reminds all that the source of this information is the aforementioned gully dwarf, Gus Fishbiter. Further action in pursuit of this goal shall, therefore, be postponed until such time as the information can be affirmed by a *reliable* source.)

Thus be it agreed that, should that confirmation be attained, the dwarves exiled from under the mountain shall seek the assistance, in a military alliance, of the Neidar. The hill dwarves shall offer such assistance as is requested and adjudged to be reasonable given the resources available. The two great clans of dwarfkind, working in concert, shall seek to restore the ancient throne of Thorbardin and establish therein a realm where all clans, kin, and breeds of dwarf shall find themselves welcome. The benefits accrued from such a reinstatement shall be shared equally between the clans, with allowances for the proportion of resources committed and losses suffered during the campaign.

For many ages, we dwarves have been forced to look back in shame and to look forward in apprehension. Let it now be decreed that our ancient shame shall become our current wisdom and that Reorx shall will that our future apprehension turn, once and for all, into hope.

It is suggested by many that the person of Tor Bellowgranite be upheld as a perfect symbol of this hope. His father hails from a mix of two of Thorbardin's great clans, while his mother traces her roots to the highest nobility of the Neidar. Thus, he may become a prince for all the dwarves, for all the ages.

Nor should it be assumed that this agreement was easily achieved or peacefully completed. All the signatories wish to note, with appreciation, the contribution of Gretchan Pax, priestess of Reorx, who served to moderate the debate and firmly kept the discussion focused and progressing.

Thus be it declared to all:

The future goal of both our peoples, the Neidar Hill Dwarves and the Mountain Dwarves in exile, is the reclamation of Thorbardin, once the greatest nation and proudest land in all the world of Krynn.

Signed,

Tarn Bellowgranite
Slate Fireforge
Otaxx Shortbeard
Mason Axeblade
Axel Carbondale
Crystal Heathstone
Tor Bellowgranite, (minor) witness

And

Gretchan Pax, priestess of Reorx

PART I

One

Fire in the Hive

The horax hissed, its segmented body rearing high above the cavern floor as the arachnoid perched upon six rear legs. An equal number of forelegs thrashed menacingly, striking with hooked talons toward the monster's tormentors. Two multifaceted eyes bulged from its melon-sized head, cold and dispassionate even as they reflected the light of several flaring torches. A pair of wicked mandibles thrashed before the monster's mouth, wickedly cutting back and forth, slashing with enough strength to slice a man—or a dwarf—in two.

Three heavily armored dwarves advanced on the horax, shoulder to shoulder, protected by long, steel shields extending from floor to nose. Each fighter was further armored in plate mail, and each wore a simple steel cap that covered his scalp, ears, and forehead, with an additional flap jutting down to guard the nose. Three pairs of cold, calculating eyes studied the monster over the tops of the shields until, in unison, a trio of sharpened spikes thrust forward, piercing the monster at the juncture of its grotesque head and the first segment of its armored body. Thrashing wildly, the horax twisted away, easily sliding free of the unbarbed tips, but by the time it dropped to the cavern floor, it was dead.

"Excellent strike, men," proclaimed Sergeant Tankard Hacksaw, stepping up behind the trio. His heavy hand came down to clap each of the dwarves, one after the other, on the shoulder, a blow that sent the young soldiers to staggering. Yet each seemed to swell, visibly warmed by the grizzled sergeant's praise.

"And good drilling, Tank," said Brandon Bluestone, coming down the narrow cavern behind the small company. "You've got them fighting like they're guided by one brain."

"They are, Captain," Hacksaw said with a hearty chuckle. "It's *my* brain!"

The two dwarves stood for a moment, catching their breath, studying the broken, bleeding monster before them. Though each was a bearded dwarf girded for war, they were a study in contrasts. Brandon was tall, open-faced, and handsome, with flowing brown hair and a broad, if slightly cruel, smile. He carried a mighty battle-axe in his right hand; his grip was a foot below the head of the weapon for perfect balance.

Tankard, on the other hand, was short, and almost was wide as he was tall. His hair and beard were black, shot through with gray, and he grinned with the sheer joy of a warrior who loves to fight. His captain's praise only made him smile all the more broadly.

But the jocularity was short-lived as Tankard stared over the shoulders of his men into the unseen depths of the winding tunnel. "How goes it with Morewood and the Second Company?" he asked.

THE FATE OF THORBARDIN

"They're making good progress too," Brandon replied. "A little slower than you—they've passed a lot of side alcoves, and every one of 'em had a couple of horax lurking. It's the standard ambush tactic; they don't seem to realize that we've caught on to them. But we're closing in on the hive from both directions."

Captain Bluestone's tone was grim, purposeful. He had stalked those deep tunnels only a few months earlier, alone and terrified, desperate to rescue his beloved Gretchan Pax from the webbing of a horax tangler. He had found her, and more, but with the blessing of Reorx, they had escaped with their lives, pursued by a hissing, clacking horde of the monstrous arachnoids. Now he had returned with a small army of his fellows, and it was his determined intention that it would be the horax who would be fleeing—those that were fortunate enough to survive the onslaught of dwarves.

"What about the Firespitter?" Tankard Hacksaw asked bluntly. The weapon was a new invention, and none of them knew how well it would work. It was large and ungainly, an iron tank that rolled forward on four small wheels, with a furnace under the nozzle and a large, insulated tank of oil forming the main body of the device. It was certainly hard to move it through the underground caverns, but the veteran dwarves knew that the Firespitter might be decisive if it could be brought to bear against their insectoid enemies.

"The crew is having trouble with some of the bottlenecks in the cave; they're having to do a lot of excavating in order to bring the thing up. So we might have to hold the line for a while before we can really burn the bastards out."

"And how much farther until we get to the hive?"

Brandon shrugged. "I was running for my life the last time I came up from here, so I wasn't paying much attention to landmarks. Still, I'd guess we're within a mile of the queen's nest."

"Good. Oh, and Captain, these awlspikes are working just like advertised," the sergeant noted, gesturing to the long, sharpened steel poles carried by each of the men.

"Good. I thought they would," Brandon noted. "The barbed heads on a normal pike or spear get caught on the horax armor—too often the weapon gets pulled right out of a dwarf's hands. But these sharpened tips come out as easy as they go in. Made to order for bug killing."

"Let's stop yapping and go kill us some bugs, then," growled Tank.

"Move out," Brandon agreed. He watched in satisfaction as Sergeant Hacksaw directed his formation forward. The trio of dwarves who formed the vanguard was trailed by a single file numbering more than two dozen comrades, and as the cavern widened, Tank ordered one after another of the reserves into the front rank. Five dwarves wide, with each soldier bearing a tall shield and long awlspike, the company proceeded deeper into the subterranean darkness underneath the nation of Kayolin.

The horax had long been a threat to that realm of dwarves, for they had dwelled in the deep caverns since the dawn of time. Ever hungry and uncaring of life, they hunted and killed whenever they could. In an age long past, the dwarves had erected walls to keep them from penetrating into Kayolin's mines and delvings, but

THE FATE OF THORBARDIN

recent sabotage—sponsored, Brandon had discovered, by the dwarves' former ruler himself—had allowed the horrific species to surge anew. It was the mission of their two-pronged offensive, commanded by Brandon and closing in on the horax hive from opposite directions, to end the threat once and for all.

They passed a narrow cavern branching off to one side, and before Brandon could remind him, Hacksaw took note of the danger, posting two dwarves to guard against a sudden flank attack. Several more stood in reserve of that pair while the main shield wall moved on. Brandon hung back momentarily to scan the secondary route.

The giant insects had shown a surprising grasp of tactics, including diversion and ambush, but in the bloody month of the campaign to date, the dwarves had grown versed in the horax style of battle. Thus, Brand was not surprised to see movement in the side cavern, even though the enemy gave off no sound to reveal its presence. He knew that augured a possible sudden attack, but he expected his dwarves would have to face only a few of the bug-monsters in the flank assault.

True to his expectations, four horax materialized quickly but in utter silence, rushing from the twisting cavern with antennae quivering and mandibles spread wide, eager to crush dwarf flesh. Their hooked, taloned feet allowed them to cling to nearly smooth surfaces of stone, and so two of them charged along the walls and one advanced, upside down, clinging to the ceiling of the cave.

But the dwarves were prepared, and the giant insects clashed hard against the shields, jarring one of the dwarves back a step but unable to strike a vulnerable limb. Instead, it was the dwarves who drew blood, each of the two driving his sharpened steel spike into the head of an attacking horax.

The monsters exploded into noise, smashing mandibles in forceful *snaps*, hissing in the shrill wail that reminded Brandon of crickets—very, very large crickets—on a hot summer's night. The dwarves grunted and cursed, driving forward, lunging repeatedly with their awlspikes. Their comrades moved up behind, ready to help, but the pair in the first rank prevailed, striking again and again until all four horax were slain, their segmented bodies lying still in spreading pools of dark ichor.

As soon as that threat was neutralized, the dwarves advanced behind the first rank. The two who had just won the skirmish moved to the back of the file, replaced by a pair of well-rested warriors. The whole company continued to push deeper into the cavern.

The corridor expanded into a large, oval chamber, and the lead dwarves stepped to the sides, allowing their trailing comrades to merge into the first line. With drilled precision, the company quickly formed a semicircular front of shields and spikes, a dozen dwarves strong. The right shoulder of the rightmost dwarf touched the chamber wall, a position mirrored by the warrior on the left. From behind the rank, Brandon studied the large space, discerning three passages leading deeper under the mountain on the sides and far wall of the chamber.

Tankard, in the middle of the shield wall, glanced over his shoulder, and Brandon held up a hand with the silent order: *Wait*. For more than a minute, the dwarves did just that, watchful and alert, making no sound beyond the slight rasp of steady respiration.

THE FATE OF THORBARDIN

The first warning was a faint hiss, like a rush of water in the distance, muffled by foliage. There was no clear source for the sound; it seemed to come from everywhere at once. It swelled gradually, then defined itself into a series of clicks and scrapes and scratches, the individual footfalls of many, many twelve-legged horax.

The creatures spilled into the large chamber from all three tunnels, sweeping forward with eyes bulging and mandibles snapping. The first horax reared upward, striking at the dwarves, punching hard against their heavy shields. The dwarves stabbed away, eliciting hisses and shrieks from the stricken monsters. Several arachnoids tumbled over, oozing ichor from the punctures, but others immediately crowded forward to take the places of the wounded.

"Look left!" shouted Brandon, spotting an unusual, red-colored horax rearing up high behind the first wave. "A tangler!"

Even as he shouted the warning, the crimson horax spit a stream of webbing from the grotesque bulge under its head. The sticky strands spattered across three adjacent shields, and the tangler pulled back. Two of the trio of dwarves stood firm, but the one in the middle, whose shield was almost completely covered by the web, lurched forward, pulled off balance by the monster's gooey strands.

The fighter let go of his shield but was too late to keep his footing. He tumbled onto his face, and a horax immediately struck at the nape of his neck. One mandible sliced into his flesh while the other bounced off the shoulder plate of his steel armor. Another of the monsters plunged in, seeking to finish the stricken dwarf.

Brandon leaped forward, straddling his felled soldier and driving the Bluestone Axe down in a powerful blow. The keen edge of his beloved blade split the head of the second horax, killing it instantly. Whipping his weapon to the side, Brandon slashed the neck of the next horax. By that time, several of his men had grabbed the fallen dwarf's ankles and pulled him back behind the safety of the shield wall. The injured warrior groaned, leaving a trail of blood across the floor, and a young cleric immediately knelt to tend to his wound.

The tangler shot a stream of webbing directly at Brandon, but by then his men were set for action. Several held lit torches, standing behind their captain. They waved the sticks in the air, the flames surging, and when the gooey strands came near they touched the brands to the flammable web. Immediately the fire flared along the tangler's web, and the crimson monster had to recoil—too slowly, as the flames burned up to the horax's neck and set the segmented creature ablaze. It writhed and shrieked, and its fellow arachnoids quickly skittered away from the dying tangler.

The surviving horax still swarmed in the cavern, climbing up the walls, scrambling across the ceiling. The dwarves stabbed at every clicking head that approached, aiming for the eyes of the creatures. The long awlspikes reached as high as the cavern ceiling, and when a horax tried to approach from above, one or two stabs was usually enough to dislodge it and send it tumbling onto the backs of its fellows down below.

For several long, tense minutes, the terrible fight raged. The horax, as usual, proved to be utterly fearless as they hurled themselves against the wall of steel. Attacking with coordination, employing feints and deception and concentrations of force, they smashed again and again against the dwarf defense. But the Kayolin fighters never wavered, nor did they break ranks or yield to the lure of advancing incautiously when the horax pulled back from the center of the line, presenting an inviting gap that would have quickly exposed charging dwarves to fatal attack from three sides.

Another dwarf fell, his leg badly gashed by a monster's bite when the shield wall wavered slightly. That gap, too, was plugged immediately and the wounded warrior eased back for treatment that quickly stanched the flow of blood from his severed artery. All the while the dead horax piled up in droves in front of the dwarves, until the mound of segmented, hard-shelled bodies rose higher than the soldiers' heads.

Finally, the last of the monsters in the cavern was slain. Still Brandon's men held their formation, watching and listening and waiting to see if another wave of attackers came up. Only when the captain gave the signal to advance did they make their next move, clearing a path through the pile of bodies and cautiously shifting to the far side of the cavern.

"Take the center passage," Brandon ordered, remembering that place from his earlier ordeal. "It won't be long now."

Once again the first rank pressed down the tunnel, which was wide enough for five dwarves to march abreast. A quintet came from the back of the file; they were fresh soldiers ready to take the brunt, giving comrades exhausted from the skirmish a chance to catch their breath in the rear of the formation. They advanced steadily but quickly, with Brandon and all of the others sensing the nearness of their objective.

Then it loomed before them: a widening of the cavern, and a huge, arched entryway leading into a vast, shadowy chamber behind. Perhaps it was the fetid smell or the moist, cloying air, but suddenly Brandon knew that they were looking at the heart of the hive and that, within that cave, the bloated queen sat high upon her mound of white, oval eggs.

"Tighten yer straps, men," Tankard Hacksaw growled, buckling his own helmet on more securely.

The awlspikes came up, and the line of dwarves headed out. Brandon clapped his sergeant on the shoulder, leaving him in command of the main attack while he jogged back to the nearest connecting corridor, where he had left a team of couriers.

"Any word about the Firespitter? Or anything from Sergeant Morewood?" he asked the first dwarf he met.

"Aye, Captain," came the reply. "He's got the machine through the last bottleneck. His men met some bugs, a good nest of them, in the cave, and he's been busy pushing them out of the way. He hopes to be in position before too long."

"Good. Send word; tell him the main attack is starting. I need that Firespitter as soon as he can bring it up!"

"Yes, sir!" The courier dwarf, wearing supple leather armor instead of the heavy metal of the combat troops, was off at a sprint even as he finished his salute. As satisfied as he could be, considering that half his troops had yet to reach the battlefield, Brandon turned back toward the hive. The cave widened there, and his nostrils filled with the stink of moist earth and the rancidness of the nearby egg chamber.

Already the infantry was advancing against a seething mass of horax, the bugs hissing and clacking and rearing across the whole of the wide cavern leading into the egg chamber. Some of the bugs were scrambling up the walls, while tanglers in the back spit their sticky strands of webs.

As always, it was the front rank of dwarves, the shield wall, that met the enemy in closest, most dangerous combat. There, in the larger space, the Kayolin troops could better expend their full arsenal of tactics. Ranks of archers carried heavy crossbows. They stood behind the shield wall and fired their deadly missiles against the bugs that attempted to climb above the armored attackers. The crossbow quarrels were not as lethal as the awlspikes, but when several of the bolts struck a single horax, the monster twitched and spasmed and lost its grip on the rough stone wall. A strike in the middle of the head was often enough to kill one of the creatures outright.

Other dwarves wielded torches, and the flames surged and flared behind the front line. Whenever a tangler's web spewed forth, the torch-bearers raced to the spot and quickly burned away the highly flammable strands. Still more Kayolin warriors stood ready with small kegs of water and used the liquid to douse the flames that threatened to sear their comrades' flesh. The webs, meanwhile, burned furiously, sizzling like fuses as the flames hissed and crackled their way back to the tanglers themselves. Sometimes the red-shelled bugs managed to break free from the webs before the flames ignited their web glands, but in other instances, the tanglers erupted into churning, oily fireballs that incinerated not only the web-spewing horax, but also those of their fellow arachnoids unfortunate enough to be nearby.

Brandon scrambled up to the top of a flat boulder behind the front rank of Kayolin dwarves. From that vantage, he observed the melee and determined that Sergeant Hacksaw was handling his company skillfully. When the horax pressed on the left, pushing a bulge into the shield wall, Tankard dispatched a dozen dwarves from the reserve. They pushed back, stabbing and killing the arachnoids that threatened to break through, then shoved alongside their comrades until the company was once more secure.

They continued to advance steadily until, behind the fight, Brandon saw the mountain of eggs, pale white spheres as big as a dwarf's torso, the whole pile looming nearly to the top of the massive cavern. At the very summit sat the queen, hideous and bloated, staring about with her massive, multifaceted eyes. She rose up on her thick, segmented legs, though the vast swell of her abdomen still rested atop the pile. She herself was no threat as a fighter, yet when she spread her mandibles and uttered a keening shriek, the teeming horde of her soldiers were spurred to charge with added intensity.

Over the queen's head was a shadowy hole in the ceiling of the cavern, and Brandon's eyes kept flashing to that aperture. Up there was the tunnel from which he had rescued Gretchan. He waited for some sign of movement there.

For some time the battle raged without clear advantage. The dwarves pressed, and the horax swarmed, the line moving a few feet forward or back in different places. More of the Kayolin warriors fell, gashed or sliced by a hooked claw or scything mandible, and the wounded were pulled back and, often enough, salved and saved, while more and more reinforcements from the dwindling reserve rushed forth to join the fray.

Finally, Brandon heard an extra-piercing shriek from the queen. She reared up on top of her mound of eggs, forelegs slashing toward the hole in the ceiling over her head. The nozzle of a great iron machine appeared there, as if on cue, and before the queen could strike at it, a stream of liquid shot downward, showering the bloated horax and spilling down the mountain of hideous eggs.

In the next instant, that stream of shimmering liquid—Brandon knew it was lantern oil—erupted into flames. The Firespitter had arrived!

A dazzling blossom of fire surged down the surface of the egg pile, engulfing the queen and spuming in the middle of the cavern into a searing ball of fire. The heat swept outward immediately, followed by a cloud of thick, black smoke.

"Fall back!" shouted Brandon, his voice a bellow that rose above even the thunderous chaos in the big cavern. Oil continued to spill onto and coat the eggs, reaching all the way to the floor and spreading outward in a burning slick. The eggs crackled and sizzled, bursting open as the pile shriveled and contracted. The horax nearest the flames shrieked and fled, propelled by instinctive terror that, as often as not, caused them to impale themselves upon the waiting awlspikes.

Brandon knew that Fister Morewood's company, the operators of the Firespitter, wore gauze masks as some protection against the choking smoke. Even so, they would be falling back as well, after leaving the machine engaged so it continued to trickle flammable oil onto the inferno raging below. The fire grew hotter and larger, billowing outward, carrying the sickening stench of burned bugs with the soot and the grit of the oil smoke.

Brandon and Tankard's dwarves, down on the floor, were forced to retreat in the face of the billowing smoke, but even so they coughed and gagged as the air grew thick. Finally they withdrew in a sprint, leaving the depths of the hive to burn, cook, and die. Even in the intense heat, the withdrawal was orderly, however, with each of the wounded aided by a pair of companions and a steadfast rearguard, eyes tearing against the acrid smoke, edging carefully backward, awlspikes raised, shields ready to block any last, desperate attack that might emerge from the egg chamber.

And with the eggs died the queen and her warriors, until the threat of the horax, ever a scourge of Kayolin, became a charred footnote in the history of dwarf war.

Two

A Trap on the Trail

Somewhat south of the Newsea, in a forest of scrubby pine, spindly trees clawed their way upward from dry, sandy soil. Marshes, ponds, and a few sluggish streams dotted the landscape, but most of the ground rose high enough that the water had drained away. In one of those places, a lone dwarf maid had set about making camp.

"One thing about a dry pine forest," Gretchan Pax remarked drolly. "There's never any shortage of firewood."

The fact that she was speaking to her dog troubled her not in the least. In fact, when she thought about it, the priestess acknowledged that she spent a great deal of time voicing prayers to Reorx, who was usually nowhere to be seen. Against that backdrop, her dog was a much more congenial—not to mention tangible—conversation partner. After all, he was right there, flopping lazily on the ground at her feet.

She tossed another limb onto the fire and watched as it crackled loudly, fueling the blaze enough that sparks were sent showering skyward. An experienced camper, Gretchen had previously cleared the dry needles and branches from a wide space around her fire, so there was no chance of the blaze spinning out of control.

It was not the fire that worried her, not there, not that night. Nevertheless, she threw a couple more branches into the blaze and settled back to scratch Kondike, the great, black dog that was her conversation partner, between the ears atop his broad, flat head. The animal huffed contentedly, but his flopped ears perked slightly upward. His brown eyes flashed as he shifted his head, and she could see his black nostrils flaring gently as he smelled the air, seeking some telltale spoor that might be carried by the faint breeze.

Leaning back, Gretchan tried to let the familiar presence of a wilderness camp surround and soothe her. She was a very beautiful woman, by dwarven or human or even elven standards. Her golden hair flowed down to her waist, and even after days on the trail, it shone with a coppery sheen as she loosed her braid. Her blue tunic fit snugly across her buxom torso, and leggings of the same color encased her shapely legs. Soft moccasins protected her feet so comfortably that even though she was done walking for the day, she felt no need to remove them.

Even so, she found it hard to relax entirely. Gretchan couldn't figure out why she was so worried and preoccupied. She had been traveling down a rutted cart track, leading away from the coast, which gradually meandered into the hill country. Before choosing a campsite, she'd broken away from the trail, making her way into the trackless woods for nearly a mile. With her usual care, she'd covered her passage, so even if anyone had been following her down the road, which was unlikely in that wilderness, they'd have a hard time tracing her path into the bush.

She'd made camp in a pleasant vale. A shallow creek nearby provided her with fresh water and a couple of fat trout for supper. To the west, the trees opened slightly, revealing the glimmering surface of a small lake; she'd spent a contented hour watching the beautiful reflections as the sun had set. Her camp was far enough back into the trees that no glow of her fire would have been visible from the lake, even if anyone had been there.

Yet it wasn't some wayward logger or even roaming band of highwaymen who worried her. She piled more dried pine logs onto her fire, watching as the flames crackled nearly as high as her head. The tops of the trees surrounding her camp were brightened by the light, a far-from-subtle declaration of her presence. But the light, the heat, even the smells of her cooking fish, were not the kinds of clues that would give her away, of that she was certain.

Uneasily, she rose to her feet and walked the circuit of her little camp, holding her precious staff in her hand. The anvil atop that staff, a symbol of Reorx, her immortal god, remained dark and cold, and from that, at least, she could take some comfort. She came back to the fire and settled onto the makeshift seat she'd made with a mossy stump as a backrest. Her backpack was nearby, and she put her hand upon it.

Unbidden, her mind drifted to Brandon, and she was annoyed with herself when she felt a palpable sense of longing. If only *he* were there . . .

"Damn it!" she whispered, shaking away the thought. Hadn't she crossed a continent by herself, safely making hundreds of camps with just her dog as a companion? In some of those places, there'd been hostile armies nearby, raiding bands of goblins, even ogre and minotaur slavers. She'd taken care of herself just fine, thank you very much!

So why was she so nervous?

It was the Redstone, she realized, as her hand tightened involuntarily over the flap of her pack. She had insisted on bringing the artifact with her; she was taking it to Tarn Bellowgranite at Pax Tharkas as proof that the exiled king's throne was within reach again.

"I'll come with you!" Brandon had pledged. "As soon as we clear out the horax hive! We'll travel together—it will be a splendid trip!"

"I have to go *now*." Her reply had been firm, unbending during the week of awkward discussion preceding her departure, and indeed, her resolve had resulted in the kind of stiffly formal farewell that, in the depths of the woods, struck her as foolishly prideful and petty. She wished she had kissed him with all the passion she felt, had held him against herself for a long time. Why hadn't they spent her last night in Kayolin in a blissful embrace, locked themselves away from the distractions of the world?

Instead, they had shared a formal dinner with his parents and some of the governor's associates. They had talked of politics and warfare until everyone was tired, and she had bade them all her weary and somewhat sulky farewell.

Of course, she knew she was doing the right thing. Her job was to seek out the exiled king in Pax Tharkas, so he could be convinced to prepare his dwarves for the upcoming campaign. When Brandon came after her, a few weeks or months later, he would be marching with a large contingent of the Kayolin Army. Together with Tarn's dwarves of Pax Tharkas and the hill dwarves of Kharolis, they would be armed with the legendary Tricolor Hammerhead—the Redstone was the final component of that hallowed artifact. Then the dwarves of three nations, acting in unison, would return to fabled Thorbardin, smash their way inside, and liberate their long-suffering countrymen from the reign of despotism, fanaticism, and dark magic that had too long held them in sway.

No, hers had been the right decision. Besides, in addition to cleaning out the horax scourge, Brandon needed to finish recruiting and supplying the large army he was raising, preparing that army for an arduous cross-country march, arranging for naval transport to move the dwarves through the Newsea, and a myriad other details that would have left him no time for Gretchan. Of course, logic and necessity dictated what they must do.

But, damn it all, she still missed him!

Almost unconsciously she pulled out her pipe, carefully cleaned and filled it, then touched it off with an ember from the fire. Inhaling the piquant smoke, she exhaled through her nostrils. Yet even her time-honored ritual couldn't dispel the melancholy that seemed to come from somewhere deep inside her.

It was Kondike's low growl that finally broke through her veil of loneliness. Immediately she stiffened, both hands closing around the Staff of Reorx. The black dog slowly rose to his feet, the fur on the nape of his neck bristling. His ears were fully raised, and he stared at one shadowy stretch of wood. After the first audible growl, he made no further sound, but when Gretchan touched his shoulder, she found that he was shivering with tension.

With a sudden gesture, she raised the staff, lifting the anvil high over her head. Immediately the clearing around the fire was revealed in a bright wash of light. The glow emanated from the anvil, so Gretchan knew that anyone looking at her would be at least partially blinded from staring at the light, while her own vision remained keen. She stared between the trees, seeking whatever it was that had alarmed Kondike.

She spotted a patch of color, like a woven shawl, and a moment later an old dwarf maid came into view, hobbling out from behind a pine tree. Her hand was held up to shield her eyes from the glowing anvil, partially blocking her face, but even so, Gretchan recognized her.

"The Mother Oracle! From Hillhome!" she declared, loud and accusing. "You worked for Harn Poleaxe!"

The old crone snorted contemptuously. "Harn Poleaxe wasn't fit to sew the heel on my moccasin," she retorted. "Don't confuse me for his tool merely because we served the same master."

Gretchan rose to her feet, in a wide stance, staff still held high. Beside her Kondike bristled and growled.

Undeterred, the old dwarf woman took a step closer.

"What do you want?" demanded Gretchan Pax. "Why do you seek me out in the wilderness?"

The oracle shrugged. "To do you a favor," she said. "To give you a warning."

"What do you have to warn me about?"

"The warning comes not from me, but from my true master."

THE FATE OF THORBARDIN

Gretchan studied the elderly female, her hand still unwavering as it held aloft the staff and its gleaming anvil. The oracle wore a patched robe, so ratty that it might have been assembled from a hundred multicolored rags. Her face was creased with deep wrinkles, her posture stooped so much that Gretchan could see the thin, white hair on top of her head.

She recalled her first meeting with the oracle, in the town of Hillhome, when the old dwarf woman had conjured up a fire around her hut, then claimed to the aroused citizenry that Gretchan had attacked her. The young priestess had been forced to flee, thwarted in her attempt to learn more about the oracle's mysterious purpose.

"Do you serve the black minion?" she asked. "The creature that rose from Harn Poleaxe when the dwarf was killed?"

Well did she remember that horrifying apparition, its ember-red eyes, clutching talons, and batlike wings spread wide. The thing had loomed high above her amid the battle in Pax Tharkas, but the power of her god had banished it, driven it back to the nether plane from which it had emerged. And even as she asked that question, Gretchan knew that the minion was not the oracle's master, that it, too, served the one who had corrupted Harn Poleaxe.

"What is it, then?" the cleric pressed. "What is the threat? Why do you warn me?"

She lowered the staff slightly, though the anvil still cast a broad swath of light. Gretchan was suspicious and alert, wondering whether the oracle brought a genuine warning or planned to spring some kind of trap.

"My master knows of your mission, and he wants you to turn back from Pax Tharkas. If you go there, you will be doomed; Tarn Bellowgranite, all the exiles, will perish."

"Doomed by what?" demanded Gretchan even as she felt a cold stab of fear. Whether or not the oracle was bluffing, she clearly knew a lot about the cleric's supposedly secret mission.

"Doomed by forces that will overwhelm the puny power of your priestly magic," the old dwarf maid sneered. "By powers of sorcery drawn from the black moon, Nuitari! The same powers that devoured the soul of Harn Poleaxe, that drew the minion into this world to serve my master's bidding!"

Gretchan stamped the butt of her staff on the ground, relishing the solid, fundamental strength of the blow. "I will stand with the power of Reorx at my back and face anything your dark arts can conjure!" she declared.

The oracle laughed, as if the cleric's pronouncement were utterly predictable. Something was strange about the confrontation and Gretchan struggled to understand what was happening. The old woman wasn't threatening her, not directly anyway, nor did she seem the least bit concerned about the power wielded by the dwarf priestess. It was as if she were content to talk, to torment and agitate Gretchan, simply holding her attention . . . to *distract* her!

The realization came with a sudden burst of insight, but it was almost too late. Gretchan spun around, instinctively crouching, grasping her staff in both hands as the light instantly faded to a pale glow.

At the same time, Kondike uttered a bestial snarl and hurled his big body toward the woods but *not* at the place where the oracle stood. Instead, the dog charged

THE FATE OF THORBARDIN

into the dark place between two trees as Gretchan lifted the staff, casting a beam of light into that area with cold, unerring accuracy.

A beautiful dwarf maid stood there, black-haired and pale-skinned, with full lips outlined in ruby, as shiny as if they were covered in a sheen of fresh blood. She wore a black robe, supple material hanging smoothly over the lush curves of her body. Her finger was extended, pointing directly at Gretchan, and as the spill of light revealed her, she uttered a single, sharp bark of sound.

But Kondike was there first. The dog barreled into the dwarf wizard, knocking her off balance. A burst of magic, like a searing bolt of lightning, erupted from her finger, crackling through the air over the cleric's head, bursting and burning in the tops of the dried pine trees across the campsite. The dog snapped at the magic-user's face and she screamed. Gretchan saw a flash of shiny steel in the dwarf's hand then heard a yelp as Kondike's skin was pierced. The dog flinched away, still growling, as the female Black Robe climbed to her feet.

Only then did the cleric remember the oracle. She spun back to see that the old woman had produced a slender stick from within her shawl. She held it in one hand, a wand pointed straight at Gretchan as she chanted to words to an unknown but clearly deadly spell.

The priestess whipped her staff over her head, calling out the name of Reorx as magic exploded from the tip of the wand. A bolt of lethal power shot toward Gretchan, but it was deflected by the swirling vortex of the glowing staff. Instead of striking the priestess, the oracle's spell rebounded, arrowing back against the caster. It struck her in the face and, with a single, splitting scream, the old crone toppled backward and lay still.

Kondike barked furiously, lunging again at the black-robed wizard. Gretchan sprang to help the dog, already glimpsing defeat in that pallid but beautiful face. The female's porcelain-doll features twisted in rage, but apparently she recognized that the fight had turned against her. She uttered a single, guttural word, and vanished from sight.

Only then did Gretchan notice that the forest was on fire all around her, the tinder-dry pines having been ignited by the magic-user's misfired lightning bolt. She trotted over to the oracle, determining at once that the old woman was dead. After a shiver of revulsion, Gretchan picked up the wand, prying it from the oracle's stiff fingers, and stuffed it into her own pack.

Kondike was limping, blood pooling at the base of his foreleg. She knelt, tracing her fingers over the knife wound and murmuring the incantation to a gentle healing spell. At once the dog shook off the injury, staring around with ears upraised and hackles still bristling.

"Yes, I agree. I think we need to get out of here. Let's go," Gretchan said, staring as the flames leaped from tree to tree, the forest fire roaring into life on the far side of the camp.

The dog and the dwarf maid jogged away from the blaze that ignited the once-pastoral camp. She didn't know how the servants of dark magic had found her, though she knew that there was no warning intended: their mission had been to kill her, and they had very nearly succeeded.

THE FATE OF THORBARDIN

Whatever the source of the threat, whatever the means at its disposal, one thing was clear: Gretchan couldn't get to Pax Tharkas too soon.

———DH———

The king's bedroom was cold, far colder than it should be that temperate, late-autumn evening. Tarn Bellowgranite looked out the window, reluctant to draw the shutters even against the chill.

For the icy grip that had settled around his heart was an even more oppressive frost, like a glacier that had settled over his whole spirit, his being.

"Father?"

Tor was there, speaking to the king's rigid back. Tarn winced, almost as if physically wounded. Then he clenched his jaw and turned to look at the boy.

"Yes, son. What is it?"

As he spoke, he appraised the sturdy, young dwarf, clearly more than a boy, though not yet quite a man. Tor stood nearly as tall as his father, but his long, brown hair had the softness of youth, and his beard was merely a foreshadowing of maturity, tufts of whiskers that dusted the sides of his face, just in front of his ears.

"Mother is down in the dungeon again, isn't she?" Tor said, his tone halfway between wounded and challenging. "Talking to Garn Bloodfist."

"I don't know where she is," the exiled king retorted, a half truth—though he hadn't seen her go down the stairs, he knew her habits and knew that his son was right.

"Why does she do that?" Tor said. "He's the one who wanted to kill all the hill dwarves! And now she's the only one who visits him in his cell! Has she forgotten that she's a Neidar herself?"

Tarn shook his head ruefully, turning back to look out the window at the darkness gathering through the foothills and the deep mountain valley. "Your mother will *never* forget that she's a hill dwarf!" he snapped, unable to keep the bitterness out of his voice.

"Then *why*? Why even listen to Garn Bloodfist, give him the comfort of her presence?"

"Your mother is a very sympathetic person," Tarn replied evenly. "She remembers Garn as a loyal lieutenant to me—wild and unpredictable as any Klar, but a fierce warrior and a good guardian of Pax Tharkas when we needed that protection."

"But you're the one who threw Garn in prison!" their son said, confused.

"Because he disobeyed my direct order!" the former monarch declared hotly. "If he'd succeeded, Pax Tharkas would be a tomb, and neither side would have emerged from the war with anything other than deep, incurable wounds."

"Do you think she's helping Garn to see that?" pressed Tor, rather insolently in his father's mind.

"We'll have to talk about that, your mother and I," Tarn replied.

Even as he replied in vague terms, his mind, his heart, focused on the real reason Crystal went down there, the reason she spent as much time away from him as she could within the constricting environment of the fortress. She was trying to forget about Tara, and Tarn and Tor were constant reminders of her loss.

Of *their* loss, damn it! Did she think that he hadn't lost a daughter as well? Tarn and Crystal both had watched their child, their beloved and beautiful girl, get taken by the fever last winter, the disease so cruel that it seemed to eat her away from the inside out.

Why, Reorx? Why did you take her?

For the thousandth time, Tarn voiced the question to the unanswering sky. The bitterness rose within him, the anger and bile that it seemed he would never escape. She had been too young, younger even than Tor. And she had been innocent of everything! Yet the illness had claimed her and not him, not Crystal, not even a deserving soul such as Garn Bloodfist, trapped in the moldering dankness of the dungeon so far below!

The door opened at that moment, and Crystal Heathstone entered the family's apartment, which consisted of four small, though nicely appointed, chambers high up in the East Tower of Pax Tharkas.

"Hi, Mother," Tor said, racing over to Crystal with what Tarn judged to be unseemly haste. He gave her a hug then went out the door, probably seeking his fellow adolescents in the training and exercise room that was several levels below the royal apartments in the tower.

His departure left his parents alone.

"Tor was asking me why you spend so much time with Garn Bloodfist," Tarn barked. "It's come to this: even the child is talking about it! Have you no sense of propriety?"

"There's nothing improper about it. He's in his cell; I'm outside. And the turnkey is right there, watching, at the foot of the stairs," Crystal replied, perhaps a little too casually.

She crossed the apartment to the small kitchen, pulled a piece of cheese from the chillbox, and started to carve thin slices. "I brought a loaf of bread from the baker. Do you want a sandwich?" she asked.

"Don't change the subject!" he snapped, though his stomach rumbled in spite of himself as the rich, pungent odor of the cheese spread through the room. "I think you should stop going down there," he said, his bristling chin jutting belligerently.

Crystal cut two more slices, the knife thunking solidly into the wooden cutting block with each stroke. When she turned around to face him, Tarn was surprised to see tears in her eyes.

His immediate reaction to her distress was anger. "Does he really mean that much to you?" he challenged. "I should think a dwarf who tried to exterminate a thousand of your kinfolk would be somewhat less attractive than, say, your own husband!"

"Stop it!" she hissed, shaking her head, setting her graying hair—still long and silky—shaking around her shoulders. "Don't you see that I'm trying to *understand* his hate? Trying to see how he could contemplate such an atrocity? How any dwarf, present company included, could cling to such ancient and outmoded hatreds!"

"I don't hate hill dwarves!" Tarn spluttered, surprised by her retort.

"But you still don't trust them, do you?" Crystal said. "Even though you signed a treaty with them, pledging an alliance for the future. You're doing everything you can to see that the agreement is never completed."

"How can I trust the cursed Neidar!" the exiled king shouted, nearly exploding. "They almost destroyed us—destroyed you too!"

"You know that was sorcery!" she replied. "And

Gretchan Pax showed you, and my own people, the power of Reorx. It is his will that we learn to get along!"

"Sometimes I think you long to return to your own people," Tarn said, suddenly losing his energy for the fight. "I don't know why you've stayed with me, and my people, for so long."

She looked at him coldly. "Perhaps I stayed for the children," she said.

And there it was again, out there for both of them to feel as a fresh wound, a cut that would never heal. Tara was gone, dead . . . and with her had gone so much hope for the future.

He stared out the window again. He heard Crystal sob, choking on an inarticulate final word. In the mountain valleys, the shadows had grown thick and oppressive. Darkness was almost upon them.

———DH———

The creature of Chaos did not so much live as it existed. Yet even in its primitive subsistence, it posed an almost immeasurable threat against every form of living being on, or within, the world of Krynn. It was made of consuming fire, an eternal flame that swelled from within the mighty, serpentine form, and it destroyed life, right down to the bare mineral foundations of the world, by its very presence.

For long years—perhaps decades, perhaps eons, for the mind of the creature did not acknowledge the existence of anything so ordinary as time—the being had been a prisoner, constrained by magic so powerful that even its unimaginable power had been thwarted. And for all that existence, it had remembered, recalling in vivid detail, a previous state of unbridled freedom, when the creature of Chaos had been accompanied by many others of its kind, had been followed by legions of deadly shadow wights, had born a mighty daemon warrior upon its broad shoulders as they embarked upon an orgy of destruction.

Their violence had been unleashed by a war between the very gods, when the deities of Krynn had faced their ultimate nightmare in the person of Chaos, himself. And while the gods battled, the armies of Chaos wreaked their gleeful destruction upon the world.

The creature and its daemon lord master had swept into an underground world peopled by dwarves. They had bored through the bedrock; mere granite simply melted away in the face of the monsters' incredible heat, and even metal barriers soon glowed red, yellow, then white before they flowed like water out of the way. The army of Chaos had swept through the subterranean nation like a hurricane assaulting a flatland shore, collapsing great cities, searing the waters of a mighty sea into clouds of suffocating steam, exterminating the pathetic dwarves wherever the foolish mortals thought to offer resistance.

The creature of Chaos had come from nothingness, knew naught of its previous existence in the Abyss. It had been called forth by the command of its immortal master, and in that summons it had taken form, learned flight, and brought flame and destruction into the world.

That freedom had been a fleeting moment in time, but it had been the formative experience of the Chaos creature's existence. Too soon, the lord of Chaos had been defeated by the gods of Krynn, and the army of Chaos had scattered back to the nothingness from whence it had emerged.

That was, all except that lone, surviving serpent. The Chaos creature had languished and burned in the depths beneath the mountain, trapped first by the weight of the mountains themselves then ultimately by the power of the black wizard. Always it had strived and struggled and fought for freedom, but for too long the magic chains had held it at bay.

Until, finally, those chains had been broken, shattered by the magic of the very wizard who had created them. The creature of Chaos had flown free again, bringing fire and death and massive destruction to the underground nation yet again. But such spurious killing seemed unworthy, pointless, after its long imprisonment.

It would seek a worthy goal. It would feast on magic, for magic was power, and magic was also an enemy. It was not an enemy to be feared. Unlike the almighty gods, magic could be mastered, magic could be tamed and used.

The gods were to be feared, the creature knew. That was a great lesson learned, one even the tangled mind of the fiery serpent could understand. It feared the power of the gods, but it hungered for the power of magic.

For the Chaos creature had learned to hate. It hated the one who had so wrongly trapped it. It hated magic and those who wielded magic.

And the Chaos creature would have its revenge.

Three

Halls of Governance

The file of Kayolin dwarves emerged from the horax caverns into the deep levels of their great nation, where their kinsmen struggled and strived and labored to carve out a world under the mountains. The victorious warriors climbed past the mines and smelting plants, through the coal yards and the sturdy pillars supporting the city of Garnet Thax. They beat their drums and chanted the news of their triumph, so by the time they reached the city's midlevels, the whole population of Kayolin had turned out to welcome the returning heroes.

"Bluestone! Bluestone!" The sound of his name was a proud roar in Brandon's ears, and he practically felt his chest swelling from the thundering accolades. He led the column, the Bluestone Axe slung easily over his shoulder, and though he tried to deflect some of the praise, to spread it to the sturdy shoulders of his lieutenants and foot soldiers, his men didn't begrudge him the honor.

Indeed, as they moved onto a large ramp, one of the avenues circling steadily upward through the vertical city of Garnet Thax, Tankard Hacksaw and Fister Morewood themselves stepped forward and bodily lifted their captain onto their shoulders without missing a step in their rhythmic marching.

"Put me down, damn it!" Brandon insisted, rocking backward so much that he had to grab Tankard's shoulder to restore his balance. But better to fall than to relinquish his axe!

"Ah, let yerself enjoy it, Captain," Fister proclaimed. Someone in the throng had handed the sergeant a foaming mug, and he took a deep draught, smacking his lips in satisfaction. Another vessel was proffered by a cheering maid, and the loyal soldier willingly passed that second mug up to his commander.

Though still teetering, Brandon decided that he might as well ride the wave of adulation to the top of the city, so he took a drink himself and left it to his carriers to make sure that he didn't take an ignominious fall. When he had drained the mug, he threw it hard, smashing it against the stone wall of the underground roadway and whooping in joy as the file of marching dwarves surged on, the drums pounding even faster.

He looked across the sea of beaming faces: the bearded men; the apple-cheeked dwarf maids; youngsters hopping up and down or, for a fortunate few, hoisted onto the shoulders of a willing adult. All the dwarves were cheering, and most of them were drinking. The crowd had continued to swell, spilling forward from the walls until the column of soldiers had barely room to march in double file down the middle of the wide avenue.

Unconsciously he found himself searching for Gretchan's face, though he knew that she was far away

THE FATE OF THORBARDIN

from there by then. For a wistful moment, he wished that she could be there waiting for him, joining the happiness of the victory celebration, though even a moment's rational reflection reminded him that if Gretchan had been in Kayolin when he had embarked on the recent campaign, she would have been down in the horax hive with the soldiers, not up there in the city waiting for Brandon's return.

But she had told him what she had to do, and he had agreed; they both had important missions, and the sooner they got going, the better. He reminded himself, also, that he had accomplished only a single, first step on the long and difficult road that lay before him. Defeating the horax had been a necessity but only because he needed to secure the safety of Kayolin before embarking on his more important tasks.

As if reading his mind, Chamberlain Wicket came into view, standing in the roadway before the column as the boisterous celebrants gave the governor's aide enough room, barely, to wave his hand at Captain Brandon Bluestone as he approached.

The drums still pounded, but Tankard and Fister came to a stuttering halt and lowered Brandon to the ground with as much dignity as they could muster. The captain felt acutely conscious of his muddy, sooty tunic and the flecks of ale foam still clinging to his mustache and beard.

"Congratulations!" Wicket declared, abandoning courtly manners to clasp the young warrior in an enthusiastic embrace. "Now come with me," he added firmly. "Your father needs to see you right away."

———DH———

"This is Dram Feldspar. He's representing the emperor of Solamnia in these negotiations," explained Garren Bluestone, the governor of Kayolin.

Brandon's father was holding court in his private office, a marble-furnished chamber with several chairs and a desk, adjoining the great throne room of Garnet Thax. He was a smaller, thinner dwarf than his son, and certainly more well groomed at the moment. Garren's beard was braided and tucked into his suspenders, his hair neatly combed, his nails trimmed and cleaned.

Brandon had reported there immediately upon receiving the summons from the chamberlain to find the two elder dwarves seated, each enjoying a small glass of pungent dwarf spirits.

"Sorry for my appearance," the younger dwarf said, acutely aware of the soot and stains upon his leather tunic, not to mention his scuffed and hobnailed boots. "I came here as soon as we returned from the campaign."

"No worries, I'm sure," his father said genially. "Dram Feldspar is no stranger to war."

"I've heard of you; all Kayolin owes you a debt," Brandon said, sizing up the stranger, who was regarding him with a friendly grin. Feldspar's skin was bronzed and weathered by long exposure to the outside world. His full, brown beard was shot with gray, and he wore a plain, woolen jersey and trousers. The only sign of his official status was a mantle of black silk, embroidered with silver thread, resting easily upon his broad shoulders.

Brandon bowed formally and extended his hand; Dram rose out of his chair to take it in a firm grip. The elder dwarf's exploits—he had helped the emperor

THE FATE OF THORBARDIN

of Solamnia, a former fugitive, to battle and defeat an army of ogres and goblins that had terrorized the Garnet Mountains and surrounding plains for several years—were well known to all Kayolin.

"I may have lived under the sky for these last years, but Garnet Thax is my home too," Dram said as if, like Brandon, he was embarrassed by too much praise. "And anyway, we dwarves can't leave it to the humans to do all of our fighting for us!"

"Well said," Garren Bluestone acknowledged. "And that leads me to our current goal, and to the reason we seek the assistance of the emperor and, specifically, of his ships."

"That's what he said when he sent me up here. He was intrigued by your request and asked me to make the trip to Garnet Thax posthaste. You want to send an army all the way down to Thorbardin?" Dram asked with seemingly genuine interest.

Garren nodded. "We have reason to believe that the elder home is in dire straits. It is our wish to restore the rightful high king to his throne."

Dram Feldspar frowned. "How can you know this?" he asked. "Isn't the kingdom sealed up tight?"

The governor gestured to his son, allowing Brandon to answer the question. "It's still sealed against physical entry. But some of the activities there have been marked by powerful sorcery. Several gully dwarves used that magic to escape and provide us key intelligence about Thorbardin. In addition, we are assembling an artifact that, we believe, will give us the means to gain entry to the place with a significant force of troops."

"Gully dwarves?" Dram's tone was droll. Brandon decided against telling him that one of the Aghar, Gus

Fishbiter, had actually escaped from Thorbardin twice. No need to flesh out the story with even more startling and barely believable details.

"Yes. They've been questioned by many of us, not the least of whom is a wise priestess of Reorx. She and I are both convinced they are telling the truth."

"Convinced enough that you're willing to send an army, then," Dram noted, making the phrase a statement, not a question.

"Exactly," the younger Bluestone replied.

"It hasn't escaped our notice that you call yourself 'governor' here, not 'king,' " the Solamnic emissary said, directing the remark at Garren. "Somewhat of a change from the previous regime, eh?"

"Many things have changed since the time of Regar Smashfingers," Garren Bluestone acknowledged. "Not the least of which is the matter of succession. No longer do we dispatch our former leaders with violence. Smashfingers, for all his faults, is enjoying a relatively comfortable retirement in a manor on the nobles' level. And I have made it my further responsibility to right the wrongs that are occurring in Thorbardin, so that we may restore all the dwarf nations of Krynn to their historic roles."

"A worthy goal," Dram acknowledged, though he suppressed a smile at the governor's fervor. "And do you know how many ships you might require? And where you will wish to embark and disembark your army?"

"My son has experience with the journey to the Kharolis Mountains and back," Garren said. He nodded at Brandon. "I believe you said that Caergoth would be the ideal port to begin?"

The younger Bluestone nodded. "It's the only large enough port in Southern Solamnia," he noted. "It has the capacity to load up an army—say, at least four thousand dwarves—over the course of a day. We could march to one of the smaller ports, which are closer, but it would take us a week to load up the transports."

"That's what I would have recommended," Dram replied approvingly. "No dwarf likes to have water under his feet—and to spend six days at anchor, waiting for your comrades to get rowed out to their ships, would give even the most hearty warrior a bad case of the nerves."

"Right! So then I thought your ships could put us ashore on the coast, just south of Xak Tsaroth," Brandon continued. "That puts us within a short week's march of Pax Tharkas, with Thorbardin's North Gate not too far beyond."

"Aye . . ."

Dram seemed to assent, but his tone, his quizzical expression, conveyed his skepticism.

"I know what you're thinking: 'The North Gate is a narrow tunnel, set high up in a cliff wall. No army could even reach it, much less attack,'" Brandon said.

Dram chuckled. "That's pretty close to the mark."

"Well, I think we've found a way to breach the mountain itself," the younger Bluestone continued. "It has to do with an artifact of Reorx, which consists of three parts or smaller artifacts, actually. We have now come into possession of the third and final part, which is being carried to Pax Tharkas. And with the army of Kayolin, Tarn Bellowgranite's brigade, an army of hill dwarves, and this artifact of Reorx on our side, I think we will prevail."

"Hill dwarves?" Dram looked pained. "Now I've heard it all."

"They are pledged by pact with Tarn Bellowgranite to aid him in this attempt," Brandon said. "I was there at the signing. All the exiled king need do is ask for their help."

"And of course, we are willing to pay for the sea passage," Garren said.

After a long, suspenseful pause, Dram nodded, accepting the offer. "Emperor Markham appreciates the wealth of Kayolin, as well as your friendship and, in this matter, the needs of the dwarves. He has instructed me to tell you that your army will be transported at the expense of the Solamnic Navy. He wishes you to see this as the gesture of enduring friendship and trust that it is. The ships will be dispatched upon my return to Palanthas, and they should be gathered in Caergoth within four weeks' time."

"We are humbled by his generosity," Garren said sincerely.

The emissary from Solamnia stood and cleared his throat. "Good luck to you," was all he said.

———DH———

In a dark cell in the dungeons far below the fortress of Pax Tharkas, a bitter dwarf slowly yielded to the insanity that had ever lurked just below the surface of his awareness. He pulled at the hair that still bristled from his head, though his scalp was marred by bloody, bare patches which he had previously violated. His eyes, always wide and startled looking, like any Klar's, darted wildly around the cell, swinging from the barred door to the ceiling, the walls, the floor, as if wary of an enemy or seeking some avenue of escape, in any direction.

"I'm mad!" his whispered, careful to keep his voice low so the turnkey couldn't hear him. He also worried about listeners in the adjacent cells, though through his long year of imprisonment, he had discerned no evidence of any other prisoner down there. Still, he wouldn't put it past the king to trick him, to post some scum eavesdropper right next door, listening for the prisoner to make a damning confession.

Garn Bloodfist had never been exceptionally well-balanced, even by the standards of the volatile and impetuous Klar. For most of his adult life, he had been a leader of that clan and a more or less loyal follower of the king in exile. But still he was a Klar.

The king had never fully recognized the threat posed by the hateful, deceitful hill dwarves who lived all around the area near Pax Tharkas. *Garn* had known! Garn had seen the danger and had led his valiant Klar on campaigns against the Neidar, up to—and sometimes even beyond—the limits imposed by his monarch.

Then, with the moment of his greatest triumph at hand, with the teeming mass of the enemy army funneled within the walls of the fortress, caught within a perfect trap—many thousands of tons of crushing rock, ready to be released, ready to kill *all* the hill dwarves—the king had finally lost his nerve. He had ordered Garn to hold his hand, to not release the trap.

But *Garn* had seen the truth! Garn knew what to do! He had disobeyed his king and pulled the lever to release the trap, and the killing mechanism had failed to release!

An idiot of a gully dwarf had, all unwittingly, ruined the trap's release. For Garn, his life had all but ended on that day, when the exiled king made peace with the hill dwarves, and the once-loyal Klar captain had been clapped in irons and hauled off to the dungeon.

He languished there, slowly going mad, or madder. He chewed on his lip, shivering, until he tasted blood. He smashed his fist into his temple and stopped his chewing, though he still shivered. He huddled on the floor, rocking back and forth. He wanted to whimper, to shriek, but he wouldn't give his imagined eavesdropper the satisfaction.

He wished that *she* would come back but knew that it was too soon since her last visit. *She* was the only bright spot in his life—odd, since she was a hill dwarf. Her visits were the only thing that kept him from falling utterly into despair. She listened to him, and he was careful to mask his insanity when he talked back to her in reasonable, calm tones. She spoke to him, offering comfort and hope, not so much through her words—which he frequently didn't understand—but merely from her presence and the soothing sounds she made.

Suddenly Garn Bloodfist stiffened. He'd heard a noise in the outer hall—something he recognized as a real noise, not the imagined sounds triggered by his paranoia.

"Who's there?" he demanded. *I'm not mad! She must not know that I'm mad!*

"It's me," came the whispered reply.

But it was not the cherished lady's voice that responded. Instead, the speaker sounded like a youngster, a dwarf male whose voice had not fully deepened into manhood. Garn shrewdly remained silent, listening, and the mystery was soon resolved.

"I'm Tor Bellowgranite. My mother is Crystal Heathstone. She comes here sometimes . . . to talk to you. Doesn't she?"

What to say? What to do? Garn's tongue froze in his mouth, and he felt a suffocating pressure close around his throat. He opened his mouth, but for seconds he could force only a hoarse croak to emerge.

"Yes," he finally articulated. "She talks to me. She is a kind woman, your mother."

"But she's a hill dwarf!" the lad replied, his voice an accusatory hiss. Even through his madness, Garn realized that his visitor was speaking in a harsh whisper and was no more interested in being overheard by eavesdroppers than was the Klar himself. "And you spent your life making war against the hill dwarves!"

"That war—that war is over," Garn said, somehow forcing his voice to be calm even as the lie spilled forth. That war would never end! "I . . . I care for her. She is good to me."

"You aren't trying to harm her?" asked the young dwarf.

"No!" wailed Garn, forgetting the need for discretion, forgetting everything in the searing hurt of the question. "No! I would never hurt her! I would never do her wrong!"

"My father thinks you're dangerous," Tor declared.

"But I'm not dangerous!" Garn replied, calming himself, putting all of his imagined sincerity into the denial.

He held that thought close to his heart as the young dwarf finally padded quietly away, back to his royal apartments, to his life of sunlight and family and good food.

I'm not dangerous! Garn argued with himself, persuasive, convincing, settling himself into a corner of the cell and repeating the truth like a mantra.

Not dangerous at all.

FOUR

A KING UNDER THE WORLD

"Er, Your Majesty," said General Blade Darkstone tentatively. "Could I have a word?"

King Willim of Thorbardin glared at his military commander—glaring, at least, as much as a dwarf with no eyes could glare. He could see Darkstone clearly enough because of the spell of true-seeing that the monarch cast upon himself at all times, but he knew that the image of his face, with eye sockets stitched shut and scars irregularly marking his facial features, presented a horrific sight to those who dared to look at him. And he liked that.

"What is it?" he asked petulantly. His mind was already wandering, bored with whatever matters his chief general wished to discuss.

"It's the security situation throughout the city. I strongly suggest we reform Norbardin's militia and resume patrols. There are unruly elements, criminals and gangs organized along clan lines, that are beginning to claim control of their neighborhoods."

Willim the Black sighed. He was an accomplished magic-user and master wizard in the Order of the Black

Robes. He had vanquished countless enemies, including the captors who had gouged out his eyes and scarred his face, not to mention the recent king who had made him an outlaw. He had killed more victims than he could possibly count. He had killed for vengeance, for practical gain, for power, and for the simple pleasure of inflicting death. He relished killing and violence, and he craved power.

At the same time, he had grown increasingly restless in his new role as high king of Thorbardin. In truth, it seemed as though the pursuit of the crown and the destruction of its previous holder had constituted a far more exciting endeavor than did actually ruling the place. He spent much of his time stalking around the capital city, terrifying his subjects and surveying a shockingly damaged and battle-scarred domain. When he sat on the rocky chair that served as his throne and looked out—quite literally since the palace walls remained broken and pockmarked, the aftermath of the war that had brought him to the throne—over his capital city, he saw a wasteland. And that wasteland held very little real interest for him.

That city, Norbardin, was indeed shattered. A pall of smoke lingered in the air, a layer of sooty murk that seemed to remain suspended a dozen feet above the ground. Neither did it reach to the lofty ceiling of the subterranean city; instead, it hung there like a stratus, a layer of gritty foulness in the cake that had once been Thorbardin's greatest city.

He tried to force himself to think about Darkstone's suggestion. There was clear danger in letting the clans organize around distinct power bases. His own clan, the Theiwar, had long been oppressed by the others—most notably the Hylar and Daergar—who feared the Theiwars' skill at magic. For the first time in modern history, one of their own had gained the throne of Thorbardin, and that certainly created an opportunity for the Theiwar to advance their status throughout the city of Norbardin and, indeed, within the entire great nation.

But Willim really didn't care that much about the fortunes of his clan or any other clan. For a moment he thought wistfully about his chief apprentice, the voluptuous Facet. She was gone from Thorbardin, sent by the wizard on an important mission. Yet even that crucial task seemed to pale in comparison to his immediate desires. He missed Facet and wished she would return to him soon.

His head remained down, but his spell of true-seeing allowed him to inspect the wasteland that was Norbardin, to scrutinize the vast plaza—still covered with the wrack and ruin of war—where his army had at last prevailed over the forces of the late king, Jungor Stonespringer. He remembered a bitter truth: it was not Willim's army that had prevailed, but his creature of Chaos, the fire dragon named Gorathian. The wizard had unleashed the monster from its magical bonds, and it had embarked upon an orgy of destruction, boring through the solid rock of Thorbardin's foundation, incinerating anything combustible, burning to death countless dwarves. It was Gorathian that had had most of the fun.

One of those victims had been the former king, and his death had sealed Willim's victory. Yet it was the fire dragon, not the victory, that most occupied Willim's attentions.

"What was that?" the wizard demanded, springing up from his chair, tense and trembling. He probed the murky distance with every fiber of his mind, injecting the spell of true-seeing into shadowy crevices, around corners, even under slabs of heavy rock.

"I didn't see anything, lord," Darkstone said firmly.

"There!" cried Willim, his voice cracking. "Can't you hear it? Can't you *feel* it?"

The great cavern seemed warmer already and was growing hotter by the second. Willim felt sick to his stomach, picturing the vicious, treacherous beast approaching from any direction. Indeed, Gorathian could fly through stone, could melt the very bedrock of the world. It was Willim's sincere belief that Gorathian would appear someday without warning, bursting from the floor—or the ceiling, or the walls—to devour the powerful wizard in one lethal, incinerating bite. Willim feared only one thing: the return of Gorathian.

"It comes!" croaked Willim. "It is near!"

"I presume you refer to the fire dragon," the general replied. "But I am sorry to say I detect no sign of the cursed beast's presence."

"It's coming!" shrieked the wizard king. "It's coming; it's here!"

And with a word of magic, Willim teleported away to the safety of his dark, cold lair.

———DH———

Yes, the creature of Chaos had a name: Gorathian; and it had a form: fire dragon.

And it had a hunger that gnawed and ached and burned within. It was a being of dark power, chaos fueled by the magic that thrummed and lurked and

THE FATE OF THORBARDIN

seethed in the very bowels of the world. And magic was the only thing that could infuse it with more power, that could soothe the ache, ease the hunger.

Willim guessed right. There was one target the fire dragon sought more than any other: the former master who had imprisoned it, taunted it, and finally released it to, he had dared to hope, serve his will.

But the fire dragon was not a subservient being nor did it willingly forgive those whom it hated. So it stalked the underworld darkness of Thorbardin, relentlessly seeking the spoor of the wizard whom it hated and that, someday, would consume. True, Willim the Black's powerful spells made him an elusive target, for he could teleport away at the first hint of danger. But the dark wizard must sleep and eat and slake his other mortal needs. Those needs could not help but distract him in the end, and the end would come; if Gorathian could strike when the wizard was distracted, the wizard would surely die.

Each narrow escape only served to fuel the fire dragon's hunger. Soon, it would feed.

Gorathian swept through the bedrock of Thorbardin, flying through solid stone with little more effort than a fish needed to pass through water. Behind it, the fire dragon left a wake of smoldering stone, a wormhole passage of melted rock and acrid, bitter smoke. The nation of the dwarves was permeated by such passages, nearly all of them created during the Chaos War, when scores of dragons like Gorathian had scourged the cities and warrens of the ancient nation.

Many of the cities had been so weakened by those boreholes that they had collapsed, in part or in total, heavy layers of pavement and stone buildings crumbling downward to crush the lower environs in cities such as Theibardin, Daebardin, and other vaunted clan homes.

The most violent destruction had been wrought upon the greatest city of all: Hybardin, the Life-Tree of the Hylar, which had tumbled and collapsed and fallen into a mass of rubble. Once the great community had been one of the wonders of the world, rising as a pillar from the middle of the Urkhan Sea, extending all the way to the ceiling of the vast cavern holding the sea, and serving as Life-Tree to so many of Thorbardin's great cities. Wracked by war, weakened by the onslaught of Chaos, the Life-Tree had collapsed, and with it had fallen the Hylar-inspired dreams of a prosperous and peaceful future for all dwarfkind.

The scar of the place where the Life-Tree had been rooted was called the Isle of the Dead. It rose from the still waters of the Urkhan Sea as a pile of loose rock, with an occasional section of shattered column or ruined facade discernible amid the broken stone.

For many years after the Chaos War, the Isle of the Dead had been truly that, a place where broken shards of rock, some of them bigger than a house, had frequently snapped free from the cracked and jagged upper tier, where the city had once supported the vast cavern ceiling. The deadly missiles had fallen steadily and relentlessly, ensuring than any dwarf—or other creature—who sought to remain upon the isle would eventually be crushed by falling stone.

Almost unnoticed by most of Thorbardin, however, that bombardment had slowed and virtually ceased over the past decade. Nearly all of the broken stones had finally broken loose, so the ceiling that remained was relatively, if not perfectly, intact.

THE FATE OF THORBARDIN

It was on the Isle of the Dead that Gorathian came to rest, to contemplate, and to wait. The wizard had a lair and a palace and other places that he frequented, and the fire dragon knew all of those places. It could go to any of them, at will, and it frequently did, sallying from the island to wherever it wanted to go in Thorbardin, killing dwarves with thoughtless abandon—often they died merely from proximity to its incendiary transit—and further eroding the bedrock of the undermountain realm.

Sooner or later it would catch its prey. It would feed. And at last its hunger would be sated.

FIVE

SOUTH ROAD TO WAR

The Great Gate of Kayolin yawned wide, opening the underground kingdom to the frosty, dry air. It was a crisp morning, early in the winter, in the Garnet Mountains. Snow formed heavy cornices on the highest ridges of Garnet Peak itself, but the lesser mountains were merely dusted with a coating of white powder.

The scene outside the gate was a festive one, with a thousand or more citizens having gathered under the sky to bid their warriors good fortune on their march to war. Vendors had set up stalls, selling everything from roasted sausages and fried mushrooms to beer, ale, and dwarf spirits. To judge from the raucous cheering that erupted when the vanguard of the army marched out of the darkness and into the sun, the vendors of strong drink had been doing a brisk business over the past several hours.

Brandon was neither surprised nor displeased. He marched at the head of the army, his mighty axe held casually on his shoulder in his left hand as he raised his right in salute, responding to the swelling cheers that came from both sides of the road. The track followed the bed of a mountain valley, with thick pine forests to both sides. Near the gates the woods had been cleared back a dozen paces or more from each banked ditch, and that clearing was the scene of festive celebration and hope.

Brandon himself couldn't quite believe the enthusiasm with which the citizens of Kayolin had responded to his plea for volunteers. In two weeks he had raised an army of exactly the size and strength that he had desired. Dwarves had come from all walks of life, leaving their jobs as miners and cooks, bartenders and brewers, to pledge their support to the mission that had captured the imagination of all Kayolin: Liberate Thorbardin! Return the true high king to his throne! Bring all the dwarf peoples back under a single crown!

Fortunately, nearly all of the recruits, as was standard in dwarf society, were skilled in combat and already owned their own armor and weapons, be they swords, crossbows, axes, hammers, or halberds. A disciplined people by nature, the dwarf recruits had accepted assignment into platoons, companies, brigades, and legions, and served under captains and commanders who, everyone knew, had proved their worth in many previous battles and wars.

Brandon marched at the head of a column more than four thousand dwarves strong, the largest force Kayolin had sent into the field in hundreds of years. And they would fight not for the safety of their own homeland, but for the restoration of dwarven pride and security, as represented by the ancient nation of Thorbardin.

THE FATE OF THORBARDIN

He wished, not for the first time, that Gretchan could be there to see the proud spectacle. But his booted feet were buoyed by the knowledge that, with each southward step, he moved closer to her.

A hundred paces or so outside of the gate, he stepped to the side of the road, accepting the congratulations of several sturdy miners who, judging by their slurred hellos and raucous demeanor, had obviously left their workplace some hours earlier to gather under the awning of a friendly beer vendor. Brandon politely declined ten or a dozen offers of free drinks and turned to face the road, watching his newly raised army as it marched past.

First came the elite company of the Garnet Guards, their red tunics looking sharp and warlike in the bright sunlight. They were led by the elderly, but still spry, General Watchler. Watchler and his splendid soldiers had fallen out of favor under the regime of Regar Smashfingers, the previous governor, who would have styled himself a king, and the red-garbed fighters had proved to be a key ally when Brandon and his father had challenged Smashfingers's right to rule. With the help of the Garnet Guards, the ambitious would-be king was deposed, Garren Bluestone had been placed in the governor's chair, and the events were set in motion that allowed the commencement of their epic campaign.

Watchler, his gray hair and beard woven into long braids, flashed Brandon a wink as he marched past, back and shoulders straight, eyes twinkling as long-banked martial fires were rekindled in his soul. His Redshirts, some three hundred strong, followed in precise formation, feet stomping to the beat set by the drummers.

Those drummers, marching right behind, were young dwarves led by a quartet of stalwarts carrying bass drums the size of beer kegs. They pounded in a steady cadence, the *boom boom boom* setting the early pace. Next came many rows of different-sized percussion instruments, ranging from rattling snares to crashing brass gongs. Altogether nearly one hundred dwarf drummers raised a cacophony, and the crowd cheered all the louder as they passed.

Next came a long file, some fifteen hundred dwarves, that formed the First Legion, under the command of a proud, strutting Tankard Hacksaw. His unit was followed by the engineers, hauling a dozen wagons, including three Firespitters and an array of oil casks, the ammunition for the lethal, incendiary weapons. The experimental device had performed so well against the horax that Brandon had commissioned two more of them, deciding that they might provide a crucial advantage on any underground battlefield. Finally, Fister Morewood led his Second Legion down the road, tromping in steady cadence to the still audible drummers who were, by then, ahead by nearly a mile.

Only when the last of Morewood's men, a lightly armored company of fast-moving scouts, had passed did Brandon step back onto the road. His flush of elation had diminished as the enormity of the task before him hit home.

His mind whirled with questions. Was the emperor of Solamnia reliable enough to provide the ships that he had promised, ships that were utterly necessary if the Kayolin Army was to make its way to southern Ansalon? Would Tarn Bellowgranite be ready to seize the opportunity of alliance presented by the strong

THE FATE OF THORBARDIN

Kayolin force? Would the hill dwarves honor their pact with the mountain dwarves of Pax Tharkas? Would Gretchan be there, waiting for him in that lofty fortress? Did she miss him as he missed her? Was she all right?

It was the last question, more than anything else, that returned him to the mood of anticipatory excitement with which he first had greeted the day. Unconsciously, he brightened, picking up the length of his strides, moving faster even as he maintained the pace of the drummers.

For every step took him closer to her.

——DH——

Willim the Black worked at the table in his laboratory, mixing a gruel consisting of finely ground dried bat wings leavened with a few drops of draconian blood. His hands and nimble fingers moved quickly, without conscious effort, grinding the wings to an even finer powder in his mortar, dripping the blood into the vessel with a hollowed quill, then using the tip to stir the ingredients into a viscous paste. When he was satisfied with the mixture, he scooped it out with his finger and smeared it onto a slab of marble, spreading it into a thin, even layer. Finally, he set it aside to dry; he would not be able to complete the next step of the process for several intervals, not until the paste was ready to crumble into dust. Only then would he add the rest of the components then heat it to create a precious dose of a potion of transformation—one of many hundreds of elixirs and lotions that he kept locked in his most cherished cabinet.

Nearby, two blue sparks shimmered and floated, aimlessly circling around within a clear bell jar. Once in a while the sparks would probe along the base of the jar, as if seeking escape. But the rim of the vessel rested securely upon a base of smooth rubber, and there was no way even a bubble of air, much less anything more concrete, could escape.

Willim turned his eyeless face toward the wall, listening, peering into the darkness with the keen sense of his spell of true-seeing. As always, he remained alert for any sign of fire or heat, any clue that might signal the stealthy, lethal approach of the vengeful fire dragon Gorathian.

His senses tingled but not because the serpent of Chaos was near. Instead, it was a prickling of magical awareness along the hairs at the back of his neck. Quickly he spun. Then he saw her, outlined even more clearly to his magical vision than she would have been to normal vision under brightest daylight.

"Facet! My pet!" he cried, a crooked smile creasing his scarred, bearded face. "I am so glad to have you back!" He reached for her, already anticipating her willing embrace, the warmth of her flesh, the softness of her skin . . .

But she hesitated and he felt a glimmer of alarm. He noticed that she was alone and he scowled. "The Mother Oracle?" he asked coldly.

Facet pressed a hand to her beautiful, blood-red lips, and shook her head. "She's dead," she said, her whisper almost a moan. "Killed by the priestess of Reorx."

Her eyes widened as she stared at Willim, noting the expression of rage that contorted his features. Before she could react, he lashed out a hand, striking

THE FATE OF THORBARDIN

her hard on the cheek and sending her whimpering away from him.

"You failed me!" he hissed.

"Please, Master—have mercy! It was a trap; she knew we were coming!"

Willim stood still except for the trembling in his hands that he could not control. He turned his face away from Facet, but she understood that his attention was still riveted upon her. "Tell me what happened," he barked.

Hesitantly, Facet began to speak. "We discovered her camp on the trail, just where your spell had told us she would be. The oracle and I approached from opposite directions. We would have had her, Master, except for that cursed hound! The animal sounded a warning, and the power of her god protected her."

"I gather that you did not recover the artifact." Willim's voice was flat, level.

"I had no chance, Master! The power of Reorx was in her; I would have perished in an instant had I not spirited myself away!" Facet's voice caught, and her large eyes moistened with tears.

She flinched but did not pull away when the wizard reached out a hand to touch her cheek. He caressed her soft skin, tracing the line of her jaw, reaching up to trace the curl of her ear, entwining his fingers in her long, dark hair . . . then he gripped that same lovely hair and pulled, hard. She dropped to her knees with a gasp of fear, staring up at him as he twisted, pulling her tresses taut, yanking tighter and tighter.

Nearby, the two blue sparks flittered around within the jar, bright and flickering, as though excited by the scene enacted before them.

"How dare you fail me?" spat the wizard, his voice low, each word stabbing like a dagger. "After all that I have given you, the training, the skills, the spells . . ." His voice softened, and he released his grip on her hair. ". . . the *affection*," he whispered, almost sadly.

"Please, Master!" Facet fell to the floor at his feet. "Allow me to make it up to you! Punish me but let me serve you."

She sobbed, her black robe heaving from the intensity of her anguish. Willim spent a long time looking down at her. He was still trembling with tension, with fury and desire, until finally he exhaled and relented.

"Very well," he said. "I shall whip you, and then you shall be forgiven."

"Oh, thank you, my lord!" Facet exclaimed, daring to raise her teary eyes toward his scarred, grisly visage. "It is more than I deserve!"

"Go to the rack," he instructed. "Remove your robe!"

Facet did as ordered while Willim went to a shelf near his workbench. A number of torture implements were arrayed there, including a half-dozen whips featuring leather strands of varying lengths and thicknesses. He considered one, an especially wicked-looking tool, in which several strands of cord were intertwined with sharp bits of steel, tiny razors that could easily tear flesh and draw blood.

He was tempted, but he shook his head; her flesh was too precious, too soft and welcoming, for him to want to scar her body. Instead, he took a shorter whip, one with four cords of supple leather, and flexed it against his leg with a sharp *snap* of sound.

Facet, her bare back exposed to him, did not look at him but instead gripped the handles on the whipping rack with white-knuckled fingers. A shiver ran down her spine as he stepped closer, and he briefly wondered if it was a tremble brought about by fear or anticipation. Slowly, relishing the moment, he raised the whip in his hand and hoisted it over his shoulder.

In the bell jar, the two blue sparks spun and whirled in a frenzy.

In that instant Willim froze. His senses tingled and a sheen of perspiration broke, unbidden, onto his forehead. He trembled and listened and felt a stab of fear lance through his bowels.

It was growing very warm in his lair.

He dropped the whip and spun around with a gasp. An orange light emanated from the dark chasm in the floor, the crevasse that should have been lightless and cool. Instead, radiant warmth rose from that crack, and the vague light grew more intense, brighter, and hotter as it swelled upward to fill his laboratory.

"Gorathian!" he screamed, even as a draconic head reared into sight, jaws gaping, flaming skin outlining the hellish contour of the fire dragon's skull.

With a blink of magic, the terrified Willim vanished from sight, teleporting away from his lair before the monster could strike.

---DH---

"I have this feeling that we're never going to see him again," Karine Bluestone admitted quietly, though no hint of doubt disturbed the serene expression of her countenance as she watched the tail end of her nation's army disappear down the mountain road. Brandon marched by himself in the rear of the military procession.

She and Garren stood upon a lofty ledge, high on the shoulder of Garnet Peak. The isolated aerie could be reached by air or through the access tunnel that connected directly to the governor's mansion. It was one of the perks of her husband's new office, that perch, the only place in Garnet Thax, other than the great gate, where a dwarf could go from the city directly to a view of the surface world.

"Did you hear what I said?" she asked, mildly surprised that her husband hadn't immediately tried to soothe her concern by contradicting her.

"Yes, I heard," Garren replied. He wrapped a strong arm around her shoulders and held her tightly, a gesture that at least helped to assuage some of her concern. "I wish I could say 'everything's going to turn out just fine,' but I'm not sure I believe that myself."

"Do you think they shouldn't be going to Thorbardin?" she asked stiffly. "Why on Krynn did you let them?"

"I don't know the answer to either of your questions," he admitted, his tone so frank she regretted her tartness. "Surely I have to question my own wisdom. I've been governor for less than a year, and I've authorized the raising of the largest army in our history. And not only that, but I've sent them off to fight a foreign war, with my son in command."

"He's the best dwarf for that job. You know that, don't you?" Karine chided gently.

"Aye, I do, beyond any doubt. He's grown into a fine figure of a man, if I say so. I'd trust him with my life. But this is even more than that."

"Is it the task itself, then?" she wondered. "Liberating Thorbardin from a fanatical king and a dark wizard?"

THE FATE OF THORBARDIN

" 'Tis a worthy goal," Garren said. "Probably the greatest thing we as Kayolin dwarves can fight for, now that our own nation is secure. The rest of the world is moving on. The elves are vanished, so far as I know. We have a new human emperor in Solamnia, and he regards us as important allies. That's a good thing. But without Thorbardin as an anchor for our people, as the place where our one crown stands, and our people are united under a council of thanes, we in Kayolin are only an outpost. An ally of Solamnia, yes, but I would not have us be a colony of any realm, human or otherwise. Rather, we should be a proud and independent nation of dwarves, a worthy supporter of our true king."

"Then Brandon and his army have to go there, don't they? They have to fight their way into Thorbardin and win. That's all there is to it," Karine declared, her tone growing confident once again.

"Yes," Garren said, holding her even more tightly. "That's all there is to it."

"Then let Reorx bless us, and bless Brandon, with his good will. And bring our son home to us again."

Again Garren didn't reply to his wife's words. They both understood that there was really nothing left to say.

---DH---

Facet clung to the whipping rack, remaining very still as the roaring fire dragon burst upward from the chasm, flaming wings beating against the floor. Willim was already gone; she had heard him bark the single-word teleport command and felt the rush of air as he had vanished. Embers swirled through the dark space, touching Facet's exposed skin as she still clutched the iron, her face averted, eyes tearing from the soot and the acrid smoke.

Gorathian flew upward and, with another pulse of those fiery wings, flashed through the air, sweeping into one of the tunnels leading outward from the wizard's lair. The monster's bellow of rage and pursuit lingered and echoed in the air as the fiery creature sped away from the place, again chasing its former master through Thorbardin.

Only when the dragon was gone, when darkness again had cloaked the cavern and the burning heat of the creature's flight slowly cooled back to the natural chill of the subterranean stone, did the apprentice magic-user release her grip on the rack and stand free. She pulled her black robe around her again and glanced once in the direction of the flying dragon—gone, leaving only a fading, orange glow from the infernal heat of its passage.

Facet was no longer weeping. Instead, her face was a mask of cold resolve as she went to the cabinet in which Willim kept his potions. From long experience, she manipulated the lock, pulled open the door, and looked inside.

Behind her, the two blue sparks in the bell jar flickered and danced, though whether from excitement or agitation it was impossible to tell.

———DH———

The road down from Garnet Peak was an easy march, on a descending grade, but even so it took the

THE FATE OF THORBARDIN

Kayolin Army more than two days to reach the edge of the foothills, where the road spilled onto the Solamnic plain. Immediately before them was a place familiar to many dwarves who had bothered to travel more than a few miles from Kayolin's gate.

The city of Garnet was a lively, raucous place—one of Brandon's favorite cities, in fact. But he knew that the presence of four thousand Kayolin dwarves, armed and thirsty and primed for battle, would be more than the thriving trading community could absorb. So in the face of some considerable grumbling and a few acts of insubordination that provided the first real test of his command authority, General Bluestone ordered that the marching army bypass the city and make camp in the forested fringe of the mountain range, some five miles beyond the city gates.

In a tree-shaded river valley, the army made bivouac along a broad, dry shelf of the riverbank. Scouts went out to hunt, and several returned with fresh-killed deer. Still, it was clear that wild game would not be enough to feed the whole force. Although the dwarves marched with stocks of grain and dried pemmican, Brandon didn't want to break into the food reserves so early in the trek. Besides, given the proximity of the city and its famed stockyards, it seemed only right that he authorize the purchase of a hundred beeves. Some he ordered to be butchered right away, while the others would be herded along, feeding the army as it continued the fortnight-long march to the port of Caergoth.

Thus, even though they were barred from the city's assortments of taverns and inns and show houses, the soldiers of the Kayolin Army were reasonably content as they settled into the camp and let their stomachs growl to the permeating odors of roasting roasts and grilling steaks.

Willing to enjoy one of the perquisites of command, Brandon invited General Watchler and Captains Hacksaw and Morewood to join him for a council—and first crack at the choicest rib steaks being grilled to rare perfection by the army's most senior cook, Cruster Flatiron. Flatiron was an innkeeper in private life back in Kayolin and presided over an establishment that was prized throughout the dwarf nation for its succulent beef dishes. When the call to arms had been passed around Garnet Thax, Cruster had signed up immediately, and Brandon had, just as quickly, placed him in charge of the army's brigade of cooks. Not unimportantly, he would supervise the staff that would cook for the general and his officers for the duration of the campaign.

The rotund Flatiron, his face beaming with pride, personally brought over the evening meal for the quartet of commanders. Each of the dwarves was presented with a slab of meat served on a metal plate, red juice still trickling from the steaks as the aroma of wood-fired meat tickled their nostrils.

"Ah, beautiful, Cruster," Brandon declared sincerely, taking his plate and inhaling deeply the pleasurable aroma of the perfectly cooked steak. The others mirrored his satisfaction as each, in turn, was presented with a splendid piece of meat.

Understandably, there was little talking for the next few minutes as each of the four carved off and gobbled a series of generous morsels.

Brandon had intended to discuss specific procedures for embarking the army when they arrived at Caergoth,

THE FATE OF THORBARDIN

but he and the others were distracted by a raucous squalling and squealing coming from the nearby kitchen tent. He leaped to his feet in alarm and, still holding his beef-blooded knife, raced toward the tent with his co-commanders and a number of soldiers who were similarly drawn by the commotion.

Only as he drew closer to the tent did he slow down and utter a short, surprised yelp of laughter. His reaction caused the other dwarves to stop and regard him with expressions ranging from mingled suspicion to surprise.

"Listen!" Brandon said, holding up his hands.

A shrill voice penetrated the smoke-filled air of the camp. "Put me down, bluphsplunging bully! Who you think are? Me fight two times, tell you dat! You put down me! Hey, that my meat!"

"You rotten, thieving little Aghar!" roared a much deeper voice, one that they recognized as belonging to Cruster Flatiron. "I oughta stick you on a spit and roast you till dawn!"

"You let him go, big doofar cooker dwarf!" squeaked a new combatant, clearly an agitated female. "You gots plenty meats! Share some with hungry army!"

"You're not in this army, damn your grubby fingers!" the cook retorted. Brandon heard multiple screams and hastily pushed his way into the tent, determined to avoid bloodshed—no matter how richly deserved such bloodshed might be.

He was just in time. Cruster held a little gully dwarf up off the ground, the burly chef's hand clasped firmly around the fellow's neck. In his other hand, Flatiron held a large butcher knife, poised as if ready to clean and gut the Aghar in preparation for running him through with the threatened spit. Two other gully dwarves, both female, screamed and pummeled the cook around his waist, but he was, for the moment at least, ignoring them.

"General!" the cook said, looking up to see Brandon entering. "I just caught this little wretch up to his elbows in my prime rib!"

Proof of the crime was visible in the red juices streaking the gully dwarf's arms and running down his jowls and chin. The culprit was staring at the butcher knife, his eyes wide, while his jaw flapped soundlessly.

"Gus!" Brandon snapped, holding up his hand in wordless command to Cruster. Scowling, the cook held back on the lethal blow, though if his eyes had been daggers, the gully dwarf's blood would already have been gushing onto the ground.

"What in the name of Reorx are you doing here?" the general finished.

When the gully dwarf's jaw flapped some more, Brandon gestured again, and Cruster, very reluctantly, released his grip around the thief's neck, dropping him unceremoniously onto the ground. "Tell me!"

Gus Fishbiter was well known to Brandon, and in fact, the Kayolin general owed more than a small debt of gratitude for accomplishments that the little Aghar, however unwittingly, had made to his and Gretchan's list of heroic deeds. Still, he was surprised and dismayed to see him.

With a typically stubborn and petulant look, Gus crossed his arms over his skinny chest and glared right back at Brandon. "What *you* do here?" he demanded.

THE FATE OF THORBARDIN

"Why, you impudent little wretch! I'll beat some manners into ya—" Tankard Hacksaw stepped forward, his fist raised for a punch.

"Hold on there, Tank," Brandon said, laying a hand on his captain's shoulder. "Let's talk about this. Now, Gus, you need to answer my question first."

"Me here for same reason you here!"

"I'm here because I'm leading this army south," Brandon said impatiently. "I don't see how that—"

"You here cuz for go see Gretchan!" Gus challenged, pointing a stubby and accusing finger until he noticed the shreds of meat caught under his fingernail and popped the digit into his mouth, noisily sucking off the residue of his raid.

Brandon blinked. "Well, that's just a part—that's not really—"

He was spared the burden of further explanation as the two female Aghar, who had been watching the exchange warily, suddenly rounded on Gus, meting out a barrage of punches and kicks.

"You big doofus liar!" one screamed, delivering a sharp kick to Gus's knee.

"Two times big booger liar!" shouted the other, landing a punch in the hapless Aghar's eye. "No say 'Gretchan'! Say 'Go Patharkas'! Highbulp go home!"

By that time several guards had arrived, and they, with expressions ranging from distaste to revulsion, separated the three gully dwarves, each sentry holding one of the outraged, filthy little figures.

"Should we turn 'em out into the night, General?" one asked. "Or would ye like a more, er, permanent solution?" He concluded the question with a decidedly hopeful expression.

"No! We go Patharkas!" shouted Gus insistently. "Gretchan my friend too!"

"Yes, she is," Brandon admitted. "And I fear she'd never forgive me if I gave you the punishment you deserve. So I take it that you've been marching along with us all the way from Kayolin?"

"Right out big gate!" Gus proclaimed proudly. "But you marches too fast. So we ride on fire wagon."

Brandon laughed in spite of himself and shook his head in defeat. "All right. You can come with us to, er, 'Patharkas.' And you can have a scrap or two of beef to eat, but stay away from the prime rib, or I'll order Cruster to put you on the spit he was talking about. Most important, stay out of trouble. Can you promise me that?"

Gus looked ready to argue, but the ring of looming dwarves, all of them armed and angry, apparently began to sink through even his thick layer of belligerence. "All right. Gus promise. Gus's girls promise too. Right?"

He glared at the two females, and each of them reluctantly nodded her head. "Now we eat?" one of them asked plaintively.

"Give them something tough to chew on," Brandon told Cruster. Already the other dwarves were dispersing, heading back to their campfires and their evening meals. Brandon thought of his perfectly grilled steak and hoped it hadn't gotten too cold.

And he hoped, even more fervently, that he hadn't just made a very bad decision.

Six

A King in Exile

Pax Tharkas loomed before Gretchan like a mountain, a massif straddling the winding road, barring all passage along the canyonlike gorge, except through the great gate itself. Kondike barked in recognition when the huge edifice gradually came into view of the two weary travelers rounding a bend in the rough, ascending trail. The dog bounded forward along the road, his large tail waving.

He finally paused, twenty or thirty paces in front of Gretchan, and turned to look back at her expectantly. As usual, she understood the question "What's taking you so long?" expressed in the upraised ears, the eager, panting tongue, and the proud flag of the fur-feathered tail.

"Just hold up for a second," she called cheerfully. "I keep telling you, you've got twice as many legs as I do!"

Even so, she shared the dog's enthusiasm and couldn't help but pick up her pace as she saw her destination so close in front of her. The great wall that was the fortress's main feature stood as lofty as a cliff, sheer and smooth, broken only by the massive gate in the center of the vast expanse of chiseled stone. To the right and left rose the high West and East Towers, each a bastion in its own right, which anchored the barrier of the fortification to the precipitous canyon walls that channeled all traffic right to the huge gate. When that gate was closed, nothing could pass from north to south, or vice versa, through that part of the mountain range.

Pax Tharkas had been built in a long-past age of Krynn. Despite its martial bearing and purpose, it had initially been created as a symbol of peace between the dwarves of Thorbardin and the elves of Qualinesti. Yet it was, at heart, an edifice built for war. Pax Tharkas straddled a very strategic pass in the Kharolis Mountains, a pass that provided the only practical land route between a wide array of southern and northern realms.

Gretchan knew the key to that protection was a great, unique trap concealed within the high walls. Pax Tharkas was built to provide a roadway through the mountains in times of peace, but in times of war, the trap could be released, dropping thousands of tons of rock into the interior of the vast, hollow chamber between the two high walls. That trap had been dropped, many years earlier, to block the advance of the Dark Queen's army during the War of the Lance.

In the recent decade, Tarn Bellowgranite had become the new master of the place, and he had made it his exiled subjects' task to carry that rubble up and out of the hall, reloading the trap for a potential future use, and in the meantime, reopening the pass to ease transit for trade and migration.

THE FATE OF THORBARDIN

Most recently, Gretchan and Brandon helped fight a battle to hold that pass against an army of hill dwarves. The attackers had spilled through one of the gates that had been intentionally left open and found themselves packed shoulder to shoulder in the great hall. One of Tarn's captains, a Klar named Garn Bloodfist, had attempted to release the trap, unleashing a crushing onslaught on the attacking Neidar; only good fortune, or as Gretchan preferred to think, the beneficence of Reorx, had prevented that catastrophe. By rallying the mountain dwarves who garrisoned the place, she and Brandon turned aside the onslaught and exposed the enemy captain, Harn Poleaxe, as a tool of unvarnished evil and blatant sorcery. With the obvious and dramatic assistance of her powerful god, Gretchan the priestess had banished Harn's dark master and, with Brandon's help, convinced the hill and mountain dwarves to agree to an uneasy truce.

It seemed that the truce was working. As she approached Pax Tharkas, she saw dwarves working the fields, harvesting the hops, wheat, and barley that ripened early in the high country. One sturdy, white-bearded farmer was hoeing a field near the road, and he gave Gretchan a cheerful wave and a "Howdy, stranger!" welcome. Kondike barked a reply, and a moment later the fellow blinked and let out a whoop of delighted recognition.

"No stranger at all, are you?" he chortled. "It's Gretchan Pax, come home to her poppa's fortress!"

Gretchan didn't recognize the farmer, but that was not surprising; as a high priestess of Reorx, she had been something of a celebrity in the small community for the year before her departure. But at the same time, she was warmed by the greeting, for it reminded her of the unexpected treasure she had discovered there upon her first visit. Otaxx Shortbeard, the father she had not known while she grew to adulthood, still served as Tarn's chief adviser. She had met him after the battle, and when the two of them had realized their connection, they had both been overcome by a powerful sense of love and destiny.

Invigorated by the memory, she waved cheerfully to the farmer and continued up the steeply climbing road.

The gates of Pax Tharkas, as always except in times of active warfare, stood open, one to the south and one to the north, allowing travelers on the road to stroll right through the great structure. As Gretchan approached, her view revealed the long, lofty hall of the central chamber in the partial shadows of the vaulted ceiling. Her eyes turned upward to the dwarves on the rampart far above her. Dozens of them waved and shouted greetings, apparently alerted to her approach by some unseen word-of-mouth network that carried the news ahead of her, even though she still moved at a brisk walk.

Kondike bounded forward into the hall to be greeted by a butcher with a fresh haunch of pork. The dog woofed appreciation and settled down to gnaw on the bloody morsel. Moments later Gretchan entered and was surrounded by well-wishers and cheerful dwarves. They clapped her on the shoulders and shouted their greetings until, like magic, the crowd parted to allow two old and familiar figures to approach.

"Father!" she cried, welcoming the embrace of Otaxx Shortbeard. He was trembling, she realized, but there was no frailty in his sturdy frame, his muscular arms, his bowed and stocky legs. It was the power of his emotion, she knew, as her own eyes grew moist and she clung to him for an extra few heartbeats, burying her head in the comforting scratchiness of his beard.

The second gray-bearded dwarf approached and held out his arms. Gretchan hugged him then stepped back and curtsied. "And King Bellowgranite," she said, smiling broadly. "You're looking well indeed!"

"Oh, posh with this 'king' business," Tarn Bellowgranite replied. "That's too lofty of a title for the leader of this little mountain outpost. But I must say, I'm glad to see you, child!"

"And I'm glad to be back here, but it's not just a homecoming. I have wonderful news, so much to tell you all! Can we go somewhere to talk?"

"Reorx knows we could use some positive news," Tarn said with a sudden, dour look, prompting a stab of concern from Gretchan. What had gone wrong there in the time since she'd left for Kayolin?

But the expression vanished from the king's face as quickly as it had appeared, and just as quickly he threw an avuncular arm around her shoulders. "Surely all the news can wait," he said. "You must be famished! I'll have the kitchen get an early start on the evening meal. We can eat and *then* we can talk."

"Really, I'm fine," Gretchan said. "And just so excited to let you know what's happening." At the same time, another burly dwarf, grinning broadly and wearing a metal breastplate, approached. Behind him was a younger fellow, and it took Gretchan a moment to recognize him.

"Oh, hi, Mason!" she said, greeting the king's garrison captain. She pecked him on the cheek then smiled broadly at the younger dwarf. "And Tor—you've grown a foot in the time since I've been gone!"

"Uh, not really," Tor said, awkwardly looking away. Gretchan frowned in puzzlement and not a little concern since the youthful Bellowgranite had always been outgoing and friendly during her previous time in Pax Tharkas.

"Where's your sister?" the priestess asked cheerfully, and in the sudden silence and with the stricken looks of the gathered dwarves, she understood at least a part of the strange, somber mood.

"She died last winter," Otaxx explained gently, his voice gruff with emotion. "The fever came through here and took her and several other youngsters."

"I'm so . . . so sorry," she said, clasping Tarn's hand in both of her own, feeling the hollowness of the words.

He sighed and shook his head sadly. "I guess it's sunk in now, though we're still grieving. For a time there, Crystal couldn't even get out of bed. But Reorx calls only the best to him at an early age."

"I know that verse," she replied, trying to keep the bitterness out of her voice. She had never believed it, and it angered her to hear others place the blame for random tragedy at the feet of her ever-just god. Yet if Tarn wanted to believe that it was the will of Reorx, she did not have the heart to contradict him.

"Are you sure you don't want a hearty meal? Our kitchen does very well for us, you know," Tarn pressed, changing the subject with forced heartiness.

"Oh, I remember," she said with a weary smile. Suddenly the import of her great news seemed to have paled. But still, she forced herself to remember that

THE FATE OF THORBARDIN

her mission was both important and urgent. "I'll look forward to joining your meal at the usual time, really I will," she said. "But I think you should hear my news. All of you—your wife too. Where is Crystal? Is she well?"

Tarn ignored the question, though that scowl flashed on his face again, fleetingly, before he clapped his hands. "Very well—we'll hear your news in my council chamber. Otaxx, Mason, come along with us. Tor, you too."

"Um, Father . . . there's something I have to do. Can you tell me about it later?" said Tor.

Tarn shrugged as though it were no matter to him. "Very well," he replied. "Now come this way," he concluded, taking Gretchan by the arm and leading her toward the official chambers at the base of the West Tower.

———DH———

The mad dwarf huddled in his cell, chewing on his lip, which was worn bloody by the relentless assault of his teeth. The salty blood was like nectar to him, and he could feel it sinking into his gullet, restoring his strength, clearing his mind, helping as always to focus his thoughts.

It had been a long time since the queen had come to speak with him, and Garn Bloodfist's thoughts had grown darker and more tormented in that interval. He hated so many things that it was getting hard to keep them straight. But he would try.

He hated the king, his former master, who had ordered him locked away there.

He hated Mason Axeblade, his former comrade, who had affixed the shackles to his wrists and brought him there.

He hated the priestess Gretchan Pax, who had preached her foolish and naive message of peace and, in doing so, thwarted the bloody victory that had stood just within reach of the mountain dwarves.

He hated the hill dwarves who had been his enemies for all his life.

But he loved the hill dwarf who was queen in that place . . . but she was the wife of the hated king . . . but she was the only one who had come there to talk to him, to soothe his anxious soul. Didn't he love her? It was hard to remember. But he had to! He should! She was good and kind and gentle!

Yet it had been very long since she had come there, so perhaps he hated her too.

It helped the mad dwarf, helped very much, for him to organize his thoughts in such an orderly fashion. For a short time, he was able to stop chewing his lip, to cease the relentless chatter in his mind as he contemplated and studied the long list of his enemies.

So intent was his meditation that he did not hear the subtle sound until several seconds had passed. Even then he wasn't sure. Had he imagined the noise, or had someone been in the hallway just outside of his cell?

Slowly, stealthily, the mad dwarf rose from his pallet of filthy straw, stepping carefully across the tiny chamber until he reached the door. The noise had come from just outside that door. He was certain that it had been more than his imagination.

"Who is it?" he hissed warily.

There was no response.

THE FATE OF THORBARDIN

Tentatively, he reached forward, touching the door, almost as if he hoped to feel the presence of his visitor through the hard, wooden planks. He strained upward and peered through the bars of the narrow window, but he could see nothing. Yet as he stood tall, he lost his balance, tumbling against the door.

He put his hands out to block his fall, and to his astonishment, the door swung open.

The sound! It had been the catch on the door being released by a stealthy visitor! That visitor was gone.

And the mad dwarf was free.

——DH——

It took but a few minutes for Gretchan and her hosts to retire to Tarn's office, but she still had to fidget impatiently as Tarn took care of getting everyone a cool glass of dwarf spirits. She knew that such imbibing was a traditional part of any high-level council of dwarves, but she could barely contain her impatience as the king filled her glass then Otaxx's, Mason's, and finally his own.

He had barely finished his courtesies when the door opened to reveal Tarn's wife, Crystal Heathstone. Gretchan had become good friends with the hill dwarf female, who was considerably younger than her husband, during the cleric's stay in Pax Tharkas, and she quickly rose and gave Crystal a warm embrace. At first glance she noticed the former queen's haggard look, the lines of tension radiating outward from her suddenly old-looking eyes. She filed that observation away for future, private conversation. For the time had finally come for her to share her astounding news.

She opened her backpack and pulled out the wedge of blood-red stone. She laid the artifact on the exiled king's desk and stood back as his eyes widened in appreciation and recognition.

"The third part of the hammer!" Tarn said at once. "But . . . how did you come to have it? You were going to Kayolin, and we all thought that it was in Thorbardin."

"You're right on both counts," Gretchan said. "It's a long story, but in brief, we owe it to a gully dwarf."

"You reached Kayolin, then?" asked her father. "And Brandon—is he well? Did you leave him there?"

"There's so much to tell," Gretchan said. "Brandon is on his way here, with several thousand Kayolin troops. I came on ahead with the Redstone so that we could meld it with the blue and green parts, and forge the Tricolor Hammerhead. You'll have to assemble your best smiths and alchemists, of course. And I'll help in any way I can—that is, if a humble priestess can be of service."

"Wait!" Tarn held up a hand. "Kayolin is sending an army? Here? Maybe you should take your time and start at the beginning."

So she did. Her four listeners found seats as Gretchan paced around the spacious office, describing the events that had resulted in Brandon Bluestone's father rising to the governorship of Kayolin and the new sense of political will and cooperation that led to the dispatching of a large force to aid Tarn in reclaiming his rightful throne in Thorbardin.

"Gus Fishbiter, of all people, is the one who brought us the Redstone. You'll all remember him; he's the Aghar who—accidentally but fortunately—disabled the trap here before Garn Bloodfist could release it on the Neidar. Anyway, he was able to magically travel from here back to Thorbardin, and he somehow stumbled onto the Redstone. He also learned that the war is actually happening there, the civil war between the black wizard and Jungor Stonespringer's fanatics. Then he used the same kind of magic—a dimension door spell, it was, cast by some Theiwar wizards—to escape. Only instead of returning here, he found himself in Kayolin. That's where Kondike found him and brought him to me."

"Stop!" Tarn ordered again, frowning. "We discovered some Hylar and Daergar here, in Pax Tharkas. They said they came here through this dimension door you speak of. They said they'd been eager to get away, that conditions in Thorbardin were very bad. But what's this about the war? You say a war's really happening? In Thorbardin?"

"Yes! Gus couldn't make up the details he gave me. He even talked about a huge dragon, a fiery serpent, fighting on the side of the wizard's army. But victory was far from settled, and the destruction, inflicted by and upon both sides, is great. Thorbardin is suffering, and her defenses are weakened and conflicted. The time is perfect for us to move against the underground nation. While they are tearing at each other's throats, we can return and claim your throne back for you and your line."

"But the Kayolin Army . . . ?"

"They're on the march by now, certainly. Garren Bluestone was going to arrange for passage across the Newsea; he thought he could get assistance from the emperor of Solamnia. I came on ahead so that we could forge the hammer. And also so that we could have time to recruit the hill dwarves to help in our campaign. Slate Fireforge, in Hillhome—can we send for him at once, enlist his help in raising troops?"

Gretchan noticed the frown creasing Tarn Bellowgranite's face. "What is it?" she asked immediately. "Have the Neidar gathered against you again? Just in the time since I've been gone?" She couldn't hide her despair. She had been convinced that the treaty signed at the end of the previous year's battle would be one that would stand the test of time. "We have their promise on the pact! Have they given some kind of word that they won't honor it?"

"No, the hill dwarves have done nothing overt," Tarn admitted. "But I'll be cursed by Reorx before I'll let them serve in any army under my command! Thorbardin is a nation of mountain dwarves! And so it shall remain!"

"But the treaty! You signed it!" she objected impulsively. "The hill dwarves agreed to help in exactly this purpose as soon as it became a real possibility!"

"Do you really think they meant that pledge?" Tarn snapped. "They signed it—and I signed it—in a moment of weakness!"

"It certainly can't hurt to ask them," Gretchan said, striving to maintain a reasonable tone in the face of such startling, stubborn intransigence.

"Yes, it *can* hurt," the exiled king replied. "Has it occurred to you that Thorbardin harbors a wealth of treasure? If the hill dwarves agree to go with us, it will only be so that they can get their hands on that treasure! It belongs to the mountain dwarves; we will not share it!"

Gretchan was trying to come up with some kind of reply when she—and the older men—were startled by the loud slam of a door. She spun in surprise and only then noticed that the number of dwarves in the room had decreased by one.

Crystal Heathstone, the king's wife and a proud daughter of the Neidar hill dwarves, had just stormed out of the room.

———DH———

"Why do you have to be so Reorx-cursed *stubborn?*" Crystal Heathstone demanded once she and her husband had retired to the privacy of their living chambers. "If you could have just listened to her and seen the wisdom of her words, you could be the greatest leader Thorbardin has ever known! You could be the kind of dwarf I thought you were when I married you!"

"That's enough, woman!" retorted Tarn Bellowgranite in a barely contained roar. "You forget who you're talking to!"

"Oh no I don't! I remember very well! I'm talking to a man who has been prejudiced for so long that he can't see wisdom unless it's slathered on a piece of bread and offered to him for breakfast!"

"That's enough, I say! Do you recall what happened the last time the hill dwarves came to Pax Tharkas? They brought an army and a minion of dark magic! If it hadn't been for that priestess and her staff, we'd—all of us!—be slaves in the Neidar mines by now!"

Crystal almost cried with exasperation. She turned and stomped across the office then spun back to face her husband. "That priestess, Gretchan Pax, is the same one who wants to reach out to the hill dwarves! Think about that if you can. This could be an historic moment in the whole history of dwarfkind. You could be the leader who finally moves our people beyond the destruction and rivalry of two thousand years!"

"No, I couldn't," Tarn retorted sternly. "Because I wouldn't trust a hill dwarf ally any farther than I could throw him across a ravine. I'd be certain that, at the moment of victory, he'd be ready to stab me in the back! There's a fortune in treasure in Thorbardin, and it is the property of the mountain dwarves. The hill dwarves only want it for themselves!"

"Think of what you're saying!" Crystal protested. "These are my people you're talking about! Do you think *I* would stab you in the back?"

Tarn glared without replying. His expression didn't change as his son suddenly, furtively, slipped through the door. Tor was apparently surprised to find his parents there, for he swiftly turned and ducked out again.

The king turned back to his wife, who glared at him with an expression of unrelieved stubbornness. He was about to challenge her again when they were both distracted by a fresh knock on the door.

"What is it?" he demanded loudly. "I'm busy."

"I'm sorry, sir," came Mason Axeblade's reply. "But it's urgent, an emergency."

Tarn stalked across the chamber and pulled the door open. "What's happened?" he snapped.

"It's Garn Bloodfist, sire," Mason explained, his eyes wide with concern. "I'm sorry to report that . . . well, it seems that he's escaped."

THE FATE OF THORBARDIN

Gretchan couldn't suppress a sigh as she sat at the window of her guest apartment, a place of honor high up in the East Tower. The sun had set an hour earlier, and the valley floor below her was dotted with torches, bobbing and weaving as their bearers moved through the fields, searching for Garn Bloodfist. Other parties of armed dwarves stormed through the fortress, sometimes pounding down the hallway directly outside of her door. Tarn had ordered a pair of guards posted right there, so at least she didn't have to endure their entering the room to search every time they passed.

Kondike lay on the floor beside the door. He looked comfortable, sprawled in a mass of gangly black legs and rough, shaggy fur. Yet one of his ears remained pricked alertly upward, and she knew that any disturbance would bring him bounding to his feet, hackles bristling and long teeth bared in the direction of the alarm.

Could it be that Garn Bloodfist was actually stalking through the halls of Pax Tharkas? She didn't think so—he was well known and had few friends there. Even the Klar troops who had served him when he had been their captain had seen the danger in his wild hatred and had accepted the wisdom of the treaty that had brought the war to an end.

She shuddered as she pictured the mad Klar. She hadn't seen Bloodfist since he had been arrested, at the very end of the battle in Pax Tharkas, but she would never forget the murderous look that he had directed at her, his wide Klar eyes staring wildly, dark spots in circles of white, as if he had been staring right through her.

How had everything become such a mess? Why did Reorx allow the affairs of dwarves to be so relentlessly cursed with violence, treachery, and murder?

She held her staff in both of her hands and closed her eyes as she pressed her forehead to the cool, smooth shaft of wood. She murmured a soft prayer to her god, the Master of the Forge. Her evening chants, as always, soothed her, the musical sound of prayer a calming force in even the most tumultuous of times.

She thought of Brandon, still so far away, and prayed for his safety, for his success in his campaign against the horax, for his speedy progress on his journey south. She continued to think of him as she undressed and slipped into bed—into the bed that was almost obscenely comfortable after all of the rough nights in her bedroll on the trail. Things would be so much better if he were there—of that, she was somehow certain.

And with that certainty, and the weariness of her long trek at last behind her, she finally allowed herself to sleep.

SEVEN

DEPARTURES AND RETURNS

The Kayolin Army continued its march southward to Caergoth, crossing the Solamnic plains like some miles-long, infinite-legged centipede. Always the dwarves maintained their precise column and held to the cadence set by the hundred drummers. The miles rolled by underfoot, and the sky swept like a vast canopy overhead—an experience that many of the dwarves, those who had spent most if not all of their lives underground, found profoundly unsettling.

As he walked along the column or stood beside the track and listened to the troops as they passed, Brandon heard many whispered conversations about the uncanny expanse of space there on the surface of the outside world—an expanse that was magnified by the stark emptiness of the plains. A regular debate was waged between those, a majority, who found the daylight hours to be most disturbing, and the vocal minority who had difficulty adjusting to the night sky and its myriad stars. Both sides could agree they couldn't wait to get back under the shelter of a good mountain range, as Reorx had intended, and escape from the disturbing and vast spaces of the surface world.

But even as the soldiers groused and complained and bickered, as soldiers have done in every army in every nation on every world throughout all history, Brandon was proud to see that the men grew stronger, leaner, and sturdier during the long hours of the march. By the second day after they had left the mountains, the Garnet Mountains had vanished over the horizon behind them, and the sameness of the plains sprawled into the distance in all four directions like a barren expanse of flatness.

Morale remained high. The troops believed in their mission, believed in the goal of restoring Thorbardin's greatness and reinstating the ancient dwarf home among the ranks of the mightiest nations of Krynn. The campaign had tapped into a vein of deep national longing that Brandon himself hadn't known existed, but he perceived that the brave dwarves, his men, desired much beyond their own personal satisfaction. It made him proud to call them his kinsmen.

In a few places the dwarves marveled at the wonders of Solamnia. At one point a long column of the emperor's cavalry fell in beside them for a day of marching, and the dwarves gawked and gossiped about the magnificent horses, some five hundred strong, and the gleaming armored riders who sat astride the magnificent chargers. They came to the great Kingsbridge, a sturdy stone span crossing the Caergoth River that had been rebuilt very recently, following the war that had brought the emperor to his throne. The dwarves marveled at the smooth stonework and nodded knowingly when Brandon informed them that dwarf engineers had aided the human stonecutters and masons in creating the beautiful, functional span.

But mostly Solamnia was just vast, flat, and empty. Each of those features was a strange thing to dwarves born and raised under the ground, and it was no surprise that they found them strange. Each served to awe and impress the troops in its own way, perhaps reminding the warriors of how small each individual was when set against the whole breadth of the world. Even their nation of Kayolin, the land they knew with such righteous pride, was a mere province when compared to the great sweep of land on the surface of Krynn.

The days were cool, which made for comfortable marching, and the nights were cold enough to encourage the men to stay put in their bedrolls. There was no brawling, little scuffling, only an occasional duel, and—perhaps most surprisingly—no further complaints about the three gully dwarves who had given their pledge that they would stay out of trouble. Gus and his girls seemed to be as good as their word: they stayed out of sight and, as far as Brandon knew, out of mischief.

The smooth ground provided no obstacle to the progress of the march, and early on Brandon had seen the wisdom in purchasing carts and wagons. The horses and mules pulling them spared his soldiers the burden of carrying all of their supplies. Morale skyrocketed when the dwarves understood that they would have plenty of food and at least a nip or two of the fermented beverages they cherished in every night's camp. Sturdy draft horses were strapped into the traces of the three Firespitters, and those great weapons, too, rolled along with good speed at little cost in dwarf sweat and blisters.

And a moment of true wonder was shared by all when, after a fortnight's march, the army crested the great hill before the city of Caergoth, overlooking that bustling seaport. Dozens of trading and merchant vessels as well as warships flying a half dozen different flags were under sail, some arriving, some leaving. But nearby, just off the harbor mouth and standing easily at anchor, were some hundred massive transport ships, and Brandon immediately recognized them as the fleet promised by the emperor to allow the Kayolin Army to cross the sea.

"They're huge!" gasped Tankard Hacksaw, who happened to be marching beside Brandon as the ships came into view. "Like castles on the water!"

"Galleons, they're called," Brandon explained breezily. As a veteran of three sea voyages, all of them across that same body of water, he felt well qualified to share his wisdom with the less-experienced dwarves—and that meant all of the troops of his army.

Each ship boasted three tall masts, bare at that moment, rising like pine trunks from the wide wooden decks. Those masts would sprout canvas sails like vast leaves, Brandon remembered, and the sheets would fill with wind and allow the sailors to drive their ships wherever they cared to go. The great hulls were round, like fat bellies on the tall, sturdy vessels, and the largest of the ships would be capable of carrying at least one of the Firespitters. Those heavy weapons, as well as the oxen and carts, would be loaded aboard by the cranes they could see dotting the wharves along the near side of the harbor.

Brandon felt a rush of affection for Dram Feldspar and, by extension, his master, the emperor of Solamnia. The human was as good as his word. The ships were waiting. The army could cross the water.

And for the first time, Brandon allowed himself to believe that their crazy plan just possibly had a chance of success.

---DH---

"This is Bardic Stonehammer, the greatest smith in Pax Tharkas. He has been the chief armorer in my army since my days as king," Tarn Bellowgranite explained to Gretchan after she had accepted his invitation to join him in the foundry below the base of the fortress's East Tower.

"My lady," said the smith with an affectionate smile and a deep bow. "It is a pleasure, indeed, to finally meet you."

"Thank you for that greeting and for offering to help us with the work," the priestess replied. She was impressed: Bardic Stonehammer was probably the largest, sturdiest-looking dwarf she had ever met. His shoulders were broad and square, and his arms were as thick and strapping as any normal dwarf's thighs. His head was bald, and his beard trimmed short—or perhaps, she wondered, to judge from the irregular cut of his whiskers, he just tended to singe it in his forge.

"It is an opportunity that I would not want to miss," the big smith said with infectious cheerfulness. Indeed, he had a broad smile that seemed to compel good humor all around. "Not since Theros Ironfeld was entrusted with the secret of the dragonlance has such a powerful artifact been placed in the hands of one of my trade," he noted solemnly.

Gretchan saw that the well-appointed smithy was ready for the task at hand. The three wedges of stone were arrayed on an anvil near a roaring oven, and a thick rod of steel, taller even than Bardic Stonehammer, had been procured to serve as a handle. A dozen assistant smiths, all of them accomplished in their own right to judge from their maturity and sturdy demeanor, stood ready to assist.

"But we need you to tell us what to do," Tarn reminded her. "These are the craftsmen, to be sure, but you must be the artist and perhaps the engineer."

"I'll do what I can," the priestess replied with more than a little anxiety. To prepare for the task, she had studied every available reference source she could find and had prayed to Reorx for guidance. While the references had been few and scanty, her prayers had resulted in a very precise dream, repeated over the past three nights, so she felt a certain confidence in her ability to offer plausible instruction. Still, it was a task far different from anything she had ever done before.

She studied the arrangement of the stones and made her first suggestion. "The Tricolor Hammerhead is depicted in one of the ancient scroll books, and it is shown with the Redstone on top, the Bluestone in the middle, and the Greenstone on the bottom."

Immediately two of the assistants rearranged the stones to match the order she described.

"Now they will all have to be heated—heated to a terribly high temperature, in fact—and then removed from the heat one at a time, starting with the Greenstone."

THE FATE OF THORBARDIN

Bardic himself responded to her instructions, lifting the Greenstone with a pair of long-handled tongs and placing the emerald-colored wedge of rock onto a shelf within the blazing oven. Even standing a dozen feet away from the oven, Gretchan wanted to raise her hands to block the heat from her face, and she wondered at the endurance—and the tolerance for pain—of the smith who stood right at the furnace door and calmly manipulated his precious component.

One by one he placed the other two wedges of colored stone into the furnace, finally closing the door and stepping back. Only then did he give sign that the heat had affected him in even the slightest; he took a towel and wiped the sheen of sweat that had seeped from his skin to cover his face. Gretchan, blinking in surprise, saw that his beard was smoking slightly, and when she inhaled, she caught the acrid scent of burned hair.

"Do you have the trough of ice water handy?" she asked, remembering another key feature of her dream. She had described it in detail to the smith in advance, but even so she was relieved to see several assistants appear, carrying the chilly bath. Blocks of glacial frost, brought down from the mountains in winter and stored in deep icehouses, floated in the liquid.

"Chill the handle," she ordered, and again her instructions were carried out, one apprentice holding the far end of the steel shaft while most of the rod was immersed in the water.

For several minutes they waited, Bardic watching her expectantly, until there came a moment when she just *knew* the time was right. "Remove the Greenstone," she said. "You should be able to see where to insert the handle."

Quickly the master smith unlatched the furnace door and pulled it open, releasing a blast of heat into the already sweltering smithy. Once again he took up his tongs and reached in to pull out the superheated emerald wedge. Gretchan was relieved to see that a hole had appeared, penetrating the wedge side to side, just a little closer to the narrow end than the wider.

"Now take the shaft directly out of the ice bath and plunge it in the hole—*hard*," she informed them.

Bardic lowered the stone onto a rack just above the floor, with the hole oriented horizontally and several feet of space underneath to allow the shaft to poke through the top. A burly assistant took the handle in both of his hands, raised it over his head, and plunged it down as though he were trying to spear a fish in the water. The icy cold metal steamed and shivered as it penetrated the hole, emerging through the top of the wedge and driving all the way to the floor.

"Put it back into the ice water now," the priestess instructed. "Quickly!"

The assistant smith gave her a look of questioning, no doubt expecting the hot stone to shatter from such a shocking, temperature-changing immersion.

"Do it!" Bardic snapped, and his instruction was followed. Steam foamed and sizzled upward from the trough, but within seconds the stone and the metal shaft had been chilled to freezing again. When the assistant pulled up the wedge of green stone, it was intact and seemed to be permanently fused to the shaft.

"Again!" Gretchan said urgently. "Now with the Bluestone!"

The master smith pulled the second wedge of rock from the oven, and out of nowhere Gretchan thought, fleetingly, of Brandon Bluestone. How proud he had been of his family's cherished heirloom, even before he had learned of its mighty purpose. If only he could be there to witness its transformation. At least, she told herself with a quick, silent prayer, he would be with them soon, when the artifact was used.

Even as those thoughts flitted through her head, the smiths were repeating the process, driving the head of the shaft through the hole in the Bluestone then chilling the device once more in the cold water. In short order, the third wedge of stone, the red one, was removed and affixed to the shaft.

Bardic Stonehammer pulled the artifact from the water. Gretchan could see that not only had the stones melded themselves tightly to the rock, but the lines of color where one wedge met the next had blurred slightly, as if the three stones had truly become one.

"Behold!" cried Stonehammer with all the pride of a master who had just crafted the work of his life. "I give you the Tricolor Hammerhead!"

"And behold," Gretchan added, quietly and reverently. "We are all witness to the greatness of Reorx."

---DH---

"Gus ride ship?" demanded the little gully dwarf female who was clinging to Gus's right arm. She glared at the subject of her query. "Then Slooshy go too!" she declared.

"No!" declared the little gully dwarf female who was clinging to Gus's left arm. "Take Berta!"

Gus was too astonished even to complain. Instead, his eyes practically popped out of his skull as he stared at the vast array of naval might gathered in the harbor of Solamnia's great southern port, Caergoth.

One of those ships lay tethered to the dock right before him, and a rather flimsy-looking gangplank led steeply upward to the crowded, teeming deck. Other ships, at least two and two more of them, their holds crowded with equipment and their decks crowded with nervous-looking dwarves, had already raised sail and moved away from the wharf. For nearly a full day, Gus had watched them cast off, knowing that there would always be another vessel taking on cargo and passengers. Two more, in fact.

And really, what was the hurry?

"Gus ride ship?" Slooshy repeated. "Me go too!"

"Alla girls go ship!" he retorted in exasperation. "But why so hurry? Alla time hurry!"

He looked around the dock anxiously. Nearby was a long file of Kayolin dwarves, each carrying a backpack bundling weapons and armor. They looked dour and surly, which was not surprising considering the dwarves' universal dislike of water, oceans, and ships.

Maybe, if he waited long enough, another magical blue door would appear, and he could just step through it and arrive at Pax Tharkas, where Gretchan—beautiful, kind, generous Gretchan!—would be waiting for him. After all, he had departed Pax Tharkas through just such a portal.

Though that journey, he remembered, had taken him to Thorbardin, where he and his girlfriends had spent their time running for their lives. On the bright side, of course, he had found the Redstone and located the magic blue door again. The second time he passed through the magical portal, he had stepped into Kayolin, where he had found Gretchan and basked in the glow of her appreciation for his cleverness in bringing the blood-red wedge of stone.

But then she had gone south without him, leaving him to the increasingly aggravating company of his girlfriends. Furthermore, the priestess had departed without so much as a good-bye, and Gus had had to eavesdrop in many different parts of Garnet Thax before he learned where she had gone. Fortunately, his spying had also revealed to him that Brandon—who the dwarves were calling "General Bluestone"—intended to lead a great army southward to rendezvous with the beautiful priestess. Gus had decided on the spot that he would follow along, and he reasoned that his frank discussion with the general, centered around the misunderstanding about the purloined steaks, ensured that Gus, too, could travel across the sea on one of the ships.

In fact, the general approached, striding down the line of soldiers, clapping men on their shoulders, and encouraging those who looked hesitant. "Just think of it as a wooden cave," he said breezily, gesturing to the nearby ship. "Why, you hardly even feel it moving!"

Something in Brandon's eyes made Gus think he was, at the very least, exaggerating the case. Still, most of the fleet was sailing out of the harbor, and the little Aghar sensed that his chances to accompany the army—and to find Gretchan—were rapidly diminishing. There were only a few ships, barely more than two, still left to board.

So he took a deep breath. Slooshy still clutched his right arm and Berta his left as he swaggered up the gangplank at the end of the column of soldiers. No sooner had they tumbled over the rail and found a place to huddle on the deck between casks of water and dwarf spirits than the sail dropped with a loud *whoomf.*

The wind blew steadily, and by the time Gus lifted himself up to peer at the shore, the dry land was at least two and two more long jumps away.

---DH---

"Facet! Come here!" barked Willim the Black.

"Yes, Master," came the immediate reply. The apprentice, draped in her silken robe, approached from behind the wizard. Her face expressionless, she stopped two paces from him and bowed deeply.

The wizard stood at his worktable, his face turned toward the far corner of the laboratory. Of course, he didn't need to direct his attention toward that which he wished to see; he was currently studying the row of bottles along one shelf on the right side of the table. At the same time, he observed the female's calm obedience and allowed a cold smile to crease his scarred, thin lips.

"Bring me a silver bowl of clean water," he ordered.

"At once, Master." The apprentice hurried away and soon returned from the water barrel with the requested bowl.

"Put in on the table. I intend to cast a spell of scrying, but my shoulders are stiff," Willim said calmly.

Immediately Facet did as she was told and more; once the bowl was resting on the table, she stepped behind the black wizard and began to gently massage his shoulders. Her fingers, as always, seemed to possess an extrasensory perception, a keen insight that allowed them to know exactly where to touch him, where to press, where to stroke. Almost immediately he felt the tension drain from his taut muscles.

He ignored her then, though of course she didn't cease her ministrations, and turned to concentrate on his spell. He dropped a few crystals of powdered silver into the water and poured in a bit of oil. Finally he muttered the words to a powerful spell.

Immediately the tingle of magic spread through his body, energizing him like a drug. Facet's touch became even more sensually pleasurable, though of course the magic-user did not allow pleasure to detract from the concentration required for his spell.

As the magic took hold, the water in the bowl, filmed with a thin coating of oil, began to glow. Images shimmered there and Willim couldn't suppress a frown, for they were images of war. He saw no sign of the fire dragon, which was something of a relief, but instead he noted martial pictures: dwarf troops waging battle against a backdrop of stone, underground. He saw a blue axe flailing and slaying and he flinched.

Then a chill of real terror ran down his spine, and even Facet's ministrations couldn't stop his trembling. The image was there, clear and menacing: a three-colored hammer, held high against the outside sky, raised like a talisman of ultimate warning.

"Leave me!" Willim shouted, turning and pushing Facet away with a violent shove. He saw that she had allowed her black robe to fall open while she was massaging him, and that effrontery enraged him further. She tumbled to the ground, shocked and bruised, but she knew him too well to cry out. Instead, she scuttled around the table, pulling her robe closed over her breasts and cowering in the shadows between the table and the potion cabinet.

But Willim had already forgotten her. His whole being was suffused with the terrifying picture of that hammer. He knew that his enemies had created the dread artifact, the only thing in the entire world—besides Gorathian—that he feared.

And he knew, too, that his enemies were coming for him.

EIGHT

TO THE MOUNTAIN TOWERS

The crossing of the sea took only four days, but that was enough time to bring the seasick, frightened, and claustrophobic dwarves almost to the point of mutiny. Conditions aboard the galleons, those ships that had looked so majestic and spacious from the land, proved to be confining and constricting and unsettling in ways that even the subterranean-dwelling dwarves found incredibly stifling. By the third day, half the army was practically in revolt, and only Brandon's calm assertion that they were only one day away from their destination—whereas it would take three days to turn around and go back to Caergoth—allowed him to calm the men enough to, however impatiently, wait for landfall.

When it came, it was a smudge of brown hill on the horizon and a harbor sheltering a small fishing village. With no wharf available, most of the dwarves had to be rowed to shore in small boats, and that alone was a harrowing enough experience to cause most of them to swear off water transport forever. More challenging still was the debarking of the Firespitters, and in fact, one of the heavy, iron machines toppled into the water and was lost. The other two were laboriously, one at a time, loaded onto hastily constructed rafts and slowly pulled to shore.

But at last the army, without losing a dwarf, had assembled on the southern coast of the Newsea. They were two score miles south of the ancient ruin known as Xak Tsaroth and, by Brandon's best estimate, about a week's march north of their first destination: the fortress of Pax Tharkas. They wasted little sorrow in watching the ships hoist sail and head for the north, and instead turned their landlubber eyes southward, seeking the road to their objective in the mountain pass.

The next week of marching took them through terrain that was far more rugged and varied than the monotonous flats of the Solamnic plain. They crossed rugged, flinty ridges that lay like barriers across their path, forged paths between swampy bottomlands, and even skirted a desolate plain where the ghastly mountain known as Skullcap—a permanent scar of the Dwarfgate War—rose into view from the western horizon.

Finally they approached a mountain range, and as the highland's extent expanded over the course of two full days' march they realized they were traversing much greater heights, loftier summits, and broader ridges than anything in the familiar Garnet Mountains back home.

"That's the High Kharolis," Brandon informed them solemnly. "Beneath that great summit, Cloudseeker Peak, lies Thorbardin itself. And those lesser mountains stand in our path to the North Gate."

THE FATE OF THORBARDIN

Despite the arduous climbing required, the dwarves were eager to return to a mountainous environment. The marching soldiers swung along easily, as always accompanied by their drums, and the miles fell behind as they climbed along rugged roads, ascending into the heights.

Finally the route became so tortuous that they were forced to narrow the column to single file, following a dusty track in a formation that stretched nearly two miles long, as all of the soldiers of Brandon's army filed southward through the rugged hill country rising toward the fortress of Pax Tharkas. Brandon himself strode along at the head of the column, setting a brisk pace. It was partly because he wanted the Kayolin Army to make good time and to march in peak condition. Once again his men were hardened, tough, and strong, and it was that strict pace that had toned and sharpened them.

But Brandon had another reason for his haste: he missed Gretchan more than he would ever have thought possible. As they began the seventh day of the march, he hoped they would come into sight of the fortress before dark—but even if the army needed to bivouac one more night on the trail, he had resolved to press on alone, so he could once again hold his beloved dwarf maid in his arms.

Under his watchful eye, and the steady guidance of his two legion commanders and General Watchler, the army had marched at a good pace, starting from the first hour after debarkation on the southern shore of the Newsea. Tankard Hacksaw, commander of the First Legion, marched right at Brandon's side, with his troops forming the first part of the column. In the middle was the baggage train, a collection of two-wheeled carts pulled by mules or sturdy dwarves, bearing the dried trail provisions that ensured the dwarves didn't have to take the time to forage for food.

Gus Fishbiter and his two girlfriends were riding along on one of those carts, since the short-legged Aghar would not have been able to maintain the pace of their larger cousins. The two remaining Firespitters were once again in the middle of the formation, and the Second Legion, under the command of Fister Morewood, brought up the rear.

The rocky ridges to either side of the road looked increasingly familiar, and as the path curved around another shoulder of mountainside, the familiar fortress towers came into view. The parapet was lined with cheering dwarves as the Kayolin Army stepped up its pace, singing a marching song in time with the drums as the newcomers crisply tromped up to their allies in the mountain fortress. A rain of flowers fell from the ramparts as the mountain dwarves of Pax Tharkas greeted their long-lost cousins with cheers and whoops of joy.

Soon all four thousand of the marching dwarves were passing through the great gate of the fortress and spreading out through a massive hall that had been equipped with tables, benches, and many tempting items of food and drink for a massive welcome feast.

Brandon had eyes for only one person, and Gretchan greeted him right inside the gate, falling into his arms with a shriek of delight that sent his blood to boiling. He inhaled the sweet smell of her hair as she clasped him in a warm embrace. For long moments they remained thus while the festivities swelled around them.

THE FATE OF THORBARDIN

When finally they broke apart, Brandon saw that Tarn's dwarves, under the command of Otaxx Shortbeard, mingled readily with the newcomers, and many kegs of ale had already been tapped in celebration of the greeting.

"Come with me," Gretchan said, taking Brandon by the hand.

Whatever he hoped for in her firm summons, he was surprised when she led him through a small door into an office where Tarn Bellowgranite himself, in the company of a huge, burly dwarf who wore the apron of a blacksmith, awaited him.

With a flourish, the exiled king pulled a cloak off an object that had been concealed on a table, and Brandon gaped at the Tricolor Hammer. The weapon was a perfect fusion of red, green, and blue, all the stones merged onto a massive, sturdy handle. The head of the artifact seemed to glow with an otherworldly light, as if the illumination were born within.

"The gates of Thorbardin await us," was all the exiled monarch had to say.

---DH---

General Blade Darkstone inspected the defenses of Thorbardin's gatehouse. The veteran Daergar warrior, commander of Willim the Black's army and, indeed, of all the garrison of the kingdom of Thorbardin, was worried. Willim the Black had been restless, irritable, and unpredictable lately. He had sent vague word that he would be joining his chief general for a very important inspection.

Darkstone jumped suddenly as a tingle of energy roused the hackles on the back of his neck. "Master!"

he gasped, spinning to see the eyeless wizard standing behind him. "You took me by surprise!"

That, he realized almost at once, was the wrong thing to say. Willim's face twisted into a snarl, and he raised a clenched fist. Darkstone was no coward—and he certainly didn't fear a physical blow from the wizard or anyone else—but he recoiled unconsciously, raising both hands before his face as if they could ward off any attack his master cared to deliver.

But Willim the Black limited himself to a verbal assault. "You cannot afford to be surprised!" he snapped. "That is the kind of failure that can doom me, doom us all, to a fate you cannot imagine."

"I am sorry, Lord Willim," General Darkstone apologized humbly. "I pledge that it shall not happen again."

"If it does, it will be the last time. And I shall not have to exact the punishment myself."

"What do you mean, my lord?"

"I mean that Thorbardin will be attacked from without. This great gate in which you place such faith may be breached. In that case, you must be prepared to defend our nation to the death."

"Of course, I could do nothing less, Master. But please allow me to ask: how is it even possible?"

Darkstone's question was sincere. He knew the gate itself was more than two dozen yards thick, a solid plug of stone that was literally screwed into the conical entryway that had once been Thorbardin's main point of access to the outside world. The gate had been sealed under the orders of the previous king, Jungor Stonespringer, who had fanatically insisted that all points of connection between the undermountain realm and the surface world be closed permanently.

THE FATE OF THORBARDIN

Darkstone knew that outside access to the gate could only be reached by climbing a long, narrow, and tortuous trail that twisted, snakelike, up the face of a lofty cliff. The path was not wide enough for more than two dwarves to walk abreast, so any attacking army would inevitably have its strength pared down to a spearhead of two attackers. If the gate were somehow breached, the defenders of Thorbardin could meet the attackers with a front of a dozen or more, ensuring a great advantage at the point of contact.

When Willim the Black had claimed the throne, he had seen no reason to change his predecessor's edict, and thus the kingdom had remained sealed against the outer world. The gate was the only point of access, and it was as impregnable as any fortification on Krynn.

"Don't worry about how it is possible; just imagine an enemy pouring in through this place. And have your troops prepared to meet that threat."

"As you wish, lord. Er, would it be advisable to open the gate momentarily, to allow me to dispatch a scouting party that might give us advance warning of any threat?"

"No! The gate remains shut for now . . . and forever! There is no need to open it! Do you understand?"

"Aye, Master. I certainly do."

Darkstone did understand. Indeed, since the wizard himself could easily and instantly teleport himself to any place he wanted to go, the sealing of the kingdom was no barrier to him. Yet it did help him to control his subjects and to hold potential adversaries at bay.

The wizard blinked out of sight in that startling, irritating way he had, and the general immediately set to work, though not without some misgivings. In fact, there were many things that Darkstone could be doing in the city of Norbardin, including crucial repairs, restoring vital services, and tracking down and eliminating the outlaws who roamed the city in large and unruly gangs. Yet his king had ordered him to come there, to inspect the gate, to make sure that the garrison—some hundred and twenty surly Theiwar dwarves, many of whom watched him as he paced back and forth in the gatehouse—was prepared for any eventuality.

So General Darkstone followed his orders. He instructed the garrison troops to double the permanent guard, to position extra stocks of weapons and other defensive materials, such as casks of precious oil that could be used to immolate an opponent, and to stand alert at all hours of the day and night.

They were hours that didn't vary much in the sunless underdark, but still, he managed to impress on them that the danger was real and, perhaps, just outside the gate.

——DH——

"The hill dwarves aren't going to join us?" Brandon repeated, turning to glare at Gretchan in astonishment.

"Don't blame me!" she retorted. "Our exiled king is every bit as stubborn as you'd expect an old dwarf to be."

Brandon groaned and leaned against the nearby parapet. The two were alone atop the West Tower of the great Tharkadan fortification. A dazzling array of stars brightened the crystalline nighttime sky over their heads, a swath of brilliance that easily outshone the hundreds of campfires marking the bivouac of the Kayolin Army as it sprawled on both sides of the ancient structure.

They had come up there specifically to get away from prying eyes and ears, to escape the celebration that was rising to a frenzy in the great hall, to share a private embrace, to express how delighted they were to once again be together. But soon their talk had turned to the task before them, and Gretchan had broken the news about the Neidar.

"But the pact we signed—the one that Tarn Bellow-granite himself signed!" Brandon declared, clenching his fists. "It was a pledge of peace and cooperation, forged by the blood of Neidar and mountain dwarves both. Why won't he honor it, now that we actually have a means of returning to Thorbardin?"

"*You* try talking to him," Gretchan said. "But I warn you, even his wife can't change his mind. I think he'd rather break her heart than soften his position on that old prejudice. Besides, Tarn is convinced the hill dwarves aren't necessary to this campaign. He thinks that your troops, plus about a thousand of his own from right here in Pax Tharkas, will be enough to retake Thorbardin."

Brandon shook his head. "I wish *I* could believe that. But we have no way of knowing what kind of enemy we'll face under the mountain. How can he not see that we'll need all the troops we can raise, even to have the slightest chance of success?"

Gretchan came close to her beloved, placing her hands on his shoulders and looking him straight in the eyes. Immediately the tension flowed out of Brandon's body, and he reached for her and pulled her close.

"I'm sorry," he said in a whisper. "I shouldn't have lost my temper. I know you did what you could."

"You're right—on both counts," she chided gently. "But look at the positives: we were able to forge the three stones into the hammer of legend. Tarn's own master smith accomplished that. Bardic Stonehammer is an amazing dwarf. I suggest you think about asking him to wield the hammer as we approach Thorbardin. And you were able to bring the army here in very good time. If we move at once, we should be able to breach the gates of Thorbardin before Willim the Black guesses what's happening."

"Still, he must suspect something, don't you think?"

Gretchan had told Brandon about the attack on her camp, when the apprentice magic-user and Mother Oracle had ambushed her and tried to steal the Redstone. Neither of them was willing to underestimate the powerful wizard who they believed was behind that attempt.

She could only nod somberly in reply.

"Perhaps we'd better get back down to the celebration," Brandon said quietly. "There's a lot to think about and a lot to do before tomorrow."

———DH———

Finally the long night of counsel and feasting and prayer and celebration was winding down to a natural ending. Brandon was exhausted by the ordeal, more exhausted than he had been, he thought wryly, from a long day of marching on the trail.

"It's the old bastard's stupidity that gets me most of all," he admitted to Gretchan as they climbed the stairs from the great hall, where he would join her in her chambers at last. He shrugged out of the ceremonial robe he had borrowed for the feast and sat down on the large, inviting bed. "But that's something to worry about tomorrow."

He arched an eyebrow as he watched her light several candles, kindling each with a word of magic and a touch from the anvil head of her staff. The room was suffused by a soft glow as she crossed to the window, set her staff against the wall, and knelt on a brown bearskin rug stretched across the floor. The head of her staff glowed with a golden light, slightly brighter than any of the candles, illuminating her skin and her hair in a gilded sheen.

"Aren't you coming to bed?" Brandon asked. He smiled slyly. "Or do you want me to join you over there?"

She shook her head, her golden hair cascading around her shoulders, which were bared as she shrugged out of her robe, remaining clad only in a filmy shift of white gauze. "You know I have a few things I have to do first," she chided him as she sat tall, crossing her short legs before her.

"I thought, tonight, under the circumstances—" he began, but she silenced him with the wave of a finger.

So instead, Brandon watched Gretchan as she tended to every little detail of her evening ritual. She closed her eyes and moved her lips in a silent prayer. After a time she seemed to relax, her posture easing, her hands resting in her lap. She breathed easily, drawing air slowly in through her nostrils then exhaling the same way. Finally, she opened her eyes and began a vocal prayer, a melodic recitation in a language so ancient that Brandon didn't recognize a single word.

So intense was his staring that she finally looked up from her musical chant, flashed him a secret smile, and told him to look at something else for the next few minutes.

"I can't," he admitted with complete candor. "And aren't you finished yet?"

She sighed and rose to her feet. The light from the head of her sacred staff faded until only the thin candles illuminated the room. She crossed on bare feet toward the bed, where Brandon sat, still watching, hardly daring to breathe.

The gauzy shift slipped from her shoulders, pooling like a liquid thing on the floor around her feet.

"I think Reorx will understand," she whispered.

Then she fell into his arms.

Nine

Partings and Joinings

Somehow the dwarves providing the food and drink and music for the festive welcome party in Pax Tharkas neglected to include the three gully dwarves who had proudly ridden into the fortress on the wagons hauled by the Kayolin Army. While kegs were tapped, mugs filled to overflowing and generously passed around, and platters laden with sumptuous mountains of food were displayed to every one of the many more than two tables in the place, not one dwarf thought to invite the Aghar to join in the festivities.

No matter: Gus and his girls quickly found themselves a comfortable space beneath a spacious banquet table, and by dint of furtive expeditions, both Slooshy and Berta were able to pluck up juicy, warm tidbits of meat; large pieces of sharp, fresh cheese; bread and fruit; and enough half-empty tankards of ale and spirits that all three Aghar were able to wind up comfortably and happily drunk.

The next morning, of course, they had been rudely rousted by a cleaning crew of dwarf maids who battered the gully dwarves with their brooms and brushes until the trio had to make a hasty escape from the great hall. They fled through a side door into the cellars and dungeons that were quite familiar to Gus and Berta and represented a whole new world of wonder to Slooshy.

In those stinking sewers and dungeons beneath Pax Tharkas, Gus quickly reestablished himself as the highbulp of the small but thriving Aghar community. That exalted position had become his to boast, mainly because of Berta's advocacy when he had first come to the mountain fortress. Of course, the position was mainly honorary and, for the most part, unacknowledged. The other gully dwarves took little notice of the newcomers, occupied as they were with the usual Aghar concerns of survival and avoiding discovery and harassment by the larger dwarves who were their near neighbors. Slooshy, who had joined Gus and Berta in the dank lair, quickly and inevitably resumed her jealous bickering with her gully dwarf rival for Gus's affections.

In part to get away from that constant caterwauling, but mainly because he had been anxious to steal a moment or two alone with Gretchan, Gus waited only two days before he ventured up the stairs and into the main halls of the fortress. There he saw the training of new companies of infantry, the ranges where row after row of crossbow troops took target practice, and the forges where new weapons were cast and older weapons were sharpened, repaired, and readied for war. Everywhere dwarves were marching and drilling and working, but fortunately they were too busy to take note of the little Aghar huddled behind a stack of

THE FATE OF THORBARDIN

shields, his bright eyes constantly alert for a sight of his beloved Gretchan.

For the whole of the long day, he didn't see her, and it was with a heavy heart that he returned to the dungeon. He was too morose even to partake of the drowned rat that Slooshy had discovered and, in a blatant attempt to win his affection away from Berta, offered to split with him.

Instead, he went to bed hungry and alone, and as soon as the sun was up the next day, he returned up the stairs, telling his suspicious partners that he was going to "go for walk and get air!"

Once again he took up his spying place, and though he didn't see Gretchan, he did notice Brandon Bluestone stroll through the hall in the middle of the afternoon. Seizing the opportunity, he broke from cover and raced after the Kayolin general, stealthily following him out the great gate and toward a meadow around a well of clean water. There he dived into a garden of rose bushes, ignoring the thorns that tore at his skin, and was delighted to see that Gretchan was there, apparently talking to some two and two and two young dwarves, saying something about Reorx.

She stopped her teaching to talk to Brandon for a minute, and when he departed, she resumed some boring stuff about healing prayers and curing bleeding wounds and other things that were too complicated for Gus to understand.

Finally, just before it started to get dark, she dismissed the young dwarves—they were clerics in training, Gus had finally figured out—and remained behind by herself, rinsing her face and hands in the cool, clean water from the well.

Mustering all of his debonair charm, Gus ambled out from the thicket of roses. His entrance was marred slightly by a treacherous vine that wrapped around his ankle and tripped him, dropping him onto his face before he could even say hello. The next thing he knew, Kondike was barking at him. Then the big dog waved his tail and licked the gully dwarf all over his face.

"Go 'way, big doofar hound!" he ordered to no avail. "Me here to talk Gretchan!"

"Gus?" the priestess said after she had stopped laughing and, with a curt gesture, called the dog to her side. "What are you doing here?"

"Me march with army! Alla way Kayolin to here! Me go to war! Take Thorbardin!"

At least she didn't laugh at that, but it was almost worse to see that his words seemed to make her sad. "Oh, Gus," she said with a sigh. "That's very brave of you. But, well, I just don't think it's going to work. Not this time."

"Why not? Gus big-time fighter! Him win war! Find Redstone for you!"

"I know you mean well," she said, sitting down on the grass beside him, "but this is different. We're going to climb a big mountain. There will be fighting . . . and killing. And, well, it's just not a place for you."

"Sure it is!" he argued with what he knew to be unimpeachable logic.

"What about Slooshy and Berta? Did they come here with you?" she asked gently.

"Why ask about Gus's girls? They not go to war!"

"No, Gus. They won't go to the war either. But they need you, don't you see? You should stay here with them. And I promise, if we prevail—I mean, if we

THE FATE OF THORBARDIN

win—I will send for you right away. You'll be welcome back in Thorbardin, and all of your people will be able to live there, just like before . . . before the king put a bounty on your heads."

He tried several more times to convince her, but none of his arguments seemed to make any headway. Finally she grew impatient and told him that she had to be going and that he had better get back to his girls, to see that they were safe.

"They plenty safe!" he shot back, but Gretchan was already walking up toward the gate. She let him accompany her as far as the great hall, but when she went to the door leading up into the East Tower, she firmly told him not to follow and closed that same door right in his face.

"Don't say Gus no follow!" he fumed, stomping his way down the stairs into the dungeon. "Gus follow every place! Gus follow, even follow alla way to war!"

And that determination, at least, made him feel a little better. That night, he even let Berta and Sloooshy argue about who would get to give him a foot rub. Of course, by the time they settled the argument, he had already fallen asleep.

——DH——

"Where are you going?" Tarn asked as he discovered Crystal Heathstone busily packing a backpack in the royal quarters. "My army marches tomorrow! I expect you to be on the parapets, leading the cheers as we march off to reclaim Thorbardin!"

His wife, still beautiful and smooth skinned after so many years of tumult and exile, glared at him, and when she spoke, her words were not really all that surprising.

"I'm leaving you," she said. "I'm going back to my people. You don't need me here." Her voice caught and she shook her head angrily. "You don't want *any* Neidar here!"

"That's not true!" he protested. "I—I don't even think of you as a Neidar!" His voice grew stern. "I think of you as my wife, by Reorx! And I will not have you marching off to the clans of my enemies!"

"They're not your enemies, you doddering old fool! But I know that I can't convince you of that! And frankly, I'm ready to give up trying. So I'm going back to Hillhome, to see if there's more honor among the hill clans than there is here, among your mountain dwarves!"

"I forbid it!" Tarn spluttered. "You will not leave Pax Tharkas!"

She laughed, a short and bitter sound. Something in her eyes caused him to hesitate, to wonder at the determination, the anger, that he had never seen in her before.

"Just try to stop me!" was all she said.

And in the end, he could only watch as she walked away.

———DH———

Willim the Black awakened from a most unpleasant nightmare in which he had been trying to teleport away from a looming, horrific firestorm. But his magic had failed him, and he could only quiver and tremble and sweat as the lethal, incinerating presence crept closer and closer.

THE FATE OF THORBARDIN

He awakened to find that he had cast off his blanket and was lying on the bare mattress, naked and soaking wet from his own perspiration. Facet was not there—he had sent her away after he had taken his pleasure from her—but he suddenly wished, very desperately, for the comfort of her embrace.

"Master, I heard you," came her musical voice from the door of his sleeping chamber. "Are you distressed? May I comfort you?"

"Yes—I need you!" he croaked. "Come to me now!"

"Of course, Master. But first, have a cool drink. Here, I brought you some wine."

He gratefully accepted the full tumbler she offered him, drinking so eagerly that the purple liquid trickled from the sides of his mouth, ran into his beard, and spattered across his chest. He was about to order her to bring him a towel, but for some reason his head was spinning.

He was groggy and terribly tired.

Before he knew it, he slept.

---DH---

Crystal had packed lightly, for there was little she desired to take away from that place. The one thing that grieved her above all was the thought of leaving her son behind. But she knew Tor would not choose the hill dwarves over his father's mountain clans. And if she compelled or persuaded him to go, Tarn Bellowgranite would make that an excuse for war.

So she would go alone.

She didn't even have any regrets, except perhaps for the fact that it had taken her so long to make the decision. But finally she understood the truth: there were too many barriers, too many chasms, existing between her world and her husband's. She would be better off without him, and he would be better off without her.

She spent a long moment grieving for her daughter, who had died there. Then she shook her head, hoisted her pack onto her back, and started down the stairs. She didn't look back, not even when she passed the guards at the main gate of Pax Tharkas, and saw them exchange worried looks. Yet neither of them challenged her.

Finally she was on the road, the fortress falling away behind her. Her home was ahead of her, many miles away, but they would be good miles. Of that she was certain.

And there was another thing she knew.

It was good to be free.

———DH———

The mad dwarf knew that he had outwitted them all. He was clever, too clever by far, for the king and his lackeys to catch him. Once the unseen benefactor had freed him from his cell, he had not gone up into the fortress of Pax Tharkas, where every corridor, every room, every hall would be watched and, as soon as his absence was noted, searched.

No, Garn Bloodfist had not climbed upward. Instead, he made his way even deeper into the Tharkadan cellars, slipping past the slumbering turnkey then making his way toward an ancient route that very few dwarves knew existed.

THE FATE OF THORBARDIN

The Sla-Mori, it was called, the secret way.

And so it was, a way out of Pax Tharkas, a passage that had carried him into a forested ravine more than a mile beyond the high walls, the ranks of torches, and the patrolling sentries.

There he had hidden for countless days, eating berries and grubs, hiding in the streambed whenever anyone approached, using the simple expedient of burying himself in mud until only his eyes and nose were exposed to the air. He kept his eyes closed, and the tactic had worked, for he had not yet been discovered.

As the days passed and the imminence of winter became more clear with each chill night, he wondered what to do. He watched the road leading away from the fortress, hiding as the hill dwarf traders and mountain dwarf hunting parties went past. He reminded himself that he hated them all, the hill dwarves and the mountain dwarves. They were all his foes, and they would pay.

Then one afternoon he was startled to see a lone female figure striding away from the fortress. He recognized the beautiful hair, gray but still soft, and the strong, determined stride. She was the former queen, the one who had visited him and calmed him in his dungeon of torment. He loved her, in his own way, for that care.

But then he remembered another truth, undeniable, and burning like a fire in his gut.

Oh, yes, he hated her too.

Part II

TEN

ROADS INTO THE WILD

"It's been too short, our time here together. I wish we weren't leaving for another week! Why'd you have to be so Reorx-cursed efficient?" groused Brandon, looking at his steel breastplate with distaste.

Gretchan sighed, making a sound that was a mixture of affection and aggravation. She was already dressed in her traveling clothes: her leather moccasins were laced tightly over her calves, and the woolen outer cloak she wore for warmth lay across the trunk, along with her sacred staff. The window's shutter was open, mountain darkness and chill yawning beyond, and he knew that she, too, would have been more than happy to simply go back to bed.

"I wish we could take some more time together right now. Believe me, I do," she said. "But we'd just be passing the hours here in a mountain fortress built for war, with another war looming as soon as we decide to take care of our responsibilities." Her voice turned sharp. "Or would you have us forget about Thorbardin, forget about everything but our own selfish desires?"

"No," Brandon acknowledged, sliding his arms through the sleeves of his metal armor. "Not when there's a real chance that the next war might be the *last* war, at least as it pertains to us dwarves. We might as well have at it."

If only the last three days hadn't been so restful, so pleasant, so . . . *loving!* In the back of his mind, he realized that he'd been hoping to spend a week or more there, assuming that it would take at least that long for the two armies to muster, gather supplies, and coalesce as a single force.

But Gretchan's early arrival had allowed Tarn Bellowgranite time to prepare his men for an expedition, and the combined army was ready to march from Pax Tharkas a mere seventy-two hours after the Kayolin troops had turned up. Supplies had been stockpiled, weapons and armor repaired and readied for the campaign, captains assigned, and units organized for war. Tarn himself had become the mission's most ardent supporter, and his own men had taken heart from their leader's resurgent energy.

Too soon the dawn of the first march had come, with gray light suffusing the valley of Pax Tharkas while the snowy massif of Cloudseeker Peak, with its corona of cornice and glacier, slowly took shape on the southern horizon. Brandon gazed at that mountain and shuddered, unable to suppress a shiver of growing apprehension and almost insurmountable reluctance.

Gretchan seemed, as usual, to know what he was feeling deep inside.

"I wish we could stay here, right under these covers," she agreed as though reading his thoughts, wistfully looking at the large, still disheveled, bed. "But you're right: this campaign could finally end these decades, even centuries, of violence. If we restore freedom to Thorbardin, we can look forward to a long and well-deserved peacetime."

"I still wish that stubborn old fellow would have agreed to bring the hill dwarves with us," Brandon complained. "I'd feel better about our chances."

"Of course, you are right about that," the female cleric agreed with maddening calm. "But even without the Neidar, we'll be marching with a very capable force."

The Kayolin general had to admit the assembled army was impressive. Right outside their window, hundreds of cookfires dotted the vast encampment to the south of the fortress wall. In addition to the four thousand troops he had brought south, Tarn Bellowgranite had mustered another thousand well-trained veterans, dwarves he called the Tharkadan Legion.

Among that force were some five hundred Klar of proven courage and loyalty. They were commanded by a one-eyed captain named Wildon Dacker. Dacker had served with Tarn Bellowgranite even before the long exile and was a much steadier and more reliable captain than his predecessor, Garn Bloodfist. And Dacker undeniably held the loyalty of his Klar warriors. Though they retained the impetuous and frenzied traits of their clan, they made for exceptional shock troops, and when they attacked in a berserking frenzy, their whoops and wails would test the courage of even the stoutest opponent.

The rest of the Tharkadan Legion consisted of heavily armed and armored Hylar and Daergar, under the command of Mason Axeblade. They, too, were seasoned veterans who had proven their loyalty to Tarn

Bellowgranite many times over through the years—so much so that all of them had chosen to follow him into exile more than a decade earlier. They were ready to march with him unto death to reclaim his rightful throne.

The former king of Thorbardin suggested that the entire force should be named the Dwarf Home Army, and so it was done. The agreement had been sealed over two nights of feasting and celebration and, dwarves being dwarves, much drinking. The captains of the two realms had gotten to know each other as friends, while the troops had sized each other up and been satisfied, even impressed, by their new comrades in arms.

Dawn was brightening toward full daylight with inexorable speed as Brandon hoisted his backpack onto his shoulders and took up the Bluestone Axe. Gretchan hoisted her staff too, and they were at last ready to go.

Near the door, Kondike whined and waved his tail halfheartedly.

"You'll have to stay here, old friend," Gretchan said sadly and fondly. She gave the dog a pat on his broad head but wouldn't let him out the door. "Tor Bellowgranite will come and let you out in a few hours," she explained as if the animal could understand. "But I'm keeping you behind the door until we're well over the horizon."

Tarn's son, like Kondike, had been disappointed at being left behind. The priestess had tried to ease his chagrin with words of encouragement about the future. Finally, though, after being charged with the dog's care while Gretchan was away, the young dwarf had seemed to accept his decidedly minor role in the master battle plan.

THE FATE OF THORBARDIN

By the time Gretchan and Brandon had descended from her room in the high tower, the whole of the Dwarf Home Army had assembled on the terraced ground just south of the great fortress. They looked ready to go to war.

Tarn Bellowgranite was at the center of a circle that included Otaxx Shortbeard, the Klar Wildon Dacker, and Mason Axeblade. He waved the couple over as soon as they emerged from the gates.

"Brandon! Gretchan! This is a great day!" he declared loudly. "Are you ready to make history?"

"Indeed we are," Brandon said, inspired in spite of himself by the old dwarf's ebullience.

Gretchan nodded, studying Tarn with slightly narrowed eyes. Brandon knew that Gretchen was worried about the absence of Crystal Heathstone and the effect that might have on the king. The Kayolin dwarf noticed Tarn glance once upward, toward the windows of his royal apartment, while an expression of sadness flickered across his face. But that look vanished immediately as the exiled king clapped a hand on the hilt of the short sword he wore at his waist and turned his eyes to the south, toward Thorbardin.

Bardic Stonehammer stood near the king. He clasped Brandon's hand and embraced Gretchan. The hulking smith carried a leather-wrapped bundle slung over his broad shoulder, and Brandon, once again, was glad to have the burly dwarf along, chosen as the best one to wield the Tricolor Hammer. All of their hopes depended on that artifact doing what it was supposed to do: cracking the unbreachable gate of Thorbardin.

And that would be only the beginning of what was certain to be a long and bloody campaign.

Still, it was a column of optimistic dwarves who started on the mountain road. They had hot food in their bellies, a worthy goal before them, and a priestess of Reorx to counsel them. As if to beckon them onward, Cloudseeker was outlined in bright sunlight, the glacial summit sparkling like a massive gemstone before them.

The hope of all their futures awaited them under the mountain.

---DH---

Meanwhile, the mad dwarf was skulking along the ridgetop, bouncing from ravine to ledge to rocky crest on all fours, peering around the corner of a boulder, watching his . . . his quarry? His friend . . . ? His woman . . . ?

More and more, he found himself thinking in terms of the latter.

Surely she recognized their bond too! Wasn't that the reason she had come to visit him so often while he languished in his cell? Her kindness had been more than mere charity. That much was obvious. As the mad dwarf remembered things, he could almost hear the quiver of longing in her voice whenever she had spoken to him. Her eyes, when he had glimpsed them, had positively shined with what must certainly have been desire.

He had located a good vantage atop a rocky crest, with the road curving around the base of the elevation, and settled himself on a flat rock, lying on his belly as he studied Crystal Heathstone's resolute progress away from Pax Tharkas.

THE FATE OF THORBARDIN

She walked as if she knew that he was observing her; at least, that was the thought in the mad dwarf's mind. The sway of her hips as she walked over the rough ground was alluring, a personal signal to him. His heart tripped. Was that a furtive look over her shoulder? A coy glance at the watcher on the hilltop? Did she suspect he was up there?

He almost convinced himself that she knew his position. Only with a great exertion of will did he restrain himself from leaping to his feet, waving wildly, and running down the steep and rocky slope to sweep her into his arms. Oh, how he wanted to!

But he had retained more than a vestige of his cunning, and he realized that, if he were wrong and he revealed himself too soon, she might flee in fear. So instead he contented himself with watching, shifting slowly along the slab of rock as she strolled along the road so far below, gradually making her way around the huge knob of granite.

As she continued on, he saw that the road wound away from him and she was already passing around the curve, vanishing behind the shoulder of the next hill. Garn sprang up, running down the slope so fast that he pitched forward and rolled all the way to the bottom, jarring to a stop in a ditch. Picking himself up, he limped on a bruised knee and wiped streaks of dust and gravel out of his beard but wasted no time in hastening after his quarry.

He jogged awkwardly along the road for several hundred paces until he sensed that he was getting too close to Crystal again. It was still too soon for him to reveal himself, so he jumped in the ditch again then started climbing up through the slope that would again carry him to a level high above the dwarf maid. His knee bothered him enough that he had to pull himself along by grasping tree trunks and outcrops of rocks.

The hill was not as steep nor as rugged as the previous one, and the forest of tall, thin pines extended all the way to the top. Using the woods as cover, he moved along as quickly as he was able and was at last awarded another glimpse of the beautiful white fur cloak worn by the former queen of Thorbardin. He limped along, grunting against the pain that stabbed through his leg, grateful for the thick concealment offered by the trees.

He was well hidden from her. He didn't have to stay so far away. And as dusk started to settle through the hills, he knew it was time to move closer to her.

———DH———

Once the army was ready to leave—and there was Gretchan, going away with all the soldiers—Gus was determined not to be left behind. He watched, innocently waving, as the troops packed up their gear, formed into companies, and made ready to march. The two Firespitters, with their accompanying carts of oil, were near the tail of the formation, and the gully dwarf casually made his way toward those ungainly vehicles.

As the great column of dwarves finally started along the southward road leading into the Kharolis Mountains, Gus Fishbiter left the shadows of Pax Tharkas and made his way to the dense center of the columns of the army, swelled by the soldiers of Tarn Bellowgranite's Tharkadan Legion. He marched along, trying to look inconspicuous. Mindful of Gretchan's orders instructing him to remain behind, he avoided going anywhere near the cleric, for the moment.

He finally found the cart in which he had ridden earlier—a vehicle carrying casks of oil for the Firespitters, the kegs stored carefully on beds of straw—and quickly scrambled up the side and into the bedding. Settling into the soft nest with a contented smile, he leaned back and stared up into the sunny sky, seeing the high ridges to either side of the valley road.

And almost immediately his view was blocked by two female faces, peering crossly down at him. Berta pulled herself over one side of the cart while Slooshy scrambled over the other.

"Hey! Almost forgot me!" Berta declared crossly, settling next to him in the hay.

"No! Almost forgot Slooshy! What kind of bluph-splunging doofar you are, anyway?"

Grumpily, Gus made room for his two bickering female consorts and spent the first day of the army's march riding along, his happiness spoiled, in gloomy silence. He didn't even spot his beloved Gretchan until late in the day, when the column started to climb a long switchback toward the first of several passes that lay between Pax Tharkas and their objective. Then, as the front of the column snaked around to pass along the road far above him, he caught a glimpse of her blue robe and golden hair. Not surprisingly, she was striding along at Brandon Bluestone's side. Berta noticed and elbowed him for looking, and Slooshy elbowed Berta.

The army crossed over the pass during sunset, hastening down the far side to spread out across a wide valley and make camp. Gus stomped off by himself, finding a small niche behind a boulder where he could sulk out of sight of the bigger dwarves. He sent Berta and Slooshy off to steal some food and cleared a space for a reasonably comfortable bed.

Slooshy returned with a half loaf of hard bread that she had somehow coaxed from an army cook. She was prepared to share it with Gus, but when Berta returned with a real prize—a half-full flask of dwarf spirits that a grizzled sergeant had misplaced while pitching his tent—the three Aghar agreed to share and share alike.

Afterward, under the influence of the spirits, things didn't seem so bad. Even as the troops of the army, exhausted from a day of marching, settled down to slumber, the three Aghar were sipping the fiery liquid, belching and burping and relishing the warmth spreading through their filthy little bodies.

Making their pleasure last, they didn't fall asleep until after the flask was empty. But when they slept, they slept very soundly indeed, notwithstanding the rocks under their heads or, hours later, the cold mountain sky slowly brightening above them. That passed unnoticed by the slumbering gully dwarves.

Gus, the first one to awaken, looked up in surprise to see a blue sky, with the sun already well above the eastern ridge. His head hurt and his mouth felt like stale cotton. He grumpily kicked his girlfriends awake.

"Come on, lazy bluphsplungers!" he croaked. "Get up! Get going! We go with army!"

Only then did he look out over the other side of the rock that concealed their campsite. He blinked and looked again, certain that his eyes must be deceiving him. But when he opened his eyes again and looked hard

THE FATE OF THORBARDIN

one more time, his initial impression was confirmed: there was no army, no carts, and no tents anywhere to be seen in the wide valley.

The Aghar had overslept.

And the king's army had marched away without them.

———DH———

Willim the Black teleported through the vast chasms of Thorbardin, never remaining in one location for more than the fleeting seconds required for him to repeat his spell. In every case, he imagined the incinerating presence, the lethal breath of the fire dragon singeing his robes, charring his skin, propelling him on a barely controlled, panic-fueled flight throughout the underworld of his domain.

Finally he launched himself upward and out, his spell carrying him far away to the slopes of Cloudseeker Peak, the rocky summit dominating the Kharolis Mountains. He shivered in the unaccustomed wind and cast a spell of levitation, rising upward a foot or two above the ground so he wouldn't have to stand in the wet snow. Slowly, carefully, he twisted through a full circle, seeking any sign of Gorathian's deadly presence.

It was broad daylight, and nothing moved on the glacial slope. Willim began to wonder if he had imagined the creature's pursuit. He understood, rationally, that even the powerful creature of chaos could not pursue him very easily when he employed his magic to vanish and remove himself with instantaneous speed. Just in case, his spell of true-seeing allowed him to inspect the lower slopes, sweeping his attention around the cliffs that skirted the base of the great summit. Good, there was no sign of the fire dragon.

He did, however, spot the immense approaching army. He was startled. So intent had he been on the constant menace of Gorathian that he had momentarily forgotten about the growing external threat to his domain. As he watched the serpentine column twisting along the narrow mountain roads, inching its way southward from the direction of Pax Tharkas, he realized that Gorathian might not be the worst threat to his existence after all.

Willim the Black was not afraid. Instead, his lip curled into a sneer of hatred and contempt. Did that motley army of dwarves dare think they could assault *his* kingdom, *his* city? With cold curiosity, he inspected the column, noting the many thousands of armored dwarves and the small carts hauling a miscellany of supplies. He saw two large, ungainly devices hauled along at the rear of the army; his cursory inspection of the devices revealed the spitting nozzles and the large tanks of oil. Clearly they were some kind of fire weapons, but the wizard almost chortled: did those fool dwarves think they could *burn* their way into Thorbardin?

Nowhere did he notice any sign of great catapults, augers, or battering rams, the kind of things that were usually required if the attacking dwarves had any hope of penetrating the solid stone of the mountain.

So the reports and predictions were true, Willim the Black concluded: Tarn Bellowgranite intended to wield some ancient artifact in order to gain entry to Thorbardin. Well—and the wizard laughed out loud at the thought—let him try!

THE FATE OF THORBARDIN

In another second he blinked out of sight, only to arrive in his subterranean lair. The great cavern was cool and dark and eerily silent with Gorathian gone. He found Facet waiting for him, and she gasped and dropped to her knees when he materialized all of a sudden. The expression of remorse and fear warmed him, and he found that his earlier anger, like the baking warmth of the fire dragon's presence, had dissipated.

"Come to me, my pet," he said gently. He settled himself in his sturdy armchair and beckoned her to kneel before him. "I am pleased to see you."

"Oh, thank you, my lord!" she cried, leaning forward and, at a gesture of acceptance from him, embracing the wizard. "You are so good to me."

"I know that," he said, leaning back. He thought about Gorathian, about the army, and about the many things he needed to do. He thought about his private needs.

As if she understood those unspoken needs, she rose and went to a nearby table. There, a crystal goblet stood, already filled by her caring hand. She raised the glass and brought it to him, holding it out hesitantly. "I suspected that you would be thirsty, Master," she offered meekly. "Would it please you to have a drink of wine?"

"Yes, my pet. It would please me to have wine. And too," he added, taking the goblet and drinking deeply, "it would please me to have you as well."

He raised his hand, a curt gesture of command, and a willing smile curled her crimson lips as, with a shrug of her shoulders, she dropped her black robe to the floor.

ELEVEN

TO THE HIGH GATE

There's the trail," Tarn Bellowgranite said to Brandon as the two of them, with Otaxx and Gretchan, stood atop the last pass before the road to the North Gate of Thorbardin. "It's been a long time now since I've laid eyes on the place. My last look up there was when I fled into exile, barely escaping with a few loyal followers and my life. Jungor Stonespringer had the gate closed behind us, and it's never been opened since."

Brandon was gazing up the narrow valley, not even sure he could make out the road, when he noticed the former king turn his eyes to look back wistfully over his shoulder for a moment. The Kayolin general suspected that Tarn, once again, was thinking of his wife. Brandon and Gretchan had witnessed Crystal Heathstone's departure from Pax Tharkas, even before the army marched, and though they had perceived her anger, they had not been able to learn the full cause of the royal couple's breakup.

Still, they could guess. Both were saddened to think that the long schism between hill and mountain dwarf had brought the royal couple to such a rupture. At one time, the marriage between Tarn and Crystal had seemed to offer the best hope of a new, peaceful future. But that hope was doused like the coals of a campfire under a steady drizzle.

In the next instant, Tarn turned back energetically to study the valley and the rising summit of Cloudseeker Peak. He clapped his hands together, rubbing them with a lively enthusiasm that seemed very different from the stoical detachment that was more his personality when the couple had first met him, more than a year previous, in Pax Tharkas.

"I say we move on the gate today!" Tarn declared heartily.

Brandon's eyes widened and he caught the look of alarm on Otaxx Shortbeard's face as well. Behind them, stretching for miles to the north, the whole column of the king's army lay visible along the twisting mountain road. It would be many hours before the bulk of that force reached and climbed the pass, and it was clear to any observer that the valley of Thorbardin's gate lay at least another six hours' march to the south.

"A worthy goal, sire, but I fear it is not possible," Otaxx demurred respectfully.

The Kayolin dwarf was grateful that the elder Daewar, Gretchan's father and Tarn's longtime and most loyal sub-commander, broached the difficulties before Brandon had to voice his opinion. "It will take at least another day to bring the whole army up here, and then they will need rest. And even a modicum of caution will require us to scout the approaches, to examine the upper slopes and uncover any traps."

THE FATE OF THORBARDIN

"How could the wizard trap five thousand men?" demanded Tarn, scowling.

"Look at the trail, sire," Gretchan said, stepping forward to gesture.

The route to the kingdom's gate was etched in plain view before them. Patches were illuminated by the afternoon sun, but even in the shadows, much of the trail was clearly visible as it twisted and clawed its way up the sheer slope. It was even more daunting than Brandon had imagined: overhung by glaciers and lofty rock slopes, it would leave any soldiers on the trail vulnerable to avalanche or rockslide or sneak attack. A single mistake or an unforeseen attack could sweep hundreds of dwarves to their deaths. It seemed that every step of the trail was exposed to danger from higher vantages.

Even Tarn seemed to grasp that reality as he stared at the road ahead. Finally he nodded reluctantly, his eyes sweeping the terrain. "Yes, well, we can make camp along the road down there," he said, pointing, "and then move in the morning."

Brandon studied the ground indicated by the king. A few things recommended the place—a stream flowed nearby, providing a source of fresh water, and several groves of stubby trees augured a ready source of firewood. But there were disadvantages: like the trail, the ground Tarn had selected for the encampment was surrounded on all sides by lofty ridges, with the heights protected by sheer cliffs. If enemy forces appeared on those cliffs, the army's position would become a trap, with the only source of escape the narrow trail leading up to the very pass where the command party currently stood.

But when he tried to raise those objections, the king brushed them away with a confident declaration. "The enemy is waiting under the mountain, not lurking about outside the gates! I am quite certain Willim the Black will not bring his troops out in the open, where we could meet and defeat them on an honorable battlefield. Instead, he will make us fight our way into Thorbardin, where he can meet us on his own sneaking terms."

So it was that, by the king's order, the army filed over the pass and down into the valley below Cloudseeker Peak. Among the first to arrive at the bivouac area was Tankard Hacksaw. He wasted no time in sending detachments of troops from his First Legion to scramble up the steep slopes and inspect the heights to either side of the trail, ensuring that, as much as possible, they were clear of traps and there were no signs of enemy dwarves.

Brandon and Gretchan, in the meantime, decided to scout the trail leading to the gate, though they both agreed with Otaxx's wise suggestion that they not approach too close to the actual entryway. But they wanted to get a sense of the difficulties they would face if Willim's men did attempt to fight outside of Thorbardin.

"It couldn't have been planned any better for defense," Brandon admitted when the couple stopped to rest at a switchback, nearly a thousand feet above the valley floor.

"No wonder it's never been taken by storm, not in more than two thousand years," Gretchan agreed almost reverentially.

They stared at the narrow trail, with the sheer rock face on one side and the plummeting precipice on the other. The pathway rose at a steep angle and was never wide enough for more than two dwarves to walk side by side. In some places it was even too narrow for a double file without exposing the outer dwarf to a possibly fatal stumble. The trail twisted forward until it met the sheer wall of the mountain, where it simply seemed to end.

"And the gate." Brandon pointed upward to the terminus of the trail, still five hundred feet above them. "It's right there, where the path ends at the mountainside. But how sturdy it must be! How much solid rock will the Tricolor Hammer have to split?"

"My father described the mechanism to me. It's a great screw of stone, carved into a plug in the mountainside. He estimated maybe fifty or sixty feet thick," Gretchan explained. "It's designed, of course, so that it can't be forced open. And if it's opened by some other means, it still allows only a very narrow point of access to Thorbardin."

"Fifty feet of stone? That sounds impossible!" Brandon protested, his heart sinking. He had heard those descriptions before, but confronted with the reality of the scene before him, the task seemed hopeless.

"It would be impervious to any normal weapon. But remember, the Tricolor Hammer is an artifact of Reorx, and it was created by our god with this sole purpose in mind. If the three pieces of stone—scattered through Thorbardin, Pax Tharkas, and Kayolin—could be assembled, it is said, then the wielder will be able gain access to the great kingdom under the mountain. I have faith in my god. Do you?"

Brandon sighed and looked at Gretchan. Her golden hair lay plastered to her scalp, sweaty and dirty from the trail. She was breathing hard and sniffling from the cold air. And she had never looked more beautiful to him.

"I have faith in you," he said. And because of that, he had faith, too, in Gretchan's knowledge of the hammer and the prophecy of the artifact's divine might.

She smiled, a trifle wistfully, as he reached out and took her hand. "I have faith in you too," she admitted almost shyly. "If I didn't, I guess none of us would be here."

"But here we are," he said, conviction and determination growing within him. He felt a surge of optimism. "And here we'll be tomorrow."

"Let's get back down to the camp," she said. "There's a lot of preparing to do."

———DH———

"What was that? Who's there?"

Crystal's voice sounded confident, even demanding, but her heart pounded in her chest as she spun through a full circle. She studied the dark, thick pine forest that seemed to reach out from both sides, several lush boughs extending almost to the middle of the narrow, winding hill road. Dusk had seemed to settle around her very quickly.

How much farther until the next inn?

She longed for the sight of a welcoming sign, the scent of wood smoke from a tavern's hearth, and the raucous sounds of dwarves relaxing. She knew there were wayfarer's houses every few miles along the road—she'd stayed in such establishments for the past three nights—but she feared she'd miscalculated that part

THE FATE OF THORBARDIN

of the journey. She didn't relish the thought of continuing down the road after dark, but she didn't seem to have any choice if she didn't happen upon any inn or farmhouse.

She tried to tell herself that her misgivings were just foolish fears. Certainly there was no one out there, lurking in the woods, watching her!

Or was there?

The sensation of being spied upon had been growing stronger and stronger throughout the past day of her trek. Often she'd scanned the heights to either side of the road, looking for some stealthy watcher, but she'd never spotted anyone. And even if someone were there, it would be merely some hill dwarf woodcutter or a goatherd tending to his flock.

Of course it would!

Straightening her back and setting her shoulders squarely, she strode along the road, projecting an air of self-confidence that she didn't really feel. She walked ten steps, ten more, and finally felt better and could chide herself on merely a girlish case of nerves.

Then she heard the sharp *snap* of a breaking stick, like a brittle branch on the ground that had just been broken by a heavy footfall.

"Hello!" she called, brightly she hoped. "Who's there?"

"Hello, my sweet Crystal."

The rasping voice emerged from the shadowy foliage, and she felt a sick feeling growing in her gut. Her first impulse was to flee, to run headlong down the road, but she forced that thought away. Better to be brave, confident . . . wait, the watcher knew her name!

"Who are you?" she demanded, a hint of royal anger creeping into her voice.

"You know me, my queen," came the answer, and the pine boughs rustled as someone edged forward.

The first thing she saw was a pair of eyes: wide, bloodshot, and staring, with rims of white surrounding dark pupils. The eyes were centered in a bearded face, a dwarf's, with bristling hair extending down over his forehead. He was filthy and wearing a tattered cloak and boots that were torn and broken, revealing his blistered, swollen toes.

Only when the breeze shifted slightly, bearing a scent of sweat and damp straw reminiscent of the Tharkadan dungeon, did she recognize the dwarf.

"Garn?" she asked as the ball of sickness churned and thickened in her gut. "What are you doing here?"

"Why, coming with you, of course," the mad Klar said, unsuccessfully trying to stifle a cackle of delight. "That's why you let me out of my cell, isn't it? So that I could follow you home?"

"But—I didn't—it wasn't me—" She bit back the denial, not certain what approach to take with her husband's former captain. It was strange enough that some mysterious person had freed him, but to encounter him on the trail! She knew from her conversations with him that Garn was suspicious to the point of paranoia, and Crystal didn't want to risk antagonizing him to a state of agitation any more intense than his normal existence. "That is, have you been following me all along? Since I left Pax Tharkas?"

"All along!" he crowed with a sense of glee that chilled her even more. "But too high and too rough on the hills. Now I follow you on the road!"

He stepped closer, and it was too late for her to flee. She stared in horror as he reached out with a surprisingly strong hand and seized her wrist. Recoiling, she pulled and twisted.

But she couldn't break away.

---DH---

"Which way go army?" Gus asked, standing on the boulder and scratching his head.

"That way!" Slooshy declared confidently, pointing toward a narrow valley that twisted away to the east.

"No, *that* way!" Berta insisted, pointing at the mouth of a gorge that climbed steeply toward the west.

To the south, a haze of dust lingered in the air, fine particles kicked up by the passing of some five thousand dwarves along a dry dirt road. Only moments before, the tail end of the column had vanished from view around a bend in the valley toward Thorbardin. The signs of that march would linger in the air, slowly settling over the next hour or so.

But observation skills had never been a strong component of the gully dwarf intellect, and so it was that Gus was left to glare and stare and stomp his feet, finally regarding his two girlfriends with a look of unconcealed contempt—beneath which lay genuine concern. Where was Gretchan? Where had she gone? And why had she not taken Gus with her?

Miserably, he slumped down on the rock and took a long moment to pick his nose. The girls were bickering down below, but he didn't really pay much attention. One called the other a "bluphsplunging doofar" while the second retorted with an even gamier insult. Meanwhile, the army was gone and—it just occurred to Gus—so was their food supply.

Not very hopefully, he looked around again. There wasn't so much as a fruit tree or berry patch in sight; even the small oak grove along the stream had been picked clean of acorns by the large army camped there. Gus's stomach growled loudly, and he thought wistfully of the splendid tunnels of Agharhome beneath Pax Tharkas. Those passages were practically teeming with plump rats and offered many deep pools crowded with tender cave-carp. What he wouldn't give for even the fin of one of those meaty fish.

Fish! He remembered there was a stream nearby, and without another word, he hopped down from his rock and made his way over to the narrow, shallow waterway. But the creek that had been clear and speckled with lively trout the previous night was a muddy mess, ruined by the passage of ten thousand boots through a shallow ford just upstream. All them fish gone, he thought glumly.

He wondered idly where all those dwarves had marched off to. The road to the north, he remembered, led back to Pax Tharkas. But the fortress was many miles away. And he was certain that Gretchan would not have gone that way. He looked toward where the army had disappeared, wondering if the dwarf soldiers were trying some tricky plan, trying to fool him and others from following. Why would they go to Pax Tharkas anyway? So instead he looked toward the two valleys and the gorge.

At that moment, a waft of breeze came down from the west, and it carried on its breath the faint smell of a cookfire. In that instant, Gus made up his mind.

"We go that way," he declared, pointing firmly toward the source of the smell.

THE FATE OF THORBARDIN

"See. I told you!" Berta said, glaring at Slooshy. "Barflooming little sloot say wrong way! Berta knows."

"Be quiet! Alla girls be quiet!" Gus demanded, starting to walk and not much caring whether his two consorts chose to accompany him or not.

But of course they did. The three gully dwarves scrambled over some large rocks at the foot of the gorge and pulled themselves up with their stubby, little fingers as they scaled the cliff steps blocking access to the gorge. Soon the floor of the steep-walled draw leveled out into a winding track that the Aghar, at least, could walk along.

For the rest of the morning and into the afternoon, Gus and his girls climbed higher and higher into the foothills, leaving the road behind and meandering far from the track that had been taken by the mountain dwarf army. All the while, Gus's stomach rumbled from emptiness, and his misery wrapped itself around him like a cloud. After the first few hours, Berta and Slooshy had even stopped complaining; indeed they stopped talking altogether.

By the time the long shadows of afternoon stretched around them, they still hadn't come upon any sign of the missing army. Nor had they discovered anything that even vaguely resembled food (and, being Aghar, their definition of *food* was a broad one, naturally). When night settled around them, it was too dark to go any farther, and the unhappy trio was forced to huddle together in a makeshift shelter between two rocks. They had no fire, and the night was cold, so they spent most of the night shivering, snuggling close, then elbowing each other in irritation whenever one of them shifted position.

The next morning they continued on their way, and at least they were fortunate enough to come upon a berry bush that still bore a few shriveled fruits. So they feasted enough to keep them going then climbed out of the ridge and into the next. But they saw only many more ridges and no sign of any dwarf army.

---DH---

Brandon didn't sleep much, and though he knew dawn was hours away, he finally crawled out of his bedroll, pulled on his boots, and started getting ready for the upcoming battle. His restlessness was widely shared as, all around him, dwarves stirred and grumbled, stomping their feet in the chill and kindling small fires for warmth and to heat water.

Sparks flew here and there as warriors scuffed whetstones across their blades, bringing their steel to razor sharpness. Given the constricted nature of the trail, the army had to advance in segments, but the leading element of the First Legion—the troops who would lead the way—were already gathering into columns at the base of the mountain trail.

"My scouts have been up on the ridges all night," Tankard Hacksaw reported to Brandon. "Each company had plenty of torches; they were to light a flare if there was any chance of an ambush. We'd see it from down here for sure."

The Kayolin commander nodded, looking around at the dark, silent summits to either side of them. "Good sign, that. Then the real fighting will come if—" He corrected himself with a confidence he still did not entirely feel. *"When* we breach the gate."

THE FATE OF THORBARDIN

"I'll be right behind you," Tankard pledged.

Brandon shook his head and put his hand on his loyal lieutenant's shoulder. "No, old friend. I want you up there with me but at least two hundred paces back. I'll stand with Bardic Stonehammer when he wields the artifact, but if the worst happens and I fall, it'll be your job to take over command of the assault."

Tankard looked as if he wanted to argue, but after a moment, he gritted his teeth and nodded. "As you command," was all he said.

"Good man," Brandon replied.

Even as they spoke, Bardic approached, bearing the long bundle wrapped in the supple leather cover made from a single cow's hide. The big smith's bald head was not protected by any metal cap, and a sheen of sweat gleamed on the smooth surface of his scalp.

"Shall we take a look at the key to Thorbardin's gate?" he asked.

Brandon had seen the Tricolor Hammer just once, when he first returned to Pax Tharkas with his army. At that time, the artifact had seemed like some arcane memento, something to be displayed in a royal museum or king's hall. It had seemed pristine, precious, but not especially powerful or dangerous.

But as Bardic unveiled the hallowed artifact, there was no mistaking the fact that it was a *weapon*. The three stones forming the head of the hammer were each bright enough that they almost seemed luminescent. The Redstone was at the top of the hammerhead, with the blue in the middle and the green at the bottom. The colors were distinct, but the lines between the three stones had vanished, as if the wedges had melted or fused together.

The haft, a bar of solid steel, extended through the widest part of the head and out the top. At that end, the smith had capped the hammer with a tiny silver anvil, a perfect match of the little icon that topped Gretchan's staff.

"Would you like to feel its heft?" Bardic asked.

Brandon nodded and took the hammer by the handle. He lifted it, feeling the solid weight of the mighty stone head. It was a good weight, and as he took a few practice swings, it seemed to glide forward with the energy of his blow, as if the hammer itself were eager to move, to strike . . . to smash.

"It's beautiful and terrifying at the same time," Brandon said, surprised to realize he was whispering.

He felt a warm hand on his shoulder and realized that Gretchan had come up to stand beside him. Her eyes were focused on the artifact, and they seemed to shine in reflection of the three colors. Her staff was in her other hand, and Brandon didn't know if it was real or his imagination, but the anvil on the head of the shaft of wood seemed to glow with a silvery shimmer brighter even than the moonlight that still washed the mountain valley. Reverently he handed the weapon back to the smith, who accepted it in the same awed way. His eyes gleamed, reflecting the light of the three-colored stone.

"I'll go up there alone," Bardic said matter-of-factly. "You'll need to give me plenty of room to swing it."

"I will but I'll be close by with the Bluestone Axe," Brandon replied. He turned to face Gretchan soberly. "Tankard will be two hundred paces behind us with the vanguard of his legion," he said, trying once again to make the argument that had failed him the evening before. "You should stand with him. That way, if anything happens—"

"I'll be too far away to do anything other than recover your remains," she said simply. "I haven't changed my mind. I'm going to be close by your side."

He felt a lump in his throat and was too moved even to be irritated by her stubbornness. "All right," he replied. "Are you ready to go?"

She was. They all were.

The advance column of the army moved out, dwarves marching two by two behind Bardic, Brandon, and Gretchan. The Kayolin commander started out with the Bluestone Axe in a sling on his back, but he found himself desiring the sturdy feel of the weapon in his hands. Quickly he freed it from its strap and continued along, holding the smooth haft in both of his hands, grateful for the comforting presence of his trusty blade.

The two hundred dwarves who followed directly behind him were all volunteers, all sturdy veterans of the First Legion. They wore steel breastplates, helmets, and greaves, but otherwise were garbed in leather. Each carried his weapon of choice, including swords, spears, and axes in their number. None bore a shield since, in the close-quarters combat they anticipated, even a small buckler could prove to be more of a hindrance than an advantage. They were the shock troops, the men who would advance into the first breach and hold the position for the rest of the army.

They followed the hammer, the general, and the priestess up the trail grimly, as silently as an army could move. The plans had been made and repeated to all the night before, so there was no need for discussion.

They would go in quickly and violently, Brandon had explained, streaming into the gatehouse as reinforcements made their way up the sinuous trail behind. When the bulk of the First Legion had made it through the gate, they would advance, leaving the Second and Tharkadan Legions to follow along.

The sun would linger long behind the eastern ridge in that deep cut of the mountains, but the sky had brightened to a pale orange horizon and finally to a faint shade of blue as the assault force marched steadily up the trail. Brandon and Gretchan reached the place where they had stopped on the previous day's scouting mission, but that morning they continued on without hesitation. The climb was steep, and it should have been arduous, but Brandon felt his energy, his anticipation, and his determination only increasing as they continued upward. Every once in a while, he heard Gretchan murmur a soft prayer, and he knew that she was calling upon their immortal god, Reorx of the Forge, for strength. He hoped fervently that the Master of All Dwarves was listening.

He cast a glance upward, knowing that Tankard's scouts were stationed on the heights to either side. That was a reassuring thought as they passed beneath overhanging shoulders of cracked rock or under cornices of ice and snow that looked ready to break free, to fall and sweep the dwarves off the mountainside like a person might swat at a bunch of ants.

Finally the shadowy terminus of the trail loomed before them, much wider and taller than it had looked from below. Even so, it seemed like a very narrow and constricted passage, when Brandon considered that for centuries it had been the main point of access and

THE FATE OF THORBARDIN

egress to the great underground realm. The path ended in a solid plug of stone, the gate that merged seamlessly with the wall of the cliff on all sides of it.

Only the perfectly smooth face of that huge plug suggested that it was something other than a piece of the natural mountainside. It was impossible to discern any more details of the entryway until Gretchan held up her staff and cast the bright light of Reorx across the gate. That revealed the outline of the entryway. The ceiling arched some twelve feet above the ground and the sides of the portal were a similar distance apart. Brandon felt strangely relieved by the vast size of it, as it meant that Bardic would have all the room he needed to swing the hammer with all of his might.

"Looks like we might as well get on with it," the smith said calmly.

Brandon took one last glance behind him, holding up his hand to halt the initial vanguard of the column several dozen paces behind him. Gretchan remained at his shoulder, though they both backed up enough to avoid the backswing of the mighty artifact, which Bardic intended to drive upward and over his head in a straightforward blow.

The cleric started to chant, invoking the name of Reorx, speaking words in an ancient tongue. Brandon did not recognize the words, but they seemed to infuse him with strength, causing the blood to pulse through his veins, the energy of his body to hum and crackle in his ears. The head of Gretchan's staff glowed, so bright he couldn't look at it.

Bardic Stonehammer stood still, with the artifact resting on his shoulders. His face was peaceful, eyes half closed, and he seemed to be listening very carefully to the priestess's prayer. Brandon took a half step forward, unable to restrain his eagerness, until the smith breathed a long sigh and shook his head.

"Don't try to help me," he warned. "I will do this alone."

So instead, Brandon stepped back alongside the priestess and waited. The face of the gate was outlined brilliantly in the glow from the cleric's anvil, and in that light he discerned a faint line, a crack no wider than a blond hair, running vertically through the surface of Thorbardin's gate.

Bardic apparently saw that possible crack too. Taking the Tricolor Hammer in both hands, he drew a deep breath, raised it high, and let the artifact drop slightly to swing it low behind his shoulders. His muscles tensed until, with a smooth exhalation, he whipped the hammer upward, impossibly high, and drove it with all his strength into the granite surface of the gate. The three stones of the hammerhead met the gate exactly above that hairline crack.

Then a storm broke around them all.

Twelve

A Wizard Unchained

Kondike paced around the upper wall of Pax Tharkas. Frequently he stopped at one of the crenellations in the battlement, rose to rest his forepaws on the stone, and stared anxiously along the winding southward road. She, his mistress, his beloved Gretchan, had gone that way, accompanied by a countless swarm of other dwarves, all girded for war. And she had bade him, Kondike, to stay there and wait for her.

He wasn't used to that kind of treatment, and he didn't like it, not one bit. Restlessly he backed down from his upright perch and paced some more, back and forth across the platform. He whined and sniffed the air, but there was neither promising scent on the breeze nor any sound that might indicate his owner's imminent return.

He looked toward the door, the way that led into the tower, that allowed passage down the stairs and eventually out the front gate. That door was still closed, so the dog resumed his pacing, broken only by the frequent looks toward the Kharolis Mountains. He ignored the two sentries who paced back and forth, just as they ignored him. Every once in a while, another anxious whimper escaped him, and he would return to the parapet, rise onto his hind legs, and once again stare southward. Seeing nothing, he'd then go back to pacing, occasionally glancing toward the door.

Finally that door opened, and the dog's ears perked up at the sight of the young dwarf emerging into view with a dish and a bucket. Kondike raced over, tail wagging, and immediately set to work chewing and swallowing the scraps of bread, gravy, and fatty meat that filled the bowl to the top.

Of course, he still missed Gretchan, but food was food. And the food was right there.

While Kondike ate and drank deeply from the bucket of fresh water, the young dwarf scratched the big dog's head or stroked the strong ridge of backbone extending down along his sturdy frame. The nice, young dwarf had been there every day since Gretchan had left, and Kondike had gone from tolerating him to welcoming him, especially since, at least once a day, the lad brought him food.

"I wish I could go too," the young dwarf said in a low voice, speaking more to himself than to the dog. "My father's going to war to get his kingdom back. Gretchan and all those other dwarves are going to help him, and I'm stuck here, waiting to find out what happened. I should be out there with them. I'm certainly old enough to wield a sword!"

The dog gave the youth an ambiguous look, swiping a sopping tongue across his smooth face. Then Kondike sat, hopeful and attentive. It would be unusual for the dwarf, or anyone, to give him a second meal immediately

THE FATE OF THORBARDIN

following the first. But in case it happened, the dog would be ready to eat. He raised his eyebrows expectantly.

Instead, the dwarf boy wanted to talk, apparently. Kondike huffed, not impatiently, and settled on his belly, resting his head on his forepaws while he listened, only half interested at first, to the sounds of the lad's voice.

"Want to know a secret?" the young dwarf was saying, his voice tense and quiet. "About Garn Bloodfist? No one else knows, but I let him out, you know? He didn't escape on his own. But I didn't like my mother talking to him all the time; I wanted him to get out of here. So I unlocked his cell door and let him go."

The dog raised his eyebrows, almost quizzically, as the quiet words reached his ears. He, like most dogs, was a good listener, nonjudgmental and very patient. The boy seemed to appreciate that.

"I never thought my mom would actually leave. Going back to Hillhome, they said. Why? Why?"

Finally he stood up and went over to the wall, to the same parapet where Kondike had been staring to the south. The dog trotted over after him, while the young dwarf simply stared into the distance, resting his beardless chin on his fist.

"This is stupid!" he said finally, his tone vehement enough to cause the dog to tilt his head in puzzlement. "I mean, we're just sitting here, doing nothing." He waved at the mountain range rising along the southern horizon. "Everything happening in the world is going on out there!"

Finally he seemed to make a decision, looking down at Kondike as if seeking some kind of agreement or validation.

171

"Come on!" he said finally, starting—at last!—for the door to the stairs, to the hall, and to freedom. "Let's go to Thorbardin," he added quietly.

Kondike wasn't sure about Thorbardin, but for the dog, it was enough just to "go."

―――DH―――

General Blade Darkstone walked once again through the ranks of his garrison troops, the veteran dwarves he had handpicked to stand at the north gate of the kingdom. His master and king, Willim the Black, had ordered him to be ready to defend the gate against attack, so Darkstone had made ready. He had been ready for days.

Scant hours earlier, the wizard had informed him that an enemy army was indeed approaching Thorbardin and that he and his men should get themselves ready to face a fierce attack. Darkstone had studied the fortifications of the great gate, seeking any potential weakness, and came away satisfied there was none. He made sure that his men were alert and sober, ready to fight if they were attacked. And he kept his own eyes open.

Still, Darkstone couldn't imagine how any army could hope to drill its way through the massive gate, not without a thunderous amount of noise and at least a week's worth of intensive labor, during which time he and his defenders would easily slaughter them. But his was not to question his ruler—that he knew from long experience—so instead he obeyed and prepared and kept his eyes open. He had even gone so far as to bring another three hundred dwarves up there, all of them trusty Theiwar, so he had five hundred veteran warriors crammed into a barracks designed to hold half that number.

"But, General," protested his captain, Dack Whiteye. "What good will all these men do here? Even if the gate is opened, the enemy can only enter two by two. Don't we run the risk of the whole garrison, all four companies, getting trapped in these close quarters if they spring some sort of surprise on us? Or what if we get attacked from inside Thorbardin? You have your best men here, where they'll be of no use in defending the city!"

"Stop with the questions! Those are my orders, and so are they yours! Or perhaps you'd like to take up your objections with the black wizard himself?"

That retort served the desired purpose: Whiteye's already pale face grew white as a sheet of snow, and he shook his head firmly. "No, my general. Of course I will obey the order."

"Good. I thought as much."

Darkstone left his captain and went into the machine room of the gate itself. The great screw of stone was mostly invisible, buried as it was in the snug, threaded socket of bedrock. A series of metal gears, connected with pulleys and levers to a large water wheel drive system, filled the chamber below him. Those gears had not turned so much as a quarter inch in more than a decade, but the general was pleased to see that they were all free of rust, well oiled, and apparently ready for immediate use—should such a use be ordained by a power greater even than Darkstone's.

The gate truly *was* impregnable, he believed. Even if someone found a way to move the massive weight of stone that was the gate, the threaded socket held it firmly in place. It could be unscrewed if the machinery within the mountain were employed. Of course, the mechanism was of no use to anyone on the outside. And he didn't see how the gate itself could possibly be smashed.

So General Darkstone stood listening, looking, and thinking. He remained certain that he had done all he could do to be ready and kept his eyes open.

Then the world exploded around him, and all his confidence, all his calm assertions vanished in the instant of destruction. The solid stone floor beneath his feet split asunder, opening a gap that, to his panicked brain, appeared to be bottomless.

Somehow *daylight* was pouring into the gatehouse.

Then he was falling, and darkness surrounded him again.

---DH---

When Willim snapped his fingers, a flickering light came into being in the air over his head. It burned as bright as the wick of a candle, only there was no fuel, no wick, not even any visible flame. The brilliant fire shed its light far and fiercely, driving back the shadows in the cavernous laboratory, illuminating even the distant corners and the lofty ceiling.

It was not for himself that the wizard conjured the light—his spell of true-seeing guaranteed that he didn't require any such mundane accessory as illumination to see—but he wanted Facet to observe what he was doing. And there was another, two others in point of fact, whose attention he also desired. He smiled privately, speculating about Facet's reaction when she learned of the other pair of living creatures secreted in that deep cavern.

Languidly, he rose from his pallet, aware of Facet's wide eyes watching him as he reached for his robe, slipping the dark silk over his scrawny, scarred frame. As always when his nakedness was displayed, he scrutinized her face, watching for any hint of revulsion or disgust. If she had displayed such a reaction, he would have killed her. But as always she looked at him with an affection verging on adoration.

"Get up. Get dressed," he ordered curtly, turning his back and walking toward his marble worktable. He heard the rustling of her movements and, even with his back to her, admired the lush curves of her flesh until her own black robe once again slid around her body.

By then, Willim had arrived at the bell jar containing the two blue sparks. Both of those glimmering flickers had paled at his approach. They retreated, cowered actually, to the far side of the jar. He reached out a hand, caressed the glass, and the blue little lights swirled around in obvious agitation as Facet came up to stand behind him.

"I have never told you about these little sparks, have I?" Willim asked casually.

"No, Master," Facet replied, her eyes downcast. They both remembered the time she had asked about them. Right after his victory over King Stonespringer, Willim had returned to his laboratory and set up the jar in the middle of his worktable. Facet had been curious then, but her innocent question had resulted in a whipping that had left her bloody and sobbing on the rack. Naturally, she had never brought the topic up again.

"They are more than tiny blue fireflies, you know," the wizard said, relishing every word of the revelation to come. His dry lips crackled into a grotesque grin as he stroked the jar with both hands, pressing on the glass as though he could squeeze it into diamond with the force of his touch. The two blue flickers, Facet saw, had shrunk to the base of the jar and quivered, barely visible, in the center of the flat plate.

"I . . . I had wondered," she replied, realizing that he was waiting for an answer. "But I would never presume to guess. Indeed, they do seem like living things."

"You are wise, my pretty one," the Theiwar mage declared with an affection—and menace—that sent a shiver down Facet's spine. "But now the time has come for me to disclose their true nature."

"Please, Master. Tell me what you will."

The wizard pointed his finger at one of the blue sparks and flicked his hand to the side. The first of the blue lights flew in reaction to his gesture, like a bug that had been swatted away. That spark struck the side of the bell jar and sank, barely flickering, back to the bottom.

Then, in a gesture that was almost too fast to see, Willim lifted up the jar and snatched out the second, still vibrant spark, with a snakelike strike of his hand. Just as quickly, the jar was replaced on its resting spot, and the wizard held out his free hand with the fist clenched and his scarred face creased by a triumphant sneer.

He spoke a word of wrenching magic so powerful that Facet's black hair stood on end and she involuntarily recoiled, flinching away. When she looked back, there was a very old woman, a stooped and withered dwarf maid, standing in front of the black wizard. She wore a tattered shawl, and her skin was creased with

THE FATE OF THORBARDIN

wrinkles; her frail shoulders were quivering underneath the rude garment. With a gasp, she wrapped her skinny arms around herself and dropped to the floor at Willim the Black's feet.

"Oh, Master!" she cried in a voice as ancient and brittle as her skin. "Please forgive me! I shall never betray you again!"

"I know that, you pathetic crone," Willim declared coldly. "For if you do, it will be the last act of your worthless life."

Facet watched, fascinated. It had taken her only a moment to realize that she hated, really *hated,* the old crone. She didn't understand the feeling or where it had come from, but the emotion was so real that she could physically taste it, like a bitter bile that rose in her gorge.

But she could only stare, eyes wide, lips parted, as the wizard stalked in a circle around the cowering, frail figure. When he was on the far side of her, he raised his face, a cruel smile twisting his scarred features.

"Facet, this is Sadie Guilder. At one time she worked for me, was one of my agents in the city of Norbardin. But she and her husband betrayed me. So I punished them."

The younger female turned to look at the lone blue spark in the bell jar. It had recovered from Willim's blow and was drifting aimlessly, weakly, in small circles within the magical prison. Facet didn't need to study or reflect very long before she understood that the remaining spark was the treacherous husband Willim referred to.

Sadie, too, was looking at the jar, her eyes wide with horror. "Peat!" she croaked, extending one clawlike hand for an instant before again cowering downward.

"Peat is alive . . . for now," Willim declared haughtily. "And he will remain that way, with my sufferance—and your cooperation."

"Wh-what do you mean?" asked Sadie. Facet couldn't help but notice that her voice, while not confident, was guarded and cautiously optimistic, no longer terrified.

"I released you because I need you. I need the assistance of true wizards. There are tasks that are beyond the ability of an apprentice, even one with as many talents as Facet here."

It was all the young dwarf maid could do to keep from moaning out loud. Her master's words cut her like a knife, deeply, almost fatally. Facet felt her knees grow weak, and she wanted to throw herself on the floor, to plead the case of her own worthiness, to convince the wizard that he needed no one besides herself at his side.

But that reaction would be tantamount to suicide, she understood. So she held her tongue and watched in dismay as Willim extended a hand to Sadie. When the crone took it, he pulled her, roughly but not viciously, to her feet.

"Come," he said, indicating the other end of his worktable. She shuffled after him as he guided her. "I must discuss a problem with you."

Facet stared after them, forgotten, forlorn . . . and increasingly furious.

——DH——

"Go! Go! *Go!*"

Brandon heard someone shouting the command, like a drumbeat of sound that somehow rose over the cacophony before him. It was several seconds before he realized that he was the one barking out the word, over and over.

He shook his head and realized that he was sitting on the ground, on a spur of rock with the wall of the cliff as a backrest behind him. Something was in his hands, and when he looked down he saw that it was the haft of the Bluestone Axe. He clutched the weapon as if it were a lifeline, feeling the cool comfort of its eternal strength.

Slowly his vision cleared further. He saw, nearby, a length of steel pipe, a shaft that seemed vaguely familiar. It was broken and bent, but had obviously been carefully crafted.

It was the haft of the Tricolor Hammer! But when he looked at the end of the pole, where the stone head of the weapon had been, he saw only a splintered terminus where the handle, considerably shorter than it had been a few seconds earlier, ended in a broken, jagged cut.

"It's gone!" he cried despairingly, lifting the handle and groping for the end as if his hands might find what his eyes could not see. "And Bardic—where is he?"

"He's gone too," came another sad voice. It was Gretchan, he realized, as she placed a comforting hand on his shoulder. He blinked and saw that she was smiling at him, though her eyes swam with tears. "He was consumed by the smash of the hammer," she explained softly. "He gave his life to achieve our goal and smash the gate."

"The hammer . . . it broke the gate?" Brandon asked, still dazed and wondering.

His memories, his thoughts and vision, all seemed to return to him haltingly. He shook his head in frustration and tried to stand, but could not shake off Gretchan's firm grip when she held him on the ground.

"Rest just for a minute. As for the Tricolor Hammer, it is as you say: It did its job. Look!"

Gretchan's voice soothed him. She stayed right there, kneeling beside him, holding one hand against his face while the other held her staff upright. The icon of Reorx still glowed like a miniature sun, casting its light against the mountainside. Kayolin dwarves of the First Legion were racing past, two by two, moving quickly away. Only then did he look at where the gate had been.

Turning his head slowly—his neck was surprisingly stiff, as was his whole body—he saw that the smooth gate at the terminus of the mountain trail was simply gone. In its place was a wide gap, like a crack that sheared right down the face of the cliff. Leaning back, he saw that it was a very tall crack, extending as far up the precipice as he could see. Below the gate, the crack continued downward, a yawning crevasse.

The troops of Tankard's legion were charging into that wide gap, advancing quickly straight into the side of the mountain. The small shelf before the gate was missing, shattered and expanded by some unimaginable force. The great crevasse dropped below, plunging hundreds of feet down through the face of the great mountain.

But there was a ledge beside that crevasse, and that's where his dwarves were massing and advancing, charging with battle cries and unhesitating courage into the great, black vastness of Thorbardin's gatehouse.

——DH——

THE FATE OF THORBARDIN

Gorathian had no need of rest, but occasionally the Chaos creature took time for stillness, a meditation and marshaling of its great strength. It had settled for a period in the deepest chasms below Thorbardin, where the soothing heat of bubbling lava warmed its skin, and the tingling explosion of Abyssal flames teased its nostrils.

Perhaps, as it absorbed the joys of the subterranean furnace, the monster was considering a course of action, even formulating the beginnings of a plan . . .

But that was unlikely. Ever a beast of impulse and whim, it had little use for plans or schemes. Its objectives were simple.

And right then its objective was clear: destroy the black wizard. The monster craved that wizard's magic, like a drunkard craves a drink, and soon it would slake its thirst on the Theiwar wizard's blood.

At the same time, a glimmer of caution still sparked in the back of its chaotic, impulsive brain. It would crave, and consume, the magic.

But it must avoid the power of the god.

Thirteen

War Within Walls

Crystal rubbed the rough cord against the squared edge of a rock until her wrists bled. She moved with agonizing slowness, watching through narrowed lids as Garn Bloodfist's head slumped forward onto his chest. His mouth dropped open, and almost immediately he began to snore loudly.

Was he finally asleep? He must be; she guessed that he was too stupid and transparent to try to fake his own drowsiness.

Then she saw the contradiction in her own reasoning. In fact, the Klar had been wily enough to capture her, to seize her before she'd even had the wits to try to run away, and to tie her hands together while she had still been trying to talk to him, to discern what he wanted, what he hoped to accomplish.

How could *I* have been so stupid? That, in all honesty, seemed like a more relevant query. She closed her eyes and tried to remain calm, but the reality of the nightmare was settling around her with all-encompassing gloom. What would he do to her? What did he want with her?

For the moment, it seemed important to avoid antagonizing him. The fact that he was sleeping might be something she could turn to her own advantage. So she sawed away at the rough cords, ignoring the chafing of her skin, the cramps that seemed to shift from muscle to muscle with every move she made. The rope was tough, but the edge of the rock was at least minimally sharp, and if she could keep at it long enough—and Garn stayed sleeping long enough—then she might be able to free herself.

And what would she do then? She tried to occupy her mind with thoughts of vengeance, but even then she couldn't see herself crushing his skull with a rock or driving a dagger through his ribs while he slept. If she fled, she'd certainly make noise, and she very much doubted her ability to get away from him if it came to a chase through the woods.

She shuddered in terror and fatigue, although she allowed herself a bare glimmer of relief. Garn, for all his power, had been content thus far merely to talk to her—at least on that, the first night of her captivity. But she had to face it: her future did not bode well.

She thought back to the incident, several hours earlier, when he had accosted her in the woods. Why hadn't she fled when she first had the feeling that someone was watching her? By the time the urge to flee had possessed her, he had already bound her wrists. Immediately thereafter he had pulled her off the road, roughly dragging her into the woods.

They had climbed a steep slope and descended another, where she had bruised her legs and buttocks sliding painfully down on rough rock. He had pulled her through a thicket with long thorns that tore at her face and hands and waded through an icy creek. Following that splashing waterway, they had pushed up through a narrow gorge, between stone walls that sometimes ran so close together that they had to wade right up through the middle of the stream, until they had arrived at the remote grotto where they stopped.

High, rocky bluffs rose to all sides, except for the twisting ravine up which they had ascended. The surrounding woods were thick, and she had seen no sign of any other inhabitants or even the work sites of a woodcutter or miner. It seemed they were really, truly alone, so much so that she felt certain that, even if she screamed, the sound of her voice would have been blocked by the stones and trees. And certainly it would awaken Garn.

When they had arrived there, the mad Klar had pushed her roughly to the ground then secured her already bound wrists to a tree trunk with a further length of the rough cord. Only when she was tightly bound had he set about making a fire.

"Garn?" she had pressed, trying to keep her voice soothing and gentle. "Why are you doing this? I thought we were friends."

"Friends?" he said, his eyes lighting up, the whites shining brightly in the growing light of the newly kindled flames. "Yes, friends," he agreed, nodding as if savoring the taste of the word.

"But then you don't have to tie me up so tightly, do you? Can't we talk about it?" She felt her voice growing shrill as her fear swelled, so she took a deep breath and tried to force herself to remain calm.

Garn, for the time being, seemed content to ignore her as he piled more and more dry branches onto the fire. He apparently didn't have any food to cook, and, to judge by his appearance, it might have been many days since he'd had a meal. But he stoked the blaze into a roaring bonfire and settled down before it.

Abruptly those wide, staring eyes fastened upon Crystal again. "Do you have food?" he asked as if the very possibility of the question was a sudden revelation.

"Why, yes. I have a little. Some bread and cheese that I was eating on the trail. Here, if you'll untie me, I'll get it for you. It's right here in my traveling pack."

The Klar pounced on the pack as if he expected it to make a break for freedom at any moment. Pulling out her spare cloak, he came upon her sleeping robe and rubbed his filthy fingers through the soft fabric for a very long time. Finally he set it aside, taking surprising care to see that it didn't get dirty from the ground, and fished out the small half loaf of bread and wedge of hard cheese that was all that remained of her traveling supplies.

"This is all?" he asked, glowering at her.

"Well, it was only food for the day," Crystal explained. "I'd planned to stay at another inn tonight and to eat the fare of their kitchen. You know, I'm sure there's an inn not far away! If you take me there, we can both have a hot meal. I'll pay for yours, happily. Imagine a roast duck! Or perhaps a ham or even a beef stew. Wouldn't that be good?"

She kept her voice light and cheerful but was surprised to feel her own stomach rumbling with hunger. Desperately, she watched the Klar, hoping for some sign that her tempting suggestions had penetrated the layer of his madness.

But he shrugged and laughed. "This is fine. I don't need more. Don't need any hill dwarf inn, that's for sure!"

THE FATE OF THORBARDIN

"But, Garn," she continued while she had his attention momentarily, "why are you doing this? Why did you follow me? Why are you holding me captive?"

"Oh, you know," he said with a sly grin. "You remember."

"Remember? Remember what? Please! I don't understand!"

"Ah, what a coy game you play!" he said with a sound like a giggle. "All those nights in the dungeon, when you were talking to me ... I could hear the sounds in your voice. You knew that I desired you. And I knew that you desired me. Now we can be together."

She almost gagged at the memory but bit back a rebuke. She had only meant to be kind, visiting him in prison. But as he continued to talk almost nonstop, Crystal was appalled to learn how much time he had spent thinking about her, desiring her, imagining things about her.

"I know, when you sleep, that you dream of me," he confided. "But know that I dream of you as well!"

She didn't try to dissuade him from his wilder fantasies—such as his belief that she desired him as much as he desired her—for she feared his rage if she made him angry. Still, she tried to reason with him.

"You know, you really don't have to tie me up," she repeated as sweetly as she could muster.

At that, his eyes narrowed, and he uttered a short cackle of laughter. But he made no move to remove her cords, and he frightened her too much for her to try and make an argument out of it. So she watched him and watched him, and finally he fell asleep. Only then did she begin to work on her tight bonds in earnest.

And finally, she was rewarded by a loosening; she felt the strands of the rope parting.

She pulled her hands apart and looked up to see her worst nightmare: Garn Bloodfist was awake and watching her. She tried to stand, but he sprang right over the mound of coals. His rough hands grasped her shoulders, pressing her back to the ground.

And his grotesque mouth, wide open and panting, pressed over her own.

"I knew you'd try to leave!" he crowed, his vile breath making her gag. "Don't you dare! We're just getting started!"

---DH---

Brandon caught up to the Redshirts at the interior fortification of the gatehouse. General Watchler's men had secured a foothold in what looked to be a barracks room. Tankard's first companies still fought at the two tunnels leading out of the gatehouse, while more and more of the Kayolin troops filed up the trail and into the breached entry to Thorbardin.

"The bastards have forted up in both guardhouses," Watchler reported. "We can't get to them without passing through a hail of crossbows. Hacksaw and I have already lost a score of men each."

"Is there any other way around?" Brandon asked, dismayed at the thought that they might have broken through Thorbardin's main gate only to be blocked a few hundred yards farther on.

"We're checking it out, but I don't think so. This place was made for defense, after all. Anyone coming in the main gate is channeled through one of these two halls, and they're both pretty much the same. There's a long, open passageway before you get to the interior doors, and the defenders have firing platforms above the floor and inside the city where they can shoot from cover and pick off our warriors almost at will."

"All right," Brandon said with a grimace. "I'll go have a look. Stay here and keep the men formed up as they come through the outer gate. If we can carry one of these doors, I want to be able to pour a thousand troops into the city in the first wave."

"All right. Good luck," the veteran campaigner said.

"You stay with Watchler," Brandon said to Gretchan, who hadn't left his side since they had breached the outer gate. "Get the troops ready for the main attack."

"You didn't think you'd get rid of me that easily, did you?" she asked with just the hint of a twinkle in her eye.

He knew better than to waste time arguing, so he muttered a curse and started forward, carrying his axe, jogging fast enough to stay a step or two in front of the cleric. He crossed through a wide room that looked like a barracks mess hall, though the tables and benches had been overturned by combat. Some dwarves of Tankard's legion were dragging the bodies of slain defenders into a large pile off to the side, while other dead fighters, wearing the blue and black of Kayolin, were laid out in neat rows. A quick glance suggested that more than two dozen of his troops had been slain in that chamber alone.

The knowledge made him sick to his stomach and more determined than ever to break through the next obstacle. Crossing to the far side of the mess hall, he found Tankard himself and a hundred of his dwarves warily looking through a wide double doorway into a long, open hallway. More Kayolin dwarves had been killed there, and their bodies—most pierced by lethal crossbow quarrels—still lay where they had fallen.

"Hullo, General," Tankard said grimly as Brandon knelt beside him to study the constricted approach. He could see the balconies near the far end, well above the floor of the hall, where the enemy archers obviously lurked.

"You can see it's a tough nut," Hacksaw continued. "They have probably fifty crossbowmen up there, back in the shadows. Even if we bring our shooters up for cover, we can only squeeze ten or a dozen around this doorway. Meanwhile, they have shots at every dwarf that tries to charge down that hall."

Brandon could see that the doors at the far end of the hall were tall, double doors of solid stone. "I assume they're barricaded?" he asked.

Tankard nodded grimly. "Pretty damned solid too. We hit them with two score men and we just bounced off, like we were slamming into a cliff wall."

"What about a ram?"

"That's the next attempt. I sent a platoon back to find something big and heavy that we could use. Ah, here they come now."

The general turned to see two dozen dwarves approaching across the debris-strewn mess hall. They had a portion of a sturdy stone column hoisted onto their shoulders and held the makeshift ram ready as they reached the officers at the entryway of the hall.

"Perfect," Tankard Hacksaw said. "Why don't you stay here and watch us work?" he suggested to Brandon.

"Forget it. I'm coming with you on the charge!" the Kayolin commander protested.

THE FATE OF THORBARDIN

"That's not your job!" Gretchan barked before Tankard could voice his own objections. But as Brandon rounded on the priestess, his subordinate chimed in.

"She's a smart one, General," Hacksaw said. "Your axe will do a lot of good once we get through that door. But until then, you'd just be making yourself a target, and a high-value one for the enemy at that."

Though it went against every instinct he possessed, Brandon was forced to agree that the captain was right and he should be cautious. "All right," he agreed through clenched teeth. "But I'm coming up with the rest of your legion the moment you bust through that door."

"And a welcome sight you'll be," Tankard agreed cheerfully. He raised his voice to address his men. "Now I need all the bowmen right here," he commanded, gesturing to the door. "We're charging down there with that ram, and I want you to do everything you can to pick off those bastard Theiwar who try to shoot at us from the balconies!"

There was no shortage of willing crossbowmen, but Brandon saw the truth of Tank's earlier complaint: at the most, twelve of the Kayolin archers would be able to crowd into the doorway to provide covering fire while many more defenders would be able to concentrate their missiles against the ram-wielding attackers.

"Tankard," Brandon said, placing a hand on his old friend's shoulder before he realized that he didn't really have anything to say, just wanted to delay the departure of the dangerous attack for another few seconds. "Be careful—and good luck," he declared.

"I'm always careful—and lucky!" the captain replied with a breezy grin. He turned to the platoon that had brought up the ram. "All right, you slugs! Carry that thing like you mean it! Now let's go!"

Gretchan held Brandon's arm almost as if she expected him to charge forward with the ram. Instead, he clasped his own hand over hers and watched as the brave Kayolin dwarves, with the stone column supported at shoulder height, sprinted into the hallway. As soon as they had charged through the door, the archers moved into position, immediately firing at the enemy crossbowmen who swarmed forward onto the balconies. A few of the Kayolin missiles found targets, but the defenders fired an initial volley that felled six or seven of the ram-bearing dwarves at once.

Others raced forward into the hall, helping to support the heavy column as Tankard urged his men onward. They closed against the double doors quickly, and the makeshift ram smashed into the barrier with a resounding boom. The attackers stumbled back, but Brandon was encouraged to see the doors shaking from the force of the impact.

"Again!" shouted Tankard Hacksaw, and his men reared back to drive the column once more into the doors. "And again!"

But the arrow fire from above was lethal. One bolt caught Tankard in the shoulder, and he stumbled and fell. More of his men were killed, and many of those who ran to assist were shot down even before they could reach the heavy ram. Under the steady hail of missiles, the Kayolin dwarves buckled and wavered, finally dropping the stone column to the floor.

Brandon broke free of Gretchan's restraining hand. He raced into the hall, feeling an arrow knock into his breastplate and ricochet away. Tankard was kneeling, trying to pull the missile out of his shoulder. Brandon grabbed his old friend by his other arm, pulled him to his feet, then stumbled and careered back to the door. Together they fell into the mess hall, where other willing dwarves pulled them out of the enemy's line of sight.

"The rest of the men!" Tankard gasped, his face covered in a sheen of sweat. "Get them out of there! Order the retreat!"

By the time Brandon rose to his feet, there was no need to issue any orders. The only Kayolin dwarves left in the corridor were the dead.

———DH———

"Smell that! Smell fire!" Slooshy chirped excitedly.

"Maybe food with fire?" Gus said, feeling the first glimmer of hope he'd felt since they had picked over the small berry bush several—two?—days earlier.

Since that time, the three Aghar had wandered through the wilds of the Kharolis foothills. They'd come upon a few farms and villages and inns of the hill dwarves but had been driven off in each case before they could even begin to try to steal some food.

In one case, a hill dwarf innkeeper had loosed several ferocious hounds on the gully dwarves, and Gus had lost the seat of his trousers to a savage bite as he'd tried to scramble up a very thorny tree. The fact that Berta and Slooshy had been laughing at him from the higher branches had only served to further fuel his anger and disappointment.

But Slooshy was right: there was a distinct odor of wood smoke on the breeze. "Come this way—find food!" Gus urged, diving into a thorny thicket and pushing through to the other side. His companions came noisily behind, but he didn't bother waiting.

Stumbling forward eagerly, Gus tumbled into a stream and came up, gagging and choking, to find that he was standing in waist-deep, very cold water. It flowed with a noisy current, and it seemed to him that the smell of the smoke was coming from upstream, so the Aghar charged right through the icy liquid, climbing over slippery rocks, advancing up a channel that seemed to be bounded by two close-set stone walls.

He was vaguely aware of the two chattering girls coming behind him, but his growling stomach would brook no delay. Instead, he scrambled and crawled and climbed upward to move himself through the water and over the rocks. Finally he saw a glint of light through the woods and knew he had found the source of the blaze!

Leaping out of the stream, he pressed through another bramble on the bank and saw a small clearing where a large fire crackled cheerfully and warmly.

Then he froze, noticing something else. Two big dwarves were in that clearing. One was a male, a Klar to judge from his unkempt hair and wildly staring eyes. The other, a female, was fighting him. She lay on the ground, her face and most of her body concealed by that violent-looking Klar.

Then she screamed, and the urgent fear in her voice set Gus's heart to pounding. He blinked and rubbed his eyes and saw strands of light-colored hair flying around, illuminated by the fire. His mind focused, and he could think of only one thing.

"Gretchan!" he shouted, charging forward without another thought. The two combatants were so fiercely engaged that neither seemed to notice him at first, but the Aghar advanced resolutely. "Leave Gretchan alone!" he shouted at the Klar.

The only answer was an inarticulate growl as the male reared back and fastened his powerful hands around the female's throat. Her next scream was choked into a gagging cough by the Klar's suffocating grip.

"You let go!" Gus cried again. He reached down, picking up a large, jagged-edged rock that was right under his feet. With an impetuous spring, he leaped forward, lifting the rock over his head in both of his hands. With stunningly accurate force, he brought it crashing down on the Klar's skull.

The attacker groaned and immediately collapsed on the female, who grunted and struggled to push the inert form away.

"Gretchan! Gus save you!" cried the gully dwarf, grabbing the insensate Klar by one hand and pulling him off to the side. The victim, still coughing and choking, pushed herself into a sitting position and struggled to regain her breath.

"Hey! You not Gretchan!" Gus declared indignantly.

"No, I'm not," she said when she finally found her voice. She wiped a hand across her face and looked at Gus with considerable relief. "But I'm very grateful to you for saving my life."

"Oh, well, all right," Gus replied, warmed by the praise—even if the dwarf maid was an impostor.

Abruptly his arms were seized by firm, small hands, one pair pulling to each side of him.

"Hey, you big dwarf sister!" declared Berta in a voice full of menace. "You stay away!"

"Yeah!" added Slooshy, tugging hard at Gus's other side. "This *my* guy!"

"Um, don't worry," said the dwarf maid whom Gus had mistaken for Gretchan. "I won't take him away. But thanks for letting him come to my rescue."

Gus, meanwhile, was thinking about other things while the three females conversed warily. "Hey," he said after a minute, addressing the dwarf he had rescued. "You got any food?"

———DH———

The courier found Brandon in the ruined mess hall, sitting with Tankard and Gretchan as the priestess worked her healing magic on the captain's deep but not lethal wound. He sprinted up and clapped his fist to his chest in salute.

"General Bluestone! Captain Morewood said to tell you that we've got the Firespitter up to the gate!"

"Bring it forward at once!" Brandon replied, seizing on the news as if it were a lifeline on a stormy sea.

And indeed, he felt direly in need of a lifeline. He'd heard from the Redshirts that General Watchler's men had fared no better against the interior hallways than had Hacksaw's. The toll was more than a hundred dead, and though both forces had tried to use battering rams against the stone doors, the men had not been able to protect themselves from the deadly crossbows long enough to use them.

But perhaps their luck was about to change.

It took another hour for the laboring crews to maneuver the first of the massive devices through the shattered gate and into the Theiwar barracks. Tankard's men worked to clear the benches and other debris out of the way, while the crewmen used levers and pulleys to winch the giant weapon along the ledge and right into the interior of the bloodstained gatehouse.

In the meantime, several lookouts kept an eye on the corridors down which the attackers would have to advance. The balconies overhead were darkened by shadows, but they knew that Theiwar defenders lurked there and that the deadly crossbows could be brought forward again within mere seconds.

Brandon and his officers anxiously watched the progress of the Firespitter as the crew pushed it into position. The weapon was large and unwieldy but not so big that it couldn't be maneuvered through the tight spaces of a subterranean battlefield. The spout of the machine was a long nozzle, a tube of steel, that extended more than a dozen feet from the round body. A portable furnace was attached to the bottom of the snout, and it was capped with a door that one of the crewmembers could open by pulling on a lever at the rear of the machine. When the furnace door was opened and pressurized oil shot down the spout, the coals incinerated the vaporous oil, and the result was the lethal incendiary attack that had proved so effective against the horax.

The mighty weapon would be turned against dwarves, something they never imagined. Brandon was suddenly acutely aware that much, perhaps too much, depended on the success of the Firespitter.

"Open fire as soon as you're ready," he instructed the crew chief. That scowling, short-bearded sergeant looked more like a mechanic than a soldier, which was probably appropriate.

"Aye aye, sir," the chief replied. "Open up the boiler," he called to one of his men, who turned a valve on a large secondary tank at the rear of the Firespitter. "Bring up the pressure."

The hissing of steam was audible in the close space. Two hundred or more Kayolin dwarves watched hopefully as the war machine rumbled and slowly came to life.

"Push 'er forward a dozen feet, no more," ordered the chief, and six of his crewmen worked levers and ratchets, clicking each wheel in unison. With each click, the Firespitter advanced another foot until the spout with its dangling furnace jutted into the hallway.

Brandon thought, with sudden regret, of all those slain dwarves in there—his dwarves. Their bodies would be burned beyond recognition, he knew. But it would cost even more lives to send in troops to bring out the dead, and that was not a sacrifice he could afford to make.

"Open the hatch," ordered the chief, and yet another crewman pulled the lever that would expose the burning coal to the vaporized oil. The sergeant glanced over at Brandon one last time, and the general nodded.

"Let 'er rip!" came the command.

Many things seemed to happen at once. Two dwarves turned valves that allowed the pressurized oil to spew out of the reservoir while another cranked up the steam pressure. The crew chief sat in his seat atop the machine and sighted down the barrel while the hissing of the pressurized steam grew to a shrieking crescendo.

Then the mist of oil shot down the long spout of the nozzle, passed over the glowing coals, and burst into flame. A billowing cloud of liquid fire spewed into the hallway, roaring like a fierce windstorm, while a wave of heat blasted back into the mess hall where the dwarves of the First Legion were gathered.

THE FATE OF THORBARDIN

From within that long corridor, Brandon thought he heard screams of pain and fear, sounds of chaos and destruction. Perhaps it was his imagination, but the noises echoed on and on in his ears, and he knew they would haunt his dreams for a long time. Gretchan, he realized, had disappeared; she had apparently gone back out to the gatehouse to avoid witnessing the carnage.

The chief held the valve open for only six or eight seconds, though it seemed like an eternity. Finally he gave the order: "Cut!" And the cessation order was instantly obeyed. The fire died away. The steam was allowed to escape with a rush, and the nimble crewmen, working with clocklike coordination, quickly backed the machine out of the doorway.

"Go, you rascals!" shouted Tankard Hacksaw to his men who had already hoisted a replacement ram. "Beat down that door! Take the war right up to them!"

With a hoarse cry, the Kayolin dwarves charged into the hot, smoky corridor, carrying their heavy ram. They smashed it once, twice, and a third time against the soot-stained, smoldering doors at the far end. No archers sniped at them from the upper, scorched balconies. On the final blow, the twin barriers collapsed inward, tumbling to shatter on the floor, revealing a roomful of terrified, and somewhat singed, Theiwar warriors.

When the rest of the First Legion charged through the breach, the defenders never had a chance.

---DH---

Facet brooded in a corner of the laboratory, watching Willim and Sadie huddle over a bowl of clear liquid. They were casting a spell of scrying there, she knew, though the spell itself was beyond her limited but growing powers. Still, a day earlier Willim would have made sure that she was at his side when he worked such important magic, so she could watch and admire and learn.

As he worked with Sadie, Facet was all but forgotten.

Abruptly she became aware that Willim had become agitated about something. Sadie recoiled from the bowl of liquid with the magical picture still shimmering on the surface. In another instant, the wizard blinked out of sight.

Immediately Facet rushed forward. She regarded the older dwarf maid through narrowed eyes. "What happened?" she demanded suspiciously.

Sadie looked at her and uttered a short bark of laughter. "Don't take that tone with me, *apprentice!*" she sneered.

Facet felt a stab of anger, an emotion so strong that her limbs quivered and her hands clenched into fists. Only with great effort did she restrain herself from attacking the elder sorceress, from scratching her eyes out or worse. For her part, Sadie watched the apprentice with an air of contempt, her fingers curled and ready for a duel of spellcasting.

What kind magic was the old crone capable of using? Suddenly, with a sick feeling in the pit of her stomach, Facet decided that she didn't want to find out.

"Who *are* you?" the younger dwarf maid demanded.

"I'm someone who sees what goes on. Someone who fears our master, like you do," Sadie said pointedly. She turned and looked at the locked potion cabinet then swung back to look at Facet with a knowing smile. "I'm someone who *knows*," she concluded.

THE FATE OF THORBARDIN

Facet could not suppress a shiver of fear. How many times had she stolen desirable potions from the cabinet while Willim had been absent? She had used some of them, especially his charm potion, with impunity, often mixing it into his wine. The subtle effect of the potion, she knew, helped keep the wizard's darker impulses under control.

Yet each time she had made one of her sly thefts, that bell jar had been sitting there, with those two blue sparks flitting around inside. It had never occurred to Facet that the minuscule bits of light might have been alive . . . or that they might have been watching her actions.

The older female smiled, a thin, cold expression devoid of humor. But Facet felt as though Sadie had been reading her mind, analyzing everything that the apprentice had been thinking and perhaps feeling.

"Your little secret is safe with me," Sadie confided in a voice that was not at all reassuring. "So long as you know your place and don't interfere with me."

The apprentice stared at the wizard for a long time, feeling as though a chilly fog had wrapped its tendrils around her. The old crone merely smacked her lips and went back to looking at the image in the bowl.

"What do you want?" asked Facet hesitantly, stepping forward. She wondered why the old woman hadn't told Willim about her treachery, and she suspected immediately that it had something to do with Sadie's own ambitions. For the first time she wondered why Willim had trapped her and her mate in the jar prison.

Sadie shrugged, not bothering to look at the younger dwarf. "I want what we all want. Power. Prosperity. Freedom. And perhaps revenge," she said finally.

Facet smiled inwardly. She could relate to all of those desires, and that gave her, for the first time, a sense of possible kinship with the older woman. Again she advanced until she, too, was standing beside the scrying bowl. "What's happening?" she asked again in a beseeching tone, peering into the bowl.

"The North Gate of Thorbardin has been breached by our master's enemies," Sadie explained, gesturing.

Yes, Facet could clearly discern an image of violent battle portrayed in the pool. Dwarves were hacking at each other with swords, stabbing with spears, charging and falling back in chaotic patterns. Flames swirled around the armies at one point, bright and vivid and so searingly real that she put a hand up in front of her face to block the illusionary heat. Eerily, she heard no sounds, but the sense of combat was so fierce and real that she was surprised that the surface of the water wasn't vibrating from the tumultuous action.

"What is the master doing?" she asked curiously.

"For now, it seems he goes to observe. He won't use his spells, won't attract attention to himself right now—not so long as the fire dragon still roams free."

"He fears that beast!" Facet burst out. "He thinks it wants to find him and kill him."

"And he's right," Sadie said, nodding. "That's why he freed me. He thinks that I might be able to help him win that fight."

"Can you?" Facet asked.

Sadie shook her head grimly. "No. That one is beyond the reach of wizardly magic."

"Then what can you do? If you fail, won't he lock you up again?"

Sadie cackled and straightened her frail shape to a surprising height. "I'll never be locked up by him, never again," she spat. "But I have found one who might be able to help him."

"Who?" Facet was intrigued in spite of herself.

The old sorceress gestured to the glimmering pool. Facet saw a dwarf there in the midst of the battle, a blond-haired female with a blue robe and a brightly glowing staff.

"Arcane magic is of no use against a creature of Chaos," Sadie declared. "But that one wields the power of a god. And we're going to seize her and use her power as our own."

FOURTEEN

A PRIESTESS VANISHED

For the first time in more than sixteen hours, Brandon allowed himself to relax his grip on the handle of the Bluestone Axe. He heard Fister Morewood barking orders to his dwarves of the Second Legion, while on a lower level of the city—visible from the balcony where he and Gretchan had finally stopped to catch their breath—Otaxx Shortbeard and Mason Axeblade directed the dispersed companies of the Tharkadan Legion to move into the alleys and byways to either side of the road. The whooping sounds of the Klar company had faded into the distance as the berserkers, barely controlled by the roaring bellows of Wildon Dacker, led the charge into the heart of the city of Norbardin.

Sounds of battle rang out from several skirmishes, but the great din of the fighting seemed to have settled down. Brandon found a stone bench that had been toppled in the fray and pulled it upright. Gretchan sat down on it and leaned back against a marble column, closing her eyes and holding her staff across her lap.

"Mind if I join you?" Brandon asked, nudging the rod to the side so there was room for him to sit on the bench beside her.

"Only if you'll show a lonely girl around a strange town, soldier," Gretchan said, smiling through her weariness.

"We've made a pretty good start, for tourists," Brandon pointed out with a grin.

And indeed, they had. The initial blast of the Firespitter had been enough to shatter the resistance in the gatehouse, and when the First Legion troops had poured through the breached doorway, the wizard's defenders had been too few, too disorganized, and in many places too fearful to put up a coherent defense. As a result, the attackers had claimed more than half of the great city in the first day of the battle. They were able to concentrate their forces wherever Willim's fighters had tried to make a stand and overwhelmed each strong point in turn before moving deeper into the legendary kingdom.

For the Tharkadan Legion, the initial victory had been a return to home. To the Kayolin dwarves, each step forward, each intersection and new building and small square or plaza, was part of the discovery of a new world that nonetheless was familiar in their hearts. None of the northern dwarves had ever seen Thorbardin before, but throughout their lives, all of them had heard of it and held the name and the place in a state of reverence and awe.

From their current resting place, Brandon and Gretchan could survey only a small portion of Norbardin, but the sight was enough to convince them both that it was the greatest underground city in all of Krynn. Even

THE FATE OF THORBARDIN

Garnet Thax, the jewel of Kayolin, looked like a piddling small town by comparison.

Great edifices rose along one wall of the vast, cavernous space. Brandon counted at least ten levels on that cliff face, each one marked by columned balconies and lofty windows, porches, and other vantages.

Between their current position and that grand facade lay a series of narrow streets and multistoried buildings, some rising far above their line of sight but others low enough that they could spot the splendid architecture beyond. The crowded lanes of the district below them no doubt usually teemed with pedestrians and vendors, but most of the citizens of Thorbardin had been content to lock themselves into their homes when the invasion began. Brandon had received encouraging reports indicating that a great portion of the populace was not enamored of either Willim the Black or his predecessor, Jungor Stonespringer. One tyrant was the same as the other, as far as they were concerned. Word of Tarn Bellowgranite's return was slowly spreading among the common people, advancing well ahead of the army.

Brandon and Gretchan looked up to see Tankard Hacksaw heading toward them. The legion commander was caked with dirt and sweat and had a bloody cut running across his forehead. But he also carried a decanter of water, and it was the most beautiful thing either of them had ever seen.

"Help yourselves," he said with a tight smile, handing the tall glass vessel to Gretchan.

The priestess took a deep draught and passed it to Brandon before pushing herself to her feet with an effort. "Here, let me have a look at that cut," she said concernedly.

"Bah!" Tankard waved her away. "It's nothing. There's them who're hurt a lot worse than me. Besides, you already did me more than fine when you plucked that arrow out of my shoulder."

"Well, it looks like you hurt yourself again. Can't you be a little more careful?" Gretchan chided good-naturedly. "Rest assured that I'll do what I can for the rest of your men. But you're a legion commander. We can't have you losing blood like that. Sets a bad example." She smiled lightly. "You'll scare the recruits."

"Ah, all right," Tankard said. His knees nearly buckled as he sank down on the bench, and Brandon saw that he was more seriously injured than he'd been letting on. But the cleric pressed her palm against the bleeding cut and murmured a prayer to Reorx. After several moments she pulled her hand away, and her palm and Tankard's forehead were both cleansed of blood.

"That's a small miracle right there," admitted the captain, wiping his own hand over his face and looking at it in amazement. "Praise be to Reorx!"

"And praise be to you too," Brandon added sincerely. "That was a masterful job of leading your legion through the barracks."

"The hardest part was getting over my astonishment, when Bardic Stonehammer broke the mountain open with that three-colored piece of rock! It was the most astounding thing I've ever seen!"

"I'll grant you that," the Bluestone dwarf replied. "I couldn't quite believe it myself."

"Now you both need to get some rest," clucked Gretchan maternally. "The war will still be going strong when you wake up, I'll warrant."

THE FATE OF THORBARDIN

"Only if you agree to get some sleep as well," Brandon said. His eyes narrowed in concern as he noted the weariness in Gretchan's face, the glaze of exhaustion that had suddenly seemed to settle over her eyes.

At first, she looked ready to argue, but apparently she took stock of his words and realized that his advice was sensible. She nodded and leaned on her staff as they looked around for a likely place to stretch out for a few hours.

For the moment, there were only the three of them on that high balcony, though hundreds of dwarves—all from their own army—were in sight on the streets and plaza below. The barracks hall connecting to the balcony was already home to dozens of sleeping dwarves, weary survivors of the First Legion, but Brandon reasoned that there'd be an office or storeroom nearby where Gretchan, at least, could have some privacy.

"You'll be safe here, far behind the battle lines," Tankard said. "And now that I feel a lot better, I think I'll go check on my men."

"Aye, old friend," Brandon said, clapping him on the shoulder. "And once again, well done."

"You too, General," Tankard said. Brandon turned to Gretchan as Tank took a step toward the door into the barracks. That was when the captain abruptly halted and cried out in alarm.

"Look out!"

The words were barely uttered when Tank flew backward and past Brandon, propelled by some unseen force that blasted him right over the railing and toward the street two dozen feet below.

Brandon was already reaching for his axe when another blast of force knocked him over, battering him like a falling wall. He heard Gretchan scream, and he struggled to turn around and go to her aid, battling a great weight that seemed to press him to the floor.

Gretchan cried out again; then he saw her, bound by some kind of web that had simply materialized in the air. But no! There were dwarves there, two of them. They were dressed in black robes. One was a strikingly attractive female, with blood red lips and flowing black hair. The other was a sturdy Theiwar male who had his back to Brandon. The web seemed to be exploding from the Theiwar's hands, wrapping Gretchan around and around until she might as well have been secured in a cocoon.

"No!" Brandon cried, pushing himself to his knees.

The black-robed Theiwar turned, flashing a wicked smile, and Brandon was shocked by his scarred visage, a hideous face with the eye sockets sewn shut. Even so, as he took in that cruel, gloating expression, he knew that the villainous dwarf could *see* him!

Then, in a flash of magic, the two black-robed wizards disappeared. With a sickening lurch of fear, Brandon saw that Gretchan had vanished too. They had taken the priestess with them.

---DH---

"I don't have any food to speak of," the rescued dwarf maid admitted to the trio of rapt gully dwarves who had fixated on the word *food*. "But I'll take you to some first thing in the morning. Eggs, bacon, milk, cheese . . . I'll treat you to a real feast."

"Sound good," Gus admitted. "All right. We eat morningtime." Suddenly he had another thought and

THE FATE OF THORBARDIN

turned to glare at the female dwarf he had rescued. "Who you, anyway?" he demanded belligerently, planting his hands on his hips. "Where you go?"

"My name is Crystal Heathstone," she said. "And I'm going to a town called Hillhome. I was, at least, on my way there, until this Klar attacked me."

She nudged the lifeless form of Garn Bloodfist with a toe and shuddered. Gus and his girls had checked out the dwarf, determining that the blow to his head had been hard enough to crush the life out of him. Gus had preened and boasted a bit, while Slooshy and Berta had cooed and awed over his bravery—until he had remembered his hunger.

"Hillhome, huh?" he said. "We go Thorbardin instead. Make war on bad wizard!"

"Oh?" Crystal said, frowning. "There was a time when I thought I was going to Thorbardin too. I was going to bring my people there to help wage that war."

"Why you not come with, then?" Gus asked. "After we eats, I mean. We go to help Gretchan," he added.

"Huh! I know Gretchan very well," Crystal said. "Now I know who you are! You must be Gus. You're quite famous, you know. Even Garn Bloodfist"—she gestured to indicate the dead Klar—"knew enough about you to hate you. You're the gully dwarf who broke the big trap before he could drop it on all the hill dwarves."

"Yep. Me do that," Gus agreed proudly, though even to that day he wasn't sure exactly what he had done to make everyone so happy with him. But he was pretty famous, that was for sure, and he was content to bask in all the accolades.

"You go Hillhome?" he said again. "Where hill dwarves be?"

211

"Yes," Crystal agreed with a laugh that reminded Gus of Gretchan. "Lots of hill dwarves be there."

"Well," said Gus, his scrunched-up face indicating that he was doing something rare and perhaps even historic; the little fellow was thinking. "I got idea. Let's go get and take 'em Thorbardin. We find Gretchan and Brandon and everyone there."

"You know," the dwarf maid said with a pensive expression. "You might just have a notion there. Anyway, I agree. Let's go to Hillhome, and I'll tell my friends all about you and maybe they'll decide to follow you and me and all of us to Thorbardin."

"That be fine!" Gus declared expansively. Then he remembered something with a scowl. "But first we eat, right?"

———DH———

"Where did she go?" Brandon cried, spinning on his heel, holding the Bluestone Axe in one hand while he reached out to brace himself against a column with the other. He threw back his head and raged. "Where is she, by Reorx?"

Dwarves of the First Legion raced to the rescue from all directions, some stumbling out of their sleep in the adjacent barracks and strapping on weapons and others, dusty and bloody from the fight, rushing up the steps to the landing. By the time the first of his men arrived on the scene, Brandon had calmed enough to realize that they would find neither Gretchan nor any of her attackers in the immediate area.

"What is it, General?" gasped one of the first to arrive, a swordsman who rushed up to Brandon and

THE FATE OF THORBARDIN

whirled to position himself as a barrier for any fresh attacker.

"Wizards! Dark magic," growled Brandon, lowering his weapon only slightly. "They came and took Gretchan Pax away . . . by sorcery. And," he added in a choked voice, looking over his shoulder as he suddenly remembered with a stab of guilt, "They might have killed my brave Commander Tankard!"

Even as more dwarves arrived on the landing, calling out in alarm, demanding information, Brandon was reaching the only logical conclusion. "It was Willim the Black himself," he groaned, stunned and near despair. "She could be a thousand miles away by now! We must find her!"

He had reached the balcony and was looking down into the street below, where several dwarves knelt around the motionless form of Tankard Hacksaw.

"Does he live?" Brandon asked with a catch in his throat.

The slumped shoulders and slowly shaking heads of the witnesses confirmed his worst fears. An overwhelming sense of despair suddenly weighed him down. The Bluestone Axe fell from his fingers, clanging unnoticed on the floor at his feet. His hands gripped the stone railing as if they could crush it, and if it had been Willim's neck, they would have done so.

But it wasn't. Angrily he pushed himself away from the brink. He turned to see two score or more dwarves surrounding him, with more arriving every second. Those who had heard Brandon's news murmured angrily, informing the newcomers. To a man, the soldiers of the First Legion looked murderous, grim, and determined.

"What are your orders, General?" asked one, a graybeard who wore the epaulets of sergeant on his shoulder.

"Resume the attack," Brandon declared. "We're going to clean out every corner of this rat-infested den. And when we find the black wizard, I'm going to kill him with my bare hands!"

The dwarves moved out immediately, rousting their comrades who still slept and gathering up those who had paused to eat or drink. They vowed to follow Brandon's orders; they would kill and search and sooner or later they would find the wizard's lair.

But would Gretchan still be alive by the time they did?

———DH———

Gretchan Pax, her face encased in gummy strands of web, could barely breathe. She tried to move her arms, but they were pinned to her sides by the same material. Her staff, too, was imprisoned, pressed tightly against her chest, so she couldn't even wrap a hand around it. The instinctive scream that tried to explode from her throat was muffled by the all-encasing netting.

She felt a sickening sensation, as if she were falling; suddenly there was no floor under her feet, and the dizzying sense of motion caused her stomach to lurch. Darkness enveloped her, and her thrashing only seemed to draw the web around her more tightly. An instant later she found herself standing on a stone floor again, but her struggles unbalanced her, and she fell heavily on her side.

Harsh sounds assailed her ears, and she recognized the sound of a magic spell being cast, spoken in a

THE FATE OF THORBARDIN

guttural, male voice. In the next instant, the web was gone, completely evaporated. Her staff clattered to the floor beside her, but before she could grab it, another dwarf, a black-robed female, snatched it away. A hideous-looking Theiwar, eyeless and grotesque and wearing the robes of a black wizard, pointed a finger at her and spit the command to another spell.

Gretchan opened her mouth to voice a spell of protection, a plea to her god for a shield, but the wizard's casting was too fast. The priestess found that her throat, her lips, her tongue could form the words normally, but no sounds emerged. She thrashed around wildly and tried to sit up, and that movement, too, was completely soundless.

Even as she pushed herself up, a loop of rope, mundane and coarse and very strong, dropped around her neck, and she was pulled roughly up but off balance, teetering in every direction. She realized that a third dwarf was behind her, and it was she who had dropped the noose around her neck. With a heaving lunge, her abductors pushed her through the door of an iron-barred cage. The door slammed shut with a metallic clang, and when Gretchan grabbed the bars and shook them, the thing rattled like a drum. But when she again cried out a challenge, a protest, the sound of her voice was swallowed entirely before it could even escape her lips.

She slumped back, realizing that she had been enchanted by a spell of silence, no doubt in an attempt to make sure that she couldn't call upon her Reorx-based powers for any help. It was a simple but utterly effective tactic.

Still, she was not about to give up or plead for mercy. Instead, she let go of the bars and backed warily away, taking stock of her captors. The young, beautiful wizard had picked her staff up from the floor and handed it to the grotesque Theiwar with obvious deference. Her gorge rose as the wizard stroked her cherished staff with obvious sensual pleasure, his cracked lips splitting into a smile, his eyeless face turning upward in apparent bliss.

Only after he had set the staff aside did he turn to regard her more closely. The smile disappeared then as his face wrinkled into a mask of pure hate. Even the two females, the old hag and the voluptuous maid, stepped away from him with expressions of wariness. But they might have been far away, for all the notice the wizard gave to them.

Gretchan could feel the full weight of his attention pitilessly focused on her. The wizard might be eyeless, but she felt as though he were stripping her with his gaze. She recoiled in horror, wrapping her arms around her breasts.

And the wizard opened his mouth and uttered a cackle of pure, vicious glee.

FIFTEEN

FIGHTING PHANTOMS

General Darkstone crawled out from under the slab of stone that had nearly crushed him flat. He stood shakily and looked around, dazed, but not so dazed that he failed to realize that the slab, caught as it was between two boulders, had actually saved his life by acting as shield against the piles of stone and debris that had rained down into the chasm when the mountain had split. Willim's army commander had fallen into that chasm, but by some miracle, General Darkstone had been spared.

He saw one of his men nearby and reached down to check on the dwarf, only to recoil when he realized it was only the head and upper torso of the soldier. The rest of his body had been crushed beneath a massive boulder. Looking up, Darkstone spotted the yawning ledges of a deep chasm. Where he had stood upon a solid floor, within a sturdily fortified gatehouse, the rock had split asunder. Some massive force had cleaved right through that immortal barrier, shattering the barrier to Thorbardin's world.

DOUGLAS NILES

Even more shocking was the bright daylight spilling in through the wide gap that had somehow been smashed into the side of the mountain. Beams of sunlight stabbed through the murk overhead, highlighting soot and dust floating in the air. Darkstone could smell the fresh mountain air, a scent he had not known for more than a decade.

He also smelled a heavy, bitter smoke, like the residue of a dense coal or oil fire.

"What in the name of Reorx?" he muttered the question aloud as he checked his limbs, somewhat surprised to find he didn't seem to have any broken bones. His stomach lurched when he tried to stand, but he leaned against a shattered stone wall and drew a few deep breaths until the heaving in his guts subsided. "How did they do such a thing?"

Groggily, he massaged a lump on his forehead, conscious of a deep, throbbing pain in his skull. He tried to think—what should he be doing? One answer seemed to be that he should be sending a prayer of thanks to Reorx, simply for being alive. He drew a deep breath and swallowed the bile rising in his throat.

"Move, damn it!" he croaked to himself. "Do something!"

Only then did he begin to take stock of the situation. He heard shouts, battle cries, and the loud clashing of steel against steel coming from high above him. A dwarf screamed loudly, in a obvious pain. Moments later a body came tumbling down, bouncing from the ledges and outcrops, armor clanging and breaking apart, until the corpse smashed to the stone floor half a dozen paces away from Darkstone. The soft plop of the body itself was accompanied by a clattering rain of debris from the fellow's broken equipment. The dwarf, his breastplate broken away, was clad in a blue tunic that bore an insignia of a crown on the chest; it was a uniform unknown to the general, who had served in virtually all of the military units within Thorbardin.

If he'd had any doubts before, that cleared it up: invaders had indeed breached Thorbardin. He could still hear the sounds of battle, though the noises seemed to be receding from the gatehouse above him. But he took heart from the fact that his garrison dwarves were clearly putting up a valiant defense.

He had to find some way to climb up from that pit and aid his men, but both sides of the crevasse seemed to form sheer cliffs with ledges and outcroppings few and far between. Rubble was piled irregularly in the bottom, but even when he scrambled up and over some of those loose boulders, he could climb only a dozen feet or so above the floor. The apparent ledge where the gatehouse had been remained more than a hundred feet over his head, well out of reach.

So instead, he started moving along the narrow floor of the chasm, stepping over slabs of stone and fallen boulders. Everywhere he looked he saw dead dwarves, many twisted and shattered from the terrible force of a long fall. Nearly all of the soldiers wore the black uniforms of his own garrison, and he suspected that most of them had met their deaths before they even knew that an attacker was upon them.

Darkstone crawled over more rocks, climbing up and over a mound of rubble at least twenty feet high, but when he descended to the lowest level of the chasm, his path was blocked. When he got down on his knees, however, he discerned an opening underneath a large slab of stone, and by crawling on his belly, he was able to push himself along, advancing away from the outer gate, toward the interior of Thorbardin.

Water flowed over his legs and hands; the surface below him proved to be very slimy. From the unpleasant stench, he judged it was an ancient remnant of an old sewer pipe, smashed open by the same brutal force that had split the mountain.

But there was no other way to go. Grimacing, forcing himself to breathe only through his mouth, the general squeezed into the old sewer pipe, which was barely large enough to allow him to squirm along. Still, he never considered halting or turning back.

His men were at war, and it was his duty, his honor, to press onward until he could join them.

---DH---

"More fire!" Brandon shouted. "Burn them out!"

He stood beside the Firespitter and watched a dozen Theiwar, some of Willim's palace guards, writhe in the throes of death as oily flames crackled in the street, burning away beards and hair, charring the leather boots and heavy gloves of the fighters. The crew chief had just spewed the liquid fire against a makeshift fortification. Even before the flames had died away, vengeful dwarves of the Kayolin First Legion swarmed over the barrier, stabbing and hacking at any defenders who still showed signs of life.

"We need to bring up more oil, General!" protested the crew chief, a soot-stained former miner named Stoker Coalman. "I only have enough fuel for one more shot, and then the tank'll be drained."

THE FATE OF THORBARDIN

"Use it up!" snarled Brandon. He spotted movement through the doorway of a nearby building, an inn carved from the bedrock of Norbardin's main level. Several of Willim's dwarves had piled benches and chairs in the open doorway. One fired a crossbow, the bolt striking a Kayolin dwarf in the neck. "Fire it right in there!"

The chief obliged, calling out his commands in a loud but surprisingly unemotional voice.

"Pressure up, there, in the boiler! All right, you men, shift us around here, thirty degrees to the right. Hop to it now!"

Six gunners set their shoulders to the handles on the side of the big machine, and the Firespitter slowly rotated in place until the long snout of the barrel was lined up on the door of the target building.

"Up the furnace, now—full draft!" Stoker barked, and another operator pulled open the vents on the firebox. That container was already a dull red from the fire held within it, but the roar of the increased heat was audible and made the crimson glow even brighter.

"Fire!"

Another gout of churning flame spewed from the machine, streaking through the open door before blossoming like a fireball, filling the inn so thoroughly with fire that tongues of orange flame licked out from the upper room onto a balcony overlooking the street. Screaming dwarves, afire from head to foot, came bursting out of the place to sprawl on the roadway, dying in a horrific stench of burned hair and flesh. In moments the massacre was over, the corpses lying in grotesque, blackened shapes. To Brandon they looked more like gnarled old tree stumps than the bodies of dwarves.

"Move out!" demanded the general. He pointed at the captain of a company of light infantry. "You! Take your men down that street to the right. Check every building—kill every dwarf that offers any resistance. The rest of you, follow me!"

Raising the Bluestone Axe, Brandon uttered a guttural battle cry and charged through the still-smoldering corpses of the slain defenders. Hundreds of Tankard Hacksaw's men followed him, echoing his battle cry with hoarse challenges and vengeful shouts. All had heard of their legion commander's death at the hands of the black wizard himself, and they intended to show no mercy toward any of Willim's dwarves.

A pair of dwarves, hiding behind a stack of kegs outside of a tavern, were flushed from cover and bloodily butchered before they could take more than a few halting steps. A little farther on, a detachment of six or eight or Willim's defenders tried to form a shield wall across the mouth of a narrow alley. The Kayolin dwarves smashed into them with a sharp, brutal charge, the weight of thirty attackers breaking apart the wall so each of the defenders could be quickly cut down from either side or from behind.

More and more, however, the invading troops seemed to be advancing without meeting any organized opposition. The enemy was dwindling somehow. Brandon smashed down the stone door to another inn, shattering the portal with a single blow of the Bluestone Axe. He rushed inside, followed by a dozen of his men, to find a score of dwarf maids and youngsters cowering against the rear wall.

"Where are your warriors?" he demanded, his voice a growl.

THE FATE OF THORBARDIN

"None here, my lord!" cried one of the women, an elderly matron who nonetheless pushed herself to her feet and faced Brandon boldly. "They have all fled to the great plaza or the roadway down to the Urkhan Sea."

"And good riddance to them!" shouted another, younger maid. "And when you find that bastard, the black wizard, may you cleave his skull with that blue axe!"

Brandon nodded vehemently. His rage still possessed him, a fury of frustration and vengefulness demanding release. But through that haze, he forced himself to remember that the dwarves before him were not his enemies; indeed, their words gave him some hope for the future of the kingdom.

Lowering his head, Brandon turned and ran from the inn, joining the charge that continued down the road. He could tell from the widening street, the vista broadening into a vast cavern before him, that they were nearing the plaza the woman had indicated. His troops were converging from all directions, and they would meet there with a powerful force. Their victory could not be denied.

But all of that paled against the truth of the questions tearing at his heart, his soul, his mind: Where was Gretchan?

And could he possibly find her in time?

———DH———

Awakened by the violence and killing, Gorathian rose from the magma-fueled furnace of the underworld, once again seeking the vitality of the dwarf world. The beast hungered for blood, for the sheer joy of killing. It had languished long enough in the lava lake of the deep caverns. So once more the rock melted away in the face of the fire dragon's advance as the creature of Chaos bored a passageway through the bedrock of Krynn.

As it rose, it was drawn to the ongoing battle as a moth is drawn to a flame. It remembered war, and it craved war.

But, too, it remembered the lure of the wizard's magic, and that caused it to hesitate in its destructive course. It came to a halt in the midst of the solid stone, probing with its nostrils, with all of its senses, seeking that alluring power, that fundamentally throbbing sorcery that had driven it for the past long intervals of its existence.

The wizard was there, somewhere, in the midst of that violent war. That much the fire dragon realized. But where he would be found and how he could be killed before he used his magic to flee remained the great and frustrating questions of the Chaos creature's awareness. So it sniffed and it pondered and it craved.

And in the midst of its seething meditation, it became aware of another power, a fresh source of great magic, even if it was not the magic of sorcery. Of course, it was warded by the power of a dangerous god, and Gorathian wanted nothing to do with any god.

Still, it was pure, arcane might, and there was nothing that would feed the fire dragon's hunger more satisfyingly than such power. So Gorathian probed with its senses, wishing to learn more about that new magical presence.

———DH———

"Why you goin' to Hillhome?" Gus asked Crystal as they strode along a rocky trail between a pair of rough ridges in the foothills.

THE FATE OF THORBARDIN

"Because it's my home," she declared simply. "I haven't been there for a while, but I've decided to go back."

Ignoring his two girlfriends, who stomped along behind them and repeatedly shot dirty looks at the back of Crystal Heathstone's fur traveling cloak, Gus strolled along and pondered the situation. In truth, his new companion reminded him a lot of Gretchan, at least insofar as she didn't try to bash him with a club or stab him with a sword just because he happened to be nearby. Yet, unlike Gretchan, Gus sensed a kind of wistful sadness in Crystal, and he wished he could do something about that. He was glad that he had killed the Klar in order to save her, but he knew that captivity in the hands of the mad dwarf was not the sole problem that had afflicted the gracious dwarf maid.

Of course, his affections had been considerably enhanced that morning, when their new companion had led them to a comfortable roadside inn, only an hour or so from her hidden camp in the woods. There she had produced a steel coin, and the innkeeper, who had at first looked askance at the trio of gully dwarves, had been persuaded to produce a loaf of bread, a pitcher of creamy milk, and even some cooked eggs that Crystal had willingly shared with the three Aghar who had rescued her in the woods.

Apparently she was still kind of lonely, for she made no attempt to shoo the gully dwarves away. Neither did she invite them to keep her close company, but that didn't stop Gus—and, by extension, the two females who had attached themselves to him like mountain ticks—from traveling along at her heels. The word *Hillhome* had triggered a vague memory, and Gus scratched his head, trying to tickle out the thought.

It wasn't until hours later, when they were descending toward a wooded valley, that the connection was finally made. "Hillhome! Gus know Hillhome dwarf!"

"Oh?" Crystal seemed surprised, even a little amused by his revelation. "And who would that be?" she asked.

"Slut Fireforge!" Gus proclaimed proudly. "Him and me was at Patharkas for Big War! Gus won Big War, but Slut help too."

"Slut Fireforge?" she repeated. "That doesn't sound—wait, do you mean *Slate* Fireforge?"

Gus frowned. He didn't like to be corrected. "Mebbe so," he admitted. "But Gus call him Slut."

Oddly, Crystal was laughing. "I'm sure you did," she said, shaking her head. "But I know Slate, and I imagine he was fairly amused. Would you like to see him again?"

"Sure! Slut big, nice guy. Even share beer with Gus."

"Well, I think you'll get your wish," the hill dwarf maid replied, gesturing to a town that was just coming into view around a bend in the forest road. "Because we'll be in Hillhome in about ten more minutes."

Sixteen

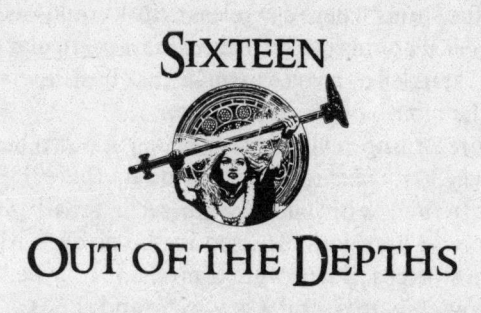

Out of the Depths

General Darkstone finally emerged from the damp, constricted drainage tunnel. The drain pipe from the ancient sewer had brought him there, but just as the tube began to drop vertically into the depths below Thorbardin, he was able to wrench aside a rusty iron grate and escape. Squirming through the narrow aperture, he rolled onto his back and breathed deeply of the city's dank but comparatively fresh air.

Mud and slime covered him from his boots to the gummy strands of his hair and beard, but he pushed himself to his feet and gave himself a shake, not unlike a dog emerging from a swamp. He stood on a narrow street, at the edge of a sewer drain. The ceiling was low overhead, filmy with mold and dripping water, and the buildings along either side of the twisting road were packed close together. Each was protected by a stout door. He didn't see any windows.

Taking stock of his surroundings, he realized he had come into Anvil's Echo, the lowest of Norbardin's hierarchy of levels. It was a place where the poorest dwarves lived, the slums where a careless drunk could easily get his throat slit or his pocket picked, in no particular order. He was startled as a voice, firm but not hostile, emerged from the mouth of a narrow alley.

"Here, stranger, you look like you got down here the hard way. Any idea what's going on up there?"

He turned with surprise to see a small platoon of Theiwar warriors, dressed in the black leather of Willim's forces. They were a mixed lot, armed with crossbows, swords, and a few axes, and they gathered behind the dwarf, wearing a sergeant's epaulets, who had addressed him. That one had an ancient scar slanting across his face, and his beard was long, gray, and wildly untamed.

"Thorbardin is attacked from without," Darkstone said bluntly. "Invaders have cracked open the great gate. Their troops are pouring into the city as we speak."

"Damn!" the sergeant replied. "It's worse than I thought."

"What word has filtered down here?" Darkstone asked.

"Well, we heard that a whole company has been burned to death, not two hundred feet over our head. My orders are to stay down here and watch for trouble in the Echo, but I've a mind to take my men up to the main level and put them to good work." He squinted, plainly appraising the mud-slicked stranger. "I'll go ahead and volunteer you into my band; you look like you could swing a sword rightly."

Darkstone almost chuckled. He found himself liking the grizzled, scarred sergeant; the fact that the fellow was willing to march headlong toward the center of the fight was the first encouraging sign he'd noted

THE FATE OF THORBARDIN

that day. He straightened up, threw back his shoulders, and mustered all the force of his command into his voice.

"Sergeant!" he barked. "What's your name?"

The dwarf blinked but then snapped to attention. "Chap Bitters, sir!" he shot back. "First Sergeant of the Third Theibardin Regiment!"

"Good man. I am General Darkstone." He looked around as the name registered. Chap Bitters blinked in astonishment. "You are hereby promoted to captain. Bring as many of your men as you can gather in five minutes; we're moving to the plaza!"

"Aye, General. Yes, sir!" Bitters turned and shouted at the dozen men in his small platoon. "You heard the honorable general! Fetch your fellows from whatever holes they're hiding in. Report to the north shaft in five minutes!"

The dwarves scattered with commendable alacrity, and by the time they'd rejoined the captain and the general at the entrance to the north shaft—which was a wide, spiraling stairway leading up to the rest of Norbardin's levels—they had collected more than a hundred other dwarves.

"Half the regiment, I'd say, sir," Bitters reported with not a little pride.

"Good," Darkstone acknowledged. "Now fall in and move up!"

They tromped up to the plaza in a serpentine column and a few minutes later emerged into a warehouse quarter where wide, straight streets passed between square buildings. The structures were two stories high, and the stone ceiling covered each street at the same height as the top of the warehouses.

In peacetime, it would have been a district bustling with pedestrians and commerce, but they found a city changed in ways that the Daergar general found hard to imagine.

Most notable was the lingering smoke and the many charred, burned bodies of soldiers they found scattered in the streets. Some of the corpses were still smoking, though it seemed as though the main fight had moved on. They heard some sounds of a clash coming from somewhere up ahead, but there was no sign of the major force that must have inflicted such terrible casualties.

"Keep your men here; have them hide in one of these warehouses," Darkstone ordered Captain Bitters. "Then come with me. We'll do a little reconnaissance."

"Aye, sir," agreed the Theiwar with the old scar. "You heard the general," he barked to his men. "Find one of these places where there's room for the whole lot of you to stay out of sight."

In a few moments, several of the Theiwar had pried open a large door to find a mostly empty space inside. Several mounds of coal along the back wall, along with a layer of black dust covering everything, suggested the commodity that was usually stored there. For the moment, fortunately, the stockpile was low, and the hundred-plus dwarves of Bitters's company were able to make themselves comfortable and, more important, stay out of sight of the street.

The men pulled the door closed as Darkstone and the captain started up the street. The two officers clung to the shadows near the dark buildings, moving stealthily, slowly advancing in the direction of the sounds of battle.

THE FATE OF THORBARDIN

Hearing the approach of a large body of warriors, the pair melted into a shadowy alcove and watched the cross street a dozen paces in front of them. They spied a file of dwarves dressed in red shirts, carrying shiny, unbloodied swords at the ready, double-time past. There were several hundred men, and they moved along one of the main avenues leading from the north gatehouse into the main center of Norbardin.

"It's clear they've come into the city in force," Darkstone said in a low voice. However brave his surviving troops at the gatehouse had been, they could not have stood for long against such overwhelming numbers.

The two officers waited a minute or two until the sounds of the marching dwarves had faded into the distance. Then they emerged to continue their scouting. They crossed the main avenue and continued down another side street; like the one where the company had hidden, it too was devoid of traffic or other activity.

"Where are all the dwarves?" Captain Bitters wondered, his voice a hoarse whisper.

"Hiding, most likely," replied Darkstone. "Probably waiting to see how this all comes out."

Once more they arrived at a main thoroughfare, and there they found a number of bodies, mostly Theiwar wearing the black tunics of Willim's troops. Some had been felled with swords and arrows, but in one place there was a wide circle of soot on the pavement with half a dozen charred and blackened bodies captured in the ring of fire.

"Did they come in with a dragon, General?" asked Captain Bitters, more angry than afraid.

"Worse than that, I think," Darkstone declared, choking on his words.

He couldn't speak as he walked past the terribly burned dwarves. Most of them were dead, and the few who still managed to open a wild, staring eye or to twitch a charred, stinking limb would perish soon enough.

He heard a groan and found one Theiwar whose legs were charred and ruined. But his eyes were bright and alert, and he uttered a hoarse curse as Darkstone knelt beside him.

"What happened here?" asked the general.

"A machine, sir! They attacked us with a great, fire-breathing machine. They pointed it at us, and it spat the huge fireball that killed half my platoon. It spit fire all the way down the street. I tried to fight them, sir—I—I really did! But I couldn't!"

"No one could, son. I'm proud of you," Darkstone said, touching the man's cheek where his beard had been burned away. Another look at that charred torso and legs confirmed that the soldier was doomed; no one could recover from a wound like that. The general looked at him with frank compassion. "I wish there was something I could do for you."

"My—my knife, General," croaked the dying soldier. "Could you put it in my hand?"

The commander found the weapon, which had a blackened, half-melted hilt but a keen, undamaged blade, lying just out of the dwarf's reach. "Here it is, lad," he said, handing him the weapon then rising and turning so he didn't see what the fellow did with the instrument.

Then he heard the sound of the cut and the spurt of arterial blood.

The Daergar general clenched his jaw and stalked onward, deadly resolve churning in his belly, his heart, and his mind. The fire cannon was the most terrible weapon he had ever seen, and the knowledge that it had been designed by dwarves and used against dwarves almost made him physically sick.

---DH---

The hill dwarves were happy to welcome Gus, Slooshy, and Berta into their village as soon as Crystal explained how the Aghar had saved her from the mad Klar. They were further delighted to find out that Gus himself had been the gully dwarf who had spared them from the lethal barrage of the Tharkadan trap. (Under the circumstances, he decided it was not really necessary to tell them that it had all been a big accident.)

Slate Fireforge had become the leader of the town, and he recognized Crystal and Gus and was quick to declare the afternoon and evening to be the occasion for a great celebration of Crystal Heathstone's homecoming. He welcomed the esteemed guests.

"Berta not wanta be 'steemed," Gus's girlfriend whispered loudly as the plans were being announced. "But they got food for us?"

Indeed, they did have food: the hill dwarves feted the gully dwarves with fresh bread; a large, smoked ham; and a whole bushel of apples and grapes. The food was placed on a table, and they ate sitting on really comfortable seats. They found themselves looking across a plaza that was growing crowded with hill dwarves as more and more of the Neidar streamed into town from the surrounding villages, almost as if a magical summons had gone out to inform them of the impromptu celebration.

For a while, Gus was too busy eating to really pay attention to anything else, but after a couple of hours, even his very expandable belly was starting to feel comfortably full. It was then that he started listening to the earnest conversation going on between Crystal Heathstone, Slate Fireforge, and a few other hill dwarf elders.

They were talking about the Big War, the same war that Gretchan was going to. Gus leaned in and tried to understand what the other dwarves were saying.

"Tarn Bellowgranite has marched on Thorbardin?" Slate Fireforge expressed surprise at the news. "Why didn't he call on our help? Like we pledged in the treaty?"

Crystal shook her head, saddened. "I'm afraid it's the old fears, the old prejudices again. Brandon Bluestone came down from the north with four thousand dwarves of Kayolin, and apparently Tarn felt that would be enough to get the job done."

"Aye. And he didn't want to share the spoils with any Neidar, unless I miss my guess," said another big hill dwarf—one who Crystal had welcomed by the name of Axel Carbondale. Gus knew that Axel had come from a different town, and in fact he looked vaguely familiar. At last it came to him: Axel had also been with the hill dwarves in the battle of Pax Tharkas.

"Is that the case?" Slate asked bluntly.

"I suppose it is," Crystal was forced to agree. "My husband is a very stubborn dwarf. And I'm afraid, sometimes, that he's getting even worse in his old age. In the end, I disagree with him. I think we should all come together. That's why I decided to come home, on my own. I came to tell you what Tarn is doing and to ask if you'd be willing to help him."

Suddenly she turned and flashed Gus a smile that, once again, reminded him very much of Gretchan. "I almost didn't make it back home, and I wouldn't have if not for Gus here."

The little gully dwarf beamed and helped himself to another thick slice of ham.

"So the old fool is willing to risk defeat?" Axel growled. "Just because he's too proud to ask for Neidar help? I say we let him face the defeat he deserves!"

That statement drew a few rumbles of assent from the gathered throng, but Gus saw that Slate, though listening carefully, wore a noncommittal expression on his face.

Crystal apparently noticed that too since she turned and put a hand on the Hillhome leader's arm. "Slate, is that what you think too? That Tarn and the exiles should go down to defeat because they failed to ask for your help?"

There was a long silence, during which even the conversations among the dwarves at the more distant feasting tables settled down to whispers, waiting for Slate's reply. Finally, Slate Fireforge shook his head. He stood up, his broad shoulders and lush mane of brown hair making him look larger than life.

"I say we should march to Tarn Bellowgranite's aid. I say we should ally ourselves with our cousins from Kayolin, cousins who have marched much, much farther than we would have to go in order to join this brave campaign."

He cleared his throat, as if embarrassed by his strong statements. But he raised his face and looked around the crowded plaza, at all the celebratory dwarves, with an expression of stern determination. He climbed onto his bench, stepped up onto the table, and from there climbed atop a huge keg. From that vantage, he could gaze all across the wide town square.

"Since when do we depend on mountain dwarves for wisdom?" he asked, his voice booming through Hillhome. He turned and addressed the dwarves on the other side of him and all around. "Since when do we depend on mountain dwarves to make our decisions or to decide our future? Hear me, brave Neidar!

"We have here the chance to right ten generations' worth of wrongs!" Slate Fireforge declared from atop the sturdy keg. "I say we seize that chance, we gird ourselves, and we march to Thorbardin!"

"And I agree!" Axel Carbondale said, pushing himself to his feet. "The time for feuding is done. Let us work together and claim the future for all dwarves!"

His bold statement roused a few cheers, but those cheers quickly swelled into a roar of acclamation as the plan for the campaign swept like wildfire through the large crowd of hill dwarves thronging the central square of Hillhome.

---DH---

Willim the Black paced back and forth before Gretchan's cage with his hands crossed behind his back and his scarred lips pressed together in an expression of concentration. Notwithstanding his grotesque visage and hunched posture, for the moment he seemed to have an aura more like a lecturing professor than a megalomaniacal magic-user.

The priestess watched him warily. She was shackled inside the cage and remained muted by the spell of silence. She had watched the wizard and his two female assistants for a long time, alert for any chance to escape. But no such opportunity had presented itself, and she could do little but listen.

"The creature of Chaos will be drawn to many things ... to your beauty, perhaps, and even your faith. But most of all, it shall be drawn to your power. That power is the key to all my hopes, so please, take care that you do not disappoint me."

The priestess leaned forward and strained against the chains binding her wrists. If she had been free, she would have cheerfully fastened her hands around Willim's neck and throttled the life out of him. For the time being, she could only glare.

He seemed to sense—and enjoy—her fury. He beamed as she glared.

"You are probably thinking that you would rather die than cooperate with me."

Her eyes widened slightly, the fury and fear in her gaze telling Willim that he was right in his assumption. The wizard shook his head, dismissing her objection. "You alone will not die. You will see: there will be many, many more who will perish."

The wizard went to his table and raised the Staff of Reorx, which had been laid there following the cleric's capture. Gretchan's stomach lurched in revulsion against the blasphemy of Willim's hands touching that sacred artifact, but she couldn't turn away as she watched in horror. Holding the staff before him, he made sure that she watched his every move then continued his tutelage in that maddeningly calm voice.

"This is a powerful tool—in some ways more powerful than any other device at my disposal."

Gretchan shook her chains, trying to stress that the Staff of Reorx was not his to use.

Again, the wizard seemed to read her mind. "Oh," he said with a deep, wet chuckle. "But it is."

———DH———

"General Bluestone! The king is coming with the rest of the Tharkadan Legion."

Brandon turned to see that Mason Axeblade had reached him. Axeblade was accompanied by a few dozen of his own men, all as sooty and bloodied as any other dwarves—proof that they had seen heavy action during their advance into the city.

The Kayolin commander stood with the front rank of his men, facing a shattered wall in the middle of Norbardin's central cavern. It was the royal palace, and though Brandon very much doubted that Willim the Black—and his prisoner Gretchan Pax—would be waiting for them in the battered but still formidable edifice, there was no way around the position. He and his captains realized they would have to storm the place.

In his fury and determination, Brandon had almost forgotten about the rest of the army, and he had to shake his head and force himself to think about Tarn Bellowgranite.

"How far away is he?" Brandon asked.

"An hour, maybe less. He got a very warm welcome from the people when he led the legion into the northern quarter of the city. It seems they're plenty sick of Willim the Black and of Jungor Stonespringer before him."

Brandon nodded, still distracted, thinking of Gretchan's dire peril. But he had to admit that Mason's

THE FATE OF THORBARDIN

report was encouraging; if the dwarves of Thorbardin were prepared to cheer for their exiled monarch, that would make the position of Willim the Black even more tenuous.

But what was the wizard doing to Gretchan?

He forced himself to think and act. "All right. You see that building there, the palace?"

Mason nodded, studying the stony edifice. It was surrounded by a stone wall; that wall was broken and cracked in many places, the damage that still remained from the recent civil war that had resulted in Willim's gaining of the throne. The large gate was barricaded with several large slabs of stone piled in place, blocking access in and out of the courtyard beyond. One tower rose into view behind the wall, but it was a jagged, broken spire. At one time it had apparently risen high above the floor of the underground city, but it looked like the trunk of a tree that had lost its top to a lightning strike.

"There are a hundred or more Theiwar holed up in there. The rest of the enemy army, mostly remnants, has moved beyond, into the widest of the roads leading down to the Urkhan Sea. But we can't get at them until we fight our way through the palace."

He looked up the road, in the direction Mason had come from. He was looking for signs of the two Firespitters, but the machines still were not moving forward. Both had exhausted their oil and coal in fighting their way into the city, and Brandon knew they were being reloaded. How much longer would that take?

Only vaguely did Brandon realize that Axeblade was waiting for the general to say something.

"I'm sorry," Brandon said. "I'm worried about this attack. What was it you asked?"

"Where do you want the king to come?" the captain repeated. "Should I ask him to wait in the north quarter or advance here to the city center?"

"Have him come here, if he's willing," Brandon replied. "Maybe the clear proof of his return will bring all the people onto our side and we can be done with this fighting sooner than we ever thought."

"Aye, General. Good idea," Mason Axeblade replied. Instead of saluting, he placed a hand on Brandon's shoulder. "And I heard about Gretchan," he added solemnly. "We're all praying for her, and I'm willing to bet that she's more than a match for that devil wizard!"

"From your mouth to Reorx's ears," was all Brandon could think of to say.

SEVENTEEN

THE FIRE DRAGON AND THE GOD

Gretchan watched warily as the wizard paced back and forth in front of her small cage. She didn't know how long she'd been imprisoned, though she guessed that it was more than one day and less than two. Working to battle despair, she had found anger to be powerful medicine, so she focused on her fury.

There were many things to hate about the vile magic-user, beginning with the very philosophy of his order. Wizards of the black robes were those who practiced the darkest forms of magic. Anything was fair business to them in the quest for power. Killing, theft, corruption, control: they were mere tools in the arsenal of any black wizard. Their god, Nuitari, was such a dark presence that his moon was invisible to all mortals, except those who dedicated themselves to the magic of that conscienceless deity.

And, too, she had seen enough of Willim's works to further fuel her contempt and her rage. She knew that he had planned to kill the hapless but innocent Aghar Gus Fishbiter, disposing of him merely as a means to study the effectiveness of some lethal concoction. It was only pure dumb luck that had allowed the gully dwarf to escape.

Furthermore, Gretchan recognized the beautiful, raven-haired apprentice as the dark wizard who had accosted her in the forest with the intention of killing her. It had only been her dog's alertness that had saved Gretchan from that assassination attempt. And the apprentice had made it clear that she was operating then under her master's instructions.

All of those facts fueled her anger and allowed her to resist the powerful urge to fall into despair. So she did not despair, but she was thirsty and hungry—ailments strange to her since her clerical powers allowed her to conjure food and drink more or less whenever she required them.

That conjuring, however, required her to speak a prayer to her god, to ask his favor and blessing. Thus far during her confinement, she had been utterly silenced by the wizard's spell, unable to vocalize so much as a whisper or even a whimper, which, in her deepest soul, was all she felt like mustering.

Still, she would not give the hideous magic-user the satisfaction of noting her distress. She watched impassively as he came closer, studying her. She sensed that there was something that he wanted to say, so she waited, keeping her guard up and her wits about her.

"You probably expect that you will die in my cage, do you not?" the Theiwar finally said, his voice a sibilant whisper. If he were going for charming, she reflected, he missed the mark by a good deal. She waited for him to continue without reacting to his question.

THE FATE OF THORBARDIN

"You *might* die here; you very well *could* die here!" he growled, leaning menacingly close to the bars of her cage. His tone dropped again. "But you do not *have* to die here," he teased.

Still she offered no reaction. The wizard frowned, paced away a few steps, and turned back. On the other side of the laboratory, his two female accomplices sat in chairs at a small table. Their backs were turned, but Gretchan sensed that they were listening carefully to every word their master spoke. The cleric spent a moment reflecting about those two, wondering how she might use them, *if* she might use them, as leverage against their master.

She had observed enough to know that the two females feared the wizard almost as much as Gretchan did. The elder one hated Willim as well for reasons that the priestess didn't know but could easily imagine. The younger one—the beautiful one—simpered and flattered and generally seemed to worship the eyeless wizard. But in that devotion Gretchan sensed a falseness, and she spent some time wondering about the apprentice's relationship with her master.

"There is a creature of Chaos in Thorbardin," Willim continued. "My powers are great, but they fall within the sphere of arcane magic—the magic powered by the three moons, and most especially by Nuitari, the black moon."

Tell me something I *don't* know, Gretchan challenged him silently, still without changing her expression or posture.

"This Chaos creature is a fire dragon and, thus, is immune to the magic of my sphere. It knows only the void, and the void is now the province of the gods. Of Reorx, too, of course—he who is lord of all dwarves."

She felt a swelling of contempt. To hear the name of her deity—a stern and powerful god to be sure, but also a god of fairness and hope—spoken by a creature such as the vile Black Robe practically turned her stomach. Still, she began to get an inkling of what the magic-user desired, and in that desire she found cause for hope— not just hope for survival, but also for freedom and, eventually, revenge.

Once again he took up her staff, holding it in his gloved hands, caressing the smooth wood in that insidious, sensual manner. Gretchan prayed to Reorx, begging her god to smite the cruel magic-user, even as she acknowledged to herself that that was not the way her deity usually worked. She knew that it was up to her to deal with her villainous foe.

For the first time, she allowed herself to display a visible reaction. She mouthed the words: I need to talk.

Willim the Black nodded and went over to the worktable, where he carefully laid the staff down amid a collection of potion bottles . . . scrolls . . . and other, not easily identified odds and ends. Turning back to the cage where she was imprisoned, he advanced and snapped his fingers. Gretchan cleared her throat and was astounded—and relieved—by how loudly the sound echoed in her ears.

"What makes you think I can defeat this monster?" she asked quickly.

He smirked, a truly grotesque smile twisting his eyeless face. "Because it will kill you if you don't. And that is a chance I am willing to take."

THE FATE OF THORBARDIN

"But if I die, then you will die as well," she challenged, though not with a great deal of confidence.

The wizard shook his head, dismissing the idea. "No, you don't understand. I shall teleport myself away. You will face the monster when it comes for me. And it *always* comes for me. But there will be many others standing in its path as well."

"You will have to let me have my staff," Gretchan asserted.

"Yes, when the time is right," Willim replied calmly. "Facet!" he barked without turning his face from the cleric's. "Take the staff and hold it ready."

The younger magic-user bowed and rose from her chair. Gretchan knew that the young female was an apprentice, and judging from her beauty and the obsequious way in which she seemed to worship the wizard, the priestess guessed that she served her master in many ways—not all of them having to do with her magical training. With another disgusted look at that scarred visage, she reflected on the thought of physical intimacy with such a dastardly creature. It was impossible for her to comprehend. She could even smell his fetid breath, like the stink of a pile of fertilizer, and he was six feet away from her.

The dwarf maid came over carrying Gretchan's staff, and when Willim turned and held out his hands, she gave it to the wizard. He took the long shaft of wood absently, running his hands up and down the smooth surface while he continued to pace. Gretchan wanted to shout at him to drop the precious talisman, to get his corrupt and filthy hands off her treasure. But she suspected that such a tantrum would only please him, so she remained silent.

"I shall give it to you when the monster approaches but not before. If your god is with you, he may—I cannot say for sure, but he *may*—consent to match his own strength with that of the fire dragon. If Reorx is willing and mighty enough, the power of this staff may be enough to vanquish the creature. If he is not willing, you will perish and many others will perish, and I will teleport away to fight another day."

The wizard scowled and shook his head, as if dismissing the thoughts of escape that had immediately popped into Gretchan's head when she heard his plan. "And you should know that these bars are protected by many traps. Should you try to work your own magic upon them, they will burst into flames, and they will burn very hot and for a long time. You will not escape, but neither will you die quickly."

"How can you claim to know what I would do?" she challenged angrily. She gestured at the two female magic-users. "And how do you know you can trust these two? How can you trust anyone? Don't you think—?"

Abruptly he snapped his fingers again, and Gretchan's voice was immediately muffled.

"I grow tired of your incessant prattle," he said, almost as though bored. He chuckled, a harsh, cruel sound. "And I do not have to trust my apprentices. It is enough that they fear me, that they know the truth and the inevitability of my vengeance. No, my dear priestess, trust is vastly overrated among those of your cloth."

He turned his back to her and resumed his aimless pacing, moving around the large cavern that was his laboratory. The apprentices watched him and stayed out of his way, and Gretchan was left alone within the cocoon of her thoughts.

The minutes ticked by, and she found her mind wandering, imagining Brandon's distress and his terrible rage. He would push himself to the limits of his strength and beyond to find her, she knew. She uttered a silent prayer, beseeching her god to watch out for her beloved warrior, to keep him from bringing disaster upon himself with any mistakes.

Abruptly, she noticed that the wizard had stopped pacing; he stood stock still in front of her. His head was cocked to the side, like a dog listening for a distant sound, and his hands gripped the staff so hard that his knuckles had turned white.

Too, it was growing steadily warmer in the cavern. She noticed a glow emanating from a wide fissure in the floor, a chasm she had not even noticed before. The glow grew brighter, and the heat increased quickly.

"Now! It is time you will see the truth of my will! You will prevail, or you will die!"

Gretchan, still silenced by his spell, shook her head and rattled the bars.

"Feel that heat! Feel the power!" Willim declared. His face had paled almost to the color of snow, and his mouth was open, his breath coming in short pants. He snapped his fingers again, and the spell of silence was dispelled; the first proof was the sound of Gretchan's distressed breathing. She turned to see what was happening behind her.

It was enough to feel the growing warmth, and the expanding brilliance swelling upward from the chasm in the floor. Fire clearly burned there, a source of heat and light growing steadily stronger.

"Tease the Chaos creature!" he barked to his two female apprentices. "See that it pursues you. Bring it to the priestess and me; you know where to find me!"

The wizard reached out and grabbed one of the bars of the cage. In another instant, the world shifted and shimmered, and they teleported. The cleric gasped at the sensation of sudden weightlessness, of rapid, whirling movement.

He was taking her somewhere else, somewhere he hoped would help the priestess to defend herself against the fire dragon. The cage came to rest, canted at a slight angle on a high elevation, allowing her to look out across a vast cavern. Gretchan stared in awe at the sight before her.

She knew at once that Willim the Black had taken her to the right place.

——DH——

Both Firespitters had been refueled and readied for battle, and their crews rolled them into position before the gate of Norbardin's royal palace. Brandon had waited impatiently for the maintenance to be completed. He had expected Tarn Bellowgranite's arrival at any minute, and in fact had heard word that the exiled king was marching at the head of the Tharkadan Legion and that the citizens of the city were turning out in great numbers to cheer and support him as he advanced. Well more than the estimated hour of the king's arrival had passed, but from the reports, the general guessed that the crowds were probably slowing the monarch's progress through the city.

So Brandon had decided to go ahead with the assault. After all, if the enemy troops could be driven out of the royal palace in short order, the structure would be the perfect headquarters for the king. Symbolically, it would make a powerful statement to the people of Thorbardin that their former monarch had returned and taken control. But there was a pesky garrison of Theiwar dwarves still sealed up in the palace, and the Kayolin commander had to root them out. His troops had caught their breath and taken advantage of the time to eat and rest, and they were ready for the assault.

Even as the two big, fire-spewing war machines rumbled forward, the dwarves of Kayolin's Second Legion, divided into two wings and advanced to either side of the tall, well-fortified gate. Fister Morewood led the right-hand wing, while Brandon himself commanded the group to the left of the gate.

The defenders behind the palace walls fired crossbows at the charging dwarves, but—unlike at the gate of the nation itself—the number of attackers far exceeded the number of defenders. A few dwarves, including one axeman sprinting right next to Brandon, fell under defensive fire, but the vast majority of them reached the base of the wall. There they wasted no time in heaving ladders against the ramparts.

From the rear ranks of the Kayolin companies, crossbowmen fired return volleys. Many of the bolts bounced off the stone wall since their targets were protected by the battlements except for visible heads and arms. Even so, the purpose of the shooting was not so much to kill the enemy archers as it was to distract their aim from the Firespitters.

The great machines included several plates of metal armor as protection for the crew, but the dwarves who manned the maneuver handles were partially exposed. If they were killed, the machines would have been unable to advance and could not employ their firepower against the gate.

Reaching the base of the wall, the attacking troops quickly hoisted their ladders, and lightly armored skirmishes began scrambling upward. The attackers were met at the top by swordsmen, but again superior numbers came into play. Steel clashed against steel as the skirmishers chopped and stabbed and tumbled over the wall, quickly seizing control of the immediate platforms.

Brandon held one of the ladders long enough for a dozen dwarves to scramble up. He had been convinced that the army commander should be not be first man over the top, but finally he could wait no longer. Slinging his axe over his shoulder, he pulled himself up hand over hand, springing to the rubble-strewn parapet and stepping to the side so still more warriors behind him could ascend.

The shattered palace nearly filled the courtyard. It looked more like an ancient and long-abandoned ruin than it did a royal edifice of dwarven construction. Great ruptures yawned in the wall, and many of them were still strewn with the stones that had been knocked free by whatever force inflicted the initial damage. The front door of the keep was gone, the entryway gaping open like a dark, silent mouth. Rising over it all was that long tower, the half spire that was missing its top.

"General, look! It's Gretchan Pax!"

The words, shouted by one of his swordsman, pulled Brandon's attention away from the crucial assault on the palace gate. He followed the man's pointing finger, and his heart leaped into his throat. He saw her at once, trapped in a metal cage, high atop the shattered spire of the palace's main tower. The cage was perched awkwardly on the stone rim of the spire, which had been broken off during the recent civil war. His priestess was there, bracing herself by clinging to the bars of the cage.

"Gretchan!" Brandon shouted, his voice rising above the chaos of the battle.

He saw, then, that the black wizard was there too. Willim's robes swirled from the lingering motion of the spell that had carried them there, and he held Gretchan's staff in both of his hands.

Then Brandon and everyone else were further distracted as a blossom of fire exploded in the great chasm. A creature made of fire, with great wings trailing sparks and smoke and a gaping mouth spread wide, roared a cry of inarticulate hunger and longing as it soared into view.

Those wings pulsed again and again as the monster flew on, and Brandon could see that the fire creature was flying directly toward the cage holding Gretchan Pax.

———DH———

"It comes!" Willim the Black croaked, his voice a mixture of thrilled anticipation and stark dread. "Make ready!"

The latter statement was accompanied by a shiver of genuine terror, and Gretchan understood how much the wizard truly feared the creature of Chaos. He certainly had reason to fear. She knew the story of the

Chaos War and the massive destruction the monsters had wrought across the face of Krynn. As she beheld the monster for the first time, she understood how its kin could have wreaked such destruction throughout all of Thorbardin.

"You must release me! And I'll need my staff," she said, somehow managing to sound calm.

The wizard refused to let her out of the cage, but he did allow her the religious talisman. "Here, take the staff! Remember, you will defeat the monster or die!" hissed Willim, suddenly thrusting the butt of the staff through the bars.

Instinctively she snatched the staff away from him, clutching it to her and murmuring a prayer of thanks. Immediately she felt the strength and serenity of Reorx flowing through her. She was ready to fight and, if it came to that, to die.

But there were all those other dwarves around her. She saw at least a thousand of the Kayolin soldiers, and guessed that Brandon must be down there with them. In the same instant that she thought of him, almost as though her magic had created him, Gretchan saw Brandon, standing on the wall almost directly below her, shouting and waving up at her.

The two female magic-users flew through the air; they were black specks that were almost impossible to see against the bright, surging flame of the Chaos creature. They swept toward the cage, following Willim's command, until, a hundred yards away from Gretchan, they vanished, presumably teleporting to safety.

The dragon roared and surged on. Gretchan grabbed the bars of the cage, but they were unyielding, and she had no doubt that the wizard had spoken the truth about his trap. Her throat was dry, so parched she could barely croak out a sound. With another whispered word, she conjured a drink of water, instantly gulping the liquid that magically appeared in her waterskin and easing her parched throat.

Then the dragon was there.

Its huge, flaming head reared upward from a long, sinuous neck. Foreclaws, like its skin and wings, made of solid fire, glowed like red-hot metal superheated in an infernal forge. The beast rippled upward. Through the waves of heat that caused it to flicker in the air, a sinuous figure of majesty and terror was outlined in crackling flames.

"Oh Reorx, grant me your strength, to stand before this horror of the Abyss. If it be your will, may I slay it. Or if it be your will, may I die with courage and grace."

She heard a cackle of laughter, like an insane giggle, coming from directly behind her, and she knew that Willim the Black lurked there, waiting for her to work Reorx's magic. The beast was so close that she dared not look away. Instead, she clutched her staff and stared at the unspeakable creature in awe.

Its head was as large as the cage imprisoning her. Atop the serpentine neck, it swiveled around, with eyes of charcoal black—the only part of the monster that didn't seem to be on fire—sweeping around the vast cavern of Norbardin's royal plaza, clearly searching, searching.

And finally those soulless eyes came to rest upon her. The dragon flew closer, looming overhead. The heat of its presence blasted Gretchan's face and hands, warmed her robe, and began to singe her hair.

"By all the power of the Forge, you are doomed!" she cried, raising the staff. "Go back to the Abyss! Go hide in your foul plane of nothingness and despair! There is nothing for you here!"

The dragon reared back, fanning the air with the great sails of its wings, dripping a cascade of sparks across the gathered throng of dwarves below. Its huge maw gaped wide, and a belch of fire erupted, an oily fireball spewing toward Gretchan, crackling and sizzling. Behind the priestess, Willim the Black shrieked, and when the sound was abruptly cut off—a split second before the fireball reached them—the cleric instantly suspected that the wizard had teleported away.

She had access to no such refuge, however, so she closed her eyes, clutched her staff, and relaxed, yielding her person and her life into the hands of her god as the dragon's fiery breath surged forward, enveloping the cage and fully engulfing her.

Then she felt Reorx's presence surround her. The Master of the Forge was like a cool blanket, insulating her against the hellish inferno that surged and churned everywhere. Even through her closed lids, she saw the fire, the brilliant orange brighter than the sun. She knew the flames were right there, but somehow she couldn't feel the terrible heat.

The fire seemed to last forever, though she realized that only a few seconds had passed. She heard the monster roar again and again as it gradually realized that it was not killing her, that, in fact, the power of Reorx was not only protecting her, but exerting itself against the Chaos creature itself.

She dared to open her eyes, and she saw the dark circles of the dragon's eyes, widening as if in astonishment or disbelief. It breathed fire again, but it seemed as though its blast of infernal breath were actually infusing her with strength and draining away the terrible potency of the fire dragon's searing presence.

"Ha!" she cried, taunting the dragon with her joy and might. "You have met your master! He will take your power! You will know death!"

She raised the staff from the floor of the cage and pointed its anvil head directly at the monster. The fire dragon bellowed again, twisting and thrashing those great wings, but it struggled like a creature caught in a trap. It writhed and roared, flailing the air with its red-hot talons, lashing with its tail, driving those vast wings in ever more desperate attempts to break away.

"No!" shouted Gretchan, exulting in the creature's defeat. "You shall not fly!"

The Chaos creature uttered one last, furious roar, a sound that resonated through the huge cavern, reverberating from the walls, echoing up and down the connecting caverns. Gretchan was pulled, hard, toward the wall of the cage, but she still held the staff, and she stabbed it like a spear, as if she would drive the head right through the monster's heart.

Then it was as though, suddenly, the fire at the dragon's core was smothered, the brightness of the flaming skin fading, the heat radiating from its horrific presence cloaked, muffled, and absorbed.

Even as she watched, the essence of the monster chilled and shrank. The flaming body cooled, flowing like smoke into the air, sucked toward the cage by the power of Reorx and the agency of his staff. Gretchan placed the head of that staff into the midst of the dense cloud of smoke and watched as it sucked away the pure, chaotic power that had wrought so much destruction.

And the staff continued to absorb the fading remnant of the fire dragon. The magical protection of Reorx still cloaked her, allowed her to survive the heat that caused the iron bars of the cage to burn hot and glow red. She could feel the shaft growing fiery in her hands, so hot that she could feel the skin on her palms blistering.

But still she held firm, not daring to let the rod even wobble or sway. Indeed, she held it straight upward, and the silver anvil at its head began to glow red, then yellow, then white, filling the underground cavern with a brilliant light such as it had never known. That illumination pierced into the far corners of Norbardin, driving back the darkness and, for a brief moment, shining as proof of Reorx's goodness and of his triumph.

Finally, the fire dragon was gone.

Gretchan stumbled backward, releasing the staff and almost gagging at the sight of her blackened palms, the smell of her own charred flesh. She muttered the words to a potent healing spell, just as blackness rose around her. She swayed, struggling to remain conscious.

She felt the cage moving. With a sickening lurch of magical power, she realized that the black wizard had returned. Quickly she reached for her staff, but it was no longer there.

Nor was her cage atop the tower of the royal palace anymore. Instead, she found herself back in the wizard's laboratory. All three of the wizards were there, gathered in a circle around her. The two females, she realized, were looking at her with expressions approaching awe.

Willim, however, was practically cackling with delight. He held her staff in his hands again, tossing it back and forth between them as if it were still too hot to hold. Once again Gretchan wished that her god would smite him for his blasphemous touch.

But instead, it seemed as though the heat inherent in the staff was dissipating, for Willim was soon able to hold it comfortably. He stroked the wood with obvious pleasure and looked at Gretchan with an expression of sudden and seemingly insatiable desire.

Part III

EIGHTEEN

A MARCH AND A LIBERATION

The night in Hillhome was one of the finest nights in Gus Fishbiter's long and eventful life. Not only did he have enough to eat and drink—so much, in fact, that necessity required him to slip away from the party occasionally so that he could throw up the contents of his full stomach, simply to make room for the next course—but he was actually privy to the council of high and mighty dwarves. They never asked his opinion about anything, of course, but they let him listen to their important debate. And if they didn't exactly seek his advice, neither did anybody clobber him on those occasions when he did dare to speak!

Even his girls were happy, both of them at the same time! That was not something he could remember ever happening before, and he made the most of it. First Slooshy fawned over him, boasting to everyone who would listen (which was, essentially, nobody but Gus) how brave he had been in Thorbardin, when the two of them had first met. She described their fight with the Theiwar bounty hunters, the flight that had caused them to plunge into a flooded, rapid underground pipe of water, and how Gus had helped her keep her head above water until he had been swept away and, she assumed, drowned like a rat.

Then Berta bragged about how Gus had been the mightiest highbulp in Pax Tharkas, and how he had taken advantage of the magical blue door that had appeared in their dungeon throne room, leading to all sorts of new adventures. Nobody could run away from danger better than Gus, according to the Aghar females.

Finally, both girls took turns flattering him about his courageous rescue of Crystal Heathstone and his slaying of the vile, mad Klar. Apparently, since Crystal was surrounded by her own people—and clearly those people were delighted to have her back—the two Aghar girls had concluded that she was not really a rival for Gus's affections. Furthermore, since it was Crystal who was more or less directly responsible for all the good food and drink that had come their way over the past day, they were inclined to view the Neidar female as rather more of a good friend than a bitter rival for the highbulp's affections.

They all got kind of drunk as the evening progressed. Still, as he paid partial attention to the earnest counsels going on around him, Gus became vaguely aware that the hill dwarves seemed to consider it a matter of pride that they go to the aid of the mountain dwarves of Pax Tharkas. They were, if anything, insulted by the fact that Tarn Bellowgranite had not called upon their assistance, as they had (rather grudgingly) agreed to provide it in the treaty signed at the end of the Tharkadan War.

THE FATE OF THORBARDIN

Encouraged by Crystal and Slate, and inflamed by the tales of corruption and villainy running rampant in Thorbardin, the Neidar became more and more determined to take forceful, assertive action. The cause was one that the Neidar could enthusiastically support.

"Thorbardin for all!" one hill dwarf proclaimed.

"Thorbardin for all!" was the cry that echoed around the great town square of Hillhome and was embraced by seemingly every newcomer who arrived in the town, and all day and all night, there continued to be a steady stream of newcomers.

"What's behind this civil war?" Slate asked Crystal at one point. "We've heard rumors, but you seem to know more than we do."

"It dates back to our exile. The fanatic pretender, Jungor Stonespringer, kidnapped my son, Tor, and used him as leverage to get Tarn to abdicate the throne. Jungor was wildly unpopular; he issued edict after edict, banning everything from gully dwarves to music, to females owning their own businesses or going about without a male escort. More recently, a powerful wizard named Willim the Black has made a move to claim the nation."

"And how fares the war in the undermountain?" pressed the Neidar leader. "Does it still rage?"

"Well, the most recent witness is right here," Crystal said, looking skeptically at the nodding, groggy Aghar. "Gus, what did you see in Thorbardin the last time you were there?"

"Black wizard kill 'em all," Gus proclaimed. It was late in the evening, and he was thoroughly drunk but more than happy to expound. "Bunty hunters hunt Aghar. Big King Stonespringer hunt Aghar. Black wizard hunt everybody. And him got big magic. Scare Gus outta there, right one, two . . . one, two . . ."

His voice trailed off. What came after two again? He shrugged, remembering that it was really not ever necessary to count higher than that. As the dwarves resumed their debating, he reached for his mug. It had been filled again by a friendly barmaid.

"This make . . . two drinks!" he said, draining the contents of the mug into his mouth and across his chin and down his chest. It splashed right onto the boards of the high platform upon which he and his girlfriends had been invited to sit.

Many more times that night, he quaffed his second drink until, finally, he tilted the mug back and leaned back to finish it and toppled right off the back of the bench. He rolled over the edge of the platform and onto the ground. There, his fall was fortunately broken by the soft, plump bodies of his two girlfriends who, he vaguely recalled, had made similarly elegant departures from the party sometime earlier in the night.

Thus cushioned, Gus spent a blissful two hours sleeping. When he dreamed, it was of bountiful tables, foaming kegs, and willing girlfriends, and when he didn't dream, his body rested, recovered, and regained its strength.

When he awakened, it was with one of the worst headaches he had ever known. But even that couldn't distract him from the excitement of the preparations. He and his girls, groaning and groggy, crawled up from the mud and back onto the platform, where they found Slate Fireforge seated at the table and a long file of hill dwarves gathered in the plaza before him. They stepped up, one by one, and signed something onto a long scroll of parchment. As they did so, Slate assigned them to the "swords" or the "crossbows" or the "spears."

Gus was about to elbow the Neidar chief aside with a firm "Hey, that my seat!" when he was accosted by Crystal Heathstone, who took him by the arm and, with his girls following, led him to a new table in the sunlight, just outside of a bakery. A cheerful, young lad brought them a fresh loaf of bread and some milk, and Gus's headache was instantly forgotten.

"You were splendid last night," Crystal told him. "I don't think we'd have mustered half this many volunteers without your testimony."

"Well, sure 'nuf," he agreed, stuffing a crusty piece of bread, heavily slathered with butter, into his mouth. Of course, he wasn't certain what *splendid* or *volunteer* or *testimony* meant, but he trusted it was all good. He looked around hopefully.

"Nuther party today?" he asked.

She smiled, though once again he detected that hint of sadness in her eyes and her manner. "Not today," she said. "We're all busy getting ready to go help Tarn—and Gretchan Pax. We thought you'd want to come along with us."

"Go Thorbardin? Why, sure," he said. "Me ready. Girls ready!"

The rest of the day he lolled about Hillhome while the Neidar busied themselves with preparations. Curious children came around to talk to them, asking him with wide eyes, "Are you the one who saved Crystal Heathstone?"

"That me," Gus replied before asking, "Got any beer?"

The children proved to be a woefully inadequate source of strong drink, and perhaps that was a good thing. In any event, the Neidar under Slate Fireforge left Hillhome the very next morning, with a force of some four hundred doughty warriors. Criers had been sent to the outlying towns and villages, and all day long more bands of warriors, coming those from places south of Hillhome where the column passed through, or from other villages that didn't have time to muster in the town itself, joined the streaming column as it marched toward Thorbardin.

The bigger towns each sent sixty or eighty men, while the smaller villages might dispatch only a dozen or so, but every one of the volunteers was welcomed, and the force grew hourly as it steadily proceeded southward. Unlike the Kayolin Army and the Dwarf Home Army, the Neidar troops didn't march with any wagons or carts in which the Aghar could ride, but Gus was surprised to realize as he strode along that his legs seemed to feel stronger than ever before. The same was true of his girls, so they had no difficulty keeping up with the steadily marching hill dwarves. Crystal even allowed the gully dwarves to keep her company for a while, right near the front of the column!

"I think you toughened up, walking all that way from Pax Tharkas," Crystal suggested.

"Hmm, yeah?" Gus said, liking the sound of that. "Gus plenty tough!"

Slate was an easygoing commander, and Gus found that the Neidar captain was even willing to talk to him when the gully dwarf made his way to the very lead position of the long, sinuous marching formation.

"You lotta times make war?" Gus asked, impressed with the way Slate's men followed his orders and seemed so willing to help him out.

"Not so much," Slate said. "The only other time was a mistake, when Harn Poleaxe convinced us to march on Pax Tharkas. Still, this kind of business sort of runs in the family."

"Runs? You runs to war alla time?"

"No," Slate laughed. "I mean my ancestors have always sort of been the adventuring type. My great-uncle was Flint Fireforge. Maybe you heard of him? He was one of the Heroes of the Lance. He went all the way to Palanthas and even rode a dragon in the war against the Dark Queen."

Gus shuddered. He didn't know which sounded worse: riding a dragon or making war against a Dark Queen. Either way, he was sort of relieved they were merely marching under the mountain and going to fight against a fearsome, spell-casting wizard. But he sensed that Slate was proud of his uncle, so he didn't say anything insulting.

They were interrupted by a large cheer that rose from the dwarves behind them, and they turned to see Axel Carbondale marching out of a side valley, leading a force of, well, more than two dwarves. (Gus heard Axel boast that he had brought "four hundred swords" to join the expedition. Since he didn't see any swords marching by themselves, he figured that each sword had also brought along a dwarf to wield itself.)

By late afternoon it was a weary band of hill dwarves who finally paused to make camp after the sun had set behind the western mountains. The Neidar made bivouac in the forested valley beside a mirror-still lake. Archers had been preceding the army all day, and they had already fanned out along the marshy shore. A steady supply of geese was being carried to the cookfires that started to blaze all over.

Gus sent his girls to find a good place for him to sleep. "No big rock to hide us this time!" he warned direly, well remembering the first night of the march, when his companions' incompetence had caused them to become separated from the Dwarf Home Army.

Then he settled down to enjoy the evening. He was pleased when Crystal Heathstone came by to see how he had handled the long march.

"Plenty good," Gus replied honestly. Before she wandered back to the army commanders, he remembered something he'd been planning to tell her.

"You know, new king gonna put Aghar back on thanes," Gus boasted. "Get a real big stone chair and everything."

"It's a nice idea, and it should happen. But who told you that?" the Neidar female wondered.

The very memory provoked a blissful sigh from Gus. "Gretchan Pax say so." He frowned, trying to recall details. "Well, she say she talk to king, want king to give Aghar a thane. Or big new highbulp at least."

"I used to live in Thorbardin," Crystal noted. "The Aghar always used to have a seat on the council of thanes."

"Yeah, but bad King Stonespringer, he take away. Him kill Aghar thane; want kill *all* Aghar."

"Well, it just so happens that I know King Bellowgranite," Crystal said with a sly smile. "And if my word has any weight with him—together with Gretchan's—you can be sure that the Aghar will once again be seated at that council."

Gus drifted off to a blissful sleep, dreaming of a crown and a very big chair and all the food he could possibly eat. Of course, at the army camp, there wasn't nearly as much beer to drink as there had been in Hillhome, but even that had its advantages as, the next morning, the Neidar and their Aghar companions awakened early. Free of any headaches or churning stomachs and eager to resume the march, they didn't even take the time for cookfires as they prepared to set out again upon the road to Thorbardin.

The North Gate, Gus heard someone say, was only two days' march away.

---DH---

Brandon had been able only to stare in horror and awe as the fire dragon had swept toward Gretchan, exposed as she had been in the cage on the lofty palace spire. He called her name, but with the monster's sudden appearance, his voice froze in his throat. His fingers clenched around the hilt of his axe so tightly that they grew numb, but there was nothing he, nor even his epic weapon, could do against the impossibly mighty beast.

All around him the dwarves of his own army, as well as Willim's defenders within the palace, had been paralyzed by fear at the monster's appearance. Warriors who had stared death in the face on a dozen battlefields, who had led charges against unassailable ramparts, who had stood and faced enemy armies numbering ten or twenty times their own, had quailed and wailed and dropped facedown onto the ground, desperately crawling under anything remotely resembling cover.

The Kayolin general stood alone, watching in awful fascination as the beast first threatened then recoiled from the brave dwarf maid and her mighty staff. He sensed the wyrm's struggles against the immortal power of Reorx and held his breath as the monster slowly dissolved into the black vapor that, obviously, was sucked into the staff itself by the Master of the Forge.

And he howled in triumph when the serpent finally disappeared. His elation surging, he raced along the parapet atop the palace wall, seeking a way across to the keep. But his elation lasted mere seconds—until he had seen Willim the Black return. He watched as the wizard snatched the staff away from the stunned, exhausted priestess.

Finally Brandon had cried out in unquenchable rage as the powerful magic-user had placed a hand on the cage and worked a spell of teleportation, removing the cage, the priestess, the staff, and the wizard himself from sight.

"Come back here and fight, you bastard!" howled the Kayolin dwarf. It was a fruitless cry, and the black wizard made no reappearance; so Brandon turned his rage on the enemy troops who were only then starting to emerge from their hiding places. Some clearly had no stomach for further battle and were turning to flee. Others looked around, hesitatingly, seeking an officer or sergeant to issue some sort of command.

Brandon leaped from the rampart down to the floor of the courtyard, a drop of a dozen feet, and he didn't even feel the impact. Instead, he sprang from his crouch, instantly on the attack. His axe slashed, chopping the heads from two Theiwar who were trying to crawl up from under a slab of rock. He whirled, his senses a blur of hatred and fury, to see more black-clad defenders emerging from the shattered, gaping door of the keep.

THE FATE OF THORBARDIN

He set upon them in a frenzy, his aim unerringly true and lethal. The Bluestone Axe fought like a living thing, hungry for Theiwar blood. He chopped and slashed and spun through a circle, lopping off limbs, slashing faces, splitting skulls. When the axe couldn't reach an enemy's flesh, it destroyed his weapon, smashing swords, slicing the heads off of spears, even blocking arrows with lightning-quick parries.

The enemy troops, already shaken by the appearance of the fire dragon and thoroughly outnumbered in their defense of the palace, recoiled in horror from the fury of Brandon's attack. Some fell before him, stumbling in panic, and he killed them before they could rise. Others, quailing but trying to master their fear, faced him and fought, and those he killed with outright glee.

He gave no quarter: If a Theiwar turned his back to run, Brandon sliced open his spine. When three of them cowered together in an alcove, protecting themselves with tall steel shields, Brandon chopped the shields into splinters then hacked the trio of enemy dwarves into bloody cutlets. He charged through the keep's entry hall, scattering a full platoon of Theiwar pikemen who tried to defend the door to the throne room. Leaving a dozen dead in his wake, he rushed into that great chamber, hoping against all rational hope that he might discover Gretchan or at least Willim within.

Instead, he found himself standing alone in a great, vaulted hall. Rubble and dust lay across the floor, and holes—the detritus of the last war, the conflict between Jungor Stonespringer and Willim the Black—pocked the walls and ceiling. Very slowly, the haze of violence fell away from his eyes, and he slumped, suddenly feeling a great weariness. The floor seemed to tilt, and he dropped to his knees, using the handle of his axe to keep from toppling onto his face.

Leaning over, pressing his face to the cool blade of his mighty weapon, uncaring of the blood that still smeared the steel surface, blood that streaked his cheek and soaked into his beard, he wept.

Vaguely, he was aware that someone was calling his name.

"General! General Bluestone!"

Footsteps clattered nearby. If it had been an enemy, Brandon would have been too dazed, too exhausted to defend himself. Instead, he felt a hand on a shoulder and looked up to see the concerned face of Fister Morewood, commander of the Second Legion.

"The palace is secure, General," said the loyal officer. "We've cleaned out the rest of the garrison." He looked around, his expression a mixture of awe and wry amusement. "That is, those few that you left for us."

The captain's face immediately grew serious again as Brandon pushed himself to his feet and shook off his subordinate's supporting hand. "Were there any prisoners?" growled the general.

Morewood looked back with a grim expression. "One, sir. He escaped the notice of the first wave, but the follow-up men found him hiding in a closet. We got some information out of him, but . . . well, he died during the interrogation."

Brandon nodded, not displeased. "What did you learn?"

"He claims that most of the men of Willim's defense forces have withdrawn from the city. Apparently they're going to make a last stand in the widest of the tunnels connecting the city to the shore of the Urkhan Sea. It's called the Urkhan Road, and it used to be a major trade route, before the Chaos War disrupted all the cities by the sea. We've already located the gatehouse leading to that road. It's well-defended, but I've taken the liberty of ordering the Firespitters moved in that direction."

"Good," Brandon said. He felt the incredible weariness again, looking around in something like surprise at the sprawl of horribly gashed bodies around him. His axe was still stained with gore, and the sight of that mess disturbed him more than the corpses of his enemy. Quickly he snatched up a piece of dusty but clean linen—apparently once an elegant tablecloth, dating back to some distant time of peace—and used it to wipe his blade to a shining brilliance.

By then, both officers could hear the sounds of loud cheering, coming from the city streets and the plaza beyond the palace wall. They made their way out of the keep to be greeted by several dwarves of the Second Legion, all of them flushed with victory and triumph.

"It's King Bellowgranite, sir!" one of them proclaimed. "He and the Tharkadan Legion are marching into the plaza. They're being followed by thousands of dwarves; that's the cheering you can hear! General, the war is won!"

"It's not won!" snapped Bluestone, his harsh tone immediately quelling the delight in the soldiers' faces. "We've won a victory, a great victory even, but the enemy army still survives, and our task is not complete until it is destroyed!"

And until I get Gretchan back, or die in the attempt.

"Yes, General! Of course—and, sorry, sir," replied the chagrined swordsman. "I—I just . . ."

"You were celebrating the victory, as you should," Brandon said, much more gently. "You, all you men, have done a splendid job and have every right to be proud. Just remember, this was a battle, not the war."

"I will, sir. And thank you."

"Go," ordered Morewood. "Tell the king that we'll be out to meet him as soon as possible."

The men jogged off, and Fister looked Brandon in the eye. He offered him a waterskin, and the general drank greedily, surprised at how thirsty he was.

"Do you need to sit down for a bit, sir? I could find you a bite to eat . . ."

"No. Thanks anyway, Fister. I'm all right. Let's go meet the king and then get this whole damned thing over with."

"Very good, sir. And . . . I saw Gretchan on the tower, in that cage. But I'm afraid I didn't see very clearly what happened up there. Did the dragon . . . ?"

Brand's reply was a sharp bark of laughter. "The dragon died. Gretchan, and her staff, slew it. But then the wizard took her away again. I don't know where they are now."

"I'm sorry, General. But you know we'll find her! There's not a man in the army who wouldn't give his life to bring her back."

"I know, Fister. And thanks, old friend. I needed your good words. Now let's go welcome Tarn Bellowgranite back to his palace."

The two officers emerged from the keep and pushed through the main gate, which had been cleared by the diligent efforts of Kayolin diggers. "We had them ready, you recall, but didn't need to use the Firespitters here," Morewood explained. "Once the dragon was gone, our

THE FATE OF THORBARDIN

men were in control of the walls, and they were able to come down and clear out the courtyard in quick time. After you set the example, of course."

Brandon blinked, realizing that he barely remembered the fight, his wild and solitary charge into the palace. For the first time, he imagined that he could understand the fury that seized a Klar when the haze of battle frenzy came over him.

Emerging onto the great plaza of Norbardin, they saw the Tharkadan Legion, with King Bellowgranite and his old general, Otaxx Shortbeard, marching at the head. The column of cheering citizenry swirled around the military formation, with maids rushing up to kiss the soldiers or to throw silken scarves at the feet of the returning monarch.

"Long live King Bellowgranite! Hail to the true king!"

The cheers resounded through the great cavern, and despite his gloom and worry, Brandon couldn't help but feel a resurgence of hope. Yet when he reached the royal party and spotted Gretchan's father, he was reminded of her absence again; and everything else seemed to pale to insignificance when compared to her dire peril.

Tarn Bellowgranite and Otaxx Shortbeard led the Tharkadan Legion to a station in the great central plaza of Norbardin, and it was there that Brandon joined them.

"Congratulations, my lad!" Tarn proclaimed expansively. "Your Kayolin troops did a magnificent job! The city is retaken!"

"And what word of Willim the Black?" asked Otaxx Shortbeard, ever more practical than his liege.

"He's taken Gretchan!" Brandon said, seizing Otaxx by the shoulder, clenching the old soldier tightly. "Willim the Black has taken Gretchan! He's magicked her away, and they've disappeared."

The veteran general's face paled. "By Reorx—do you have any idea where they have gone?"

"There's no way to tell. We've learned that his army, such of it as survives, is fortifying the main road to the Urkhan Sea. We're making ready an attack there."

"By all means, make haste," Tarn said, overhearing the conversation and immediately growing serious. "We'll find that villain—and get Gretchan back, I trust."

Brandon nodded and turned back to the war. He hoped the king was right. But that was all he could go on . . .

Hope.

——DH——

Chap Bitters proved to be an inventive and hardworking captain. Operating under Blade Darkstone's orders, he had sent out numerous small parties of his men, ordering them to quietly muster any of Willim's troops they could find. Hour by hour he gathered a steadily expanding force in the concealment of the warehouse district.

The rest of the company had set to work expanding and fortifying their space. By knocking out the walls connecting the coal storage building to several neighboring structures, they had created a large hideaway in which to gather and wait. All the external doors except their initial entrance were fortified and guarded around the clock.

THE FATE OF THORBARDIN

By the time some forty-eight hours had passed, General Darkstone had assembled more than a thousand loyal Theiwar. For the time being, they kept a low profile, concealed in the bank of warehouses along the darkest streets of Norbardin's industrial quarter.

Most of the citizens in the area had been frightened away, and those who weren't and could be found were given a quick choice: either join Darkstone's force or die.

Most of them, of course, volunteered.

At the same time, the general's spies brought him steady reports about the enemy's progress. The fall of the palace was reported to him, though it did not come as a surprise: Darkstone knew that the battered structure was ill suited for defense.

More significant were the reports that Willim's troops were massing to make a stand on the Urkhan Road. Though they had suffered tremendous casualties thus far, the general knew that his troops, added to the black wizard's, meant they still had a sizable force at their disposal.

Then he looked up to see that, in a breath of magic, his master had come to him.

"Welcome, sire," Darkstone said, bowing deeply. He didn't know whether he would be allowed to live through to the end of his report, but he was not ashamed of his recent activities. And when he explained about all the recruiting he had done, boasting of the nearly twelve hundred loyal soldiers collected there in secret, poised on the enemy's flank and, as yet, undiscovered by the invaders, Willim the Black was not displeased.

"It is as if you have read my mind," the wizard said with uncharacteristic praise. "I have been preparing a bit of a surprise for our enemies. First, I will lead them away from here, into a perfect trap. I am certain that, flushed with victory as they are, they will follow me..."

Then, Blade Darkstone would have a great ambush ready—an ambush that would either win the war or leave a scar of blood and despair across the breadth of the new king's realm.

Nineteen

Retreat and Regroup

Gretchan sat in her cage and watched the two black-robed females talking in low tones, looking frequently in her direction. Sadie, Facet, and the imprisoned cleric were alone in the vast cavern of the wizard's lair, Willim having teleported away to an unknown location several minutes earlier.

The priestess stared at her staff, resting on the wizard's worktable, well out of her reach. To her, that sacred artifact seemed almost to thrum with power. The anvil on the head retained a faint glow, which was very unusual when she wasn't holding onto it. She remembered how the device had seemed to absorb the dissolving essence of the fire dragon, and she couldn't help but wonder how the presence of so much uncontained power could affect the thing.

The black wizard's worktable, as usual, was covered by a scattered assortment of vials and jars, dishes and boxes filled with components too vile and mysterious for the cleric to identify. Among them lay scrolls, some rolled into tubes, while others were spread flat for reading. In her rare glimpses, Gretchan had seen that some of the pages contained various arcane symbols, none of which made sense to her. But she knew enough about the ways of wizards to understand that the scrolls contained written versions of his spells, some of them undoubtedly very powerful. Through the medium of a scroll, even a wizard who was not powerful enough to learn a specific casting could obtain the means of using certain elaborate magics, by carefully reading the words aloud.

Among all the detritus on the table, rising higher than anything else, stood the bell jar that had caught the cleric's eyes long before. A lone blue spark drifted around in that jar like a wistful firefly, seeming to fly without pattern or purpose. Gretchan had noticed the elder apprentice, Sadie, paying a great deal of attention to that jar, frequently glancing at it with a frown of concern or worry on her face. Once, when neither of the other wizards was looking, she had gone over to it and placed a tender hand on the glass, almost stroking it affectionately.

Beyond the table stood a large cabinet closed and locked. But Facet and Willim had opened it several times during Gretchan's captivity, and she had noticed that it contained rows and rows of bottles in a variety of sizes and shapes and colors. Some were so large, they looked like wine jugs, and they were opaque, as if made of clay. Others were tiny vials of clear, delicate glass, with liquids that were colorless and watery or dark and thick as syrup. She had guessed that it was the wizard's potion cabinet, and she knew enough about sorcery to know that such dangerous elixirs could offer the one who drank them any of a wide variety of powerful, albeit temporary, powers. She'd heard of potions that allowed the imbiber to fly or to become invisible or to move at a speed far faster than any mortal could attain. Others were known to bewitch the drinker into viewing the one who had offered the drink as a great friend, a person to be trusted and favored in every way possible. There were even more sinister and vile applications, up to and including lethal poison. In fact, it had been the wizard's intent to test one such potion on Gus, an incident which had led to the gully dwarf's fortuitous escape from Thorbardin, when he had drunk a potion of teleportation instead of poison.

Gretchan couldn't offer any comments or start a conversation with the other dwarf maids because, before he had departed, Willim the Black had once again muffled her with a spell of silence. In fact, he had even ordered Facet, the younger apprentice, to bring the priestess food and water. Gretchan had unquestionably been drained and exhausted by the confrontation with the fire dragon, and after quenching her hunger and thirst, she had, for the first time since her capture, fallen into a deep sleep.

When she awakened, Sadie had been absent and Facet had been servicing her master in a very personal way, much to the dark wizard's loud and groaning delight. Stomach turning, Gretchan had turned her back and tried to ignore the activity, which was punctuated by Willim's cruel cries of ecstasy and, eventually, the whimpering submission of the young, beautiful apprentice. Not long after that, Sadie had returned via teleportation. The wizard had spoken to them both quietly before departing.

Gretchan spotted Facet looking in her direction. The priestess raised a hand and beckoned her to come closer, taking care to move slowly, to mask any threat that might be implied by her gesture. The two black-robed females whispered together again, both of them glancing over at her, and finally they rose and, side by side, and walked slowly and cautiously over to Gretchan, stopping several paces back from the bars of the cage.

Gretchan gestured to her mouth then spread her hands and reached out, a clear gesture of beseeching. *Let me talk to you,* she mouthed silently.

She could see the hesitation and fear on both the wrinkled face of the elder Sadie and the beautiful but haunted visage of Facet. Once again she was struck by the contrast in appearance between the two, the only wizards she had observed in Willim's company and service. Sadie was wary and guarded, her eyes deeply set in her skull, her expression cautious and, in some unknowable way, sad. Facet was brazen and haughty, meeting Gretchan's look with a glare of frank hostility. With her crimson lips and alabaster, sculpted face, she was almost indescribably beautiful. Yet her eyes remained hooded with a look not so much of sadness, like Sadie's, but of constant, lurking fear.

The priestess spread her hands, palms up, in the universal gesture of peaceful intent. The apprentice younger whispered something to the elder, and finally the older one approached the cage and snapped her fingers.

Immediately Gretchan heard all the sounds of her own body, the things she had so often taken for granted. As the breath rasped through her nose, her pulse thrumming audibly again, she nodded and said, "Thank you."

"Beware," cautioned Sadie. "If he returns, this will not go well . . . for any of us."

"I know. But I'm so grateful. I was afraid I'd go mad, being cooped up in that silence. It's a powerful spell," she added, nodding appreciatively at Sadie.

The old dwarf maid snorted skeptically. "It's basic magic. Real power . . . well, that's what you demonstrated when you vanquished the fire dragon like that. I wouldn't have believed it if I hadn't seen it with my own eyes."

Remembering that the two apprentices had teleported away as the dragon arrived, Gretchan looked at her quizzically. "I didn't know you saw it. I thought you had gone somewhere safer."

Sadie smiled unapologetically. "We were on the far side of the city. We expected you to die and, well . . ."

"We wanted to watch," Facet said sharply. She scowled, clearly disappointed by the cleric's survival. "How did you defeat the monster, anyway?" Facet demanded. "We thought the Chaos creature was immortal!"

"I didn't vanquish the creature," Gretchan said. "All the glory goes to Reorx, Master of the Forge and Father God of All Dwarves," she added pointedly, reminding her captors of the shared kinship of their ancestry. "I was merely his tool, and a prisoner at that, as you well know."

"I do know," Sadie said, nodding. "About being a prisoner as well."

"Oh?" Gretchan prodded, grateful to have the conversation and curious as to what she might learn. "Who made you a prisoner?"

"Why, Willim, of course," the elder apprentice declared as if surprised at the question. Her eyes flickered to the side, toward the laboratory table, and Gretchan remembered the bell jar, the blue spark, and Sadie's constant attention to that mysterious light.

"Is that a prison? A glass cage?" she asked.

Sadie stared at her again, frankly. "Yes. I was there too until very recently. Willim thought my husband and I were betraying him, and in his rage he was . . . not kind to us."

Gretchan nodded sympathetically then turned her eyes to Facet, who was watching them, her face an unreadable mask. "And you? Were you his prisoner as well?"

"I am here by my own choice!" she asserted fiercely. "My master has taught me very much. He is training me, and I am learning from him. I serve him, and he shares the deepest secrets of the Order of the Black Robes with me."

"I have noticed that he doesn't seem to treat you very well, however," Gretchan declared gently. "And it seems he forces you to do some . . . unsavory . . . things."

For the first time, the pale female's face colored. Facet tossed back her hair and lifted her chin proudly. "I use all the tools at my disposal," she said coldly and with a little too much bravado.

The priestess nodded, maintaining her sympathetic tone. "I understand. We all live in a man's world. We must all do what we can to get along."

"Why are you even talking to us?" Facet blurted. "Surely you remember that it was I who tried to kill you in the woods, on your way to Pax Tharkas?" She sneered. "You were a fool, traveling by yourself, sleeping with a big fire."

"Oh, I remember. You scared the daylights out of me. And you were skilled with your magic—you almost killed me. But if I am such a fool, doesn't that make you a greater fool for your failure?"

THE FATE OF THORBARDIN

Gretchan again saw fear flicker across the young woman's face. "I . . . I was already punished, severely, for my failure," she said sullenly. "You will not survive me again."

"I apologize for my words and am sorry you were punished," the cleric said. "Of course I had to defend myself, but I can attest that you tried very hard to do your job. Your master must be very cruel, indeed."

"You didn't answer my question. Why are you talking to us?" Facet demanded again, her tone thick with suspicion.

The cleric shrugged, choosing her words carefully. "I'm lonely, for one thing. I'm used to being surrounded by people. And I'm a talker and a writer by nature. To be locked up in a cage and especially muffled under a spell of silence . . . well, it's almost enough to drive me mad."

The discussion ended with a sudden gasp from Facet, who quickly spun away from the cage and dropped to her knees. Sadie, more slowly, turned and bowed as the wizard materialized abruptly in the space in front of his table. He was frowning, agitated, and at first didn't even take note of his accomplices or their reactions. He smashed a fist down against the stone surface then paced angrily away in the direction of the chasm.

"My master, is there news?" asked Sadie, shooting Gretchan a look of warning.

Instead of answering, he took up the cleric's staff and stalked over to the cage where Gretchan, taking care to utter no sound, sat watching him. With a snap of his fingers he dispelled the magic of the silence spell, doing so with such distracted haste that he apparently didn't notice the magic had already been neutralized.

"You must be ready to travel," he said. "Have you eaten and drunk your fill?"

"Yes," she replied calmly.

"Good. Now get ready, all of you!" he barked in a tone of command. "We're going to the Isle of the Dead. Facet, gather a case of potions—a large case, for we may be gone for a while. You and I shall go at once, taking our prisoner.

"Sadie," he continued. "I want you to collect my spellbooks and the scrolls. Bring them all; use a bag of holding to contain them. Follow us as soon as you can." Willim himself took Gretchan's staff from his worktable, holding it in both hands and pausing for a moment as if to savor the touch of the powerful artifact.

Gretchan watched in silent apprehension as the two apprentices set about their tasks, obeying their master's commands. She saw Sadie looking around with alarm and felt a stab of sympathy for the elder female, who obviously didn't want to leave the jar with the blue spark behind.

Facet looked at Sadie only once, but when she did, her dark eyes were pinpoints of seething, jealous rage.

Gretchan felt no sympathy for the younger wizard, who only caused her a cold, penetrating fear.

---DH---

"We've confirmed the prisoner's report and located the main body of Willim's army," Fister Morewood reported breathlessly, speaking to Brandon and ignoring Otaxx and King Bellowgranite, who kept clearing his throat ostentatiously. With a gesture, Brandon directed his lieutenant to address his words to the monarch.

THE FATE OF THORBARDIN

"Uh, sorry, my liege. The enemy seems to be falling back to the Urkhan Sea," the Second Legion commander reported. "But they're putting up a pretty stiff fight in the gatehouse. The fort blocks our path, but we've confirmed that there's a wide avenue that runs from the city's main gate down to the water."

"That's right," Tarn said. "It's nearly a hundred feet wide and perhaps four miles long. It ends at a wharf at the edge of the lake."

"We've interrogated a number of prisoners," Morewood explained. "All claim that Willim has more than a thousand men on the Urkhan Road, gathered in that tunnel. They're waiting for his command, so it may be that we can catch them by surprise if we move quickly."

"What kind of fight are they mounting at the gatehouse?" asked the king.

"I sent a probe that way, and they were attacked by at least two hundred archers. When I sent a reconnaissance against the gates with a heavy ram, they found it securely fastened and well defended. My men have come to a dead stop."

"Get the army in motion, then!" declared Tarn. "Send the Tharkadan Legion after them, and bring up your Kayolin troops in reserve!"

Brandon was as anxious to get after the black wizard's army as anyone else, but a cautionary note sounded in the back of his mind. He couldn't leave the plan unchallenged.

"King Bellowgranite, why would Willim position his army in a tunnel? It makes no sense! He denies himself any room to maneuver, and as soon as we carry this gatehouse he'd be vulnerable to our attack."

"Well, perhaps he feels he can hold the gatehouse indefinitely," the monarch suggested. "His men are fierce fighters, as you know."

"Yes, I realize that. But the potential for disaster is too great. It may cost us a lot of casualties, but we will carry the outer fortification, no matter how long it takes. Do you think he doubts our determination, after we forged the Tricolor Hammer and fought our way into his kingdom?"

"Probably not. But in that tunnel, he only has to defend a narrow front. We can't bring the bulk of our army to bear against him." Tarn frowned, brooding on the situation.

"No, but we can match him man for man. And with the Firespitters, any defense in a descending tunnel would turn into a deathtrap! He must know that and have some devious strategy in mind."

"But surely he didn't know about the Firespitters when he made his plan. It seems to me that he simply failed to take them into consideration."

Brandon drew a deep breath and tried a new tack. "Sire," he said. "We need to attack. But even if the main bulk of the enemy troops are on this Urkhan Road, the city of Norbardin is far from secure. I suggest we leave one legion here, to finish clearing the streets, sweeping the buildings. There are whole quarters of Norbardin, including Anvil's Echo, that we haven't even begun to explore."

"No!" barked the king. "You've seen the welcome I received from the citizens! They wouldn't be celebrating like that if they were still worried about Willim's army. Obviously, he's abandoned the city and is massing one last defense elsewhere. We need to strike fast, to take advantage of the crucial intelligence we've gained at such a cost."

"But, sire—"

Tarn's tone softened as he reached out to touch Brandon with affection and obvious respect. "Look, I understand your concern. And we all owe you a great debt; if you hadn't made the long march from Kayolin, the Dwarf Home Army wouldn't even exist. But there'll be time enough for a thorough search when the main body of his army is destroyed. Now it seems clear that we have that army on the run! I want to send every man we have after Willim's soldiers and not stop till the last of his swordsmen has fallen or surrendered. If he retreats all the way to the Isle of the Dead, then we must take to the boats and follow him."

Brandon felt a stir of misgiving, but he himself was too eager to get on with the fight to argue any further. So instead, he merely nodded and said, "Yes, Your Majesty. As you command."

"How do you propose to take the gatehouse, sir?" asked Morewood.

"The Firespitters are ready again, aren't they?" Brandon asked.

"Yes, sir. They've already been moved into position, a hundred yards or so back from the gates to keep them out of arrow range."

"All right. Let's organize the troops and get this done." He turned to the king. "But, sire, one last request. Please allow the Kayolin troops to carry this fight, and let us leave the Tharkadan Legion in reserve. After all, your men are familiar with the city, while mine are not. If we can finish the campaign on the road to the lake, your troops will be fresh and ready to search Norbardin to make sure it's all secure."

Tarn scowled for a moment, and Brandon could see that the king, his power and confidence returning by the minute, didn't like being superseded. But the Kayolin general's argument made too much sense. After a moment's contemplation, Bellowgranite nodded. "Do it," he ordered. "Without wasting any more time."

It took less than an hour for Brandon and Fister Morewood to gather the Second Legion and the freshest troops of the battered First Legion and array them against the formidable gatehouse. The troops, like their leaders, sensed that total victory was imminent. They were buoyed by the exuberant reception the returning king had received from the city's populace and ready to put the short, violent war behind them.

Studying their position, Brandon could see at once that it would be a much tougher objective than the royal palace. The gatehouse was a fortress in its own right but built into the wall of the great cavern that housed Norbardin. Thus, his army would be able to attack from only one side. The key to the gatehouse was a high, wide tunnel leading from Norbardin onto the Urkhan Road, the wide route to the lake that the king had described. That avenue was screened and defended by a pair of high, stone gates.

To either side of the gates rose formidable towers, lined with battlements and pocked with arrow slits. The towers jutted out from the wall, offering fields of fire in three directions, but to the rear they were firmly anchored in the bedrock of Norbardin. They rose from the cavern floor all the way to the ceiling and, from the looks of the battlements and windows, appeared to have walls that were six or eight feet thick.

Larger, wide platforms were carved right into the cliff wall and extended for more than two hundred yards to the right and left of the gate. Morewood explained that all of those platforms seemed to be garrisoned by Willim's troops. The attackers faced a formidable defense while having to advance uphill.

Since the Kayolin troops were reasonably rested and the Second Legion had suffered few casualties, neither Morewood nor Brandon saw any point in waiting any longer. While Mason Axeblade, in tactical command of the Tharkadan Legion, moved his men into a supporting position, the two Kayolin commanders prepared their troops for the assault.

Instead of directing the Firespitters against the gates themselves, which were so wide and sturdy—and made of solid stone—that they appeared to be impervious to fire, they decided to use the great weapons in concert to sweep the defensive positions to the right of the main gatehouse. Brandon was glad to be back in action; anything to take his mind off of Gretchan's peril. So it was with cold, direct purpose that he ordered the attack to commence.

They began with a diversionary strike against the positions to the left of the main gate. The troops of the First Legion surged forward there, directing a hail of missile fire against the enemy warriors on the multileveled platforms along the cavern wall and into the fighters' niches that dotted the left of the two towers. First Legion drummers pounded out a loud, rhythmic beat in a further attempt to confuse the enemy.

In the meantime, the Firespitters were stoked, boilers heated, and furnaces ignited. They were kept behind an intervening wall for as long as possible, so the enemy couldn't see them. Brandon knew that, once the attack began, it would take some time for the lumbering machines to move up to the wall. He grimaced at the thought, knowing many brave dwarves would fall to the enemy archers while the deadly devices inched close enough for use. Fortunately, they had been designed with the ability to crank the firing snouts up to nearly a forty-five-degree angle above the ground; so if they could get close enough to the battle platforms, they should be able to inflict serious damage against the lower ramparts.

The diversion worked splendidly. For half an hour, the Kayolin troops on the ground of the plaza and the Theiwar troops on the battle platforms maintained a spirited exchange of missile fire, though with few casualties on either side. The drummers did their job as well, raising a thunderous and rhythmic din. Brandon could only hope that the defending commander was sending some of his reinforcements to that flank in anticipation of a major assault.

Finally, the time was right for the main push. Fister Morewood ordered his legion forward, and the dwarves surged against the right flank of the mighty gatehouse, boots pounding the stone floor as they rushed from concealment behind walls, ditches, small buildings, and other obstacles. Carrying ladders, advancing under the covering fire of their own archers, they raced to the base of the wall and tried to force their way up the ladders. Hundreds of defending troops met them on the lower parapets, and hundreds of steel blades clashed against shield or met flesh in a savage melee.

Meanwhile, the crews of the Firespitters, augmented by a hundred extra dwarves who helped to haul each machine, moved the devices forward with as much alacrity as possible. As they drew near to the walls, the lethal weapons came under resolute fire, but the archers of the Second Legion were numerous enough to keep the defenders' heads down for the most part. Shields had been propped up on the crucial positions of the war machines' controls, providing at least partial cover to the crew from the missile fire that, as expected, rained down from the enemy battlements.

When the Firespitters reached the base of the wall, their crew chiefs opened up with full gouts of oily flame. The billowing, incendiary clouds swept across the lower levels of the defensive platforms, slowly spreading out to each side.

Specially armored infantry, wearing fire-retardant leather uniforms, heavy gloves, and masks, swarmed up ladders and claimed the still-smoldering platform that had been swept free of living defenders by the lethal flames. More dwarves followed as the battlefield cooled until a steady stream of Kayolin warriors charged up and over the wall, spreading out, attacking savagely, and cleaning the outnumbered defenders out of every corner of the great gatehouse.

One detachment, led by Fister Morewood himself, scrambled up to the interior of the great gates and released the barriers to a great cheer. They swung open slowly, and the dwarves of Kayolin spilled through the gatehouse and onto the lake road, where all reports indicated that the rest of Willim's army awaited them.

"General! I'm almost out of oil!" called the crew chief on the first machine. "Do you want us to push forward with the army?"

"No," Brandon called back, eyeing the passage onto the road. He knew that the Tharkadan Legion troops were still in the plaza, and those thousand dwarves would be capable of defending the war machines against any surprise attack.

"Stay here and refuel. We'll send for you if we need you!"

With that command, he took up his axe, which had not been blooded in that fight, and followed his troops onto the long, wide road to the Urkhan Sea.

———DH———

Tor Bellowgranite was having the time of his young life. Accompanied by the powerful, enthusiastic dog left in his care by Gretchan, he made his way south through the lofty, rugged terrain of the Kharolis Mountains. For several days, the pair had strolled through a stunning wilderness of forests, lakes, and mountain peaks. They didn't see another soul, which certainly suited Tor's desires.

Every step of the way, Kondike bounded ahead of the young dwarf, but the dog never ventured out of his sight. His deep bark seemed proof against any of nature's threats, as witnessed by the way he chased a hungry bear away from their camp on the pair's second night in the wild. Tor, who had a bow and arrows with him in addition to a short sword, was relieved that he didn't have to shoot the hulking, shaggy creature. He suspected that even a well-aimed arrow would have only served to make it angry.

And the dog was good company too, plopping down on the ground nearby whenever Tor sat down to rest or lay down to sleep. Kondike always welcomed a scratch on the head or shoulder, showing his appreciation with the heavy thumping of his tail against the ground. He even proved to be something of a hunter, several times

THE FATE OF THORBARDIN

returning to Tor with a fat rabbit or, once even, a goose clamped in his powerful jaws.

Mindful of the presence of adult dwarves, all of whom he regarded as, if not enemies, potential authority figures who would certainly compel him to return home, Tor led Kondike on paths away from the main road to Thorbardin. That suited them both, for their route took them through alpine meadows and high, sparse forests.

It was in one of the woodlands that Tor, who was quite a good shot, killed a deer, and the two wayfarers enjoyed a sumptuous feast of warm, fresh meat. Sizzling the fresh steaks over the coals of his fire, the young dwarf felt as though, for the first time, he was truly master of his world.

All the time Cloudseeker Peak towered over them, and with each passing hour and every passing day, Tor knew that he drawing closer and closer to his destination: the great dwarven nation of Krynn.

It was the place where he had been born.

———DH———

King Bellowgranite watched the Kayolin troops march down the dark road, and he almost immediately felt abandoned and restless. He didn't like the sensation of sitting and doing nothing while the dwarves from the northern realm did all the real fighting. He went to inspect the palace and was deeply saddened to note the destruction that had wrecked the once-splendid edifice. General Watchler, whose company of Redshirts had been left to garrison the place, invited him to stay there and occupy his old royal quarters, but

Tarn didn't have the stomach for that, and besides, he still felt that restlessness.

In part, he realized, it was because he missed Crystal, more than he had ever imagined he would. He kept reviewing, in the privacy of his own thoughts, the quarrel that had sent her away, and each time he thought of something he should have said or done differently. Sure, she was a stubborn woman—what dwarf wasn't?—and she had clearly been misguided when she claimed that the hill dwarves should have been included in the campaign.

But Tarn could have made his case much more diplomatically. Indeed, if including the hill dwarves was so important to her, perhaps he could have even yielded the point. So the hill dwarves would have been superfluous in the campaign. Did he really think that they would have charged in there seeking to plunder the treasures of Thorbardin? He only had to look around, at the waste and the damage and the ruin that had been wrought in the place during the more than twelve years since his exile, to realize the absurdity of that belief.

Thorbardin wasn't a source of treasure to anyone, not anymore. Indeed, it would take massive expenditures, and great amounts of work, to restore the nation to the glory it had possessed even a few decades before.

And even that was nothing compared to Thorbardin as it had been in its heyday, before the Chaos War, when the Life-Tree of the Hylar had sprouted proudly from the middle of the Urkhan Sea, rising all the way to the ceiling of the great cavern, bedecked with lights and noise and laughter. It was heartbreaking to think of the wonders that had been and that were no longer and could never be again.

THE FATE OF THORBARDIN

He was thus wrapped in a cloud of gloom as he emerged from the palace, accompanied by a pair of bodyguards who, sensing their liege's mood, stayed well behind the brooding king. Tarn made his way toward the legion's camp, on the plaza of Norbardin before the city's main gate and the Urkhan Road, lost in his dark thoughts. He looked at the massive gatehouse, carried at such a cost in blood, and wondered how Brandon's troops were faring against the concentration of enemy troops reported to be waiting there.

As if in response to his very thoughts, a dwarf soldier appeared, wearing the patch of the Second Legion. Tarn didn't recognize the soldier, but he was running down the ramp from the gatehouse with an unmistakable air of urgency. He spotted the king and his entourage of guards and immediately changed course to intercept him.

"King Bellowgranite!" he called. "Your Majesty!"

"Yes, man, what is it?" Tarn demanded.

"It's a message from General Bluestone! He's marched into a trap! The wizard has altered the tunnel to include an ambuscade! The Kayolin troops are under attack from two sides! He begs you to bring up your legion at once—before it's too late."

"I knew I'd be needed!" Tarn muttered almost gratefully as he saw Mason Axeblade running over to him from the legion headquarters.

"What's the commotion?" asked the loyal captain.

"Bluestone's army is under attack. We need to go to him at once!" Tarn insisted. He turned to the messenger, noting that the fellow was smeared with blood. "Isn't that right, son?"

"I'm afraid so," the dwarf gasped. "The situation is in crisis. Please, come at once!"

Axeblade looked for a moment as if he wanted to argue or waste time asking questions. One look at his king's fierce face dissuaded him, and Tarn didn't have to repeat his order.

"All right, dwarves of the Tharkadan Legion!" Mason Axeblade cried, addressing the captains who were gathered at his command post and all the other dwarves within earshot. "We're needed on the Urkhan Road! Gird yourselves and make ready to march. We charge to the rescue of Kayolin!"

———DH———

Darkstone's spies had continued to watch the enemy's movements during the day after Willim the Black had outlined the plan for his commander. The general had kept his restive troops silent and hidden for all that time, gathering even more stragglers whenever he could surreptitiously draw them into his ranks. The troops numbered more than two thousand, and every one of them had lost valued comrades to the enemy invasion. Each man, like the general himself, was thirsting for vengeance and eager to go to war.

The general was poring over maps of the city that one of his men had found in a nearby scribe's shop when he felt the familiar tingling of nearby teleportation. He looked up to find Willim the Black standing in front of him, wearing a bloody uniform. Slowly that gore-streaked garment faded into the wizard's black robe, and Darkstone understood that it had been a guise, an illusion.

"The trap is nearly ready," the wizard crowed. "I myself have given them the final, false lead. The fool of a king will lead his troops onto the road in the next hour. When he does so, it will be time for you to move!"

"Aye, Master—with pleasure!" Darkstone growled, truly eager to join the battle, to avenge the losses that had been eating at his conscience since the first assault against the outer gate. "We are ready to move!"

"Good! You know what to do!"

And with that, the wizard was gone.

It was only a few minutes later that Darkstone received the report that confirmed Willim's trap. A stealthy scout, a former thief who dressed all in black and slipped easily through the shadowy byways of Norbardin's seedier neighborhoods, came to him with news.

"General, the False King's army has marched onto the road leading to the Urkhan Sea. The fools have taken almost all of their troops down that single road. If we move now, we can cut them off from behind and trap them against the lake!"

"Splendid!" Darkstone declared, clenching his fist. All around, his bored and well-rested troops watched him, waiting for the next command. "On your feet, men," he declared. "Weapons ready. We move out at once!"

The troops wasted no time in obeying. Under the immediate command of Chap Bitters and several other loyal captains, the force was divided into four equal-sized columns. Each followed a different road, but they all would converge on the great plaza of Norbardin. Moving silently, jogging along at a good speed, they killed any citizens they encountered along the way to guarantee that they retained the element of surprise.

Finally they came to the end of the roads, where each avenue spilled into the wide plaza. There Darkstone stopped to take stock of the situation. He'd heard the reports, but he couldn't believe his eyes: There, right before him, were the two Firespitters, the enemy's most lethal and deadly weapons.

And the fools had left no troops behind to defend them!

Twenty

Fuel for the Fires of War

The teleportation magic, as always, left Gretchan feeling dizzy and disoriented. She grabbed hold of the bars of the cage to steady herself and blinked and looked around. Feeling sick, she braced herself and breathed deeply until the unrest in her seething stomach slowly settled.

As soon as she had her wits about her, she looked around more widely, seeking any information she could detect through her senses. Her first impression was one of vast, immense space and absolute darkness. She wondered, momentarily, if the wizard might have brought her to some vague and empty place, such as the Abyss or a plane of nothingness in some ambiguous location between the physical worlds of the universe.

Then she heard the scuff of a footstep on what sounded like loose rocks. Gravel skittered away, and her own feet, through the bottom bars of the cage, discerned an irregular but solid surface. Finally, as her eyes began to adjust to darkness even more extreme than that in the wizard's lair, she was able to see that Willim was nearby, right next to the cage, and that Facet was not much farther away, just a little beyond the wizard and apparently standing on a lower surface. The younger female held the case of potions she had packed before departing the lair.

Gretchan's cherished possession, the Staff of Reorx, was still held in the wizard's two hands. The light on the anvil had been totally extinguished, but she could see the shape of the long pole as he stood still studying something . . . what? It was impossible to know, with his eyeless face, but she had the keen impression that he was inspecting their surroundings very carefully.

As she looked around, Gretchan realized she must be on some kind of hilltop. The ground below her was rough and rocky and sloped away in all directions, as if her cage had been placed right on the summit of a cone-shaped elevation. A glance overhead convinced her that she was still underground, however; there was no hint of a sky, not even the diffuse glow that starlight inevitably cast through even the heaviest haze of clouds.

Like all dwarves, she had keen vision in almost total darkness, and as she strained to see some kind of ceiling overhead, she began to discern a rocky vault far, far above her. She sniffed, tasting and smelling the air, seeking more clues, and gradually she became aware of a cold humidity. There must be a lot of water there or very nearby for the air to feel so moist. Could it be that the liquid nearly filled the whole, vast cavern?

The Urkhan Sea!

That would explain the vastness of the chamber, the moisture in the air, and the high ceiling. But how could she be on a hilltop or high peak? The sea was surrounded by sheer cliffs, and by the ruins of the great

THE FATE OF THORBARDIN

cities of Thorbardin. Those cities had been abandoned since the damage inflicted, primarily by fire dragons, during the Chaos War. But those cities had been built upon cliffs, their open faces, toward the lake, rising in a series of terraces and steps. They were not rugged hills.

Only then did she remember Willim's words as he had appeared in the lair and snatched her away.

"What is the Isle of the Dead?" she asked, the sound of her voice hollow and loud in the wide space. As if to confirm the vastness of the cavern, she didn't even hear the faintest of echoes following her words.

"Ah, you were paying attention," the wizard said as if praising a wise student. "Surely a well-read woman such as yourself knows of the Life-Tree of the Hylar?"

He placed her staff on the ground, well away from her reach, and as he turned back to her, she noticed that the anvil on the head of the artifact once again began to glow, faint and pale but still visible to the priestess in the vault of darkness.

"Of course I do. It was the most splendid city in all the realms of the dwarves, more magnificent than Garnet Thax or any place else in Thorbardin or even in the most ancient of dwarf homes. It was carved from a pillar of stone that rose from the middle of the Urkhan Sea and extended more than a hundred levels from the water all the way up to the ceiling of the cavern."

"Correct. And have your studies informed you of what happened to the Life-Tree?"

"Yes, my mother told me. It collapsed during the Chaos War, crumbled away into the water because it was so weakened by the fire dragons who bored right through the supporting structures of the bedrock."

"Yes, indeed. It collapsed. But it didn't vanish into the water. Instead, the base of the pillar became an island—an island of barren stone."

"An island of death . . ." Gretchan concluded.

"Well, yes. For a while, anyway. For years after the war, pieces of rock were continually breaking off from the ceiling and falling down onto this place. It was merely a matter of odds that made it almost certainly fatal to anyone who tried to spend more than a day or two here. Hence its name. But in the more recent years, the last of the loose rocks seemed to have fallen. So we're really quite . . . well, *mostly* safe out here."

"Why did you bring me here?" she challenged him, seeing his scarred face more clearly as he strutted just beyond the bars. "What are you going to do with me?"

"With you?" Willim's voice was an evil chuckle. "Perhaps I want to do something *to* you. You're a very attractive female, after all. And I'm a male, normal in some respects at least. I have needs and you have the means of satisfying them."

Gretchan felt a growing sickness in the pit of her stomach. She glanced at Facet's pale face, her red lips clenched in anger as she stood behind and below the wizard. Her eyes shot daggers at Gretchan, while the cleric wondered if there weren't some way she could turn the apprentice's jealousy to her advantage.

As if sensing the young female's attention, Willim turned and addressed her curtly. "Take the case of potions into the space below, and store it for me."

"Yes, Master," Facet said softly. She turned to obey but still flashed Gretchan a look of fierce resentment that made the cleric all the more determined to try to exploit such a weakness in one of her captors.

THE FATE OF THORBARDIN

Her musings on that track were interrupted by another arrival as Sadie materialized nearby. She held a sack, presumably the bag of holding with the wizard's spellbooks and scrolls, in one hand, and she clutched something to her frail chest with the other. When she moved to set it down, Gretchan—and Willim—recognized it as the bell jar containing the lone blue spark of light.

"I did not give you permission to bring that," the wizard said coldly.

"I didn't ask," Sadie replied, meeting his eyeless face with an impassive gaze. "But I sensed that we are departing the lair, perhaps for good. I was not about to leave Peat behind."

The wizard snorted but didn't argue. Finally, he uttered a short, cold laugh. "Very well. It's not like you have the power to change him back to his true form; only I can do that. Really, it's good that you brought him here. It simply guarantees that my power over you will remain secure."

Facet returned to the hilltop without the case. She did, however, carry a glass of red wine in her hand. Apparently tired of being left out of the conversation, she stepped forward and knelt at the wizard's feet. "Your power over me remains absolute, Master," she offered. "Make your wishes known, and I shall obey."

"This I know, my pet," Willim said absently, stepping around her to regard Sadie with his eyeless face.

"Would you like me to give you a drink?' she asked, offering the glass she held in both hands.

"Not now," Willim declared, lost in thought.

"Do you want me to kill the priestess?" Facet asked suddenly. "I failed you once at that task, but I would not fail again."

"No, of course you wouldn't," the wizard snapped. "Not when I have imprisoned her in a cage and stolen her most precious possession and most powerful weapon. But I do not want her slain, not yet. You see, I have a use for her. It pleases me to keep her alive."

"What use?" Gretchan demanded, realizing that Facet had asked the same question at the same time.

Willim seemed to find the echoing duet amusing, for he threw back his head and laughed aloud.

"Very well," he said. "I'll answer your questions." He planted his fists on his hips, and turned his scarred, stitched visage toward Gretchan. "You, my dear priestess, are here to serve as bait. And this"—he nudged the Staff of Reorx with his toe—"might just be the weapon that can bring about the end of our world."

———DH———

The plaza of Norbardin was, if not crowded, at least populated with some evidence of commerce and celebration. A few vendors had taken advantage of Tarn's return to bring out their carts and set up stalls—acts that would have been risky under the lawless regime of Willim the Black since his leather-clad enforcers had a habit of plundering food and drink and other goods from honest merchants without feeling any obligation to pay for the same.

More than a few paying customers had emerged from the shattered city's silent quarters, gathering around the stalls, especially those selling food and drink, and discussing the stunning changes wrought in the city, and the kingdom, over the past few days. They had watched in awe as the Firespitter had spewed liquid hell into the gatehouse, and they had cheered as the Kayolin dwarves had stormed the ramparts and finally opened the great gates.

Then they had remained there, congregating in a festive mood as the Kayolin, and later Tharkadan, troops had vanished down the long tunnel of the Urkhan Road.

The impromptu gatherings were rudely shattered as General Darkstone's four columns burst from four different streets with perfect coordination. They ignored the ruined edifice of the royal palace, where some of the invading troops had set up stations, and raced right across the plaza, where the panicked citizenry immediately scattered toward the streets and buildings around the plaza's fringe.

The attackers moved with focus and speed, heading for the most important objective in all Thorbardin: the two Firespitters, currently being cleaned and reloaded just outside the gates of the roadway to the Urkhan Sea.

Chap Bitters was the first to reach one of the machines, which was defended by only a company of light infantry and its regular crew. The chief of that crew leaped down from his seat and pulled out a long sword, but the Theiwar captain stabbed him through the heart in the first instant of contact. The rest of Bitters's men swarmed around the base of the massive iron contraption. The crew tried to put up a spirited fight, but they had been taken by surprise and, thoroughly outnumbered, had no hope of resisting the attack.

Darkstone himself followed the column that attacked the second Firespitter. That one was farther away, and thus, its crew had a little more warning of the attack. A few brave dwarves started to move the huge machine into a pivot, trying vainly to bring it around to face the charging Theiwar, but it quickly became apparent that the thing was too ungainly for rapid redeployment. Witnessing the fate of the Kayolin dwarves who tried to defend the first Firespitter, the crew of the second then wisely abandoned the machine and sprinted through the gates leading toward the Urkhan Road.

A third column of Theiwar moved to screen off the palace, where a few dozen occupying troops, men wearing bright red shirts, had started to sortie from the gates. Faced by five hundred angry, steady veterans, those dwarves quickly fell back to the relative safety of the palace, piling benches, blocks of stone, and other obstacles in the gaping gateway.

"D'ye want us to clean out the rats in the palace?" one of his captains asked General Darkstone.

The Daergar commander shook his head. "No, I want to keep our force concentrated. See if you can find me a prisoner—I want to find out what the enemy's up to."

As the captain hurried to comply, Darkstone handed out assignments to other Theiwar, those who had experience with things such as smithing, steam fitting, and other trades; they were asked to study the Firespitters, to determine if they thought they could operate the lethal war machines. He made it very clear that he didn't expect them to respond in the negative.

Soon, one bleeding Hylar, his right arm half amputated by the blow of sword, was dragged up to Darkstone and roughly tossed to the ground before the general.

"Where is Tarn Bellowgranite?" demanded the Daergar commander.

In response, the prisoner spit a gob that narrowly missed Darkstone's boot.

THE FATE OF THORBARDIN

"Cut off his other arm!" barked the general, reaching down to brutally twist the wounded limb. His words and actions brought a scream from the stricken dwarf, and the fellow flopped onto his back, his face breaking out in a sheen of sweat.

"No!" cried the prisoner. "I'll tell you!"

"I thought you might," Darkstone acknowledged coldly. "Now speak quickly."

"He took his legion to the lake, down the Urkhan Road," the wounded Hylar explained in a burst. "A messenger came from the Kayolin dwarves—told him that there was a Theiwar garrison down there. They were said to be ambushing the Kayolins, and the king hurried to their assistance!"

"How amusing," Darkstone said, pleased with the news. "And what of the other roads?"

He knew that the East Road and West Road were two other tunnels, not so wide as the Urkhan Road there at the main gate, but parallel routes that connected the city to the lakeshore. He had sent units up all three roads when attacking the city some months earlier, as commander of Willim's forces during the civil war against Jungor Stonespringer.

"They haven't been explored, sir. Not that I've heard anyway."

"And the main body. The rest of those Kayolin scum? Where did they go?"

"They also marched down the Urkhan Road," the prisoner reported, looking helplessly around at his captors. "Brandon Bluestone is leading them against the Theiwar he heard were down there."

"Perfect!" Darkstone declared with a bark of laughter. Willim the Black's trap could not have worked better.

"Please, lord," said the prisoner, gasping in pain, swaying on his knees from the lack of blood. "Can you not find some treatment for my wound in return for the information I have provided?"

"Oh, you've earned a reward, all right," the general said contemptuously. He looked at the Theiwar swordsman standing behind the kneeling prisoner. "See that he doesn't feel any more pain," he ordered.

Darkstone turned to inspect his two iron-bellied prizes and was so entranced with their amazing potential that he didn't even hear the dwarf's head bounce off the stone floor.

——DH——

"That's the gate to Thorbardin!" Crystal Heathstone declared. "But it didn't look like this when we left!"

The hill dwarves, after a forced march of several days, had come up to the valley at the foot of Cloudseeker Peak. The column had swelled to some fifteen hundred warriors, all of them eager to have a crack at the land of their ancient mountain dwarf foes. Crystal, who had spent much of her life living in the undermountain kingdom, had led them on the shortest route to the gate. But as she gazed upward at the face of the mountain, she didn't even recognize the place.

A jagged crack scored its way down the mountainside, at least five hundred feet from top to bottom. The trail leading up to the gate still twisted along the lower slope of the peak then vanished into the shadow of the massive gap. From below, they couldn't see where the trail led, but they were hopeful that it would provide access; after all, they were passing through the debris of a large army camp, and there was no sign of Tarn Bellowgranite's force. They had to have gone *somewhere!*

"Let's go, then. This looks like the front door, or the back door, to Thorbardin," Slate declared.

"Yep!" Gus proclaimed loudly. "Let's go! Up to Thorbardin, fight wizard's dwarves!"

Crystal knelt and addressed the gully dwarf directly. "You're coming in there with us, Gus; you know you are. And we all know that you're very brave. But right now I'd like you to march at the back of our army until I'm sure what lies ahead. You can see how narrow the trail is, and well, we wouldn't want to take a chance on something happening to you."

"But—!"

"I'm afraid I must insist," Crystal said with a hitherto unnoticed—by Gus, at least—sternness.

Sulking, the Aghar and his two girlfriends slumped at the side of the road, watching the Neidar warriors push past. Slate Fireforge wasted no time in starting up the trail, leading the long column that was forced to narrow and squeeze along the precipitous pathway. Crystal followed close behind him, and the rest of the hill dwarves came after.

Marching two by two, the Neidar advanced up the steep trail, crossing back and forth on the switchbacks, the formation creeping like a long snake until the leaders reached the gap in the mountainside. Even from below, Gus perceived that the roadway continued into the cliff, as if the force that had smashed open the mountain had been controlled by some power that had made certain the blast would create a passage into Thorbardin.

So they entered the mountain kingdom and pressed on through the obvious detritus of battle and war. And the three gully dwarves, panting and puffing from the steep climb, hurried along behind.

---DH---

Brandon stood at the edge of the water. The Urkhan Road ended at a broad wharf with a series of docks where long, metal-hulled boats could be berthed. There were many boats there, his men had reported, but every one of them had been holed, and they all rested on the bottom of the shallow lake.

"Can they be repaired?" he asked.

"Aye, General," replied a captain of one of the scout companies, the dwarf whose men had been the first on the scene. "But it'll take a smithy with some metal plate and a good forge. And it'll take time. Do you want me to get started on that chore?"

"Make some preparations," he said absently. He didn't know that he needed boats, but considering that it was the end of the road for the Kayolin Army's advance, he wanted to be ready for the possibility.

All around him, troops of the entire Kayolin force, including both legions, stood at the edge of the water or lined the sides of the long, wide Urkhan Road. Looking around glumly at their fallen faces, Brandon was forced to accept the inescapable conclusion that he had been duped by the prisoners he and his men had interrogated.

At least half a dozen captured Theiwar had sworn that Willim the Black and his army had come down that road and intended to make a last stand before the lake. Yet his scouts had searched thoroughly as they advanced, and there was no sign of even a small company of Willim's troops, much less the bulk of his army. The prisoners had been lying.

"We've come on a wild goose chase," he admitted to Otaxx Shortbeard, who had been detached from service to the king in order to help Brandon seek his daughter. "I didn't really expect to find Willim or Gretchan here, but I can't believe there's nothing! No point to it at all."

"There must have been a point, though," the old campaigner suggested grimly. "Even if the purpose is not our own, we were sent here because someone wanted us here."

"Just to waste our time?" he wondered aloud. "That doesn't make sense."

"No, it doesn't," Otaxx agreed.

Fister Morewood, looking perplexed, came up to join them at the water's edge. "Not a damned sign of a Theiwar anywhere along this road," he reported. "Anything down here?"

"Not a bit," Brandon replied. "Where do we go from here?"

"I'm thinking we'd better get out of this road, this tunnel, before we get some unpleasant information," Morewood suggested.

"You're right," Brandon agreed. "Can you start the legions marching back to the plaza? I'll be along shortly. I want to study this lakeshore a little more."

"Sure thing," the legion commander agreed. "Just don't dawdle."

The Kayolin dwarf turned and started up the road, a grade that climbed gently away from the water. "All right, you lazy lugs!" he barked to the hundreds of Kayolin dwarves waiting within earshot. "Strap on your helmets and put down your flasks! We're marching back to the city. Now move out!"

Brandon couldn't help but smile at the good-natured grumbling of the weary soldiers who, nonetheless, began to follow orders and start back up the four-mile-long road they had just marched down.

But his good humor quickly vanished as he remembered Gretchan's predicament and considered the fact that he might have brought his men on a wasted mission.

Or was it a trap? He didn't see how it could be. Sure, the men on the road were vulnerable to attack from the city, but the Tharkadan Legion held the gatehouse and was maintaining a garrison in the square. No army could reach the Kayolin troops, not so long as Tarn Bellowgranite and his legion were posted astride that key route.

Otaxx seemed to be deeply troubled by his own thoughts. He kept looking out over the water, as if the mystery might be solved by something floating on the Urkhan Sea.

"I'm going to head back up to the city," Brandon said to the old campaigner. "But I'd like you to stay down here and keep an eye on things. Would you do that?"

"Yes, yes, of course," Shortbeard agreed. "Although this whole place smells like a gully dwarf latrine."

"I'll leave a company of scouts here as well. I'm going to ask some of these men to try and set up a smithy, see if they can start repairs on the boats. Can you supervise them?"

"Sure. Good luck to you, and I'll let you know if there's anything amiss."

"Thanks."

THE FATE OF THORBARDIN

Still Brandon didn't leave, not just yet. Instead, he found himself staring out over the water. Somewhere out there, he knew, was the rocky pile called the Isle of the Dead—once the site of the greatest city in all dwarvendom. He tried to spot it, but the lake was too big, the darkness too intense, for his vision to penetrate that far. Remembering tales of the Urkhan Sea as once it had been, before the Chaos War, he pictured glittering cities lining the rocky shore of the vast, underground lake, lights shining from thousands of windows. Boat traffic had been common back then, which explained the existence of wharves such as the one they stood on and the many others that were positioned all around the shore.

Of course, there was no commerce there anymore; there was not much of anything actually. It saddened him to think of that great age, when Thorbardin had flourished so, and to compare it to the sorry state of the nation as it currently existed. So much of it could be blamed on the Chaos War, he knew, and dwarves never hesitated to do that.

But much of the blame lies with us, ourselves.

He didn't like to admit that—no dwarf did—but he knew it was true.

Finally, Brandon's eyes alighted on the captain who had informed him about the boats, and he went over and told him to keep an eye on the wharf as well as set up a temporary forge to repair the boats. He was relieved, at least, that Otaxx would be there to oversee things. Something about that place made him think it needed watching.

Frustrated, melancholy, and very worried about his priestess, Brandon started up the road. He trudged wearily, feeling the hunger, the fatigue, the stultifying exhaustion of so many days of almost constant battle. The victories seemed like tiny, intangible things at such moments, while the challenges still facing him and his army seemed almost insurmountable.

Deeply wrapped in that gloom, he didn't even notice the commotion ahead of him, not until a breathless courier jogged into view. The dwarf's face was streaked with sweat, and even more alarming, he smelled of soot and fire.

"What is it?" demanded Brandon. "What's the news?"

"The Theiwar have attacked from the rear. They've captured the Firespitters, General," the dwarf reported. The veteran warrior's face was streaked with blood too, Brandon noticed once he saw him up close. The whites of his eyes were like two beacons shining from a murky night, and they shone with a message of real alarm.

"What about the Tharkadan Legion?" the Kayolin general demanded.

"They're right up here in the tunnel with us, sir. I hear they got the same reports we did, and the king didn't want to sit around picking his nose—no offense intended, sir—while we were busy killing Theiwar. So it's all of us, the whole of the Dwarf Home Army. The enemy has us trapped on this road. And they're pouring fire in from the high end!"

Twenty-One

Battle in the Balance

Crystal looked around in awe. She almost had to pinch herself to remember she was returning to the place that had been her home for most of her adult life. Beginning with the shattered ruin of the gatehouse, she had felt a growing apprehension. When she and Tarn had left Norbardin, the place had been a splendid tribute to her husband's wisdom and foresight, a truly great city that had risen from the terrible wreckage of the Chaos War. Moving through the smoky and soot-stained halls of what had once been an immaculate barracks and into the streets, though, she felt horror and dismay.

She barely recognized a thing.

"This is terrible," she whispered, half to herself and half to Slate Fireforge. "So much destruction . . . so much damage."

"All from the civil war, do you think?" asked the Neidar commander.

"It must be," she said, pointing to a row of houses, an entire block where the front walls had all been smashed inward. The dwellings revealed were empty, pathetic little cubicles, from which everything of value had long been removed; whatever remained was covered with a thick layer of dust. "That didn't happen in the last fortnight, certainly."

"No, it didn't." Slate pointed to a once-grand edifice, a broken structure rising at the end of the street they were on. It blocked their view of the central plaza, but from there they could see that the surrounding wall was shattered in many places, and the once-splendid building beyond the wall showed gaping holes in the roof. A crooked, shattered spire of a broken tower rising only a short distance beyond. "What was that?"

"That was Tarn's—was *our*—palace," she said in dismay. "It was a beautiful building, surrounded by ornate columns. That wall was high and straight, with a beautifully carved parapet surrounding it. We had colored banners hanging all along the rampart, with tall spires on the corners. There was a marketplace on each side of the palace, and the merchants thrived at all hours; there were always customers, of course. The palace gate was never closed, and people came and went with complete freedom."

She drew a breath, trying to stem the emotions, the grief and sadness, that threatened to choke her voice. In a moment she went on, retrieving the happy memories.

"And the keep—it had a high roof, supported by flying buttresses. It had a slate roof, not because it needed one, but because it looked so beautiful. Now it looks like it was smashed by a meteor shower."

The gaping hill dwarves continued to advance. They spotted a dwarf watching them from a niche in the broken wall. The fellow was wearing a bright red shirt, and he raised a crossbow as the front of the Neidar column drew close.

"Halt!" he ordered. "And name yourselves!"

"Or what?" Slate retorted belligerently. "You'll fire your lone arrow at nearly two thousand dwarves?"

"If the alternative is surrendering this palace to the enemies of King Bellowgranite, then yes, I will!" the sentry replied boldly.

"Then there is no need to shoot," Crystal said, stepping in front of Slate. "For I am the king's wife, and I bring a force of hill dwarves to aid him in his campaign."

"Hill dwarves? Here to help the king? Well, that's different, then—and some good news indeed. Come forward."

As the Neidar advanced, more than a hundred other dwarves, all wearing that distinctive red tunic, popped into view along the jagged top of the wall. Each wielded a heavy crossbow, and though the sentry held his at ease after Crystal spoke, it looked as if he would not have hesitated to let loose a lethal volley.

"Of course, I might have met you with more than a single arrow," the archer said with a twinkle in his eye.

Another dwarf in red, older and bearing himself with immense dignity, stepped through the gap in the wall to meet them. He was unarmed, saved for a short sword, but he had the unmistakable air of a warrior, a commander, about him.

"I'm General Watchler," he said, "of the Kayolin Army. Did you say you are here to assist the king's cause?"

"Yes!" Crystal said, sensing the tension in the general's question. "We see that the Tricolor Hammer did its job. But how fares the campaign against Willim the Black?"

DOUGLAS NILES

"Poorly, up until now," Watchler replied. "But you just might be the folks to turn the tide. Come here and let me show you what I mean."

---DH---

Gus was having a hard time keeping up, the hill dwarves were moving so quickly. He jogged along, chasing the last of the warriors, wishing he were up front close beside Crystal or Slate or someone who could stop and tell him what was going on. Maybe he really had toughened up, as Crystal had said, but climbing was *hard*. He didn't really understand why they had climbed up the steep trail and filed along the high ledge next to the deep, steep-walled crevasse.

He had followed loyally, though, as the Neidar army moved through a large, battered room that smelled of smoke and soot and blood. He had gaped at a huge stone door that had been shattered as if by a giant fist. He even spotted many bodies, wearing black leather armor, of dwarves who had apparently been crushed under the weight of the collapsing doors. Many other shapes, black and weirdly twisted like some kind of strange carvings, intrigued him until he looked closer, and with a yelp of alarm, he jumped away.

"Those things *bodies!*" he exclaimed, wondering what kind of horrible thing had happened to those dwarves that would make them look like half-burned firewood.

Still, he kept pushing forward, ignoring the fatigue and the cramps in his legs and knees that made him really want to sit down for a spell. Instead, he tried to keep the hill dwarves in view, realizing that they were

THE FATE OF THORBARDIN

constantly getting ahead of him and his two female tagalongs—very far ahead of them.

Next they had proceeded down a long tunnel, a roadway that descended from the mountain gateway toward an unknown destination, with the little Aghar, his legs and lungs pumping, plunging after the main body. It wasn't until the hill dwarves broke into a run and spilled out of the tunnel and Gus emerged after them into a wide cavern that he skidded to a stop and stared in surprise and wonder at the scene spread out before him.

It was the city! It was dotted with buildings, crossed with a regular network of streets. Some of the structures reached all the way to the ceiling, but enough of them were lower in height that he could see most of the way across the place. The roads were wide and straight, and one huge structure was in plain view; Gus recognized the former palace of King Jungor Stonespringer in the center of the city.

"Hey!" he cried in delight to no one in particular. "We got to Thorbardin! This big-time city! Called Norbardin!"

He watched the tail of the hill dwarf column as it vanished around a corner of the wide avenue before him. Looking over his shoulder, he spotted two tiny specks and decided it was a good time to sit and wait for his girls, who had fallen behind their hero and leader. Smugly he realized that he'd been able to outrun at least *them!*

There was a bench nearby, set up on a little balcony right where the road departed from the tunnel and entered the city proper. From there, a downward-sloping ramp provided a route to the city streets, but he didn't feel the need to go down there, not just yet.

Instead, he settled himself there with a sigh of comfortable pleasure. The place was higher than most of the buildings, and as such, it offered an excellent view of the subterranean cavern. At one point, it had been an outdoor serving area for a traveler's inn, though Gus noticed the door to the inn was spiked shut and, to judge from the dust over everything, the place hadn't been open for business for quite some time. Gus didn't mind, actually, since, from what he remembered of Thorbardin, if the inn had been open, either the proprietor or some of the customers would have, at the very least, picked up any gully dwarf who dared to sit down there and pitched him right back onto the street.

Or over the balcony, he reflected with a gulp, stepping up to the railing to see that the floor of the city proper was a very, very long way—at least two feet—below him. Certainly the fall was far enough to kill him, if he should be so careless as to stumble. He sat back down on the bench.

"Hey, you bluphsplunging doofar! Why you run away?" demanded Slooshy, finally catching him and coming to sit on one side of him.

A panting Berta came right behind and firmly sat on his other side. "Yeah! Berta wants come too!"

"You girls shut up now. Gus watching Thorbardin. Gus back home! You can stay, or you can go," he added pointedly. "Gus not care."

"Oh yeah? Well Berta not care neither! Berta goin' back to Patharkas!"

Slooshy snorted. "Not too soon, Berta go back Patharkas! Go now!"

But Gus wasn't listening. His eyes were drawn to a spectacular scene across the city. He saw billowing balls of flame and thick clouds of oily smoke rising into the air.

"Girls hush mouths!" he barked, his tone so unusually commanding that his two companions obeyed. "Look!" he said, pointing at the conflagration. "We watchin' the war!"

The three Aghar stared, open mouthed, as the scene unfolded.

The Neidar troops had formed into two wings, and somehow Gus understood, even without knowing the plan, that half the hill dwarves were commanded by Slate Fireforge, the other half by Axel Carbondale. The troops flowed around the shattered edifice of the palace, which Gus recognized as the place where, fortuitously—long, long past it seemed—he had found the Redstone.

And speaking of "red," he counted many soldiers wearing shirts of that same color and remembered that the red ones had come all the way from Kayolin. The two armies were fighting together, just like Crystal and Gretchan had wanted!

All his attention was on the Neidar as, with whoops of war that carried distantly, the two wings of the hill dwarf army broke into a charge and swept toward the gatehouse where the two fire-breathing machines were creating their oily, seething inferno.

The battle was on!

And the gully dwarves had perfect seats.

———DH———

General Darkstone paced along the wide platform atop Norbardin's main gatehouse. It was the same spot from which he had commanded Willim's first attack against the city during the civil war, when his offensive was directed against Norbardin itself. His orientation of battle was reversed, centered around the two Firespitters, with his men directing their destruction into the tightly constricted tunnel of the Urkhan Road.

"More fire!" he ordered when the crew operating one of the war machines seemed to be slowing down. "Bury them in flames!"

"I'm trying, General!" replied the Theiwar who operated the controls. He was still trying to master the fine mechanical points of the Firespitter, though he had done a good job with the initial onslaught. "The furnace has gone out. It needs to be rekindled!"

"Well, hop to it, man!" roared the general. "I want to smell Tarn Bellowgranite's beard toasting in the flames!"

"Aye, sir!" Theiwar frantically swarmed around the machine, some of them burning their hands on the hot metal as they tried to reload coal into the furnace dangling under the smoldering spout.

Darkstone watched in satisfaction as the second Firespitter, still operational, shot another plume of fire down the tunnel of the Urkhan Road. The enemy dwarves inside the tunnel had stopped screaming, for the time being, but he knew they were trapped—and, he hoped, doomed.

He still remembered the cold anger he'd felt upon finding his men burned to a crisp, incinerated by that cursed, unholy weapon. He had no regrets about using it upon its makers, though; in fact, it seemed a perfect fate for the fiends who had come up with the idea. And

THE FATE OF THORBARDIN

to think, the exiled king had been foolish enough to march his whole legion into Willim the Black's trap!

He looked down at the mouth of the roadway, where frantic Theiwar still swarmed over the disabled Firespitter. Two were shoveling coal into the hungry furnace, though in their haste they were dropping more of the fuel onto the ground than into the hopper. Another was twisting a dial on the side of the boiler then screamed as a searing blast of steam erupted from a vent to catch him full in the face. He fell, writhing and moaning, clutching his blistered cheeks, but another dwarf bravely stepped in, manipulated the valve, and cut off the flow of steam.

"When are you gonna have that thing ready?" the general demanded, feeling a stab of satisfaction as the crew chief glanced at him in alarm. "Fix it or I'll find someone else who can!"

He didn't hear the panicked soldier's reply. Someone else was running up the nearby stairs, calling for his attention. "General! We're attacked from behind! Look!"

"What?" he roared, turning to confront the messenger. He didn't need to ask for the alarm to be repeated, however, for the proof was plain to see in the vast plaza between the gatehouse and the shattered palace.

Two long lines of dwarves had appeared there, seemingly materializing out of nowhere. They were charging at a run, racing across the plaza, converging directly on the gatehouse and the Theiwar position.

"Who in blazes are they?" he asked incredulously as the messenger stopped before him and knelt.

"As incredible as it sounds, it would seem they're hill dwarves, sir. At least, that was the best guess of our scout, who got a look at their leather capes and their faces."

Darkstone hadn't seen a hill dwarf in more than twenty years, but he remembered the leathery skin, the weathered faces and hands that distinguished those clans who chose to live on the surface, the result of being exposed to aboveground weather. It was not a difficult identification to make, for there was no weather in Thorbardin.

But how had hill dwarves come to be there?

In the next instant, he threw back his shoulders, reassessing the situation. Things were not good, but they were not automatically disastrous. It didn't matter how the hill dwarves had come there; they were certainly there, and hostile, and that was all he needed to know.

"You men!" he roared to a group of companies preparing to charge down the Urkhan Road. "Turn around! We're being attacked from behind!"

Immediately the Theiwar reversed the direction of their advance, streaming out of the gatehouse, hurrying to form a line in the face of the onrushing hill dwarves. Darkstone could see at once that they wouldn't be enough to stem the tide; the attackers would sweep around both ends of their line, even if they managed to form up cohesively in time.

"Captain Bitters!" he roared, calling to the loyal officer who commanded his reserve, some five hundred well-rested, well-equipped Theiwar, all of them anxious for blood and vengeance. The reserve was only for emergencies, but they were in the midst of one, Darkstone decided.

Bitters, with his men, was waiting stolidly in the wide entry to the gatehouse. He looked up at his name, a grin spreading.

Darkstone pointed to the charging Neidar. "There's your enemy! Make 'em pay!"

"Aye, General!" cried the captain. With a few choice curses and many a well-placed kick, he got his unit turned around and sent his men streaming out of the gatehouse. Barely a minute later, they smashed into the wave of hill dwarves, and the general looked down at thousands of dwarves battling furiously in the fight of their lives.

Would the reserve be enough to win the day? Only time would tell.

——DH——

Brandon raced up the Urkhan Road, past long files of Kayolin dwarves who were waiting for orders, grimly resting along the sides of the avenue. There was no point in sending them forward, he knew; if the enemy shot the Firespitters down the tunnel, packing more troops near the gatehouse was only an invitation to slaughter.

His most urgent question—Why had the Tharkadan Legion followed the Kayolin dwarves onto the road?—could at last be addressed as he all but bumped into Tarn Bellowgranite, coming toward him barely a half mile down from the gatehouse.

"Sire!" Brandon gasped in astonishment. "What are you doing here?"

"I heard the Theiwar were down this road, that you'd been ambushed and suffered horrible losses!" the king declared defensively. "I moved the legion in here to support you!"

"You were tricked!" the Kayolin general snarled, forgetting in his fury any deference to his listener's royalty. "It was a trap!"

"Well, I know that now!" Tarn snapped back. "But what are we going to do about it?"

"I'm trying to figure that out right now," Brandon said, speaking through clenched teeth. "Sire, please. Wait here, and I'll see what the situation is up there!"

He left the chagrined monarch at a sprint and quickly found Fister Morewood. The stalwart captain was nursing a badly burned arm; the limb was bleeding through the gauze wrapped around it. Fister looked to the side in shame as Brandon approached.

"I'm sorry, sir," he began. "I thought the king—"

"I know," Brandon cut him off. "But what's happening?"

"The Theiwar came out of hiding in the city somewhere. They have seized the Firespitters and turned them against us. We lost a hundred men in the first attack and a hundred more when we tried to engage them. General, they have turned the whole road into a firestorm!"

Brandon grimaced. He could easily picture how the lethal weapons might control a narrow avenue such as the Urkhan Road; the enemy held the high ground after all and could pour the heavy, burning oil right down the throats of the trapped Dwarf Home Army. What could they do about it?

"The scouts, the men who climbed the ladders onto the burning balcony when we first stormed the gatehouse," Brandon blurted, thinking aloud. "They were wearing armor that resisted the fire and masks. There were more than a hundred of them, weren't there? Are they trapped in here with us?"

Fister's face twisted in shame and grief. "Aye, General, they are. Only, half of them perished in the first counterattack. Their suits protect them if they move into a hot area, but they can't withstand the direct force of a Firespitter's attack."

"All right. Still, they're the best hope we have. Lead me to their captain."

Five minutes later Brandon was speaking earnestly to a young Hylar, Dane Forestall. His unusual appearance was marked by very short hair, and a neatly trimmed beard—grooming that made perfect sense for one who might have to walk through fire.

"I have sixty men left, sir," the captain said, meeting Brandon's eyes. "Every one of us is willing to die for you and for the king. But what do you expect us to do?"

"First, you can give up one of those suits and a mask. I'd like to go with you," Brandon declared.

He waved away the captain's objections, and a few minutes later, after removing his metal breastplate and helmet, Brandon donned a bulky shirt of leather and a helm of the same material. There were gloves to match, though they were not exactly supple and, in fact, made his fingers resemble sausages. They just barely allowed him to grip his axe, but they would have to do. The mask, made of several layers of padded silk, he slid into place.

"All right," he said to Dane Forestall, his voice muffled a bit by the thick mask. "You and your men follow me. We're not going to charge right into the spout of the thing, but we've got to be ready to seize any chance."

Impressed by the general's courage and silent resolve, the men of Forestall's company fell into line behind Brandon. They moved forward, closer to the massive, open gates leading into the city, and soon thick, choking smoke surrounded them. Too many bodies to count lay in grisly fashion along the floor; they were men of the

Dwarf Home Army caught in the first lethal onslaught. The advancing warriors had to step around the charred, blackened corpses. Brandon's only spot of hope was the fact that the smoke was so thick that, perhaps, the enemy wouldn't see their approach until it was too late.

As they drew nearer to the wide portal, Brandon was puzzled to hear sounds of violent conflict. He heard a piercing scream, and the distinct clash of steel meeting steel. Peering ahead through the thinning murk, he saw the hulking, sinister bulk of the two Firespitters. Many dwarves swarmed around the bases of the machines, but through a gap in the smoke, he ascertained that neither crew chief's seat was occupied.

That meant they had an opening, maybe only a few seconds of opportunity, before the Firespitters could be used again.

"Charge!" he barked, raising his axe, the weapon feeling strange and unwieldy through the heavy gloves.

The dwarves of Forestall's company charged after him as Brandon rushed out of the gates. He homed in on a large, soot-stained Theiwar as the black-clad dwarf looked up in shock to see the Bluestone Axe plunging toward his forehead.

It was the last thing that dwarf would ever see.

Seconds later the Kayolin dwarves were swarming around the Firespitters.

Everywhere the Theiwar were beset by assailants, with sunburned troops clad in fur and leather shouting the name of Reorx as they chopped and slashed at the outnumbered defenders. The fresh recruits to the war seemed to be everywhere at once, killing and fighting with frenzied violence.

Hill dwarves!

THE FATE OF THORBARDIN

There was no time to wonder how hill dwarves had come to be there. Brandon grabbed one of his own soldiers by the arm. "Go back down the road. Tell Fister Morewood to make haste in this direction with everyone who can still walk. Go!"

As the messenger sprinted back into the tunnel, Brandon led the charge up one stairway at the side of the great gate. Two Theiwar tried to block his path, and they both fell to a single, wild sideways slash of the Bluestone Axe. But the clumsy gloves almost caused him to drop the weapon, so he paused just long enough to pull them off. At the same time he tore the hood and mask away from his face and, thus unencumbered, sprang higher up the stairs.

From somewhere he heard crazed shouting, the battle cries of a soldier bent on killing and destruction. Dimly, he realized that the sounds were pouring out of his own mouth.

At the top of the gate, Brandon found a brace of guards protecting an officer, and he knew he had cornered the enemy commander.

"General Darkstone!" one of the guards shouted. "Get to safety, sir. We'll handle this one!"

Those were his last words as the Bluestone Axe sliced a great gash sideways across his belly. Gore spilled from the wound as the Theiwar toppled. One of his comrades stepped up to meet the same fate.

"Ah," said the dwarf called General Darkstone. He nodded, knowingly, at the potent axe in Brandon's hands. "I believe you must be General Bluestone. It is fitting, is it not, that we should face each other?"

"It is fitting," Brandon agreed. He felt a stirring of respect for the Daergar who faced him with dignity and pride. But that respect wouldn't keep him from killing the dwarf if he had the chance.

He felt reasonably confident that Darkstone felt the same way.

The Daergar raised a sword, an ancient weapon with a silver blade and arcane scrollwork running up and down the metal. Like Brandon, he carried no shield. He settled into a fighter's crouch and sidestepped to move away from the stairs as the Kayolin general moved onto the high platform.

They were the only two dwarves up there; the other guards had fled. The parapet blocked any view of the fight from those on the plaza or within the gates, but plenty of other dwarf warriors, those on the gatehouse walls or in the two battle towers rising to either side, could see the combatants. Those witnesses, often engaged in their own desperate skirmishes, gradually put up their weapons; hill dwarves and Theiwar came to a gradual halt and stood side by side, watching the duel.

Brandon struck first, swinging the axe in roundhouse fashion from the right, the left, and the right again, advancing carefully with each attack. Darkstone fell back but grudgingly, moving just enough to stay beyond his opponent's reach. Suddenly, after Brandon's fourth swing, the Daergar struck back, stabbing with lightning quickness. Twisting his axe, the Kayolin dwarf parried the blow with the handle of his weapon. Then it was his turn to give ground, backing away from a series of stabs and chops, each one coming fast.

When he had retreated almost to the top of the stairs, he paused, flexed his knees, and charged again, wielding the axe with short, controlled chops. Darkstone didn't retreat, and for ten seconds, the two commanders met in a furious clash of steel. The Bluestone Axe slammed against the Daergar's blade, but that was no mortal weapon; it withstood the blow. Brandon's weapon stung in his hands. Darkstone met the same result, a slashing blow ringing off the flat of the axe blade, sending him stumbling backward.

For a moment each dwarf paused, breathing hard, trying to catch his wind. Brandon used the back of his bare hand to wipe the sweat from his eyes while Darkstone pinched the bridge of his nose, shaking his head as if to clear it. Then they were at it again, swinging overhand, chopping and stabbing, dancing away from each other, then charging in with a succession of aggressive blows.

Brandon's hands stung, and sweat once more streamed into his eyes. He danced away to the side, feinting to the right then hopping to the left and coming in with another series of hacking blows. Darkstone pivoted, desperately blocking those attacks and circling away so he was the one with his back to the stairs. He lunged, sword point extended, his lead foot stomping heavily; then he repeated the attack, forcing Brandon backward with each thrust.

The Kayolin dwarf sensed the parapet's nearness, and he once again slipped to the side. But he'd miscalculated, misjudging the whereabouts of one of the dead guards, the man he'd cut down on his first charge. His foot slipped in the man's blood, and there was an audible gasp from the watching dwarves as Brandon fell heavily onto his back.

Darkstone wasted no time in capitalizing on the error, leaping forward and driving his sword down, its keen tip plunging toward Brandon's chest. But the prone dwarf rolled away with a speed he didn't know he possessed, and the metal tip of Darkstone's sword clanged loudly off the flagstone platform.

His axe was badly out of position, but his feet weren't. Brandon made a sweeping, sideways kick and knocked his foe's legs out from under him. Darkstone went down with a thud as Brandon swiveled into a sitting position, holding his axe in both hands. He brought the weapon over his head while the Daergar tried to parry.

But the Daergar commander misjudged the moment, and the Bluestone Axe came sweeping down, biting through flesh and bone. Darkstone grunted, dropping the sword from a nerveless hand, a hand that dangled by less than half of a wrist.

Brandon pulled his weapon free and sprang to his feet. His opponent, moving more slowly, hissing from the pain of his deep wound, also managed to stand. But the Daergar no longer had a weapon.

"Surrender, and you will live," Brandon declared, holding his axe at the ready.

Instead, Darkstone edged away until he was trapped at the edge of the parapet. There the Daergar leaped to the top of the rampart wall. He was fifty feet above the floor.

Then General Darkstone smiled, almost sadly, before offering Brandon a salute with his grisly, half-severed hand and toppling backward off the edge.

Twenty-Two

A Mistress Betrayed

Gretchan awakened from another restless sleep. She was sore from lying on the bars of the cage; the grid was broken irregularly by crags of rock that jutted upward. She sat up and leaned her back against the side of her prison, trying to be very silent as she looked around.

Not much had changed since the last time she had taken stock of her surroundings. She couldn't see any of the three wizards, though she didn't know if that meant that they were elsewhere or merely within some of the chambers that existed in the porous hilltop upon which she rested. More than once she had seen one or more of her captors duck behind a rock or stoop beneath an overhanging slab, disappearing into unseen spaces.

The case of potions and the bag of spellbooks had been placed within her view. She wished that her staff were nearby as well, but she had noticed, with alarm, that the wizard seemed to be almost obsessed with the artifact of Reorx, and she suspected that it meant far more to him than merely the talisman of his powerful captive.

DOUGLAS NILES

What did he want it for? Why did it fascinate him so much?

It had not been long since she had watched as Sadie had descended from the hilltop and vanished into an unseen opening on one side. An hour later, she had reappeared on the other side of the crest. While it was always possible that the crone had teleported herself from one place to the other, it seemed more likely to Gretchan that her sojourn indicated the existence of a network of connecting passages, with an unknown number of entrances, leading to an unfathomable complex of rooms, corridors, and compartments.

She knew that Sadie had placed the bell jar somewhere that wasn't out there on the surface of the hilltop, for the priestess hadn't seen that container and its precious blue spark since the elder apprentice had first arrived with it. It was odd to think of that aimlessly drifting spot of light as a living thing, but Gretchan had no doubt that Sadie had been speaking the truth when she talked about it being Peat, her husband. Not for the first time, she wondered what Sadie and Peat had done to provoke Willim's wrath.

A soft footstep scuffed on the rocks behind her, and Gretchan twisted around to see Facet approaching. The younger apprentice was alone, climbing the rough surface of the hill with her black robe swirling around her. Her light eyes were fastened upon the priestess; her face was devoid of emotion.

"Hello," Gretchan said as cheerfully as she could. "What's going on out there today?"

Facet didn't answer and as she continued her silent, purposeful approach, Gretchan felt a growing prickle of alarm.

"What's wrong?" she asked. "Where are Willim and Sadie?"

It was odd to think that the wizard's presence might make her feel safer, but the more she studied the young apprentice's ice-cold expression, with her glacially pale face and frigid, darting eyes, the more worried she became.

"You would steal him from me, wouldn't you?" Facet suddenly declared, her tone slicing like a blade.

"I don't know what you mean!" Gretchan protested, though of course she did suspect Facet's jealousy.

"Oh, yes, you do," Facet declared. "You would supplant me—with your golden hair, your lush figure . . . your eyes! You would make him forget, abandon me!"

"I would not!" Gretchan argued. "He's—"

She was about to say how much Willim disgusted her, how grotesque she found him to be. Yet she knew that was the wrong tactic to take in that particular argument. "I can see that he's too much in love with you," she found herself saying.

"He doesn't love me!" Facet replied scornfully. "He doesn't love anybody! But he needs me! He has to have me!"

"Yes, you're right. Love . . . love is hard for him. But he does need you. You should never think that I could take your place!"

"No, you won't. You will never take my place."

Abruptly Facet raised her hand and pointed a finger at Gretchan. She spat the command of a powerful spell, and a bolt of lightning burst from her flesh, crackling and sizzling toward the cleric like a living, hungry thing.

The blast of electricity struck the bars of the cage, and Gretchan felt the blow in the pit of her stomach.

She screamed and fell down, watching in horror as a cascade of sparks illuminated the metal grid, causing the bars to glow so brightly, she had to cover her eyes.

But when the sizzling stopped, the cleric sat up again, realizing that she was unharmed.

"How did you do that?" Facet demanded, taking a step closer.

How, indeed? Gretchan hadn't done anything, though she didn't think it was wise to admit that, not at the moment. Then a thought occurred to her.

The cage! Willim had told her that the bars themselves were enchanted by his power, infused with traps that would prevent her from escaping. Was it possible that the same sorcery would block the spells of an external attacker?

She didn't get a chance to pursue that train of thought as more magic crackled in the air. Two more figures appeared, and Gretchan saw that Willim and Sadie had arrived.

The black wizard did not look pleased. He sniffed the air, no doubt detecting the lingering smell of ozone, and rounded on his young apprentice.

"What are you doing?" he demanded.

"She—she was trying to escape!" Facet declared, pointing at Gretchan. "I used magic to stop her!"

"That's a lie!" the cleric protested. "She was trying to kill me!"

"You be quiet," Willim commanded, and Gretchan could only obey. She feared his power too much to argue. At the same time, she was fascinated to see what he would do about his apprentice's disobedience.

"Here, my master," said Facet. "Let me soothe you. Have a drink of wine! I saved it for you!"

THE FATE OF THORBARDIN

She produced a flask from within a pocket of her robe and stepped forward, tentatively offering it to the black wizard.

"You do seem to know when I have a thirst," Willim acknowledged approvingly. "It seems you understand *all* of my needs, my pet."

"Perhaps you should have a closer look at that drink, my lord," Sadie interjected coldly, keeping her eyes fixed upon Facet.

"No!" cried the younger woman, immediately pulling the flask to herself. "Don't listen to her!" Even as she protested, her eyes widened in horror, and Willim the Black put a pensive finger to his lips.

"Why, Sadie," the wizard asked calmly but intrigued, "what do you mean?"

"I mean just what I say, Master. Perhaps you would wish to examine the drink she offers you."

"There really is no need, is there?" Willim said, addressing Facet.

"No, Master," she returned miserably. "There is no need."

The black wizard sighed, a sound that seemed to mock and rebuke Facet. "I have taught you so much, and I have trusted you," he said to the beautiful apprentice. "I have given you understanding of my power. I have given you access . . . to my potion cabinet. Haven't I?"

"Yes, Master," Facet replied in a whisper.

"Such power to be found there, in those potions. The power of flight, of invisibility . . . you could have tried to poison me with my own potion if you'd wanted to. Couldn't you?"

"I would never poison you, never harm you, Master. Surely you must know that!"

"Oh, I do. I do. You could never harm me. Just as you could never deceive me."

"Nor would I try, Master!" croaked the terrified Theiwar female.

"But you did!" Willim pointed out with a great air of wounded feelings. "You have deceived me for a long time. Do you think I didn't notice that I had less charm potion in my cabinet than I should have? Do you think I don't know what that potion has been used for, these years—these too-short years—that you have served me?"

Facet sobbed and dropped to her knees, covering her face, which was even more pale than its usual alabaster whiteness, with her hands.

"For you see, my dear apprentice, my charm potion doesn't work on me. I let you believe that it did, for it amused me to know your treachery. It amused me to let you please me, to serve me . . ."

"Please, Master! I will serve you faithfully! Punish me; I deserve it! Let me please you as only I can do."

"Oh, there are many who can please me the way you do. You were an amusing diversion, a tempting morsel, for a time. But I am through with you now."

Facet groaned piteously. Gretchan watched in horror, her own stomach twisting into a knot. Despite her situation, she felt a powerful sympathy for the young woman and a frustrating knowledge that there was nothing she could do to help her.

"I wish I didn't have to do this," Willim said softly. "I really do."

Then he snapped his fingers, the sound as harsh as the crack of a dry pine branch. Facet toppled backward, gagging, clawing at her neck with her hands, her crimson fingernails. She struggled and thrashed, groping as if

THE FATE OF THORBARDIN

trying to pull a noose away from herself. She scratched so desperately that she cut her skin, left her beautiful, ice-white throat slashed and bleeding.

But there was no succor there. Her face, so pale a moment earlier, grew red, bright red from the concentration of blood. Her tongue protruded, swelling grotesquely, and her eyes bulged from their sockets, staring wildly, seeing nothing.

Facet rolled on the ground, kicking her feet, arching her back. She made no sound as she thrashed and struggled, trying to pull away from the invisible thing that was choking her.

But there was no noose there, no physical thing that she could pull away, to relieve the suffocating pressure, to give her the freedom to breathe again.

There was only the wizard's dark, lethal magic.

And soon its work was done.

———DH———

The very public suicide of General Blade Darkstone sapped the fight out of those few of his soldiers who had survived the ferocious wave of the hill dwarf onslaught. Perhaps because they had fewer immediate grudges and scars from their brief but decisive participation in the campaign to reclaim Thorbardin, the Neidar—unlike the vengeance-minded mountain dwarves—actually accepted the Theiwar as prisoners. Many who had served in Willim the Black's force surrendered to the new regime.

That regime, in the person of Tarn Bellowgranite, emerged from the Urkhan Road in the wake of the victory to find soldiers of his own Tharkadan Legion, the Kayolin Army, and the hill dwarves celebrating wildly in the great plaza of Norbardin.

An exhausted Brandon Bluestone, still numbed from his ferocious fight with Darkstone, was trudging down the steps from the gatehouse platform when he encountered the king.

"What happened?" Tarn Bellowgranite asked rather plaintively. He looked around grimly, seeing the sooty residue of the Firespitter attack and the hundreds of charred or bloody corpses scattered in every direction.

"We—you, me, our whole army—was saved by a counterattack by the hill dwarves," Brandon informed him sharply. "Somehow, they decided it would be a good idea to honor the treaty that they signed, even though their allies didn't ask them for help. Apparently they aren't as stubborn as some of our people."

Tarn's face flushed—with shame, not anger. "They came out of the hills, even after I refused to ask for their help?" he asked in wonder.

"Let's go find out; there's Slate Fireforge," Brandon said, feeling little warmth for Tarn at the moment. "And unless I'm mistaken, there's the woman who used to be your queen."

Indeed, the Hillhome commander and Crystal Heathstone, together with Axel Carbondale, General Watchler, and Mason Axeblade, were exchanging weary embraces in the very shadow of the gatehouse. Beyond them and to both sides, the victorious dwarves of the Dwarf Home Army and the Neidar of the hills were rolling out kegs of ale and spirits, cracking them open with axes—there was no time to use a proper tapper— and dipping in with mugs, bowls, helmets, and any other containers they could find.

Many of the citizens of Norbardin, too, were emerging from the side streets, cautiously poking out of the apartments and houses that ringed the square, and coming forward with greater and greater enthusiasm to join the growing celebration.

"I . . . I need to talk to Crystal. To all of them," Tarn said, making to excuse himself.

"Yes, you do. And I'm coming along," Brandon said firmly.

Side by side, they approached the other commanders, who looked up with varying measures of satisfaction, suspicion, and joy as they recognized the former and finally restored king.

"Crystal . . ." Tarn began nervously. "And Slate, Axel . . . there are no proper words to thank you enough for what you have done, in spite of my stubbornness, my foolishness. My mistake, my upholding of an old prejudice over a new alliance, almost doomed us. And you were wise enough to see through my error and to have come anyway."

"You can start by thanking your wife," Slate began. He tried to appear stern and angry, but a smile of delight and victory kept forcing its way through the tangle of his beard. "She makes a fine recruiter! And just to hear you apologize and to see your face as you came out of that tunnel—why, that made the whole thing worthwhile!"

"And you can thank a gully dwarf," Crystal said, "or I never would have made it to Hillhome." To Tarn's puzzled expression, she merely replied. "It's a long story. I'll tell you about it . . . later. But you shouldn't be surprised to know the gully dwarf is Gus Fishbiter."

"Gus?" It was Brandon's turn to be freshly amazed. "He's here with you? He sure does have a knack for being in the right place when he needs to be."

Crystal's noble and beautiful features were still tinged with sadness. Tarn took another step toward her, raising his hands tentatively. "Can you ever forgive me?" he asked.

She joined him in an embrace, her eyes wet with tears and her face still drawn with melancholy. "I don't know that I should," she said frankly. "But thanks to Slate and Brandon and all these brave dwarves, at least I'll have a chance to try."

"Where is Gus anyway?" asked Brandon.

Crystal opened her mouth to reply when suddenly she looked around then regarded Brandon with an expression of deep concern. "Wait, where's Gretchan?" she asked.

"Gone," he replied grimly. "Taken by the wizard. Still alive but captive, so far as we know. But to be honest, we don't know where she or Willim the Black are."

"Then there's still work to be done," the former and future queen acknowledged.

"General Bluestone!" It was a breathless messenger, red-faced and panting from exertion. He hailed them from the direction of the Urkhan Road as he raced closer.

"Yes! What is it?"

"I bring a message from Otaxx Shortbeard. He says you must come at once! He told me that he thinks he knows where she is!"

———DH———

THE FATE OF THORBARDIN

Tor and Kondike made their way along a lofty ridge, looking down at the valley so far below. They could see a narrow track twisting through marshy meadows before vanishing into a small grove of pines. The young dwarf wasn't even sure if that was the route to Thorbardin; for too long, he had been traversing the alpine meadows, always working his way higher and higher. Plus, it seemed that a road followed by an army, especially one hauling machines like the Firespitters, would have to be more obvious than that.

Yet he was not displeased to think that he had drifted farther and farther from the path followed by the Dwarf Home Army. He was enjoying the solitude and the wilderness. It made him happy to be by himself, with only the big dog for company. He loved the heights, the mountains and glaciers and secluded lakes and groves.

He was a mountain dwarf, after all, but he was a hill dwarf too. He might find himself at home under the mountains, but he felt equally at home under the sky. He couldn't even recall life in the subterranean realm—he'd been barely one year old when his mother and father had been exiled from Thorbardin—but he wasn't sure he'd ever want to go back to living in a place where one never saw the sun, never felt the rain or the wind or the snow on his face. There was no place that he felt happier than on those high slopes.

Having made his way south for many days, there was really only one destination that drew him on, and it was not a destination that lay under the mountain.

Oddly, the summit of Cloudseeker Peak seemed as far away as it had appeared three days earlier. Every time he thought they were getting closer to the peak, they'd stumbled upon a deep chasm blocking their path.

Going around obstacles, still climbing, he'd approach an elevation that he was certain would prove to be the top of the mountain. Eagerly he'd increase his pace, with the dog loping along, sometimes kicking up clots of snow from a glacier or skirting along the rim of a precipitous cliff, while the young Bellowgranite stayed on the crest of the ridge and drew ever closer to the top.

Except that whenever he reached that crest, he invariably discovered that it was a false summit. His position on the high ridge caused every next knob to look like the top of the mountain, but then there always seemed to be a higher knob a mile or two beyond. He continued onward and upward, and he was always fooled, but he loved the discovery of the new vista, the mystery of what lay beyond. He was determined to keep climbing.

Of course, he had enough experience in the mountains to know that it was dangerous to spend a night on the unprotected slopes, so each afternoon he and the dog would descend into a narrow valley, dropping down at least until they reached the tree line. There, amid scraggly cedars that were sometimes no taller than a grown dwarf, he would scrounge enough wood for a fire and kindle a blaze that would keep the two of them, if not warm, at least alive through another chilly night.

But when the sun came up the next morning, the young dwarf felt anew the allure, the purity, the summons of the mountain heights. Always accompanied by the black dog, he'd once again set out to climb some sloping, but still steep, shoulder of the great mountains until, one more time, he crested a hopeful ridge and set his sights toward the distant summit that, he was certain, could only be the very top of the world.

THE FATE OF THORBARDIN

―――DH―――

Brandon ran down the Urkhan Road, reaching the lake as soon as he could. He was out of breath, panting and sweating, but he found Otaxx Shortbeard standing at the wharf beside the water, staring out over the darkened sea.

"What is it?" the Kayolin general gasped. "I got your message; the courier said it was urgent, so I came as fast as I could."

"Out there," the elderly soldier pointed. "I was looking across the water, barely more than an hour ago. And I saw ... something."

"What?" demanded Brandon. "What did you see?"

"It was a flash of light, very brief. But bright, explosive even. Like a flash of lightning in the darkness."

"It must have been magic!" Brandon said excitedly. "There can't be real lightning in Thorbardin."

"Aye, and more than that ... revealed in the glow, if my old eyes aren't deceiving me, I think I saw a cage!"

"Gretchan!" Brandon was certain that there could be no other explanation.

"I can only hope so," said the old dwarf. "But yes, I believe it was a cage like the one that held my daughter when last we saw her on the palace tower. It was too far away and fleeting to see if anything, or anyone, was inside the cage. But I thought you should know."

"Yes! It has to be her! Of course, it makes sense that the wizard would take her to the Isle of the Dead. It's a perfect place for him to hide, to watch, to observe what's happening in the kingdom!"

"I am thinking the same thing," replied Otaxx. "I thought you would want to go there as soon as possible."

"Yes, of course!" Brandon's mind whirled through the possibilities. "A boat! I need a boat!"

"Yes, we need a boat," Otaxx replied. "For I intend to go with you. And as for a watercraft . . ."

He pointed down and Brandon saw a sleek metal hull lashed to the dock at his feet. Unlike all the other boats, it seemed whole and was floating.

"The smith has been working hard. He's been making patches, and he welded one onto the hull of this watercraft just a few minutes ago."

"Then let's go at once!"

"I thought you would say that," the old warrior agreed. "I have here two oars and leather rags to muffle the oarlocks. It seems we would be wise to row as silently as possible."

"Certainly, yes. Good thinking." Brandon said.

In another minute, they slipped away from the shoreline at the end of the Urkhan Road. Brandon stroked the oars while Otaxx sat in the bow, trying to peer through the darkness, staring toward their destination.

---DH---

Willim the Black approached Gretchan, but her eyes were not on the wizard; they were fixed on the precious artifact he carried in his hands. He had hidden the Staff of Reorx away some time earlier, and she had wrestled with despair at the thought that, somehow, he had figured out a way to destroy it.

But there it was, still intact, resting in both of his hands as he casually swung it around before him. He stopped a dozen paces away from the cage, his eyeless face turned toward the priestess.

"I have lost the war," he announced bluntly. "My army has failed me. My general has killed himself, to save me the bother. I am no longer the king in this place."

Though his comments were the first good news she had heard in the long days of captivity, Gretchan refrained from making any comment. Instead, she watched him warily, sensing that he had not come there merely to explain that his life was over. Indeed, he did not sound even vaguely disappointed. His mood seemed, almost, weirdly upbeat.

But he waited before saying anything else, seeming to be very patient, and finally she could contain her curiosity no longer. "What are you going to do, then?" she asked.

To her surprise, he giggled.

"What's funny?" she probed. "Didn't you just tell me that all your plans have ended in failure?"

"I said no such thing!" he declared, seeming to enjoy the verbal jousting. "I merely said that I lost the war, that I have no troops to command. But I don't need troops, and I don't need a throne. In fact, both have proved far more trouble than they are worth."

"Are you leaving here, then?" Gretchan asked, not daring to hope that he'd answer in the affirmative.

"Well, you might say that," he replied with a brief, private chuckle.

"Where's Sadie?" the priestess demanded, looking around, realizing suddenly that the elder female wizard had vanished. "Did you kill her, just like you killed Facet?"

Like you're going to kill me? She couldn't suppress the terrible thought, though she didn't speak it aloud. She shivered, wondering if her life would end the way Facet's had.

Strangely, the grotesque face of the wizard twisted into a wounded expression. "Of course not!" he replied. "I need her!"

Gretchan saw, however, that he spoke the truth, for just then Sadie appeared behind him, climbing up toward the cage that remained where it had been placed on the rocky summit. The cleric saw that the elderly wizard carried the bell jar in her arms, a fact that apparently took Willim by surprise, for he turned around with a frown and confronted her with a question.

"Why are you bringing that silly thing up here?" he demanded.

"Because you need more than just me. You need two of us! I want you to free Peat from this spell."

"You *want* me to?" Willim sounded incredulous.

"Well, of course, that is what I said," Sadie replied firmly, refusing to back down. "It's because I think you need him to be free as well. He can stay here and keep an eye on the priestess while you and I go and do what else needs to be done."

Gretchan listened to the conversation with a growing sense of unease. The two wizards were talking almost as though they had forgotten about her presence, so she wasn't about to interrupt and remind them. Instead, she watched and listened warily.

Strangely, the wizard seemed to be pondering his assistant's suggestion. "Very well," he said finally. "You're right. It will be easier to coordinate the casting with three, rather than two."

He gestured. "Put the jar down. Tip it over, off its base."

Sadie did so but then hesitated, giving the wizard a penetrating look. Finally, she backed away. The blue spark hovered near the jar, drifting toward Sadie, then floating back to the base of the jar, apparently unwilling to leave its safe confines.

Willim gestured and snarled the command, a sound like the growl of an angry animal, to a spell. Magic shimmered in the air, and Gretchan felt the powerful sorcery as a pulse deep in her belly.

Instantly, the blue spark disappeared, and an old Theiwar dwarf, stooped and balding and looking around in startled fright, stood there. His blinking eyes fastened upon his wife, and he croaked out her name.

"Sadie!"

"Peat!" she replied.

Hobbling awkwardly, like someone who hadn't used his legs or the rest of his body for a very long time, he made his way over to her and, for a second, the pair embraced.

"Thank you," Sadie said to Willim.

He snorted, whether in amusement or contempt the cleric couldn't tell.

Sadie nodded obeisantly to him, her chin firm. "Shall we make ready to go now?"

"Wait!" Gretchan protested. "Where are you going? And what do you want with my staff?"

Willim didn't face her, but his cold chuckle was the most sinister sound she had ever heard. "I am going many places," he said. He hoisted the rod with its anvil and the smooth shaft that the cleric knew so well.

"And as to this," he said. "You will see soon enough. It's a little surprise." He turned to Sadie. "Come," he said. "Let us go get the teeth."

———DH———

The prow of the boat nudged against the rocky shore of the island with a sound that seemed shockingly loud against the silence of the long, stealthy crossing. Brandon winced, certain they had announced their presence as surely as if they had come with a full complement of Kayolin drummers, but Otaxx merely tapped him on the shoulder, and together, gingerly, they climbed out of the boat.

They pulled the bow of the craft up out of the water far enough that it wouldn't drift away, resting it on a flat rock. Carefully they stored the oars inside.

Looking around, Brandon saw that they were on a barren shore. The Isle of the Dead was aptly named, he decided, for there was not so much as a flake of lichen or a slimy, clinging fungus to be seen.

The two dwarves communicated by sign language, wishing to avoid any excessive noisemaking. Otaxx drew his short sword and pointed up the slope leading directly away from the water. Brandon nodded and raised the Bluestone Axe, the handle held in both of his hands.

Side by side, the two dwarves started up the hill.

TWENTY-THREE

THE ISLE OF THE DEAD

The cleric was left alone with the old Theiwar male as Sadie and Willim disappeared into one of the passages below the hilltop.

"What happened to cause you and Sadie to get punished by Willim like that?" Gretchan said after she watched Peat look around in confusion then seat himself awkwardly on a flat rock nearby.

"Eh?" he replied as if surprised he could hear again. "Who are you again?" he asked. "Oh, I saw the master bring you into his lair. At least, I think I did. My eyes ain't too good."

"My name is Gretchan Pax. I'm a priestess—of Reorx. I'm a friend of Sadie's," she added, not certain if it was entirely the truth. But she could hope. "And no friend of Willim's. I know he trapped you in that jar. But why?"

"Er, that is . . . well, we just had a little scheme going. You know, to make some profit on the side. The thing is, Sadie always had a little bit of greed to her. She, um, borrowed one of his spells—a dimension door—and we used it to get dwarves out of Thorbardin. You know, those who wanted to leave . . . and who could pay."

Their discussion was interrupted by the return of Willim and Sadie, the two Theiwar climbing into view from just below the crest of the hill. They carried three conical objects, Sadie carrying one in both her hands, Willim carrying two, one in each hand, holding them by their narrow points. They set them on the ground, bases down and points up, and the cleric remembered that Willim had referred to them as "teeth."

Each was about a foot high and at least six inches wide at the base. They were not perfect cones, but rather they had a bit of a curve to them, so that although the bases rested flat, the sharply pointed tips curved slightly. They were as black as coal.

"What kind of teeth are those?" Gretchan asked, deciding she had nothing to lose by being curious.

"Dragon teeth, of course. But not the teeth of any mortal dragon." Willim the Black stood tall and all but beamed at her. Clearly, he was very proud of his rare treasures. "These are the teeth of a fire dragon, discovered by me after the Chaos War. Now, like their owner before them, they are about to change Thorbardin for all time."

Once again Willim picked up Gretchan's staff, and when he touched the wooden rod, she felt a stab of pain penetrate right through her chest.

"What are you doing?" she demanded angrily.

He chuckled. "To you, this pathetic stick is a symbol, perhaps even a tool, of your god. But to me, it is much, much more. You see, when you faced Gorathian and used the power of Reorx to defeat it, all of that power, that unspeakable, chaotic, destructive force, was absorbed by

THE FATE OF THORBARDIN

your staff, for it had no place else to go. If Reorx hadn't claimed it, it would have been unleashed in an explosion powerful enough to destroy the whole city. And of course your god—excuse me, *our* god—would never allow that to happen." He smirked and lifted the staff as he stepped over to the dragon teeth.

"But now," he explained. "I give that monstrous power back to its rightful owner—three of its rightful owners, to be more precise."

With that, he touched the butt of the staff to the tip of one of the teeth. Light flashed briefly, and Gretchan retched loudly, crippled by a sudden wave of nausea.

When Willim moved the staff away, the black tooth looked unchanged except for a faint reflection, like a glow that seemed to lie deep within it. The priestess, blinded by tears, watched him with dread.

Quickly he repeated the process with the other two teeth, each casting compounding Gretchan's agony by an order of magnitude. Finally, he handed the staff to Sadie. "Go put this away," he ordered. While she was gone, he removed two small bottles of potion from a pocket in his cloak. The crone returned a minute later, and the black wizard extended one of the bottles to her and handed the other to her husband.

"Now drink those," Willim ordered.

"What for?" Peat asked suspiciously, studying the murky liquid in the unlabeled bottle.

"Because we have a job to do, and you will have to be able to fly to do it. And if we do it quickly, this potion will even give you enough time to come back down to land safely before the enchantment wears off!"

Not surprisingly, neither of the elder Theiwar seemed inclined to argue with their evil master. Each pulled the stopper from his or her bottle and quickly quaffed the contents.

"Good," Willim said approvingly. "Now each of you take one of the teeth."

Again, they obeyed.

"Now we fly!" the black wizard declared. Clutching one of the teeth, he rose from the ground, slowly ascending higher and looking back to make sure his elderly assistants followed his instructions.

And so they did, each of them stooping awkwardly to pick up a tooth then using the magic of flight to rise from the hilltop. In another minute, the three magic-users had disappeared into the dark air, soaring far above the Urkhan Sea, rising quickly toward the ceiling of the large, domed cavern.

Left behind, Gretchen clutched herself, still in pain, and moaned.

———DH———

Acutely conscious of the need to work silently, Brandon raced as quickly as he could up the irregular surface of the steeply sloping hill. Nevertheless, since the Isle of the Dead was in reality simply a mound of loose rock that had piled up over the years as more and more stone had broken free from the ceiling of the Urkhan Sea's cavern, it was impossible to avoid sliding on gravel or kicking small boulders with almost every step. It seemed to him he was making a cacophony of sound, that each footstep certainly would attract the attention of the black wizard or one of his minions.

The need for haste overrode caution, however, and as the seconds ticked past, he moved faster and faster until

THE FATE OF THORBARDIN

he was sprinting madly upward, holding his axe in his right hand while he used the left to aid his balance. In places where the slope was unusually steep, he needed his free hand just to pull himself along, and he clawed and scrambled for height.

Otaxx Shortbeard climbed with him at first, but the old general lacked Brandon's speed and strength, and the Kayolin dwarf couldn't force himself to wait. He sprinted on, knowing that Otaxx would arrive at the summit as quickly as he could. Brandon's whole focus was on Gretchan, on the powerful, abiding hope that he would find her up above.

Finally he made out the crest, and as he came up to the lip there, he spotted the shape of a cage, silhouetted against the broader darkness beyond. He scrambled up the last distance, a sloping slab of intact rock that carried him right to the top of the hill.

His heart thudded as he spotted a dwarf maid in the cage. She was kneeling, with her back to him, and seemed to be staring upward into the vault of the cavern. There was not a sliver of doubt in Brandon's mind that the figure was Gretchan, but he was afraid to shout her name or otherwise attract her attention. Perhaps there was someone else, someone unfriendly, around.

Instead, he squatted at the lip of the slab, one hand braced on the top, while he allowed his breathing and heart rate to slow to normal levels. At the same time, he looked around carefully, eyeing the surrounding rocky landscape, looking for some sign of the black wizard.

When he saw nothing of his enemy and he could breathe normally again, he crept over the edge of the rock and moved toward the cage. His foot crunched into a patch of gravel, and the prisoner turned, gasping and pressing a hand to her mouth. The shining reflection of her eyes, full of love and terror, proved she recognized him, and he sprinted the last distance to the cage.

They embraced through the bars, both of them silently cursing the metal barrier that separated them. Brandon pressed his face close, inhaling the scent of her hair and her skin, as his hands clutched at her shoulders, her back, and he felt her own arms reaching as far as they could around him.

"Hurry!" she whispered. "The wizards are gone for now, but I don't know when they'll be back."

Brandon looked at the bars of the cage. They seemed to be made of steel, each as thick as his thumb and spaced only six inches or so apart. "Maybe I can smash them with my axe," he said hopefully.

She shook her head. "They're enchanted. And the noise would surely attract Willim's attention."

"What can I do, then?" he whispered, hoarse with frustration and despair.

"My staff!" she said. "It's down below, somewhere. If you can find it and bring it to me, I might be able to use the power of Reorx."

"Down below where?" he wondered, thinking of the whole massive, irregular surface of the island. There were thousands, probably millions of places where a rod of wood could be concealed.

"I think there's some kind of space hollowed out on the hilltop, not too far down," she told him, her voice whispering but urgent. "Like a network of caves or a series of rooms. There are at least two entrances, and I think he would keep it in there."

Once he was holding her, Brandon wanted nothing to do with leaving Gretchan alone again in her cage, but

THE FATE OF THORBARDIN

he could understand the rationale of her plan. "Your father came here with me; he's still climbing the hill. I'll have him help me look!"

"Yes, yes—but please, hurry!"

The Kayolin dwarf scuttled back to the edge of the hilltop and slipped off the crest. Otaxx was a dozen feet below, red faced and puffing, but still laboring upward. Quickly, Brandon told him what they were looking for. "You go around that way," he said. "I'll take the other direction. If you find an entrance, go inside and start looking."

The old Daewar nodded and immediately moved off to the left on a lateral search. Brandon went the opposite way, dropping down to peer under an overhanging boulder, scrambling sideways and up to investigate a shadowy niche.

In only a few minutes, miraculously, he found it: a flat, smooth floor beneath a square mantel of doorway. Without hesitation, he plunged into the dark space. His eyes, already attuned to the almost lightless vault of the Urkhan Sea, quickly adjusted, and he saw that there were several arched corridors leading out of the entryway.

Which way? He almost groaned but then he felt a conviction, a thought insinuating itself into his subconscious: go to the right! He obeyed the instinct and found himself in a small room. Next to one wall was an array of scrolls and books scattered across the floor. It was not there, but he spun around and saw what he sought almost immediately.

The Staff of Reorx leaned against the wall in a niche between two stones. Quickly Brandon grabbed it and raced back outside. Holding the shaft in one hand

and his axe in the other, he picked his way carefully back up to the summit. He saw Gretchan watching for him with wide, perfect eyes. She gestured him toward her, and he broke into a run.

Then he heard something soaring through the air, something that was flying but didn't have any wings.

———DH———

Gus and his girls mingled as much as possible in the celebration currently sweeping across the great plaza of Norbardin. They couldn't locate any of their friends in the chaotic, frenzied throng, and naturally the strangers were less than enthusiastic about sharing their food and drink with mere gully dwarves, so in the end, the trio was forced to revert to time-honored Aghar tactics: stealth; theft; and speedy, panic-fueled flight.

Surprisingly, they were able to stick together (loosely speaking) and gather at the appointed meeting place, a niche under the palace wall, with an assortment of bread crusts; cheese rinds; one large, marinated mushroom; and several mugs that still had some tasty ale, not much tainted with backwash, sloshing in the bottom. There, relatively safe from discovery, they settled down to share, with no more than the usual bickering.

"Dwarf folk pretty happy," Slooshy said.

"Big party!" Berta agreed.

"Thorbardin always happy place," Gus intoned knowingly. "Lotsa big party here, alla day, every day."

"Gus bluphsplunging stoopar!" Berta retorted. "Last time come here, alla time killing and fire. Big dragon try to eat Berta!"

THE FATE OF THORBARDIN

"Yeah!" Slooshy remembered. "We runnin' from big, kill'em dwarf too. Wanna stick Slooshy and Gus with spear! No party, two times! Not dat day!"

In truth, Gus did have a vague memory of the events the two females were recalling. When he stopped to think about it, he also recalled being a prisoner in a cage in the black wizard's laboratory and running for his life from the Theiwar bounty hunters that stalked around the shore of the Urkhan Sea, looking for gully dwarves so they could kill them and cut off their heads. That was all pretty long past, he thought, scratching himself.

Then he remembered finding the Redstone, almost in that very spot. The fire dragon had tried to kill the old king, who had been holding it. Then he sneaked through the magical blue door in the old magic-users' shop. Those two Theiwar, Peat and Sadie had been their names, had sure been surprised when three gully dwarves came strolling into the back room of their little store! Gus still remembered his adroit duck and dodge as Sadie had hurled unmentionable things at him while he fled out the door.

"Ah, those was days," he sighed, leaning back on a jagged pile of bricks and sighing contentedly. Contented to a point, that was, until he remembered they had drained the last of their partial ale mugs.

"Hey," he said, kicking a bit of cheese out of Berta's hands. "Girls get Gus more beer. Who gets biggest glass get to rub Gus's feet!"

Surprisingly, that enticing bit of persuasion didn't result in any takers. Instead, the girls actually laughed at him and went right back to chewing. Gus sulked for a little while, listening as the celebration in the plaza grew ever more raucous. There were certainly two dwarves, and maybe two more, out there, whooping and singing and cheering the new king. Everyone seemed to want Tarn Bellowgranite to live a long time—at least, they kept yelling that he should do that.

Finally, Gus realized that if he were going to get more beer, he would have to do it himself. He'd had plenty to eat and drink already but wasn't so bloated that he couldn't move, so he pushed himself to his feet and climbed up over the lip of the hole where he had been hiding.

The plaza truly was a scene of chaos and delight. Large fires burned here and there, and dwarves were dancing and singing wildly. The Kayolin drummers were moving through the crowd, pounding out different beats, so the whole mingling of sound was a rousing thunder, a steady rumble that seemed to underscore the shared joy of the celebrating, liberated Thorbardin.

"Hey, Gus no sneak off!"

One of the girls—he didn't even bother to see which one—tugged at his right arm, and the other tugged at his left. He smiled contentedly, realizing that, at last, he had come back to where he belonged.

That thought triggered an even stronger one, a memory of a little house off of a sewer pipe, on the steep cliff face above the Urkhan Sea. He remembered the affectionate wallops his pap used to give him, the way his big brothers would always steal his food and his mam would kick him out of the house to find more. A tear surprised him by welling up in his eye, and he felt a strange urge, something he'd never known before.

"Come this way," he said, striding across the plaza, toward one of the tunnels leading down to the lake.

THE FATE OF THORBARDIN

Perhaps there was an unusual pleading tone in his voice, for his order was greeted with not bickering and argument, but meek compliance. The two females accompanied him, hurrying along in silence for a full two minutes, until Berta spoke.

"Where Gus goin'? Where we goin'?"

"This way," he said, pointing a stubby finger. "Gus going home!"

———DH———

Floating in the air, Willim admired his handiwork: he had taken one of the fire dragon's teeth and punched it into the solid rock in the vast ceiling of stone spanning the Urkhan Sea. It was almost invisible stuck there, except for the faint glow it emitted, the merest suggestion of the power lurking within that potent artifact.

Satisfied, he flew along under the ceiling, first to Sadie, who had done as he had instructed and sank her tooth into a different part of the ceiling, then to Peat, who had done the same thing. The three fire dragon teeth, each infused with the power stored within the Staff of Reorx—the power that once had been Gorathian—formed a triangle on the top of the cavern with equal sides nearly a quarter mile apart.

"Why are we doing this?" Peat whispered to Sadie, loudly enough for the black wizard to hear. The old female merely shrugged and pointed to her master. Willim had already determined that the two assistants didn't need to know the purpose of the exercise.

"Come—we fly back to the Isle of the Dead now," he said.

Their task completed, Willim, Sadie, and Peat glided downward on the wings of the flying spells that had borne them aloft—Willim through his own casting, and the two elderly Theiwar by dint of the potion he had given them to drink. The black wizard was satisfied that, soon enough, he would leave his mark on Thorbardin in a way that history would never forget.

He wondered for a moment where he would choose to go after his task was done. He didn't have a place in mind, but he knew that his power would carry him anywhere, allow him to become the master of any place he chose to reside. He considered, briefly, visiting the Tower of High Sorcery in Wayreth Forest. Willim the Black, together with Dalamar the Dark and a host of other wizards of all three orders, had been instrumental in reclaiming that enchanted spire from the powers of corruption that had seized it earlier in the Fifth Age.

But there were likely to be other wizards there, strangers, powerful wizards, and Willim was not inclined to share his time with the likes of them.

Perhaps he would go east. He'd heard that many changes were occurring there, including a new wave of minotaur invasion. That would surely result in some nicely chaotic circumstances, just the sort of thing that was appealing to Willim.

He saw the priestess, Gretchan Pax, gazing up at him as he swooped down to land on the hilltop. He smiled, admiring her beauty, and his emotions stirred with the kind of feeling Facet used to arouse in him. Perhaps, before he killed Gretchan, he would slake that lust, either against her will or with her magically compelled compliance.

THE FATE OF THORBARDIN

So intrigued was he by those prospects that he didn't notice the other dwarf until it was almost too late.

Bluestone! Where did he come from all of a sudden? The Kayolin dwarf was sprinting onto the hilltop, racing toward the cage. And he had Gretchan's staff!

"No!" barked the black wizard. He pointed his finger and launched a stream of magic missiles, sparkling darts that streaked unerringly at the Kayolin dwarf. The first one struck Brandon in the left shoulder, knocking him down. The staff tumbled from his fingers, falling—or was it thrown?—a dozen feet short of the cage.

Brandon twisted, crying out in pain. His left arm hung uselessly, the joint shattered, and he lay on his back with the Bluestone Axe across his chest. More and more of the magic missiles spewed from Willim's finger, sparking and sizzling as they struck him right in the heart. By the time Willim had settled to the ground, the spell was exhausted, but the Kayolin general had been smashed with more magical power than any mortal could survive.

Willim smiled as he landed, a hideous grimace creasing his features. Behind him, he heard Gretchan sobbing, her voice raw with grief.

"You think you are suffering now," he said to her. She looked up at him, hatred glaring from her moisture-shedding eyes.

"Just wait," he promised as he took a step toward the cage.

——DH——

Otaxx Shortbeard was gasping for breath. His chest felt as if it were being squeezed in a vice, and he could barely see. Damn his old age! He didn't have the endurance of a young child anymore.

Still, he pushed himself up the last bit of the hilltop, each breath rasping in his throat. The sound of his blood pulsing was a roar in his ears, and he shook his head, trying to clear his thoughts. Finally he clawed his way over the lip of the summit and pulled himself to his knees and finally to his feet.

The first thing he saw was Brandon Bluestone, lying on his back, his shoulder and chest shiny with blood. Then he saw the black wizard, advancing toward Gretchan, still trapped in the cage. She rose to her full height and spit at the Theiwar magic-user, and Otaxx wanted to rush to her, to stop her from antagonizing the brutal wizard.

But of course, it was too late. Willim raised his hands, reaching toward the cleric, and Gretchan gasped and fell, rolling on the ground as if she were being physically attacked, though the wizard stood several feet outside of the cage.

The scene was too much for the old general. He drew his short sword and lumbered forward as fast as his tired legs could carry him.

"You leave her alone, you bastard!" he cried. "You leave my daughter alone!"

Then the wizard turned that hideous face toward Otaxx, and he knew he was doomed.

———DH———

Sadie watched the old Daewar charge, and she knew that he was going to die, that Willim would kill him as certainly as he had killed Facet and Brandon . . . and would kill Gretchan Pax, and undoubtedly her and Peat after that, probably sooner rather than later.

The old woman felt a strange mix of emotions. Fatigue was high among them: it had been too long that she had known fear every minute, every day, every step she took, every breath she took. She looked to the side, where Peat had come to rest on the ground beside her, and recognized the same fear, the hopelessness, in his eyes.

He had just come back to her, less than an hour past, and it was all going to end. Even more powerful than fatigue was the crushing sadness: she had managed to get Willim to reverse the spell that had condemned him to the glass bell jar, but for what?

Only to die on the rocky hilltop. That place was all too appropriately named, she reflected bitterly.

The Isle of the Dead.

She looked again at Willim, who had driven the old Daewar onto his back with a blow from a force spell, like a powerful punch that required no physical contact on the wizard's part. The elderly dwarf, his face already reddened to an unhealthy degree, was grunting as the wizard's intangible blows swatted him back and forth. Willim was taking a long time to kill the old fellow, she realized. Probably he was enjoying it.

Gretchan was sobbing, tugging on the bars of her cage as if that would do any good. She called out to the Daewar, called him "Father" in a tone full of grief and heartache. Sadie actually felt sorry for her.

Only then did she notice the staff on the ground, lying very near her feet, where Brandon had dropped it when Willim's magic missile barrage had smashed him down. Sadie looked up again. The wizard was fully engaged in his gradual, deliberate murder. He was paying no attention to his elderly apprentice or to her equally elderly husband.

Slowly, not sure why she was doing it, Sadie reached down and picked up the Staff of Reorx. She caressed the smooth wood, which felt very nice and solid in her hands. And she noticed that the priestess had stopped crying.

Instead, Gretchan was looking at Sadie with wide, disbelieving eyes.

---DH---

Gretchan was almost blinded by grief. She could see Brandon's bloody, immobile form on the ground and was watching the black wizard pummel her father to death. Those two images were enough to make her want to blind herself, to tear out her eyes.

Then a strange calm possessed her, and her grief slowly dissipated.

She felt the presence of Reorx, a benign and comforting embrace, easing her despair, somehow even infusing her with a measure of hope.

It was then that she looked around, spotting Sadie a mere ten feet away. The old Theiwar woman was holding the sacred staff, looking at it in wonder. Perhaps she, too, felt the presence of Reorx, Master of the Forge, Father God of All Dwarves.

"Please!" Gretchan begged, her voice a hoarse croak. "Give me the staff!"

Sadie stared at her for what seemed like a lifetime but was perhaps only five seconds. Then she inched closer and extended the staff, anvil head first, and the cleric seized it as if it were a lifeline thrown to a drowning woman. She pulled the sacred artifact to her, clutched it to her breast, and spun around to locate the wizard.

Willim stood over her father's body, gloating. Then the wizard turned his eyeless face toward Gretchan, his expression distorted with fury.

"He died!" cried the wizard in a monstrous rage. "He died before I could kill—"

Abruptly he stopped, growing stiff and still. "Oh, your staff," he said calmly. "Do you think that will save you? It won't. But it will make your dying all that much sweeter . . . for me."

He took a step toward her, and she planted the butt of the rod on the ground and seized the middle with both hands. "Oh, mighty Reorx," she intoned. "Father God of All Dwarves! Free me from this unholy cage."

As the bars burst apart around her, Willim the Black took another step closer and raised his hands for the casting of yet another mighty, lethal spell.

———DH———

Brandon lay on the rocky ground, his body wracked with pain. This is what dying feels like, he thought. The Bluestone Axe he still held in his right hand, the only hand he could use as his left shoulder had been smashed to a bloody pulp by the wizard's deadly missiles.

At least they would have been deadly if the Kayolin dwarf hadn't been able to pull up his axe as he fell and use the wide, Reorx-blessed blade as a makeshift shield. The last dozen of Willim's bolts had blasted into the metal axe head and been absorbed there without inflicting further damage to their target.

Still, he was brutally wounded. It was all he could do to keep his eyes open, to watch the events swirl around him. He knew that Otaxx was dead; the old Daewar had sacrificed himself to distract the wizard's attention away from Brandon.

Then he had watched with numb disbelief as Sadie had snatched up the staff and handed it to Gretchan. He had seen the cage burst to pieces as the power of the god was made real. And he witnessed Willim, his back to Brandon, slowly advancing on Gretchan. The priestess did not seem to be afraid, but the Kayolin dwarf knew that neither could she hope to stand, to survive, in the face of the wizard's murderous rage.

Gasping from the pain, Brandon tried to move. His left arm was on fire, and his shoulder grated sickeningly as the broken bones shifted and twisted against each other. Somehow he managed to block out the agony, to use his right arm to push himself to a sitting position while he rested the axe in his lap. When next he looked up, Willim was only two steps away from Gretchan. She held her staff before her, as if to ward off the villainous wizard, but her power couldn't match his. With a single, sharp gesture, Willim the Black swept his hand to the side, and the staff was torn from Gretchan's hands. It went clattering helplessly onto the rocks of the hilltop.

The handle of the Bluestone Axe was in Brandon's hand. He hoisted that hand, pulled it back over his shoulder, and hurled the artifact with all his might, aiming for the middle of the black robe shrouding the back of the eyeless wizard.

The throw was true: The axe spiraled through the air and struck the wizard squarely between the shoulder blades. The keen edge sliced through the black robe, the withered skin, and the scrawny, scarred frame of its intended target. Willim tumbled onto his face with a gagging cry, clawing at the stony ground. He twisted, trying to reach the weapon that was killing him, but it was behind him, beyond the grasp of his fingers.

With one last croak of sound, he died.

In that death his body became fire, and the fire spumed into smoke. It rose from his corrupt flesh like a living thing, the manifest remnant of foul magic, consuming evil, and nearly absolute power. The smoke, thick and dark and acrid, exploded from the vanishing flesh, swirling and churning, gathering strength near the ground for a few moments.

Then it began to billow upward. The murky cloud rose quickly, surging and churning and climbing. As it spumed upward from the Isle of the Dead, it separated into three columns, and each column swelled higher, flying like a living creature, a dragon of smoke perhaps, roaring and churning toward the three dragon teeth embedded in the ceiling of Thorbardin.

Twenty-Four

A Tree Regrown

There is nothing that terrifies a population of underground-dwelling mountain dwarves as much as an earthquake. Nothing can rain death upon a cavern as soundly, as quickly, as thoroughly as a great convulsion that shakes the bedrock of the world and collapses structures and caverns and pillars and caves that have long been considered solid and permanent. The crushing weight of such a cave-in can mark a permanent and fatal end, not just to lives, but to houses, villages, cities, even whole nations of dwarves.

Thus, when the ground shivered underneath and rumbles of sound, louder than thunder and twice as violent, shot through the great plaza of Norbardin, the celebration of victory and the triumph of King Bellowgranite's return to the throne came to an immediate end. Cheers of laughter and hope, songs of delight and praise, all were replaced with cries of terror. The pounding of the drums ceased, though the loud percussion continued as rocks split free from the ceiling to crash into the streets and onto the buildings. Screams of pain replaced the sounds of revelry from one end of the city to the other.

The floor buckled and pitched underfoot. Dwarves who were dancing crazily lost their balance and tumbled to the ground. Youngsters screamed in fear, and elders shouted prayers or curses, depending on temperament. Everywhere dwarves dived for cover or fled, screaming, into the side streets or the imagined safety of sturdy buildings.

In the heart of the celebration, near the center of the great plaza, Tarn Bellowgranite wrapped his arms around his wife and bore her to the ground, protecting her body with his own. For a second he lay on top of her, heart pounding, eyes tightly closed as he waited for the lethal, crushing force of collapse.

But then the ground grew still again, and it seemed that the danger had passed.

"I appreciate the sentiment," the restored queen said, grunting for breath. "But if a ten-ton rock falls on you, I don't think you're going to offer much protection."

"Sorry," Tarn said, quickly rolling to the side. "But it's a quake—!"

"And your first instinct was to protect me," Crystal replied, not unkindly, as she sat up and brushed herself off. "I think that's marvelous. But doesn't it seem strange that there would be an earthquake now, of all times?"

Indeed, her voice had a calming effect on the king, and it seemed to have the same effect on the world itself. At least, after the initial shock, the ground seemed to have grown still, and the rumbling slowly faded into echoes.

"Could it be over already?" Tarn wondered, standing on shaky legs and helping his wife climb to her feet. "It seemed terribly abrupt and quick."

"I don't think that was a natural earthquake," Crystal said. "I'm rather more worried that it had something to do with the black wizard. I think we should investigate. Where can we go to get a look at what's happening?"

"The Urkhan Sea!" Tarn said, holding on to his wife rather more than was strictly necessary for safety's sake. Thankfully, the ground remained still, though the deep, thrumming rumble of unsettled bedrock continued to assault their ears, forcing them to shout just to be heard. "That's where Otaxx and Brandon were going. Maybe there."

"Let's go!" Crystal agreed.

---DH---

Gretchan knelt over Brandon's bloodied form and touched his shoulder, closing her eyes as she concentrated on a prayer of healing. Almost immediately she felt him twitch then heard him groan—at least, she thought she did, though the roar of the churning smoke consuming the wizard's body was all around, making it difficult to hear anything else.

Willim's corpse had disappeared, but the unholy murk still churned, and the three columns continued to spume upward, reaching all the way to the ceiling. Each of the pillars extended like a great, black tentacle, the whole resembling a three-taloned paw reaching upward from some monstrous being, claws extended to scrape the sky itself.

"It's the black wizard!" Sadie screamed. "He wants to bring all of Cloudseeker Peak down upon us! Look!"

That appeared to be the case. The cleric looked upward and saw that three great fires burned at the places where the smoke touched the top of the dome over the sea. They burned like cancerous sores, boring holes in the ceiling, eating away at the foundation of the rock, rotting the very roof over the mountain kingdom. They seemed to shed no heat, but they were terribly bright, casting a pale, sickeningly yellow light.

Tons of rocks were already breaking free, falling into the lake on three sides, breaking loose from each of the oozing sores on the upper dome of rock. The collapsing stone, some of it in the form of house-sized boulders, sent huge waves churning across the waters that had never been troubled by so much as a breath of wind.

In the glaring light of the unholy fires, it was possible to see to all sides of the great cavern, much as if the whole place had been thrown open to a noonday sun.

"Do something!" Sadie screamed while Peat dropped to his knees and covered his face with his frail, spotted hands.

Seeing that Brandon was sitting up, touching his healed shoulder in wonder even as he looked around at the monstrous scope of destruction, Gretchan rose to her feet and strode to the very summit of the Isle of the Dead, to the place where her cage had rested before the power of Reorx had blasted it asunder.

The priestess stood tall, resting the butt of her staff on the ground, and she leaned back to expose her face to the ceiling, to the blinding light of the infernal fires. Closing her eyes in concentration, clutching the rod of her sacred artifact in both hands, she raised her voice in a chant that pierced through even the thunderous chaos roaring through the chamber.

"O Father God of All Dwarves, Master of the Forge—hear my prayer!" cried the priestess. Her words echoed and resounded like a chorus of singing voices. The anvil on the tip of her staff glowed with a brilliance that outshone even the hellish fires on the dome overhead.

Suddenly, with a shocking lurch, the ground moved under her feet, and for an instant the cleric thought they were all doomed, that they were going to fall amid the rocks, tumble into the water, drown or be buried by the massive, cataclysmic collapse of the entire mountain range. But they were not falling. In fact, it was the lake that seemed to be going down and away from them as, with each passing second, the surface of the water appeared to recede farther and farther away.

Still, Gretchan kept her feet and sensed the movement as a steady, stable force. She held firm in her position upon the crest of the hill, with Brandon, Sadie, and Peat huddling nearby. It was clear to all by then that they were not falling.

Instead, they were being borne upward, lifted by the power of her immortal god.

——DH——

Tarn and Crystal led a mass procession of dwarves out of Norbardin and down the Urkhan Road. When they reached the terminus, at the shore of the sea, they found hundreds of dwarves already thronging there, staring out over the underground lake. Whispered word of their arrival spread, and the crowd parted to allow the king and queen to move down near the edge of the water, though none dared venture onto the wharf because it was steadily inundated by the fierce, unnatural waves that pounded against the shore.

At first, Tarn thought they were seeing a place exposed to daylight, and he wondered if the whole top of the mountain had been shorn away. Very quickly he determined that the brilliance came from three distinct fires, places where the rocky ceiling of the cavern was being consumed by a foul, yellow fire that seemed to cut right through the stone. The brilliance was intense and surreal, surrounded by thick and churning smoke. The smell of sulfur and brimstone was thick in the air, and he had a terrible flashing memory of the Chaos War, when the fires had been living things, a scourge of destruction sweeping through Thorbardin.

And in that light, he saw movement in the center of the lake. He wondered if it were a volcanic eruption, some kind of disaster that sent the Isle of the Dead exploding upward. For that was what they witnessed: a movement of solid ground, an upthrust of the rocky knob climbing away from the water, rising toward the ceiling of the massive cavern. It was the whole island, and it was moving upward, away from the lake and into the air.

But it was not an explosion, and it was not flying; it was a true, living growth. Solid rock supported the upper surface, like a shaft of green plant shooting upward to seek the sun. The rock continued to grow, emerging from the water, pushing higher and higher through the vault of the great cavern. The yellow fires on the ceiling smoked and smoldered in the face of such power, but those blazes were corrupt, and they were dying, as the rising stone pillar was genuine, no illusion, and it was pure.

The rocky, shattered island continued to be elevated into the air, borne upward by a massive pillar of rock that emerged from the lake, lifting it ever higher. Water gushed away from it in a steady cascade, a churning whitewash of foam and current. It spilled down the sides of the stone surface, and it churned and tossed around the base, radiating outward with the force of huge waves. The swells struck the shores of the sea and rolled back upon themselves until the whole surface of the water was tossed like a gale-swept ocean, waves colliding and crashing, spray flying, breakers smashing against the shore.

And the force that caused the storm was not a natural pillar of stone, the king realized, as more water spilled away from the exposed rock and the pillar continued to grow, rising hundreds of feet above the lake, with water draining away enough that the watchers could make out details. Dwarves began to mutter or pray or shout in reverence and awe. For they all knew they were witnessing a miracle, the real power of their deity, the Father God of All Dwarves, giving his people a great and wonderful gift.

Crystal gripped Tarn's hand tightly, and together, barely daring to believe, they made out the outlines of wide porticos and columned balconies, as pure and pristine as if they had just been carved by master craftsmen. Buildings and platforms came into view, with rows of windows and ornate, marbled vantages swiftly drying as the water spilled away. Tarn scarcely dared to believe it as he saw the outline of his father's palace, the wonderful edifice near to the top of the city that had been destroyed during the Chaos War.

And it was coming into being again, all immaculate, still rising, with the top of the island pressing ever higher, toward the ceiling of the cavern. Where that ceiling had started to sag, weakened by the three fires of corruption, it would be supported, stronger than ever, by the might of the renewed stone pillar.

Tarn realized what was happening, though he scarcely dared to believe it. But he recognized the truth, and he spoke that truth to his wife:

"By the power of Reorx," he murmured. "The Life-Tree is restored!"

———DH———

Brandon was swept away by a sense of wonder—amazement at his own survival, at Willim's death, and at the power of the god, made manifest in Gretchan's prayer. He knew they rose higher and higher, and very rapidly at that, but the movement was so smooth that he didn't even feel any difficulty in standing or maintaining his balance. They were drawing closer to the vile, yellow fires that had burned into the ceiling, but those infernal sores were being gradually doused, defeated by the glory of Reorx.

"The teeth of the dragon are no match for the power of our god," Gretchan told him, and though he had no idea what dragon she was referring to, he was willing to acknowledge that the power of their growing pillar

THE FATE OF THORBARDIN

of stone was the most awe-inspiring display of force he had ever seen.

He became aware of a new problem, one that would affect only the four of them who happened to be on the Isle of the Dead as the miracle transpired. The surface of the lake was far below them as the pillar of rock continued to grow. The ceiling over them was very close and coming ever closer. They could look up and see the cracks and fissures in the roof, and it seemed clear that the pillar would continue to rise until the two surfaces met. That meeting would save Thorbardin, for the pillar would support the roof and prevent the catastrophic collapse that had seemed so imminent.

But it might be very bad news for the four dwarves standing on top of the pillar.

"Do something!" Sadie screamed. "We'll be crushed!" She rushed toward Gretchan, but both Peat and Brandon seized her and pulled her away from the priestess.

"Sit still, woman!" Peat barked. "Can't you see she's doing the best miracle she knows how to do?"

"It may be the will of Reorx that we die here," Gretchan replied calmly. "The pillar is rising, and it will support the dome of the mountaintop. But to do that, it must reach the ceiling. I would prefer to give my life to this cause rather than to have my death serve as entertainment for the black wizard. May Reorx's will be done."

"At least we can look for shelter," Brandon pointed out, touching Gretchan on the shoulder. "Here, let's find a niche or a crevasse where we might have a chance."

A quick survey revealed a wide crack, just past the crest where the cage had been.

"A lot of good that will do," Sadie said sourly. "So we suffocate instead of getting crushed."

"Choose your poison," Brandon said. In another minute he brought Gretchan, Sadie, and Peat to the edge and helped each of them climb down. The gap was narrow, only a couple of feet wide, but it was also more than eight feet deep. The four of them huddled there, feeling the mountain shudder around them, the pillar of rock continuing to rise.

Soon they could see the cavern ceiling in complete detail. It was close enough to strike with a thrown rock. The four of them ducked instinctively. Then there came a solid *thunk,* and the movement ceased. Rock spilled and gravel tumbled into the crack around them. It was completely dark and utterly still.

"But the Urkhan Sea is saved," Gretchan said. "Glory be to Reorx."

"Glory may be," Sadie said sourly. "But it looks like we're trapped in here. I wonder how long it will be until our air runs out."

---DH---

At last Tor stood at the top of the world. The summit of Cloudseeker Peak offered a magnificent vista on such a clear, cold day. After days of climbing, he and Kondike had mastered the last of the false summits, had moved along a knifelike, rocky ridge, and finally found themselves standing upon the crest of a huge dome of rock. They could see for—maybe for a hundred!—miles in every direction. Not even the eagles flew so high, the young dwarf thought with wonder.

THE FATE OF THORBARDIN

When the mountain began to shake, he wasn't even afraid. He turned his face skyward and trusted fate, and the mountain, to hold him aloft. The shaking stopped soon enough, in any event, and the minor earthquake did nothing to detract from the thrill of his accomplishment.

He did notice a few places where the ground had shifted and cracked, where some of the loose scree on the summit had actually trickled away, falling inward and down as if draining into some hollow cavity.

Then the dog began to bark frantically, even more urgently than he had when he had chased away the bear. He was circling one of those sinkholes, looking down, his tail wagging with undeniable urgency. The dog looked up at Tor then down into the hole and barked again.

"What is it?" Tor asked. "Do you smell something down there?"

In response, the dog scrambled into the depression. Kondike began to dig, frantically clawing at the rock, barking in agitation. Tor went over and helped him, using his hands to pull away the rocks and digging deeper and deeper toward he knew not what.

An hour later they had opened a hole into a compartment in the mountaintop, revealing a narrow space, and they heard voices! Tor scrambled back, alarmed and excited at the presence of the first people he had seen since departing Pax Tharkas.

He could only gape in astonishment and witness the teary reunion and the joy as Gretchan Pax climbed out of the hole and hugged her dog. Brandon Bluestone came next, and they were followed by two more dwarves he didn't know. They blinked in astonishment and squinted into the sunlight.

They told Tor Bellowgranite that they were lucky to be alive . . . and that his mother and father were king and queen in Thorbardin once more.

——DH——

"Look at lights on water!" Gus declared in awe.

He and his girls had come down to the lake via the East Road since the Urkhan Road had been crowded with so many big dwarves. The East Road was little used, and besides, it went the closest to the part of the shore where Gus intended to go.

The three Aghar stood alone on the shore and stared in wonder at a sight never before imagined. At least, as far as Gus knew, the Urkhan Sea had never looked like that before.

Beams of brilliant sunlight shot downward, penetrating the dome of the mountaintop in three places. The light reflected off the water, dazzling in the waves that were slowly settling back to the usual placid surface. There was a big pillar of rock in the middle of the lake, and Gus was pretty sure *that* hadn't been there before either.

He didn't know about the fire dragon teeth placed by the black wizard, of course, but even to a gully dwarf, the trio of holes seemed nicely spaced, the points of an equilateral triangle having a symmetry all its own. They were like splendid skylights, openings in the mountaintop that allowed light and fresh air into the undermountain kingdom. The three Aghar squealed in delight as they spied a bird, probably the first one ever to come to Thorbardin, swoop down through one of the holes, fly across the lake, then

THE FATE OF THORBARDIN

wing its way upward to fly out another one of the new openings.

"This way. We go to fine Agharhome," he boasted, following his memory as they made their way along the steep, cliff-lined shore. "Plenty good town for gully dwarves," he said. (Given recent events, he might be forgiven if his memory was a little sketchy on the latter point.)

Finally they reached a familiar spot, where several sewers from the ancient dwarf cities converged to run down toward the lake.

"Come down here," he told his girls, sliding down the ravine, ducking beneath the low-hanging shelf of a familiar tunnel. Already he could smell it: rotten cave carp, freshly hauled up from the spawning shelf!

Unerringly he made his way back to the Fishbiter house, a doorless hovel along a shelf of rock, one of many doorless hovels where unknown numbers of gully dwarves had tried to eke out an existence over the years.

"Girls wait here," he whispered conspiratorially as he stood outside the entrance. Reluctantly, they agreed, and so he strode inside.

"Mam!" he cried. "Pap! It's me, Gus! Me come home!"

"Huh?" Pap said, looking up in irritation from the flat rock that was the only piece of furniture in the Fishbiter house. "This my seat!"

"Gus?" Mam said. "You still alive?"

She looked rather confused.

"And this my carp!" declared his big brothers Ooz and Birt, elbowing each other as they hovered over the decaying scrap of fish. They glowered at Gus, though for some reason they weren't glowering *down* at him as much as they used to. In fact, if he didn't know any better, Gus would have thought that they were glowering *up*.

In fact, they were.

With an easy cuff, Gus knocked his bullying siblings out of the way and picked up the skeletal remains of the fish.

"Hey, Berta, Slooshy!" he said, calling to the girls who were still waiting out in the sewer trough. "Come here, see! Gus got food!"

DUNGEONS & DRAGONS

FROM THE RUINS OF FALLEN EMPIRES, A NEW AGE OF HEROES ARISES

It is a time of magic and monsters, a time when the world struggles against a rising tide of shadow. Only a few scattered points of light glow with stubborn determination in the deepening darkness.

It is a time where everything is new in an ancient and mysterious world.

BE THERE AS THE FIRST ADVENTURES UNFOLD.

THE MARK OF NERATH
Bill Slavicsek
August 2010

THE SEAL OF KARGA KUL
Alex Irvine
December 2010

The first two novels in a new line set in the evolving world of the DUNGEONS & DRAGONS® game setting. If you haven't played . . . or read D&D® in a while, your reintroduction starts in August!

ALSO AVAILABLE AS E-BOOKS!

DUNGEONS & DRAGONS, WIZARDS OF THE COAST, and their respective logos, and D&D are trademarks of Wizards of the Coast LLC in the U.S.A. and other countries. ©2010 Wizards.

FORGOTTEN REALMS

RICHARD LEE BYERS

BROTHERHOOD OF THE GRIFFON

NOBODY DARED TO CROSS CHESSENTA...

BOOK I
THE CAPTIVE FLAME
APRIL 2010

BOOK II
WHISPER OF VENOM
FEBRUARY 2011

BOOK III
THE SPECTRAL BLAZE
FEBRUARY 2012

...WHEN THE RED DRAGON WAS KING.

"This is Thay as it's never been shown before... Dark, sinister, foreboding and downright disturbing!"
—Alaundo, Candlekeep.com on Richard Byers's *Unclean*

ALSO AVAILABLE AS E-BOOKS!

FORGOTTEN REALMS, DUNGEONS & DRAGONS, WIZARDS OF THE COAST, and their respective logos are trademarks of Wizards of the Coast LLC in the U.S.A. and other countries. Other trademarks are property of their respective owners.
©2010 Wizards.

"Now, when I hear FORGOTTEN REALMS, I think Paul S. Kemp."
— fantasy book spot.

FORGOTTEN REALMS

From *The New York Times* Best-Selling Author

PAUL S. KEMP

He never knew his father, a dark figure that history remembers only as the Shadowman. But as a young paladin, he'll have to confront the shadows within him, a birthright that leads all the way back to a lost and forgotten god.

CYCLE OF NIGHT

BOOK I
GODBORN
JULY 2010

BOOK II
GODBOUND
MAY 2011

BOOK III
GODSLAYER
EARLY 2012

"Paul S. Kemp has . . . barreled into dark fantasy with a quick wit, incomparable style, and an unabashed desire to portray the human psyche in all of its horrific and uplifting glory."
— Pat Ferrara, Mania.com

ALSO AVAILABLE AS E-BOOKS!

FORGOTTEN REALMS, DUNGEONS & DRAGONS, WIZARDS OF THE COAST, and their respective logos are trademarks of Wizards of the Coast LLC in the U.S.A. and other countries. Other trademarks are property of their respective owners.
©2010 Wizards.

FORGOTTEN REALMS

R.A. SALVATORE & GENO
STONE OF TYMORA TRILOGY

Sail the treacherous seas of the Forgotten Realms® world with Maimun, a boy who couldn't imagine how unlucky it would be to be blessed by the goddess of luck. Chased by a demon, hunted by pirates, Maimun must discover the secret of the Stone of Tymora, before his luck runs out!

Book 1: The Stowaway
Hardcover: 978-0-7869-5094-2
Paperback: 978-0-7869-5257-1

Book 2: The Shadowmask
Hardcover: 978-0-7869-5147-5
Paperback: available June 2010: 978-0-7869-5501-5

Book 3: The Sentinels
Hardcover: available September 2010: 978-0-7869-5505-3
Paperback: available in Fall 2011

"An exciting new tale from R.A. Salvatore, complete with his famously pulse-quickening action scenes and, of course, lots and lots of swordplay. If you're a fan of fantasy fiction, this book is not to be missed!"
—Kidzworld on *The Stowaway*

FORGOTTEN REALMS, DUNGEONS & DRAGONS, WIZARDS OF THE COAST, and their respective logos are trademarks of Wizards of the Coast LLC in the U.S.A. and other countries. Other trademarks are property of their respective owners ©2010 Wizards.

A DUNGEONS & DRAGONS NOVEL

Wizards of the Coast
Books for Young Readers

Want to Know Everything About Dragons?
Immerse yourself in these stories inspired by *The New York Times* best-selling

A Practical Guide to
DRAGONS

Red Dragon Codex
978-0-7869-4925-0

Bronze Dragon Codex
978-0-7869-4930-4

Black Dragon Codex
978-0-7869-4972-4

Brass Dragon Codex
978-0-7869-5108-6

Green Dragon Codex
978-0-7869-5145-1

Silver Dragon Codex
978-0-7869-5253-3

Gold Dragon Codex
978-0-7869-5348-6

Experience the power and magic of dragonkind!

A DUNGEONS & DRAGONS NOVEL

DUNGEONS & DRAGONS, WIZARDS OF THE COAST, and their respective logos are trademarks of Wizards of the Coast LLC in the U.S.A. and other countries. Other trademarks are property of their respective owners ©2010 Wizards.

Wizards of the Coast
Books for Young Readers

WELCOME TO THE DESERT WORLD
OF ATHAS, A LAND RULED BY A HARSH
AND UNFORGIVING CLIMATE, A LAND
GOVERNED BY THE ANCIENT AND
TYRANNICAL SORCERER KINGS.
THIS IS THE LAND OF

CITY UNDER THE SAND
Jeff Mariotte
OCTOBER 2010

*Sometimes lost knowledge is
knowledge best left unknown.*

FIND OUT WHAT YOU'RE MISSING IN THIS
BRAND NEW DARK SUN® ADVENTURE BY
THE AUTHOR OF *COLD BLACK HEARTS*.

ALSO AVAILABLE AS AN E-BOOK!

THE PRISM PENTAD
Troy Denning's classic DARK SUN
series revisited! Check out the great new editions of
The Verdant Passage, *The Crimson Legion*,
The Amber Enchantress, *The Obsidian Oracle*,
and *The Cerulean Storm*.

DARK SUN, DUNGEONS & DRAGONS, WIZARDS OF THE COAST, and their respective logos are trademarks of Wizards of the Coast LLC in the U.S.A. and other countries. ©2010 Wizards.

RETURN TO A WORLD OF PERIL, DECEIT, AND INTRIGUE, A WORLD REBORN IN THE WAKE OF A GLOBAL WAR.

EBERRON

TIM WAGGONER'S
LADY RUIN

She dedicated her life to the nation of Karrnath. With the war ended, and the army asleep—waiting—in their crypts, Karrnath assigned her to a new project: find a way to harness the dark powers of the Plane of Madness.

REVEL IN THE RUIN
DECEMBER 2010

ALSO AVAILABLE AS AN E-BOOK!

Eberron, Dungeons & Dragons, Wizards of the Coast, and their respective logos are trademarks of Wizards of the Coast LLC in the U.S.A. and other countries. ©2010 Wizards.

Don't wait until you're accepted into wizardry school to begin your career of adventure.

This go-to guide is filled with essential activities for wannabe wizards who want to start

RIGHT NOW!
Ever wonder how to:

Make a monster-catching net?
Improvise a wand?
Capture a werewolf?
Escape a griffon?
Check a room for traps?

Find step-by-step answers to these questions and many more in:

Young Wizards Handbook:

HOW TO TRAP A ZOMBIE, TRACK A VAMPIRE,
AND OTHER HANDS-ON ACTIVITIES FOR MONSTER HUNTERS

by A.R. Rotruck

DUNGEONS & DRAGONS, WIZARDS OF THE COAST, and their respective logos are trademarks of Wizards of the Coast LLC in the U.S.A. and other countries. ©2010 Wizards.

Books for Young Readers